Operatio

Alfred Draper

PIATKUS

This is a work of fiction, and apart from some obvious
exceptions the characters are entirely imaginary.
I am deeply grateful for the considerable assistance I
received from the Imperial War Museum, the Submarine
Museum, Gosport, numerous ex-Commandos and the
Wilkinson Sword Company.

Copyright © 1993 by Alfred Draper

First published in Great Britain in 1993 by
Judy Piatkus (Publishers) Ltd of
5 Windmill Street, London W1P 1HF

**The moral right of the author
has been asserted**

*A catalogue record for this book is available
from the British Library*

ISBN 0-7499-0171-3

Set in Linotron Times by
Computerset, Harmondsworth, Middlesex
Printed and bound in Great Britain

Chapter One

The sergeant lay flat on his back in a field of slowly ripening corn, his head resting against a rolled-up gas cape which he had placed on his pack to cushion the hardness of the improvised pillow. He gazed indifferently through half-lidded eyes at the cloudless sky above. Swallows darted and skimmed above the wheat which was speckled with blood-red poppies, and unseen larks could be heard singing endlessly high above. He closed his eyes and thought how incongruous it was that such incredible beauty could exist when chaos and carnage were only a few yards away.

His mind wandered back to his childhood when the entire school had to stand at attention every Armistice Day and recite, parrot-fashion, the same poem: 'Scarce heard amid the guns below.' He had found the words stirring and ennobling.

Christ, he asked himself, how could a soldier, even if he was a poet, wax so lyrical in conditions that must have been every bit as bad as these? He recalled the headmaster, tears rolling unashamedly down his cheeks, as he read from the red leather Book of Remembrance that was removed every November the 11th from its glass-fronted case as soon as they had intoned:

> 'We shall not sleep, though poppies grow
> In Flanders Fields.'

This was always followed by two minutes' silence in honour of the men who had paid the supreme sacrifice for God, King

1

and Country. Even the trams and buses which rumbled past the ruin of a school came to a halt, and men doffed their hats and clasped them to their chests.

Now, having seen the cock-up the generals had made of things, he realized for the first time the prophetic warning in the poet's words. It certainly would not be wise, he mused, for any general to put in an appearance right now. He would hear a few things that would make him blush as red as the tabs he wore, or those ruddy poppies that were such an obsession with people. *'When the poppies bloom again, I'll remember you!'* People still sang it; half-pissed at parties, as if there were something romantic about being blown to bits in a pretty field. Well, the top brass had certainly broken faith with the long dead, and the more recent ones to boot, through their incompetence. Not one lesson had been learned since the War To End All Wars.

Six months ago, Sergeant Harry Keith would have thought it impossible to entertain such mutinous thoughts.

Thirty yards to his left and less than six feet above his head was a narrow, poorly surfaced road jammed with an immobile mass of traffic and humanity. There were army lorries – French and British – packed with weary, dust-caked men, the drivers angrily sounding their horns in a futile endeavour to make the refugees give way; but the civilians paid no heed. They were concerned only with saving their own skins, oblivious to the fact that their only hope lay with the soldiers who were falling back to take up defensive positions against the army sweeping inexorably towards them like an avalanche. Bogged down with the infantry were tanks whose commanders stood upright in the turrets, bellowing torrents of abuse in sheer frustration; ambulances filled with groaning, whimpering wounded suffering from every conceivable wound, and field guns whose muzzles drooped as if in utter despair.

The refugees had no idea where they were heading for. All they knew was that they wanted to get away from the fighters which appeared as if from nowhere to strafe them with machine gun and cannon fire, and the terrifying Stukas which descended on them in almost vertical dives, their sirens screaming the most bloodcurdling sound, to drop high explo-

2

sive and anti-personnel bombs which cut great swathes through them and left behind heaps of mutilated men, women and children.

It did not occur to them in their panic that the road to which they clung so tenaciously offered them the poorest chance of survival; for the Germans, with no heed to morality, had quickly realized that the mass slaughter of civilians was the ideal means of impeding the progress of the Allied armies throwing them into total confusion. They employed the same ruthless tactics on the railways, which were also cluttered with troop trains and others packed with refugees, and any towns and villages which stood in the path of their advance. It was inhuman but effective, and all part of the carefully planned and premeditated Blitzkrieg.

Sergeant Harry Keith swore loudly, cursing the ineptitude which had resulted in the Allies being caught with their pants down. He sat up, reached for his pack and rummaged inside until he found a clean pair of socks. He removed his boots, took off the socks he was wearing – gamey as camembert and stiff with sweat – and meticulously examined his feet, toe by toe, before putting on the clean pair. At the first opportunity he would wash the filthy ones. Napoleon, he told himself, may have thought an army marched on its stomach; but *he* was an artillery man, whereas any footslogger who had put in any time knew bloody well it was the feet that did the marching.

Using his rifle as a prop he hauled himself upright. He fastened his pack on his back and contemplated whether or not to jettison his greatcoat and gas cape, but decided against it. Apart from the discipline which had been instilled in him over the years, he was reluctant to discard anything at all, weighed down though he was. The gas cape was useful as a ground sheet, and although the weather was intolerably hot one never knew when it might change for the worse; then he would be grateful for the greatcoat. He also kept the three pouches of ammunition, reasoning that there was no point in getting rid of them if he was going to hang on to his rifle, something he would be parted from only when he copped the one with his name on it. Anyway, he reminded himself, he was still a fighting soldier.

3

He ached in every joint and had no idea how far he had travelled since his battalion had been attacked at night by panzers, mortars and heavy machine guns. They had fought ferociously and stubbornly, exacting a high price for every yard the enemy advanced, but the outcome had never been in question. They possessed no mortars of their own, no supporting artillery and no anti-tank guns, and the Germans had smashed through in three places so that the battalion had been scattered and its members had lost contact. His own company had been virtually wiped out, and the remaining handful had been told by the one surviving officer, mortally wounded himself, to break out and withdraw until they could attach themselves to the nearest line of defence.

Sergeant Keith had set off with three privates, but two had been captured when they called at a farmhouse to ask for food, only to find it occupied by Germans. The third had been blown to pieces when he inadvertently stepped on a landmine laid by the retreating British.

Sergeant Keith's problem was that no one he had so far encountered had the vaguest idea where the new line of defence had been established. The only advice he had been offered was to keep going as best he could until he learned something definite. And so he had trudged along with the long queue of troops and refugees who clogged the road before him.

He had quickly learned the wisdom of not sticking to the road, for when the Stukas and fighters came over there was no time to take cover and wholesale slaughter was inevitable. Now he marched parallel to the road, and although slow, his personal progress had been steady.

He poured a little water from his bottle into his dixie, enough to dip his razor in, and shaved the rough stubble off his chin. If he bought it at least he would look like a soldier.

He climbed the steep incline leading up to the road and walked along the verge, looking for someone who might possibly have some up to date information. He had never encountered such a sight. People were carrying what pitiful possessions they had managed to salvage in every conceivable form of transport: baby prams, handcarts, wheelbarrows, horse-drawn wagons, and strange-looking vehicles that looked as if they had been lying forgotten for years in some barn or outhouse. One old woman sat on the handlebars of a cycle, being pushed by an equally aged man. There were bleating sheep being chided along by men armed with long switches, lowing herds of cows being urged on by savage blows on their hindquarters, and squealing pigs which squealed all the louder when attempts were made to beat them into silence.

The humid, sticky air was filled with the grinding of engines in low gear, the stench of exhaust fumes and the ordure of petrified animals and unwashed humans. But overriding all was the almost tangible odour of defeat.

He walked, the sun beating down on to his steel helmet with such intensity he thought his head would explode, until he came abreast of a British tank whose young commander was leaning out of the turret, his head tilted sideways as if willing some coherent message to arrive through his earphones.

Keith heaved himself onto a track and tapped on his shoulder. The officer removed his headphones and asked brusquely: 'What the hell do you want, Sergeant?'

Keith saluted. 'Just wondered if you've managed to pick up any useful gen, sir. I'm looking for the new line. Was told to make for it when Jerry broke through and wiped my lot out.'

'Only wish I could help – but I've had these ruddy things on for the past forty-eight hours and haven't been able to pick up anything that makes sense. What a ruddy shambles! We were ordered up to the front and no sooner had we got there than we were ordered to withdraw! Didn't fire a single shot. Not that these tin cans someone had the effrontery to call tanks would have put up much of a show against the Jerry tanks and guns, but it would have been nice to have had the chance.'

Keith glanced at the tank and had to admit to himself that they were death traps. They were lightly armoured, lacking in fire power, but fast and extremely manoeuvrable, as if the designer had been told to produce something as close as possible to a horse.

He wondered whether any of the top brass had ever bothered to find out what kind of tanks the German army had. If they had, they should have realized the horse was a relic of the past. What was needed in modern warfare was a battleship on steel tracks.

The officer said: 'When we were ordered to fall back I don't think anyone at HQ had the foggiest idea what conditions on the roads were like. We're going to get nowhere at this rate.'

Keith could see the lines of fatigue deeply etched in his face, and his eyes had the look of a man humiliated. To have withdrawn as he had done after a valiant fight against over-whelming odds was one thing, but to be shunted back and forth as if tanks and men were no more than coloured pins on a map was totally demoralizing.

'Not to worry, sir,' said Keith. 'You know what they say about the British: we may lose battles, but we win the wars.'

'We muddle through, you mean. The trouble is that your theory permeates the whole of Whitehall. They're still think-ing in terms of '14-18': stick it out and we're bound to win. But the Germans have introduced a new kind of warfare which those silly buggers never knew existed. So fast and pulveriz-ing, time might not be on our side . .' He broke off and quickly donned his headphones. 'Something's coming through!'

The sergeant watched intently as the officer listened to the message. Then, after what seemed an interminable wait but was in fact a matter of minutes, the officer removed his headphones. 'Seems the withdrawal's became a rout. We've been ordered to fall back towards Arras and Belgium and Holland are likely to toss the towel in any minute. Know what the daft bastard at the other end said? "Stick to the roads as we must not alienate the farming community by destroying their crops." Well, fuck that for a game of soldiers! I'm taking my lads and our tanks across country, and if any farmer's deprived of his bread for breakfast that's just too bloody bad.'

Keith realized just how serious things must be. He couldn't imagine an officer talking like that to an NCO if things weren't pretty desperate.

Keith was not privy to the plans of the British High Command, but he did know that Arras was where General Lord Gort, Commander-in-Chief of the Expeditionary Force, had his HQ. If the tanks were heading there, then events must have taken a rapid turn for the worse.

'Which direction's Arras, sir?'

The tank commander pointed vaguely with a forefinger. 'Somewhere over there. Jump aboard and I'll give you a lift.'

'Thanks all the same, sir, but I'll make my own way.'

He did not like to tell the young officer that he reckoned he would get there a damn sight quicker on foot. In any case, it was more than likely that the order to withdraw to Arras would be countermanded and the tanks told to make a last-ditch stand, so as to provide the army with precious time in which to regroup.

Sergeant Keith hitched his rifle over his shoulder and began to march through the waist-high corn. The ears pecked at his bare arms like birds picking insects off a plant, and he could hear the crunch as his boots trampled down the corn. He felt a certain satisfaction in the thought that every step was depriving some Frenchman of his morning croissant. He knew he was being unreasonable in thinking the French should have put up a stiffer resistance, yet he could not help but contrast their present mood with the spirit he had encountered when he first arrived in France. Then the cry, 'Ils ne passeront pas!' had been on everyone's lips as they cockily pointed out the impregnability of the Maginot Line. No army, they had assured their ally, stood a hope of breaking through.

The feeling of frustration tasted like bile in his mouth, and bitterness welled within him. The army was his life and had been for the past fifteen years, ever since the day he had revolted against the soul-destroying task of job hunting and shortened the dole queue by walking into the nearest recruiting office to sign on as a regular. It had been a spur of the moment decision, borne more out of despair than anything else; but it had been one he had never regretted. Within a remarkably short time he knew he had found his vocation in life, and the regiment became the be-all and end-all of his existence. What had started out as a marriage of convenience had developed into a passionate love affair.

From the outset he was determined to be a good soldier. To that end he had worked hard and enthusiastically, revelling in the comradeship and the sense of tradition that could mould men from such contrasting backgrounds into a close-knit family. They were cultured, well-educated men, seeking

7

anonymity from a past they never discussed; men who had known power and authority but now sought a life in which the most insignificant detail was decided by somebody else; men who had known nothing but grinding poverty, and men who had tired of the pursuit of wealth. There were atheists, agnostics, and men who were not embarrassed to kneel by their bunks every night praying loudly and openly. There were married men, single men, bigamists, celibates and reprobates. There were men who endured everything without complaining, and others who did nothing but moan.

Keith had quickly realized that if he were to succeed in his chosen profession he would have to do something about his totally inadequate education. He had left school at fourteen with only a rudimentary knowledge of what were called the Three Rs. So he had assiduously attended evening classes until he was as well educated as any sixth form grammar school boy. During the process of 'improving his mind' he had discovered an unexpected bonus: the pleasure obtained far outweighed the benefits of pure acquisition of knowledge. And so he became an avid if indiscriminate reader and as nature had endowed him with a strong, powerful physique and a natural love of games, he had been able to avoid being tagged a bookworm. He also had a good head and a taste for beer; qualities which ensured he was never short of friends.

Promotion had been slow, but that was the norm in the peacetime army, and although he took with the proverbial pinch of salt the assurance that every ranker had a Field Marshal's baton in his knapsack, he knew talent and initiative were ultimately rewarded. And so he had climbed the ladder of promotion in the traditional rung-by-rung fashion: lance-jack, corporal, and finally sergeant. Ambitious though he was, the thought of becoming an officer had never entered his head – the army was too class conscious to encourage such pipe dreams. There was a strongly-held feeling in high places, vocally expressed in every officers' mess, that there were those who were born to lead and those who were born to follow. What mattered was *where* you were educated, not how well. And how you spoke was more important than what you said. To be an officer, it was essential, first and foremost, to be a gentleman.

No one, least of all Sergeant Keith, questioned the wisdom of such beliefs: they were engraved in stone. And it did not worry him in the least. One day he might reach the dizzy heights of Sergeant Major, but if he did not he would be quite content to remain a sergeant. After all, they were the backbone of the British army.

He had also learned that the hoary old cliche 'travel broadens the mind' was a statement of fact. He had served in India, been blooded on the North-West Frontier, had been awakened to the fact that a man should not be judged by the colour of his skin. He had savoured the exotic delights of Singapore and Burma, and in Palestine learned the hard way that maintaining the peace often made more enemies than friends. He had also discovered that bullying did not make for leadership: guiding by example did, and men would follow and obey without question someone they respected.

Like all good soldiers he had not hankered after war, but if it did come was determined not to disgrace himself or the regiment. Then, when the crunch had come, the army had let everybody down: routed in a ridiculously short period of time. There was no hiding the fact that they had been beaten by an army better equipped with everything, bar courage, and led by true professionals.

As he thrust his way through the cornfields, Sergeant Keith was aware of the rumble of artillery which seemed to be getting closer. High in the sky, in the far distance, he could see an observation balloon, obviously directing the German guns. He could see no sign of anti-aircraft fire, and deduced that the enemy had gained complete control of that particular sector.

The heat was so unbearable he took off his steel helmet, attached it to a shoulder strap on his battle-dress blouse and put on his forage cap. He was so tired it was sheer will power forcing one leg to go before the other. He paused to take a sip of water, and his mind went back to the day the battalion had first arrived in France.

Not so long before Britain had been in an almost euphoric state of exhilaration. Chamberlain, the 'umbrella man', had assured the people there would be 'peace in our time', ably abetted by a cohort of appeasers.

Sergeant Keith, along with many others, had seen it as a welcome but temporary reprieve; time in which to build up the nation's strength. He was unaware of the fitness of the Royal Air Force or Royal Navy to wage war, but he knew to his chagrin that the army was certainly ill-prepared. Even as the war clouds gathered he had taken part in manoeuvres in which officers had stalked the battle area carrying placards denoting tanks or guns because there was an acute shortage of both. In fact there was a desperate shortage of many items essential to the conduct of a modern war: mortars, anti-tank guns, machine guns, and light automatic weapons. Whitehall, it seemed, was still populated by blinkered men who firmly believed that any foe would run at the sight of cold steel.

He knew it was only a deep sense of loyalty that had prevented many junior officers from voicing their misgivings: not that they would have achieved much if they had. There were too many people in high office who had been strongly opposed to a powerful army for a variety of reasons: financial considerations, the worst depression in living memory, pacifism and appeasement. There was also the defeatist school which believed any money spent on the army was a waste, because bombers alone would decide the fate of the world. So the best thing to do was enjoy life while you could.

There was also a genuinely-held belief that Hitler was bluffing. So strong was this belief, that France and Britain had pledged themselves to go to the aid of Poland if it was invaded, and an ultimatum had been issued to that effect. That in itself would guarantee peace.

But the ultimatum had been ignored, and Sergeant Keith's battalion was among the first to be sent to France.

He vividly recalled arriving at Calais, disembarking from a cross-Channel ferry that had been commandeered for troops. They had stomped down the gangways, burdened down with enough useless equipment to tax the strength of a mule, and marched through the streets lustily singing of their intention to hang out the washing on the Siegfried Line. Women had darted forward to thrust posies of flowers into their hands, and old men who had fought alongside 'Tommy' in the First War presented bottles of wine. Union Jacks fluttered from flag poles and balconies.

After a brief rest they travelled to the French-Belgian frontier where they had dug in and built fortifications, laying miles and miles of barbed wire because the Dutch and Belgians had stubbornly refused to allow their borders with Germany to be fortified, fearing that such a step would provide Hitler with an excuse to attack.

It marked what became known as the Phoney War. The winter was bitterly cold and boredom quickly set in among the troops, who played endless games of football to curb the monotony of their lives in which the only casualties were caused by over-enthusiastic tackles, accidents in the blackout or over-indulgence in the local *estaminets*.

To their right was the comforting presence of the Maginot Line. Admittedly it ended rather abruptly at Longuyon on the French-Belgian border, which meant there was a big gap from there to the sea, but no one seriously contemplated Hitler violating the neutrality of the Low Countries. As the weeks passed and nothing happened, the feeling grew that the war, like old soldiers, would simply fade away.

It did not. The dawn of May 10th was one that Sergeant Keith would never forget. The tranquility had been abruptly shattered by the thunderous rumble of heavy artillery, growing louder and more incessant by the minute. He had been standing outside the guard room when he saw a private with a signal in his hand running across the parade ground like a hare pursued by lurchers.

He had shouted in the voice that sent a chill through many a fresh recruit: 'Steady , lad! You should know better than to run like a scalded cat. You're in the army, not a relay team. No need to get the wind up because you've heard a few guns.'

The soldier halted beside him, panting heavily. 'I gotta hand this to the Colonel, Sarge. If you was to see what's on it, you'd understand the 'urry.'

Keith took the signal, read it and said: 'I'd better take this to him myself.'

The message was short but devastating. The Germans had invaded France, Belgium and Holland. The 'invulnerable' Maginot Line on which such high hopes had rested might just as well not have existed.

The colonel seemed remarkably unperturbed when Keith handed him the signal. 'Well, Sergeant, the balloon's gone up

11

at last. About time too; we'd have died of boredom otherwise. We may not be the best equipped battalion in the British army, but I know we'll give a bloody good account of ourselves. There's one good thing we can be grateful for: Chamberlain's gone, and we have a new leader in Churchill who'll give us the inspiration that's been so sadly lacking.' He sounded as if they were about to take part in a knock-out soccer competition.

There was a flurry of bugle calls and the men took up their positions behind the fortifications they had spent so many weeks erecting. An hour later orders came through for the battalion to leave its entrenched positions and advance to meet the Germans.

With hindsight, Keith reflected, it had not been a wise decision. Behind their well-fortified line they might have been able to hold off the enemy for a while longer. As it was, they met an enemy who swept them aside as nonchalantly as a man swatting a mosquito. Sheer guts were no match for the highly mechanized army commanded by Rommel and other brilliant generals. He wished the British army commanders were as shrewd as their German counterparts; but the British had always placed more emphasis on courage than on brains. And that was certainly the case with John Standish Surtees Prendergast Vereker, 6th Viscount Gort.

No one could question his valour, for he was the holder of the Victoria Cross, three DSO's and the MC. But he was no strategist, and was often referred to despairingly by his junior officers as 'Fat Boy Gort'. His denigrators had coined the phrase: 'Oh, Gort, our help in ages past' to emphasize the point that he was a military dinosaur.

Sergeant Keith marched steadily throughout the day, pausing briefly every two hours to take a sip of water and relieve his shoulders of the heavy pack he was carrying. Although he was in the peak of condition and knew he could march all day without halting – he had done enough route marches to justify this faith in himself – he rigorously kept to his self-imposed schedule. He wanted to be in a fit state to fight when he did eventually reach the lines. He would have preferred to travel by night; a solitary figure trudging across the fields was a tempting target for the low-flying fighters which roamed at will and shot up anything they spotted, but as he had no compass that was out of the question.

As the hours passed the sound of battle seemed to envelop him on all sides. He was plagued with doubts as to which direction he should head. One thing was certain: the magnitude of the disaster that had overtaken the Allies. He passed solitary farmhouses where white sheets fluttered from windows, and went through half-deserted villages where pillowslips and tablecloths now occupied the place where tricolours and Union Jacks had fluttered so proudly such a short time before.

As he moved cautiously through one village he was surprised to see an elderly woman frantically beckoning to him from the doorway of a stone cottage. She had a black scarf over her head and wore a shapeless, grimy dress and a pair of wooden sabots. Her filthy stockings were rolled down below her knees. He was unable to understand what she was saying, but it was obvious she wanted him to follow her inside. Remembering the fate of his two comrades in arms, he removed his rifle from his shoulder and worked a bullet into the breech. She looked harmless enough, but there could be a gun at her back.

He called back: '*Je ne peux pas parler francais*,' – the only words he had learned during his sojourn on the frontier.

She gabbled something incoherent and disappeared inside the house, to emerge a few seconds later brandishing a British steel helmet. She gesticulated towards the interior of the house, a bemused expression on her weather-wrinkled face. She was obviously searching for words he would understand. Suddenly her face brightened. 'Tommy *ici*,' she said, and rapped a knuckle against the tin hat.

Sergeant Keith moved towards her, his rifle ready to be fired at the slightest hint of danger. She tugged anxiously at the sleeve of his battle-dress blouse, urging him to follow her inside.

The room was dark; no lights burned even though the shutters were closed. The woman shuffled her way tentatively to a large scrubbed table and lit a lantern. In the gloom Keith could just discern the shapes of two hard-backed chairs and an unlit cooking stove. There was no other furniture and the only adornment on the whitewashed walls was a crude wooden crucifix.

The woman held the lantern in front of her and moved towards a rickety ladder which led to a loft of some kind. She kicked off her clogs and began to climb it, glancing over her shoulder every now and then to make sure he was following.

He ascended the ladder warily, holding the rung above him with one hand. The other gripped his rifle, his finger on the trigger. The loft stank of old cattle fodder, and as his eyes became accustomed to the dark he saw a dark shape huddled in a corner. The old woman pointed at it and said, 'Tommy. *Ici.*'

A voice unmistakably English called: 'I can't see in the dark if you're friend or foe. If you're German I demand the right to be treated under the rules of the Geneva Convention. And, to make my point, I've got a .303 pointed at your navel. If you're a friend, it's a different matter altogether.'

The voice was soft, and by Keith's standards rather refined.

'Take it easy. I'm a friend all right, so put your rifle down before there's a nasty accident. Sergeant Keith, Second Battalion Hop Pickers, and wet nurse to every mummy's boy in C Company.'

He heard a clatter as the soldier put the rifle on the floor. 'Let's have a closer look at you, lad.'

He took the lantern from the woman's hand and knelt beside the recumbent form.

'Thank God you're one of ours – because I'm not really in any fit state to make a nuisance of myself,' the soldier said. 'Can't stand. Got a lump of shrapnel in my leg.'

Sergeant Keith moved the lantern closer to the soldier's face. He was boyishly good-looking, with dark hair and deep-set blue eyes. He could not have been older than nineteen. There were beads of perspiration on his forehead, and he was obviously in considerable pain.

'Better let me take a look at the leg,' he said. 'I wish I could ask the old lady if she has a torch. This lantern's useless.'

'I'll ask her to get something. She wanted to put a light on, but I was against it. Thought it would be safer if the place looked deserted, if any Krauts happened to pass.' He spoke fluently in French to the woman, who promptly scurried down the ladder.

'How did you come to get here?' Keith asked. 'She's taking an awful risk.'

'Don't think she doesn't know that. I warned her, but she said she was too old to worry about that. She's been absolutely marvellous – God knows where she got the strength to help me up the ladder. Poor old soul had to lie down for an hour afterwards.'

'Better tell me how you came to be here in the first place.'

'I was in the rear truck of a small convoy heading towards the front, or where we had been led to believe the front was. It was so hot the canvas top had been rolled down, and we were sunning ourselves as if we hadn't a care in the world. Somewhere one of the lads was playing a mouth organ and everyone was singing. All the old favourites: "Nellie Dean", 'Tipperary", "Run Rabbit Run" . . . it was difficult to imagine there was a war on. Lookouts had been posted in each truck, standing upright behind the cabins, although no one thought they would be needed. Then, suddenly, it happened. They came at us from out of the sun and we heard them before we saw them.' He spoke slowly, with frequent pauses, and Keith knew he was fighting the pain. 'Messerschmitt 109s, three of them. They were so low we thought they would hit us. They opened up with cannon and machine guns. Everyone grabbed for his rifle, and a couple of Brens fired off bursts, but they were away before anyone could take proper aim. They made four attacks, killing goodness knows how many men. Several of the trucks caught fire and exploded in great balls of flame. Men were jumping out and rolling in the dust in an attempt to put out the flames that enveloped them. Then the Stukas came in, screaming like banshees, to plaster us with fragmentation bombs. The order was given for everyone to bail out and take cover in the hedges, but it came too late; the damage had been done. I nosedived out of the truck and was hit above the knee by something which felt like a sledgehammer. There were blazing trucks everywhere, and the order was given for everyone to pile into the few that were still mobile. The fit helped the wounded, the dead were left behind. No one needed any encouragement, because any moment the planes might have returned. I must have passed out for a short time; when I came to I was lying at the bottom of a hedge. I could see what was happening and I shouted and screamed until I thought my lungs would burst, but no one heard me, and by the time I managed to crawl back to the road I was the only living person around.'

Sergeant Keith heard the old woman wheezily and laboriously making her way up the ladder.

'Save the rest till later, lad. Let's see what she's managed to dig up.'

The woman scrambled through the hatch, clutching another oil lamp in one hand and a torch in the other. She lit the lamp and handed him the torch. mumbling something in his ear; her breath reeked of garlic.

'What's she saying?' asked Keith irritably.

'She says she thinks I'm going to die, and would you help her bury me in the manure heap; the Boche will never think of looking there.'

'Thank her for the offer, but tell her you're not going to snuff it, you're coming with me. Tell her I want plenty of hot water and some disinfectant, iodine, carbolic: anything suitable she can lay her hands on.'

The soldier spoke to her and she nodded gravely, then went down the ladder again.

'Think you can roll up your trouser leg so's I can take a dekko?'

'I've tried, but my leg's like a balloon. Couldn't get it as far as my calf.'

'Not to worry, I'll use my bayonet.' He looked at the soldier and saw his look of apprehension. 'Not on your leg, you fool! On your trousers.'

He took his bayonet from his scabbard and slit the trouser leg from just above the canvas puttee to the thigh. When the bare leg was exposed, Keith directed the beam of the torch on to the wound and whistled silently. 'You've copped a real beauty there, lad.'

He took a cartridge from one of his pouches and put it in the soldier's mouth. 'Bite hard on it. You may think it's something that only happens in cowboy films – but, take it from me, it works. What I'm going to do will make you want to

16

scream the place down, but we don't want any passing Jerry to hear. So if you can avoid that, I'll be most grateful.'

The wound was not large, but the shrapnel was deeply embedded in the flesh above the knee. Keith probed as gently as he could to see if any bones were broken.

'I'm no sawbones, but I don't think there's any break or fracture. Thankfully it's not bleeding and there's no sign of gangrene, for which you should be eternally grateful. That's the real danger with this kind of wound.'

'Are you going to try to dig it out?'

'Not on your life, lad. You'd lose your leg for sure if I tried that. No, I'm just going to clean it up.'

When the old lady reappeared she was carrying a kettle of boiling water. No sooner had she handed it to Sergeant Keith than she vanished again, to return with a large can. Her gestures indicated that she wanted him to rub it on the wound.

He unscrewed the cap and sniffed. It smelled like lysol or some other strong disinfectant. 'Want to read what it says on the label?' he asked the soldier with a grin.

'No thanks. It might be bad news, and that's the last thing I need. Just let me live – or die – in hope.'

Keith filled his mess tin with hot water and poured in some of the disinfectant. Then he rummaged around in his pack until he found a field dressing, dipped it in the mixture and began to clean the wound. He was as gentle as he could be, but he had no idea if he was causing pain because the soldier remained absolutely silent.

He found another dressing, doused it with the liquid and applied it to the wound. 'You can spit the bullet out now, lad. Your mother would be proud of you. Now, if it's not expecting to much of the old dear, would you tell her I'd be grateful if she could sew your pants up?'

The soldier spoke to the woman who grinned toothily and disappeared down the ladder.

'You certainly struck gold when you came across her,' said Keith. 'You'd be food for the crows otherwise.'

'I didn't find her. She found me – I was incapable of moving when she passed me in her donkey cart. I don't know how she managed it, but she got me into it somehow and brought me here.'

17

'Is there a man about the house?'

'No, she's a widow. Her husband was gassed in the last war and didn't live to see forty. Since then she's run the place on her own: a few chickens, a couple of pigs, one milk cow and a vegetable patch. Just eking out an existence.'

When the old lady had finished repairing the trouser leg, Keith said, 'Ask her which direction Arras is in. While she's explaining I'd better go and see if I can find something to make a rough crutch from, 'cos I don't intend giving you a fireman's lift.'

'You'd be better off on your own,' said the soldier.

'I wouldn't leave my mother-in-law, if I had one, to the tender mercies of the Jerries. Apart from that, I'd hate to think of the old lady being stood up against the wall and shot for harbouring a British soldier.'

Sergeant Keith went out into the garden looking for something to fashion into a crutch. Embedded into a sawn off section of tree trunk which served as a chopping block was a large axe. He pulled it out and went in search of a suitable branch. It took him some time before he found one with a large enough fork to fit under a man's armpit. He lopped it off the tree, trimmed it and went back to the farmhouse where he searched for something that would serve as padding. He found an old horse collar hanging on a wall and he took it down and cut off a large section which he nailed to the crutch. It was far from ideal but the horsehair stuffing would make life a little more bearable for the wounded man. He also found an ancient block and tackle that had once been used to haul bales of hay into the loft. It was mildewed and rusty, but still serviceable.

When he climbed back into the loft, he said to the soldier, 'If I can find something to attach this to I'll have a go at lowering you down.'

The old woman read his thoughts and pointed to a large eye bolt screwed into one of the beams. He attached one end of the tackle to it and said to the soldier, 'Stick the hook through your belt and hang on like grim death.'

Then he dragged him to the hatch. 'Now just relax and let me do all the work. All you've got to do is enjoy the free ride.'

When the hook was secured he wound the rope round his own waist and braced himself to take the weight as the soldier

18

lowered himself through the gap. The sudden jerk almost threw Keith off his feet, but he steadied himself and slowly paid out the rope.

'Give a shout when you reach terra firma,' he called out.

The pain in his back and shoulders was excruciating, and he heaved an audible sigh of relief when he heard: 'You can let go now. I'm on the floor. Sadly not vertical, but very horizontal.'

'Not to worry – the hard part's over. The rest is a piece of cake. Just a nice long stroll through the countryside in the sun.'

Sergeant Keith picked up the soldier's rifle and slung it on the shoulder opposite the one on which he carried his own weapon, then he came backwards down the ladder.

'Thank the old lady for all she's done and apologize for not having anything tangible with which to express our gratitude.'

'I've done that, and she says it doesn't matter. Wouldn't have taken anything if we'd offered.'

Sergeant Keith picked up the makeshift crutch and handed it to the soldier. 'Try that for size, then let's get cracking.'

The soldier fitted it under his arms and grinned. 'Tailor-made.'

Tears were spilling down the old woman's cheeks as she embraced them and kissed them on both cheeks before handing then a small basket containing some bread and cheese and a bottle of rough wine.

'*Merci, merci madame*,' Keith murmured, knowing how inadequate were his words.

'I must give her *something*. Not payment – just a keepsake,' muttered the private. He unstrapped his gold watch from his wrist and thrust it into her hand. She protested volubly, but he insisted on her keeping it.

When they emerged into the sunlight they stood for several seconds letting their eyes become accustomed to the bright light after the darkness of the loft before setting off in the direction of a distant steeple.

'That's the direction she said we should take,' said the soldier.

They turned and waved back to the old lady who stood framed in the doorway, her black scarf fluttering in her hand.

'The old girl was reluctant to take your watch. Pity you insisted in a way. It won't be much use to her, whereas it could be to us later on. It could buy food and possibly shelter. Apart from telling us the time.'

'I insisted because it's the most valuable thing I have,' the soldier retorted.

'Well, it was a nice gesture. Now put one arm round my shoulder and take the weight off your gammy leg on the crutch. We've got a lot of ground to cover and not much time to do it in.'

They trudged on in silence for an hour, Sergeant Keith acutely aware that each step was sheer agony to the young private. Although he had not uttered a whimper of complaint, his lips were bloodless and his face ashen.

Another hour passed and the steeple seemed no nearer. 'Time for a breather,' said the sergeant. 'I'm knackered.' He did not like to say the private seemed all -in and desperately in need of a rest.

They sat beneath the shade of a huge chestnut tree, and Keith cut off chunks of bread and cheese which they washed down with the rough wine.

'It's about time you introduced yourself, lad. I don't even know your name,' said the sergeant.

The private extended his hand, saying almost apologetically, 'It's Emmanuel Gluckstein, actually.'

'Christ almighty! That's quite a mouthful. You sure you're on the right side in this war, lad?'

'I'm as British as you are,' Gluckstein snapped angrily.

'Sorry. Just being facetious.'

'My father was born in Germany, but he fled to England when he saw what was happening in his country. My mother was pregnant and he was determined I wouldn't be born in a country where Jews were reviled and persecuted.'

'When was that?'

'1920. Adolf Hitler, a mob orator and rabid anti-semite, was beginning to make his mark in Munich. He blamed the Jews for Germany's defeat in the First War and for all its subsequent ills. He called for the union of all Germans in a Greater Germany, which meant the annexation of Austria, the Sudetenland and the return of German Danzig. Jews were

20

to be denied office, even citizenship, and all who had entered the Reich after August 1914 were to be expelled.'

'I hadn't realized he'd been going for so long.'

'Most of the outside world was happy to turn a blind eye. And in Germany some scoffed, but a lot listened. Nazism was on the way. Hitler chose as his party emblem the *Hakenkreuz* – or swastika – which to him personified the struggle for victory of Aryan man.'

'Didn't the people know what they were letting themselves in for?'

'Some were very apprehensive, but Hitler set up strong-arm squads, mostly war veterans, to silence any hecklers and break up the meetings of political opponents. They wore brown uniforms and sported the swastika. My father didn't hang around; he packed two suitcases and left with my mother.'

'Where are they now?'

'Mother's dead. Father's interned on the Isle of Man under Section 18B. He took out British nationality as soon as he could, but it didn't help when the war came.'

Sergeant Keith shook his head in bewilderment. 'It's a rum old world and no mistake. Your Dad's behind barbed wire, and here you are in the British army. Doesn't make sense.'

'The old man isn't in the least bitter. I gather he goes round the camp boasting about his boy in the army. I'm allowed to write to him, but I didn't tell him that when I joined up I was advised to change my name. Anti-semitism, I was told, was not confined to Germans.'

'You didn't though?'

'Of course not. That would have made a mockery of me enlisting in the first place.'

'Did you have a rough ride?'

'Only to start with.' He shrugged. 'I had a few good pals who stood by me and thumped anyone who insulted me. They told me that if I was prepared to fight for my country they didn't give a damn what my name was.'

Sergeant Keith felt in his tunic pocket and produced his last packet of Woodbines. When they had finished their cigarettes he said, 'How's the leg? Feel up to moving?'

21

'Ready when you are. It's going to get a lot worse before it gets any better, so I might as well make hay when the sun shines.'

Keith slapped him on the back. 'You know, your old man has every right to be proud of you, Emmanuel.'

'Sergeant, would you mind not calling me Emmanuel? My pals call me Ted.'

'Ted it'll be from now on, lad.'

They had no idea how far they had walked before they reached the church. It was the only undamaged building in the entire village. Fires glowed in the gathering darkness, and the deserted streets were littered with the corpses of humans and animals, already smelling of the charnel-house. When they entered the church they were appalled to see the bodies of forty children laid out in the main aisle like the sculptured effigies on medieval tombs.

An ancient-looking priest wearing a shabby and much patched *soutane* emerged from behind the altar and shuffled towards them. He spoke in a hushed, reverential voice that was quavering with age.

Sergeant Keith said impatiently: 'What's he saying?'

'He's telling us we're welcome to take sanctuary in the house of God. We will not disturb the peace of the slaughtered innocents.'

'Ask him what happened.'

The private spoke to the priest, then interpreted his reply. 'He says the bombers came over yesterday and bombed indiscriminately. The children were in the school, which received a direct hit. The villagers brought the bodies here promising to return to bury them when the danger had passed.'

'Tell him we're very tired and would like to rest for a while, but only if he's sure the Germans will not punish him.'

Private Gluckstein passed on the message and repeated his answer. 'He says he's sure the Germans will not come here, because there's nothing to find. They just wanted to terrify everyone. Now, if we'll excuse him, he'll find us something to eat and drink.'

The priest returned with some bread and a jug of steaming coffee.

'He apologizes for the frugality of the fare, but his house-keeper is among those who have temporarily departed,' said Gluckstein.

The priest shuffled out and soon afterwards they heard the big bell in the steeple summoning the faithful to prayer, sending out the message that the villagers should return to the one thing that really mattered in life.

When Keith and Gluckstein had eaten they stretched out on one of the long pews and drifted into a deep sleep, exhaustion blotting out all fears for the future.

Chapter Two

The first fitful rays of the early morning sun were casting long multi-coloured beams through the big stained glass window above the altar when Sergeant Keith woke up. He had slept longer than he had intended. The church was silent; the bodies of the children still lay as if in deep slumber on the centre aisle.

He sat up and leaned across the pew and shook the still sleeping private. There was no response, and he feared he had lapsed into unconsciousness. He shook him several more times before Gluckstein sat up and groaned 'I wish you had a shot of morphine.'

'If I had one, Ted, I wouldn't give it to you. It would only put you to sleep, and then you wouldn't be able to walk. Ready to move?'

'What's the alternative?' he asked wearily.

'You stay here and end up in the bag, or maybe join those kids lying on the floor,' said Keith savagely.

'You're a hard bastard, Sergeant, anyone ever told you that?'

'Many times. But I'm an old softie really, heart of gold . . .'

'I know, and twice as hard,' said Gluckstein. 'Just give me five minutes.'

'Sorry lad. We've been here too long as it is. So grab your crutch and let's get cracking.'

He knew he was being unduly harsh; the shrapnel wound required the attention of a doctor, but the last thing the private needed was sympathy.

Private Gluckstein picked up his crutch and levered himself upright, teeth clenched and his face a pewter grey. Keith could see that every movement was agony, and it was only sheer will power that prevented him from screaming out loud.

The decrepit priest shambled in and handed the sergeant a small bundle of food and a bottle of wine. He spoke urgently to the private. 'Some villagers have returned to warn me the Boche is coming – they are perhaps less than twenty-five kilometres away. You must leave immediately.'

The private repeated the words to Keith.

'Tell him we're on our way.'

The priest put his hands together in a gesture of prayer and mumbled something. A smile flickered across Gluckstein's face, forcing Keith to ask angrily: 'What's he say that's so amusing? Share the ruddy joke!'

'He says, "Go in peace, and may God be with us." He also said the bottle contains Communion wine, but as it's all he has the Almighty will surely overlook such sacrilege.'

Keith laughed aloud. 'Well, no one can accuse the old boy of not having a sense of humour. Go in peace! What wouldn't I give to make that a reality.'

'I liked the bit about the wine myself. I wonder what he would say if he knew what faith I followed?'

Sergeant Keith shook the old man vigorously by the hand, and said to Gluckstein, 'Tell him we'll be back.' It sounded banal, but was the only thing he could think of to express their gratitude.

They emerged from the church and the sergeant paused to study the terrain. Taking the main street was out of the question; one of the narrow lanes surmounted on either side by high stone banks offered the best chance of survival. He pointed in the direction he intended to take. 'Jerry will stick to the main roads because he won't be able to get his armour and mechanized transport down those lanes.'

They walked for an hour before the sergeant ordered a halt. They were bathed in perspiration, their faces and bare arms mottled with insect bites. The sergeant thought half an hour's rest was not taking too much of a risk. Overhanging branches shielded them from the occasional aircraft flying low overhead, and they could hear nothing that indicated the presence of enemy troops.

'You know, I had an awful dream in that church,' Gluckstein said. 'Dreamt I had lost two fingers in the air attack rather

26

than being wounded in the leg. Was I relieved when I woke and found it was a dream!'

'Funny sense of priorities you have, young Ted,' Sergeant Keith commented drily. 'If you'd lost an entire hand at least you'd still be able to walk properly, and we'd be a good twenty miles nearer to where we're heading.'

'Hands are the most important thing I possess,' said the private gravely. 'Without two I wouldn't want to live.'

'Come off it, lad! I've known men lose a hand and think nothing of it. They quickly adapted.'

'They weren't pianists.'

'And you *are*?'

Gluckstein nodded, as if apologizing for the admission.

'You play in a dance band?'

The private smiled ruefully. 'Afraid not. It's not the kind of stuff you can dance to, more what you would call highbrow. Classical music.' He leaned forward, saying with great intensity, 'I'm going to be famous one day, Sergeant.'

He saw the look of amusement on Keith's face and added hastily, in case the sergeant thought he was bragging: 'Not so much for myself, but for my parents. They made some incredible sacrifices.'

The sergeant passed him one of the few remaining Woodbines.

'As we're going to be stuck with each other for some time, you might as well tell me the whole story. It might even convince me it's been worth all the trouble you've put me to.'

Gluckstein extended his hands. Keith could not help noticing how long and sensitive the fingers were.

'My mother used to play in cinemas in Germany, just for the sheer pleasure of it. That was before talkies. You know the kind of stuff – thundering chords and a lot of pedal work for the dramatic scenes, sentimental melodies for the romantic episodes. When she and my father fled to England she started giving music lessons to make some extra cash, and she began to teach me when I was still so small I had to be lifted onto the stool. She quickly realized that I needed far more expert tuition than she could give. But lessons cost money, and my parents were very hard up. My father's English wasn't that hot, and he'd been forced to take on the most menial jobs. Between them they scrimped and scraped to pay for lessons. Fortunately I managed to win a scholarship to the Royal Academy of Music where my tutor decided I needed even more expert guidance, and he got me into the Paris Conservatoire.'

'That's how you learned French so well?'

Gluckstein nodded. 'It still cost my parents money – money they could ill afford – but they never begrudged it. I gave one or two recitals in London, nothing big you understand, but I got some kindly reviews, especially after a concert in the Wigmore Hall. My mother died soon afterwards.' He clicked his fingers. 'Just like that: no illness, no warning. Just worn out. Then the war came.' He shrugged. 'You know the rest.'

'Listen, Ted, and listen carefully. All their sacrifices won't amount to a row of beans if you don't survive. So when I yank you to your feet I want you to be playing the piano all the way to where we're going. Forget your leg and imagine yourself in a boiled shirt playing at one of those Albert Hall concerts. Hear the applause ringing in your head, and see yourself taking bow after bow. You won't even notice the miles passing.'

Gluckstein hoisted himself upright and began swinging his leg like a pendulum. He hummed out loud, pausing to yell out: 'Tchaikovsky! Wonderful stuff to march to.'

When he had finished that he started something else. He was still humming two hours later when Keith called a brief halt. 'Look, Ted, I told you to *imagine* it, not treat me to a dress rehearsal of a full-scale concert! Now if you want to strike up with some regimental march I could bear it, but what you're subjecting me to isn't music to my ears.'

'How about "Soldiers of the Queen"?' said Gluckstein, unabashed. 'Even you must know that.'

'Not my favourite, by a long chalk, but preferable to what you've been bashing my ears with.'

They rested for half an hour before setting off again, singing lustily the words of the song that had echoed through-out the world to the sound of tramping feet. When they had sung that three times they switched to Kipling's 'Boots', then to 'Tipperary', then 'The Road to Mandalay'.

When the private began to flag and music was no longer a stimulus, Keith called another halt. They ate, drank some wine and smoked a cigarette. When they resumed the sergeant insisted they would walk for an hour, then rest for twenty minutes. When nightfall approached he estimated they had covered eight or nine miles at the most. By then their entire repertoire of songs was exhausted.

They slept under the shelter of a hedgerow, protecting themselves from the morning dew with their gas capes and cushioning the hard ground with their greatcoats.

Keith was the first to wake, aroused by the sound of heavy gunfire and the sharp crump of mortars. It seemed to be coming from all directions at once and he had no idea if it was friend or foe, or both. But he did know that it was uncomfortably close.

He woke the private. 'Ted, I'm going to leave you alone for a while. I need to find out exactly where we are and who's making all that din and I can do it more quickly on my own. You just wait and have a good kip – I'll be back. Promise.' He removed the private's rifle from his shoulder and laid it on the ground.

The private watched the retreating figure of the sergeant, stocky and compact, shoulders thrown back, head erect. *What a remarkable man, he thought. He's made of ruddy steel. A lesser man would have abandoned me long ago.*

He lay back under the hedge and closed his eyes. He could hear the bees buzzing in the cowslips in the nearby field. When he woke from a short doze a fox passed so close to him he could have reached out and touched it. There were occasional lulls in the gunfire but never of long duration. High above flights of bombers flew in perfect formation, black and white crosses and swastikas clearly visible on the underside of their wings and tailplanes.

Time passed agonizingly slowly, and he began to regret having parted with his watch. He tried counting off the minutes, but soon tired of that. He tried to measure the passage of time by watching the sun, but it seemed to hang motionless in the sky. His leg now ached intolerably and he doubted if he would be able to get up again. He dozed off, and when he woke he saw the sun had moved, but had no way of determining what it indicated in terms of time. He tried to think of something to take his mind off the pain that was searing through him like a red hot poker, but his brain refused to co-operate. He tried humming some of his favourite Chopin *études*, but that did not work either.

The next time he woke up the sun had moved appreciably. He ruefully accepted that Sergeant Keith had either been killed or captured, unable to accept the possibility that he had decided to press on alone. Well, he told himself, being a POW isn't the end of the world. He would be no worse off than his father languishing away on the Isle of Man, a prisoner of the country he so admired and whose nationality he had so eagerly embraced, while he would become a prisoner of the country of his father's birth, a country he detested. It was all rather ironic. But even the Germans were signatories to the Geneva Convention, which meant they were honour-bound to treat prisoners according to the rules of war. Then it suddenly occurred to him that he might never be found in the lonely country lane and he felt a cold chill of fear sweep through him. He shivered at the thought of a slow death from starvation, of crows picking out his eyes and rats gnawing at his flesh.

His hand reached out for the rifle that lay within easy reach. All it needed was a few seconds of courage: just the time it took to put the muzzle in his mouth and pull the trigger. Then all would be oblivion. He groped around until he found a forked twig long enough to reach the trigger, then struggled into an upright position, his back resting against a small trunk. He worked the bolt, put a bullet into the breech, then put the twig against the trigger and placed his mouth over the barrel. He felt remarkably calm.

He heard the crunch of boots. Guiltily he tossed the rifle aside so that it was no longer within reach. Sergeant Keith's voice was low and rebuking. 'Now, you weren't planning anything daft, were you?'

'Of course not. I knew you'd be back.'

Keith stooped and retrieved the Lee-Enfield and slung it over his shoulder, then tossed aside the forked stick which lay at the private's feet. 'Glad of that, Ted, because it would have been a terrible waste. Think of all those music lovers who'd have been denied the pleasure of your genius!' He sounded jocular, but Gluckstein detected a note of reproof.

Keith felt inside his battle dress and produced a bottle of cognac, a tin of bully beef and a bar of Cadbury's chocolate. He uncorked the brandy and passed the bottle to the private. 'Take a long swig of that. Nothing like getting half-pissed to chase the blues away and make you feel up to a ten mile hike.'

He opened the corned beef with his bayonet, sat down beside the private and carefully measured the contents into two equal portions which he put into their mess tins. 'I've found our Army, Ted – but it isn't all good news. It's a total shambles out there,' he said morosely. 'The guns you can hear are mostly theirs. Our discipline is holding and the willingness to fight is there, but no one has the foggiest idea what's going on. Without any clear-cut orders they're like dogs chasing their own tails. The lines of communication are non-existent and DRs are rushing off in all directions like blue-arsed flies to get some coherent orders.'

He took two cigarettes from a fresh packet and handed one to the private. 'At least I was able to stock up with NAAFI frees. No one has any money to buy them, so they're handing them out with the rations.'

'Seriously, Sergeant, what *is* the position?'

Sergeant Keith shook his head. 'Honestly, if I knew I'd level with you. I spoke to dozens of our lads, and I'm no wiser than when I started off. According to some the swastika is flying over every town hall in France. I'm sure it isn't, but the problem is sorting out the wheat from the chaff.'

'What's the next move?'

'We press on and link up with some outfit or other and just go where they go. If we stay on our own we don't stand a snowball in hell's chance. Anyway, I need to get you to an MO.'

It took them over eight hours before they caught up with the tail end of a small convoy of British troops. They encountered a scene of indescribable confusion. Refugees were travelling in opposite directions and insisting they were only doing as they had been told. As a result, the bogged-down column was forced to abandon all thoughts of compassion and batter a path through them. There were lorries packed to suffocation with badly wounded men; lorries filled with soldiers taking a short respite from the constant footslogging

31

before changing places with the men trudging like sleep-walkers beside the vehicles.

Sergeant Keith forced his way through to one of the ambulances, calling out at the top of his voice, 'Is there a medical officer around?'

A head appeared between the gap in the canvas at the end. 'What do you want, Sergeant?'

'I've got a badly wounded man with me, sir. He's in urgent need of proper attention.'

'What's wrong with him?'

'Shrapnel in his leg, sir. Been marching on it for several days now, and he's dead beat.'

'If he's walked this far he can walk a little further. Sorry to be so callous, but I've got men in here with their guts spilling out, and others with no legs at all. And I can't do a thing for them – I've run out of drugs and morphia. All I can do is utter meaningless words of comfort and promise them there'll be proper facilities available very soon. What they need is a padre, not a doctor. The best advice I can give is get him aboard one of the trucks.'

Keith managed to find space aboard one of the already overcrowded trucks, the men who were travelling in acute discomfort willingly making room for a man they clearly saw could walk no further. Keith took up a position by the tailboard. 'A bit cramped, lad, but better than Shank's pony!'

The convoy moved like a crippled centipede. Red, green and yellow Very lights continuously exploded over head, and occasionally a white rocket soared upwards to indicate the enemy had seized another objective. The sound of battle raged unabated, but by some miracle the column was not bombed or shelled.

Hours passed with no sign of a field hospital, and when night came the pitiful cries of the wounded could be clearly heard above the constant growl of the engines. Some of the marching soldiers tried to raise morale by singing, but their voices soon petered out; they needed to breath to keep them going.

When the sun came up, blistering in its intensity, the exhausted men began to discard items of equipment and the sides of the road became littered with gas masks, back-packs, greatcoats and entrenching tools; anything that would lighten their load. Lorries broke down and were manhandled off the road, and when an ambulance seized up the wounded were crammed into another one, so that conditions became even more intolerable. It was inevitable that when men were transferred from one vehicle to another the whole column was brought to a grinding halt, and it was during one such hold up that Sergeant Keith decided to walk ahead and make a personal reconnaissance.

He arrived at a deserted village and advanced cautiously down the cobbled main street, lined on either side by shuttered shops bearing the words '*Charcuterie*', '*Boulangerie*', '*Crêpes*' and '*Patisserie*'. It was uncannily quiet. He unslung his rifle and held it crosswise with both hands, ready to fire at the slightest hint of danger. Despite his caution his footsteps sounded alarmingly loud.

Then, to his surprise, he saw an open Humber staff car parked outside an *estaminet*. There were tables on the pavement with big sunshades covering them, but no customers. Sitting at the wheel of the Humber was an army corporal who was glancing anxiously around, as if afraid the enemy might suddenly put in an appearance. He had kept the engine running in readiness for a sudden and swift departure.

Sergeant Keith hurried towards it and said: 'Admiring the view, Corporal?' He did not wait for a reply. 'You wouldn't by any chance have room aboard for a badly wounded kid?'

'Sorry, Sarge,' said the driver, jerking his head sideways. 'There's a couple of officers – a colonel and a captain – inside the cafe, trying to rustle up some grub and anything fit to drink. They're trying to make it to Arras to find out what the hell's going on. No other way of contacting HQ – all their signal equipment's up the spout. If they give a lift to one man they'll have hundreds demanding the same.'

'You keep looking around like a bookie's runner. You think Jerry might appear?'

'That's always on the cards; but I'm more worried about some of our lads taking it into their heads to hi-jack this motor. I've seem some rum things on the way here. Soldiers nicking bikes, trying to start up cars abandoned by civvies; even saw one bloke trying to round up a horse in a field. Can't take no chances.'

When the two officers emerged clutching some bread, sausage and a stone flagon of cider, Keith saluted. 'Any up-to-date gen, sir, that I can pass on to my outfit?'

'The last message we received from Divisional HQ before we lost all contact was so garbled it didn't make a lot of sense. For what it's worth, it seems that a rearguard action is being mounted to provide valuable time for the bulk of the BEF to withdraw to the Dunkirk salient. We're heading there in an attempt to clarify things,' said the captain.

The colonel leaned forward and tapped the driver on the shoulder with his swagger stick. 'No time to dawdle. Off you go, Corporal.'

The Humber had only travelled some two hundred yards when there was the harsh staccato bark of a machine gun, followed almost immediately by a single, much louder bang. Keith watched with amazement as a door flew into the air and the Humber disintegrated in a vivid ball of flame.

The blast threw him off his feet, and when he picked himself up he turned and began to run back towards the column. If the tank, or whatever it was, caught up with it, the massacre would be horrendous. Suddenly, from the corner of his eye, he spotted an abandoned 25mm anti-tank gun on the pavement. He thought briefly of getting a couple of men to help him, but realized he did not have the time. He crouched beside the gun and was relieved to see the firing pin had not been removed or the breech destroyed. He studied the strange weapon and shrugged; one gun was very much like another. You rammed a shell home, lined it up, and pulled the trigger. He opened one of the ammunition boxes and offered up a silent prayer: it was full. He removed a shell and loaded the gun, moving swiftly back and forth between the layer's seat and the trainer's, aiming the gun until it was pointing directly up the street in the direction of the burning Humber. His hands were shaking, and he could feel beads of sweat dripping into his eyes. He gulped down great lungfuls of air to steady himself. *Don't panic. You're only going to have one chance, so make the most of it.* He scurried from one side of the weapon to the other, traversing and lowering the barrel. Only when it was parallel to the ground and aiming at the gap between the Humber and a wall was he satisfied.

Whatever had written off the staff car would have to pass through that little space.

His chest felt so tight he had trouble breathing. Then he heard the clatter of tank tracks on the cobbled street, and he waited for it to appear. His heart was beating like a trip hammer. *Dear God, don't make it a dud shell.*

Then the tank appeared and he felt as if an impossible burden had been lifted from his shoulders. He did not know what class it was, but it certainly wasn't a big tank. It was more like an armoured car, high with a square-shaped turret. There was a gun in the middle that didn't look too imposing, and a couple of machine gun slits. He could see an officer standing upright in the open turret, his binoculars focused on the burning Humber, anxious to make sure the occupants were dead and he would not be suddenly confronted by a hail of bullets. It slewed sideways like a wary crab as it edged its way past the car, and was virtually stationary when Keith fired. The recoil tossed him backwards and the noise almost burst his eardrums. The explosion that followed was tremendous, and he heard the sound of shattering glass as the windows of nearby shops and houses were blown out by the blast and a huge cloud of black smoke filled the street. He waited for the machine guns to open up, but they remained silent. It seemed an eternity before the smoke cleared, and when it did he saw that the tank was lying on its side. Beside it was a man, screaming loudly, rolling himself on the ground in an attempt to extinguish the flames that shrouded him. There was no other sign of life. He raised his rifle, took aim and fired twice. The man jerked convulsively and was still.

He counted slowly up to three hundred before darting down a side street, making a detour so that he could approach the wreckage from behind. The commander's body lay slumped half in and half out of the turret, which had a gaping hole in the side as big as a dustbin lid. He approached cautiously, rifle at the ready. He peered through the hole and had to force himself not to vomit; the remains of the crew were plastered around the interior like jam on a sandwich. He thought he discerned a slight movement of the commander's head and he shot him, hoping that someone would do the same for him if the situation were ever reversed. He cocked his head to one side, listening intently, but could hear nothing but the crackling of flames from the Humber. With a bit of luck, he mused, the armoured car had been scouting ahead of a bigger force which would wait until it reported back.

The Humber had stopped burning and he paused to peer inside. The two officers and driver were unrecognizable, the strips of cloth adhering to their remains the only indication that they had once been human beings.

He ran back down the main street, making no attempt at concealment, only too anxious to rejoin the convoy. When he reached the leading vehicle he told an officer what had happened.

'The main street is impassable, sir, so I think we should make a detour and bypass the place. When Jerry arrives, and that can't be long now, and sees what's happened, he's not going to be in a friendly mood.'

'Good work, Sergeant. We'll do as you say and skirt the place. We're going to meet up with him sooner or later, but there's no point in inviting disaster.'

Surprisingly they did not encounter the enemy, although the convoy was subjected to heavy air and artillery attacks as it approached the coast. The sky was filled with the non-stop drone of engines as Dorniers, Heinkels and Stukas bombed the retreating column.

Sergeant Keith, who had resumed his position at the rear of the truck in which Private Gluckstein was lying in a semi-coma, gazed at the ever increasing disorder as more and more troops converged on the coastal area. He knew in his heart of hearts that the army was doomed. Even if it did reach the Dunkirk salient, there was not a hope in hell of the army being able to regroup into any coherent fighting force. He suspected he was not alone in his conclusions, because he could see sappers laying demolition charges on bridges and canal locks, and placing booby traps in strategic spots on the roads and railway lines. To put it bluntly, they were walking into a death trap.

Dusk was approaching as the column reached the outskirts of Dunkirk. Military policemen were doing their utmost to restore some semblance of order and cohesion to the milling masses arriving from every direction. When they entered the town itself men and equipment were everywhere. The streets were filled with panic-stricken civilians, many of them hopelessly drunk. Shops were being looted for food, and hotels which had not yet opened for the season were being broken into and their stores and cellars plundered. Soldiers who had not tasted water for many hours were so desperate to quench their thirst they drank from the lavatory cisterns.

There were bodies everywhere; the stench was overpowering. Some of the corpses were bloated and beginning to putrefy in the heat. There were civilian corpses, but the majority were soldiers. Many covered with greatcoats and gas capes, their big army boots protruding at grotesque angles.

In the distance oil tanks were blazing in the docks, and the flames from burning warehouses gave the sky a pink glow. Bombs rained down, creating even greater havoc, replaced from time to time by artillery and mortar shells as the enemy revelled in an orgy of destruction. Ironically, as death plummeted from the sky, the promise of life came too. Leaflets fluttered down urging the army to surrender. *'Throw down your arms. We take prisoners.'*

The British contributed to the mayhem by destroying their own ammunition dumps, and when word of this reached Sergeant Keith he knew there would be no last stand. This was confirmed when a Frenchman staggered unsteadily towards him and thrust a bottle of Calvados into his hands, as with tears coursing down his cheeks he cried, *'La guerre est finit!'*

In the darkness and turmoil men became separated from their units and the night was filled with the cries: 'Anyone around from the Duke of Wellington's?' 'You there, Bill?' or 'Any KOYLIS, fall in over here.'

A major, surprisingly immaculate, approached the officer who had been leading the small convoy and gave his orders. 'Everyone is to disembark. All transport and heavy equipment is to be destroyed. Only personal and light automatic weapons are to be retained. Then you are to make you way through the dock area to the beaches.'

'What happens, then, sir?'

'With luck you go home. The navy's going to evacuate as many of us as possible.'

The young officer turned to Sergeant Keith. 'You heard what the major said. I want you to help make sure nothing – and I mean *nothing* – is left behind that can be of any use to the enemy.'

For the next two hours Keith watched men smash wireless sets, stave in radiators and engines with sledge hammers, rip tyres to shreds, then set fire to what was left. Artillery was rendered useless and motor cycles doused with petrol and burned. A soldier standing by an abandoned NAAFI lorry was handing out cartons of cigarettes. 'Compliments of the house,' he cried.

As the wounded were unloaded from the ambulances, fit and able men stepped forward to volunteer as stretcher bearers. Others singled out their personal friends and slung them over their shoulders. The walking wounded had to make their own way to the beach.

When the destruction of the transport and heavy equipment had been completed, Sergeant Keith sought out Private Gluckstein. 'Stick close to me, lad. And holler your head off if we get separated.'

The men were formed into some semblance of a column to begin the slow trek towards the dock area. France's third largest port had been pounded to rubble, and the destruction was continuing without pause. Huge cranes tilted at crazy angles, and fires raged. Sunken ships littered the basins, and the dry docks were filled with the wreckage of engines and goods wagons which had been hurled through the air by the blast of heavy bombs. Pumping stations were tangled heaps of steel and bricks; the quays were cratered and pot-holed. Water mains had fractured and many of the surrounding streets were flooded and drinking water contaminated.

Hardly anyone spoke as they made their way to the dunes, and the only sound apart from the ceaseless bombardment was the scuffing of their boots. Suddenly Sergeant Keith was aware of the thud of hooves and jingle of harness, and he turned to see a company of French cavalry ride past, the eyes of the horses wide with fear. He could not believe his eyes when they halted and the men dismounted, embraced their mounts, then calmly shot them before joining the long queues of troops.

The beaches from which the army was being evacuated stretched for twenty-five miles, from Gravelines in the west through Malo-les-Bains, Bray Dunes and La Panne, to Nieuport on the Belgian frontier. Dawn was breaking when the column caught their first sight of them. They were wide, flat, largely featureless and a dirty grey in colour. Thousands of men were packed on to the beach ahead and on the dunes which lay behind. Long lines of lorries had been driven seawards to form improvised piers, and stretching out into the water were long lines of soldiers waiting patiently to clamber aboard the small boats that were coming close inshore. Further out to sea were destroyers, trawlers, paddle-steamers, hospital ships, pleasure boats and cross-Channel ferries, standing by to take aboard the men from the small boats. Every vessel capable of making the crossing from England had been mobilized.

The guns of the warships kept up a constant barrage in a desperate attempt to delay the advancing Germans, the blue cloudless sky dotted with shell bursts as anti-aircraft guns fought off the attacking bombers and fighters. The beleaguered troops had prayed for deliverance but resigned themselves to death or captivity; but God, in the form of Vice-Admiral Sir Bertram Ramsey, had come to their aid. Although no plans had been made for the evacuation of the army, for the simple reason that no one had anticipated such a swift and comprehensive defeat, Ramsey had responded quickly and brilliantly as soon as the plight of the BEF became apparent. From his Dover Command headquarters, in a series of rooms hewn out of the cliffs below the famous castle, he had issued orders for every available naval ship to head for Dunkirk. In addition to the warships, he also enlisted the aid of countless other vessels. The first the encircled troops knew of it was when the vast armada suddenly appeared on the horizon.

When Sergeant Keith's column reached the beach, Stukas and Me 109s were strafing and bombing it. Some of the troops had dug fox holes, but they afforded little protection. Others hid among the thick murram grass which covered the dunes, patiently waiting their turn to move. The men standing chest-high in the water stubbornly refused to take cover when rescue was so close at hand.

Sergeant Keith realized it would be hours before they stood the slightest chance of getting a passage and Private Gluckstein was in no condition to stand in the sea for any length of time. The shock alone would kill him. He spotted a row of shabby, paint-peeling holiday homes that lay back from the beach behind the dunes. 'Think you can make it up there, lad? At least you'll have a place to kip down till our turn comes.'

'I'll manage all right. I'm not going to give up after coming this far,' said the private grimly.

The sand on the dunes was fine and soft, and they sank into it until their boots were so filled it was an effort to drag one foot after the other.

The beach house had clearly not been used for a long time. The bare wooden floor was carpeted with sand and seaweed which had blown under the door and smelt of damp and mildew. Keith went into the kitchen to find some water, but when he turned on a tap nothing came out but a thin trickle of rust-stained liquid. He settled the private against the wall below the one window where he would be safe from flying glass if the hut were hit. 'I'm going down to the beach to see if there are any alternatives to wading out to one of the boats.'

When he reached the beach the stench of blood and mutilated flesh was so overpowering he almost vomited. Some of the bodies had been there so long they were decomposing in the heat and he might have been walking through an abattoir. He moved gingerly among the dead and living towards the edge of the beach where the sand was firmer. There were men standing in the shallows cooling their blistered feet, their boots suspended by their laces round their necks. Others had stripped down to their underpants and were planning to swim out to one of the ships.

Keith paused beside one group of men. 'Is there any other way out of this hell hole? I've got a lad who's been badly knocked about.'

'Well, there are two moles, the East and West,' replied one soldier 'but the chances aren't much better than if you stay here. Big ships are able to go alongside, but they're being bombed and shelled to buggery. Personally I'm going to stick it out here. If things get too hot we can always retire to the dunes. That's right, isn't it, Bob?'

A voice responded. 'What? And lose your place in the queue? Not on your nelly. If I cop one, I cop one, but I'm not budging for anyone or anything.'

Suddenly the air was filled with the drone of aircraft engines as the Germans launched another attack. Men dived for their fox holes and reached for their weapons, working the bolts of their rifles faster than ever before. Others bent low while their comrades used their backs as rests for Bren guns. The soldiers knew retaliation was futile, but at least it showed the enemy they had not lost the will to fight.

The attack lasted minutes that seemed like hours, and by the time it ended the number of bodies had increased considerably. One man turned to Keith and said bitterly: 'Where the fuck are the Brylcreem boys?' It was a remark he was to hear quite frequently, and one with which he sympathized, for like all the hemmed-in soldiers he did not know the RAF was fighting countless sorties further inland in a desperate attempt to prevent the bombers reaching the beaches.

Keith decided he would head for the West Mole. It was a solid structure stretching so far out to sea the far end was barely visible to the human eye. He thought it offered a better chance than the East Mole, which was no more than a series of rickety wooden piles and planks.

Water lapped over his boots and he buried his head between his shoulders like a tortoise withdrawing into its shell, his ears waiting for the dreaded sound that heralded the return of the Luftwaffe. Flames leapt hundreds of feet into the air from blazing oil tankers near the mole, and shells burst around it with pin-point accuracy.

As he approached the inshore end he saw large groups of soldiers wearily trudging along. There was no whistling or singing and very little talk, but they were remarkably orderly. Officers and sergeants were calling out names and ticking them off their lists as the men responded.

He went up to a captain and saluted. 'I've got a badly wounded chap on my hands, sir. He can't wade out to one of the boats, and he really deserves to get out of this after all he's been through.'

'You could say the same for every man jack here, Sergeant,' the captain said. 'No queue jumping, I'm afraid.'

Sergeant Keith's voice hardened. He would never have dreamed of pleading for himself, but he had no qualms about doing so for the young private he considered his personal responsibility. 'His father's behind bars, even though he's British; his only crime was to realize what an evil bastard Hitler was long before our own politicians got around to sharing his view. But his lad still volunteered!'

'That's quite enough, Sergeant. Don't say anything you'll regret.'

'Can't you make an exception, just this once, sir? Makes this ruddy war rather pointless otherwise.'

The officer's voice mellowed. 'If you can get him down here, I'll see he gets a berth.'

It was almost dusk by the time Keith reached the dunes which loomed like stranded whales in the gloom. He cursed out loud as he stumbled into the charred skeletons of trucks and equipment half-buried in the sand. Several of the beach houses were burning and he quickened his pace, desperately worried that Gluckstein might be trapped. He was relieved to find the house intact and the private in exactly the same position as when he had left.

'Time to leave. I've got you a berth.'

Gluckstein heaved himself up. 'Lead on, Macduff,' he said cheerfully.

'It's bad enough when you're whistling and humming tunes I've never heard of, but when you start spouting Shakespeare at me – that's the last straw!'

The private gave a mock salute; he could see the sergeant was amused.

As they slithered down the dunes to the beach the private's crutch sank deep into the sand, and he wrestled it free before taking another step forward. Keith realized that in the encroaching darkness it would take them a long time to reach the mole: so long that by the time they got there the captain might already have sailed.

'Better chuck the ruddy crutch away – it's worse than useless.'

'I can't move without it.'

'You can't move *with* it,' said the sergeant savagely, 'so do as I say.'

'How am I going to make it?' asked the private wearily.

'On my shoulders. Piggyback, they call it.'

He bent low and the private straddled his back like a tired child. 'You'll have to be navigator, lad. Bent double I won't be able to see a thing. Just imagine you're riding the Derby winner. Tap my shoulder to signal which way you want me to go.'

The sergeant walked for a hundred yards, then rested a few minutes before resuming. But not once did he lower the private to the ground. Gluckstein was amazed at his prodigious strength and tenacity, because Keith was not a big man. He tried several times to whisper words of encouragement but got no response, and he was aware that the sergeant needed every ounce of concentration to keep going.

When they reached the mole Keith rested the private against a bollard, then went in search of the captain, determined to hold him to his promise. Two destroyers and two paddle steamers were alongside the mole and men were clambering aboard with a newfound energy. Close by the masts of a Grimsby trawler could be seen rising from the water, steam still hissing from the half-submerged funnel. Two hundred yards out a destroyer had received a direct hit from a high explosive bomb and was listing badly. Men were leaping over the side, while attempts were being made to lower lifeboats. Then, as the ship listed sharply and began to sink by the stern, the order to abandon ship was clearly heard.

Sergeant Keith was relieved to find the officer. 'I've got the boy here, sir.'

'I'll send two lads back to give you a hand. Get him aboard one of the destroyers.'

With the help of two soldiers, Keith carried him along the mole to the waiting ship. They found a small space between the torpedo tubes and settled down to make themselves as comfortable as conditions permitted. The destroyer frequently shuddered from bow to stern as a bomb or shell fell perilously close and great gouts of water were thrown into the air to cascade down onto the deck, drenching everyone to the skin. Every inch of space above and below decks were filled with exhausted soldiers, and still more were pouring aboard. Keith saw the ship's captain lean over the bridge wing, megaphone in hand, and heard him bellow, 'Cast off.'

An immense feeling of relief flooded through him, and he turned to the private. 'Well lad, the worst part's over. We're Blighty bound!'

'Thank God for that,' Gluckstein said. 'By the way, I haven't had the chance to ask before, but did you knock out a Jerry tank single-handed? Someone said you did. You deserve a medal.'

'Hearsay – just hearsay. No one witnessed it,' he replied indifferently. 'An award is only given when there's an eye witness.'

Black smoke belched from the funnel as the destroyer slid astern away from the mole. It was barely clear before another ship steamed in to occupy the vacated berth. The sea was dotted with hundreds of ships, some heading for England, others arriving to pick up more troops from the moles and beaches.

Sergeant Keith settled down snugly against the comforting protective shield of the torpedo tubes and dozed off, only to be awakened by the bark of the ship's anti-aircraft guns. He opened his eyes and saw a Heinkel III flying in at masthead height. The destroyer's Oerlikons and machine guns joined the cacophony of the bigger guns until the bomber was surrounded by shell bursts and looping tracers. The aircraft veered away, climbing steeply to escape the curtain of steel and seek out an easier unarmed target.

Keith dozed off again but was roused by a hand shaking his shoulder. He looked up and saw a sailor standing over him with a steaming mug in his hand. 'Fancy a cup of pusser's ki, laced with a tot of Nelson's blood? Get that down you and you'll feel like going on the town when we land.'

Keith felt the strong rum-laced cocoa burning its way to his stomach. Never had a drink tasted so wonderful.

'We nearly there?'

'You'll be seeing the white cliffs of Dover any time now, though we can't guarantee any blue birds. Fag?'

Keith took the proffered cigarette. 'You lads must have a pretty low opinion of the army after this shambles.'

'I don't deny there's a lot of talk back home about the need for a few arses to be kicked, and a bit of room made at the top for men with more imagination than those who landed you in

44

this mess. But you can take it from me, Sarge, no one has a bad word for the ordinary pongo.'

'What day is it?' Keith said. 'I've lost all count.'

'May 28th. Two days ago was a National Day of Prayer, and the churches were packed with people who normally never set foot in them. Now it's beginning to look as if it paid off.'

The destroyer's siren hooted. 'Better buzz. Be going alongside soon.'

'What'll you do then?'

'Offload you lot, then turn round and go back. We've only made five trips so far, which is two less than our chummy ship. When this little caper is over and done with we don't want them bragging they did more than us.'

Keith stood up and looked towards the bow. The white cliffs were clearly visible.

'Any chance of having a quick shave and a spruce-up before we dock?'

'Stone the crows, Sarge! They aren't going to inspect you when you land.'

'Perhaps not, but I feel thoroughly ashamed at being kicked out of France like this, and I'm not going to arrive home in shit order.'

'I'll take you down to the seamen's mess. You can have a shit, shave and shampoo there.'

He escorted the sergeant below decks to a compartment where there were rows of zinc basins and several showers. Keith stripped off, revelling in the first hot water he had felt since the retreat began. He shaved, lathering his chin with a bar of yellow soap. Then when he had dried himself he cleaned up his battle dress with a scrubbing brush that was lying on the deck.

You haven't exactly covered yourself in glory, he told himself, *but at least you can arrive looking like a soldier*.

He went back on deck and looked towards the harbour. There were ships everywhere and the air was filled with the hoot of sirens and the wail of klaxons. High above the ships silver-grey barrage balloons tugged at their hawsers like playful St Bernards straining at their leads.

The destroyer bumped alongside a stone quay and men began scrambling ashore before the order, 'Finished with engines', had been given. Rows of ambulances stood waiting to take the wounded to hospitals as far afield as Croydon, and there were members of the Women's Voluntary Service and the Women's Institute standing behind trestle tables on which were steaming urns of tea and piles of sandwiches, cakes, pies and apples.

Sergeant Keith helped Gluckstein across the deck, stepping warily to avoid the shell cases littering it, and on to the quay where a group of nurses and medical orderlies were standing.

'Look after him.'

One of the nurses detached herself from the group, saying: 'Follow me. Can't risk losing a handsome fellow like you!' She led them to a civilian ambulance. 'Nip in and we'll be off.'

Gluckstein climbed inside. It was already filled with wounded men, and judging from their cries he reckoned he had got off pretty lightly.

Sergeant Keith held out his hand. 'Get well soon, lad.'

'Thanks for everything, Sarge' Gluckstein said. 'I don't suppose we'll be seeing each other again.'

''Course we will – at the Albert Hall when this is all over. Send me a complimentary ticket. I may not understand what you're playing, but I'll do my best to stay awake.' He patted him on the shoulder. 'I'm proud of you, Ted. You'd make a bloody good Hop Picker.'

Gluckstein experienced an unexpected glow of pride, aware that the sergeant could not have paid him a higher tribute. He had no idea of the official name of Keith's regiment, but knew that it was famous, recruiting most of its men from Kent, and that whenever the sergeant spoke of it it was in terms of near-reverence.

Keith watched the ambulance speed away, its lights flashing, its bell ringing furiously, until it disappeared from view.

He turned, shouldered his rifle, and walked across to an officer who seemed to be dealing with movement control. He saluted. 'I wonder if you can help me with rejoining my regiment, sir. Lost contact early on.'

The officer eyed him doubtfully. 'You seem to have got off remarkably lightly, Sergeant. All spick and span and ready for a spot of leave.'

46

Keith was aware he as vaguely hinting at cowardice, but he was too tired to rise to the bait. 'Naturally I was interested in getting back in one piece, sir, but leave is the last thing I had in mind. Nowhere to go.'

The officer said, less aggressively: 'Report to one of the RTOs. They're dealing with warrants, and money if you need any. And good luck.'

Keith was driven in a convoy of lorries to the main station where he boarded a train for London. There he was put on another train which took him north where transport was provided to take him to a transit camp.

At the camp he was issued with a new uniform and given a warrant to travel to his regimental headquarters in Kent: the county in which he had landed.

Chapter Three

Sergeant Keith stared out of the window at the rain that was falling in penny-sized drops. It hammered against the glass and cascaded down in a torrent of transparent beads from the overflowing guttering. He had never known rain like it; it had not stopped for more than ten minutes in the past seven days. Visibility was down to a few yards, he could never have imagined the place was hemmed in on three sides by towering snow-capped mountains and skirted on the fourth by a lead-coloured loch that was as deep as it was cold, had he not known it to be a fact. The person who had chosen the spot for a training camp had to be a real sadistic bastard, he mused.

He turned away from the window and looked with distaste around the spacious hall with its flagstone floor, enormous (unlit) fireplace and massive (unlit) chandeliers. He shivered involuntarily. The castle was as cold as charity, and it did not come much colder than that. Even if you did not venture outside, where the wind pierced like a rapier thrust and the rain soaked through the thickest oilskin, the castle itself was a stark reminder that you were in one of the remotest spots in the Scottish Highlands.

The entire wall above the hearth – big enough to accommodate the trunk of a sizeable fir tree – was lined with portraits of fierce-looking men with red whiskers, all wearing kilts, sporrans and tartan stockings with daggers in the top and sporting patterned shawls across their shoulders, their right hands clasping deadly looking claymores. Their eyes seemed to follow you everywhere. On the other walls were the mounted heads of prize stags, their glassy eyes every bit as

49

suspicious as those in the paintings. In showcases, in which the taxidermist had tried unsuccessfully to create their natural habitat, were golden eagles, otters, and strange-looking birds called capercaillie, which Keith, after consulting the dictionary, had discovered was Gaelic for 'horse of the woods'.

He let his eyes wander to the ceiling: vaulted and timbered and riddled with deathwatch beetle, it reminded him of an unfinished cathedral. By accident or intention the curved canopy acted as an extremely efficiient alarm system. Footsteps on the stone sounded like pistol shots that kept eechoing long after anyone entering had halted. Sergeant Keith had never been able to shed the feeling that army boots were particularly unwelcome; they were a painful reminder of the castle's turbulent past. Culloden and The Forty-Five were remembered as if it weree yesterday.

The gaunt granite bastion had been in the hands of the same family for six centuries, and it was their proud boast that no Sassenach had ever been invited inside as a guest. But that had not deterred the War Office from taking it over and consigning the present laird to a cottage once occupied by his head gillie. Keith saw him only infrequently; an old man walking forlornly around his estate dressed like his ancestors, looking bewildered and perplexed at the strange happenings around him. Men in khaki battle dress and woollen cap comforterss abseiled down the cliff-like walls of his home; waded across his famous salmon river under a hail of live ammunition and the crump of real grenades; clambered all over the moors and mountains scaring the living daylights out of the grouse and deer, while on the loch they carried out mock landings using every kind of craft from unwieldy cutters to portable rubber canoes. They snared and ate birds and animals that any self-respecting highlander would dismiss as vermin – rats, rabbits, hedgehogs, crows and magpies – packed then in clay and cooked them over open fires.

Once, when he had asked Sergeant Keith what it was all in aid of and been politely but firmly snubbed, he had shrugged and said: 'I'm too old to care, really. I'm only glad I don't have to go through it myself, it would kill me. What surprises me, Sergeant, is that you idiots seem to enjoy it. Bloody lot of nonsense if you ask me.' To emphasize his contempt he had spat on the ground and stalked off. But he never failed to put in an appearance when one group marched off as mysteriously as they had arrived, and a fresh bunch took their place.

As Sergeant Keith waited in the gloomy hall for the Colonel to call him into his office, his mind went back to the time he had volunteered for the Commandos. When he had returned to England, after his escape from Dunkirk, he had been bemused at the euphoria sweeping through the nation. The *Daily Mirror*, the soldiers' paper, had carried a headline above its leader: BLOODY MARVELLOUS. Below it: 'Praise in words is a poor thing for this huge and heroic effort. But praise we must offer for all engaged, and for the brilliant leadership in the field that shows us we have found a great soldier in our hour of need.'

Alongside the editorial was a Zec cartoon showing a smiling, neatly uniformed sailor wading out to sea with an equally cheerful looking soldier on his back. The captain said: 'This way, chum.' They were idealized, identical twins, straight out of the *Wizard* or *Hotspur*, no fear in their eyes, no slump of fatigue in their shoulders.

As for the 'great soldier' who had emerged, he had been put out to grass; a scapegoat who would never be given another field command.

Sergeant Keith had been unable to share the sense of jubilation; relief and gratitude were certainly in order, but not such blatant jingoism. It had been a humiliating defeat, and as Churchill had pointed out: 'Wars are not won by evacuations.' But everyone seemed to act as if the Germans had been given a thorough trouncing. It was true 338,226 men, of which 139,911 were French, had been rescued, but the bulk of their arms and equipment, so difficult to replace, had been abandoned. He remembered making his way back to battalion headquarters, then sitting in the sergeants' mess listening to a broadcast by the Prime Minister. The gravelly, slightly lisping voice had been rousingly defiant, even cocky: 'We shall defend out island whatever the cost may be. We shall fight on the beaches, we shall fight on the landing grounds, in the fields, in the streets, and in the hills.'

It was all very inspiring, but he could not help wondering what they were going to fight with.

51

Soon afterwards the battalion had moved to the South Coast in readiness to repel Hitler's threatened invasion. Beaches which had once echoed to the laughter of children were cordoned off with barbed wire, and pillboxes sprang up over night like mushrooms. Rifle ranges and amusement arcades were shuttered and closed, and boarding houses and cafes displayed 'Closed for the duration' notices in their windows. Overhead the sky was laced with vapour trails as the RAF fought the Battle of Britain. The nearest he and his battalion got to real action was picking up shrapnel from the parade ground.

Sergeant Keith found himself instructing the conscripts and volunteers who had replaced the men lost in France, and his dismay plummeted even further. There was a shortage of uniforms, and he was drilling men who had to make do with broomsticks for rifles. When they were allowed to fire a real one – which was not very often – six had to be shared among twenty men. Everyone was assured that the factories were working overtime to provide the much needed arms and equipment to add to the steady flow that was flooding in from America. In the meantime, they would have to improvise.

On the rare occasions when he managed to get into the nearby town for a pint if bitter, he wondered if the public really knew how badly off the army was. If they did, they remained sublimely cheerful and confident. They endured the constant air raids with remarkable stoicism, put up without complaint the food and clothes rationing, and happily went to work after a sleepless night in a street shelter or Anderson in the garden or under a Morrison that also served as a dining table. They sang with marked enthusiasm the patriotic tunes churned out by Tin Pan Alley, and really took notice of the rash of posters that sprung up everywhere urging them to: 'Be Like Dad and Keep Mum', 'Dig for Victory', reminding them that no such words as defeat or despondency existed.

Sergeant Keith was far from defeatist, but he was despondent. He wanted to fight, to hit back at the enemy; not on the beaches or in the streets, but in occupied territory.

After one particularly frustrating day, when he had been asked to instruct the local Home Guard on how to make anti-tank bombs from milk-bottles, petrol and a wad of cloth, he had returned to the camp thoroughly disillusioned. Then while idly reading the order board, he had come across something that offered the answer to his problems. It was a notice appealing for volunteers for the Commandos. Only men of superior physique, with a streak of cunning and ruthlessness and the ability to adapt and improvise, need apply.

He had submitted his request through the Colonel, who had been far from pleased and threatened to tear it up until Sergeant Keith had pointed out that he had no authority to stop him. All requests *had* to be forwarded to the selection board.

The Colonel had tried a more placatory approach. 'Sergeant, senior NCOs such as yourself are the backbone of the regiment. I'm relying on the likes of you to knock the new recruits into shape. Remember, they're all that stands between us and defeat. Please think again.'

'Sorry sir – made up my mind.'

The Colonel had pleaded and appealed to his sense of regimental pride. 'You've been with us, man and boy, far too long to just bugger off and join some elitist group of thugs. I'm all against private armies. The strength of the British army has always relied on the regimental system, the family tradition. What you want to do is join an undisciplined rabble with no background at all: a load of ruddy gangsters.'

Keith suspected that the Colonel's opinions had been formed by what he had read in the press. With so little good to write about, the press tended to depict the newly formed Commandos as either supermen or villains recruited from the dregs of society and the country's prisons. It was a view that was endorsed, even encouraged, by several highly ranked officers who feared it would drain regiments of their best men. Unfortunately for them, the Commandos had a champion in Winston Churchill, who favoured the formation of specially trained troops who could develop a reign of terror on a 'butcher and bolt' basis. From his own experiences in the Boer War, he knew that small guerilla units could thwart and harass a large army vastly superior in numbers and equipment. Even the name had been borrowed from the Dutchmen

53

who had to supply their own horse and rifle, received no pay, and wore no uniform, but had nevertheless denied the British victory for a long time.

Churchill told his cabinet and chiefs of staff: 'The completely defensive habit of mind, which has ruined the French, must not be allowed to ruin all our initiative. It is of the highest consequence to keep the largest number of German forces all along the coasts of the countries they have conquered, and we could immediately set to work to organize raiding forces on those coasts where the populations are friendly.'

He had appointed as Director of Combined Operations, Admiral Sir Roger Keyes of Zeebrugge fame, a man of tremendous enthusiasm and well versed in hit and run tactics.

A month after his brush with the Colonel, Sergeant Keith appeared before a selection board. He had been a trifle disconcerted by the opening question from the presiding officer: 'Do you know what you are volunteering for, Sergeant?'

'Not really, sir.'

'Then you're a bloody fool! You may be landed on enemy territory by boat or submarine, and left to find your own way back. We can't promise to rescue you. If you want to change your mind now it won't be held against you.'

'I've a few old scores to settle, sir.'

'Good. There's nothing like a little hatred to spur a man on.'

He was asked a few more questions, none of which seemed particularly relevant, but he saw the three officers turn towards each other and nod their heads in agreement.

'You'll get an extra six shillings and eight pence a day when you've completed your training, but you'll have to feed yourself and find your own billet. Any questions?'

'No, sir.'

He was told he would very shortly receive orders telling him where to report.

They came through a week later, telling him to make his own way to a remote spot on the Yorkshire moors: the first test of his personal initiative. He had not been able to find it on any map, and his long journey from the South Coast had been made more difficult by the absence of any road signs and the fact that it had not been deemed necessary to issue him with a rail warrant. But he had made it at last, first by smuggling himself aboard a train, then hiding in a locked toilet with a sympathetic sailor who had shoved his own warrant under the door when a ticket inspector had hammered on it, then by hitching a series of lifts; from a farmer going to market, with a vicar doing his rounds, and finally from an elderly lady who was misusing her petrol ration to make an illicit visit to the home of the Bronte sisters. The journey had ended with a nine mile walk through a blinding snow-storm. The 'school', when he did eventually find it, turned out to be in the middle of nowhere, a cluster of Nissen huts on a windsept headland overlooking the North Sea.

Ten arduous weeks later Keith was a fully fledged Commando, skilled in the arts of unarmed combat, demolition, and the ability to kill silently and stealthily with a knife or a length of cheese wire. Because he had proved so proficient, to his chagrin and annoyance he had not been sent to a combat unit but to the God-forsaken hole in Scotland as a senior instructor in a recently opened Commando school. Since then he had taught hundreds of men and seen them go off to do what he most wanted to do himself: fight the Boche.

He heard the now familiar voice that had terrified thousands of soldiers bellow: 'Come into the lion's den, Sergeant! Got important things to discuss.'

He turned and saw Lieutenant-Colonel Rutherford standing in the oak doorway that led into what had once been the laird's private snuggery, but was now the Colonel's office. Looking at the portly figure he felt a tug of affection. The old boy was a soldier's soldier who, despite his rank, was still a regimental sergeant major at heart. When Keith had arrived to take up his post as a senior instructor, Rutherford had said: 'Remember this, Sergeant, and you won't go far wrong – the real war is always the one between the front line soldier and the Staff. Win that and the war's won. We're up against that here. They dislike what I'm doing, and they'll bend over backwards to discredit it. They still hold to the view that the battlefield is a place of honour, and the kind of soldier we're producing here puts a strain on that. Well, I fought in the trenches in the last lot, and you can take it from me that the idea that it's some kind of sporting contest is a sick joke.'

Keith knew the Colonel had been an almost legendary figure before his retirement. He had been RSM to a famous infantry regiment where he had acquired a considerable reputation for his articulate lectures. He liked to claim that his bark was every bit as bad as his bite, but beneath the harsh exterior was a man who cared passionately for the welfare of the ordinary soldier. Having survived the First World War he had no time for the strategy of attrition in which thousands had to die for a few yards of mud. As long as an enemy was defeated it did not matter if the means were fair or foul. But his views had fallen on deaf ears, and it was only when the idea of one specialized school to replace the several dotted around the country was conceived that someone remembered Rutherford. He had been called out of retirement and hastily promoted, considered the best man for the task of running an establishment whose sole task was to produce an entirely new brand of soldier.

Sergeant Keith followed the beckoning finger into the office where there was a large desk with In and Out trays on top, both of which were empty. In front of the Colonel's comfortable hide chair were two glasses and a bottle of malt whisky from the laird's own distillery five miles up the glen. Rutherford had never had qualms about reminding the laird that it was his duty to ensure there was always a plentiful supply, because goodness knows what VIPs might descend on the place without warning, and it would be a grave reflection on Scottish hospitality if there was a shortage of the best tipple on God's earth.

When he saw the bottle and glasses, Sergeant Keith experienced a surge of relief. It was going to be a friendly session.

Rutherford poured two massive measures of Scotch, and motioned Keith to the seat opposite.

'There's a new batch of lads arriving in three days time.' He passed a packet of Players across the top of his desk. 'I'm going to talk off the record for a few minutes. The PM and some top brass are going to visit us – Winston apparently wants to see for himself just what we're up to. The others, I suspect, are going to look for reasons to close the school down: raise doubts in the old man's mind as to the value of what we're doing. Mustn't let that happen.'

'I don't think we need worry too much, sir. We've got Admiral Keyes on our side and he's got Mr. Churchill's ear.'

'*Had* it, you mean. He's been promoted sideways because he protested at the negative approach of those in Whitehall who control the war machine. They tried to silence him with the Official Secrets Act, so you can see what we're up against.'

Sergeant Keith wondered what all this was leading up to. The Colonel must have read his thoughts because he said; 'You must be wondering what this has got to do with you? Answer's simple: I'm seeing all instructors individually, so no one can accuse us of hatching anything. Everyone who comes in here is sworn to secrecy; this is not to be discussed even among yourselves. Cloak and dagger stuff maybe, but then that's our job.'

Rutherford poured more whisky. 'The course so far has been tough, but it's going to be even harder. As I've said, when the PM arrives with his posse of advisers they're going to pour poison down his ears – we're going to to make sure they're wasting their time. Winnie wants to show the world the old lion can still bite. We're going to show him it's not a pious hope. He'll see men being welded into the finest and most efficient fighting machine the world has ever seen.'

Sergeant Keith grinned. 'I can't see how we can make it any tougher, sir. We drive them to the limit as it is.'

'Sergeant, we're going to drive them beyond that! They'll cry themselves to sleep; that's if we give them time to get their heads down. I want the PM to leave here wishing we had a dozen similar schools in existence.'

Keith saw an opportunity to raise a more personal problem. 'Any fresh views on my own request to be transferred to an active service unit, sir?'

'Convince the PM and the doubting Thomases that we're indispensable and you'll have my personal blessing to go and get your balls shot off.'

Keith grinned widely. 'Thank you, sir.'

Chapter Four

Euston Station resembled a Stygian cavern. The vast glass canopy enclosing the platforms had been painted black, and only a handful of blue light bulbs illuminated the gloom. Even the windows of the carriages of the waiting trains had been blacked out, except for a small cross in each to enable the passengers to peer out and see if they had reached a station or merely stopped at signals.

The platforms were cluttered with heaps of equipment: kit bags, backpacks and rifles, with recumbent forms keeping a watchful eye on them. Long queues trailed outside the bars and buffets hoping to get a cup of tea, a sandwich or a glass of beer. There were sailors returning from leave, and fresh recruits joining regiments for the first time. RTOs with clipboards paced the platforms bellowing instructions at the top of their voices, and calling out the names of the various units and which trains they had been allocated. The air was thick with tobacco smoke.

At the barrier leading to Number One Platform, a small group of men remained aloof from everyone else. They all wore different regimental insignia, but were destined for the same place – the Commando training school. They looked no different to the other soldiers thronging the station, but each of them felt special. They hoped that one day they would be allowed to wear a distinctive uniform to show they were a class apart, but Whitehall jibbed at the suggestion that they should have their own badge and shoulder flashes.

There were sergeants who had readily become privates in order to join the Commandos, and officers who had sacrificed a pip for the honour. There were men who had past records they were proud of, and some who had backgrounds best forgotten. These were Colonel Rutherford's fresh batch on whom so much depended. They seemed an unlikely group on which to pin such high hopes.

Private Gluckstein sat on his kit bag deep in thought, assailed by all kinds of doubts. He wondered if he was really cut out to be a Commando. Did he have the mental and physical tenacity? He was far from ruthless by nature, and went out of his way to avoid trouble. While he never turned the other cheek, he did not deliberately stick his jaw out. He had been perfectly frank with the selection board when asked why he had volunteered, recounting his experiences in France, and how he owed his life to Sergeant Keith. (He had not mentioned the mounting need to avenge atrocities carried out by the Germans on the Jews; that was a personal matter.)

'When I was discharged from hospital I wanted to thank him properly, stand him a few beers. Let him know I made it. I went to his battalion headquarters and was told he had become a Commando. I decided to volunteer too, because I couldn't think of any outfit I'd rather serve with. It had to be good if he'd left the regiment he thought so much of to join.'

To his surprise the explanation had been accepted as perfectly valid, although one of the officers had said: 'We'll have to do something about your name. It might be OK above a tobacconists' but it won't do for the Commandos. If you were captured you wouldn't be taken to a POW camp – they'd shoot you like a rabid dog.'

'I was asked to change it once before, sir, and declined,' he replied defiantly.

'No question of that: it's an order. We have French, Dutch, Belgians and Norwegians who've volunteered, and because their countries have all signed peace terms with Germany they're considered traitors. So they've all been given new identities – no exceptions are made.'

'But I'm British, sir,' he protested.

'You're also Jewish, and we all know how Hitler feels about people of your faith. So be sensible, lad; you're being asked to change your name, not your religion.'

'Will it be permanent, sir?'

'Not unless you want it to be.'

After he had been accepted he was taken into an adjoining room, handed a telephone directory, and told to choose a new name. 'Pick something you won't have trouble remembering, as near to your own as possible. Then we'll provide you with new papers and an entirely false family background.' He had chosen Luck as his surname, because that was what Gluck almost meant in German, and he had a feeling that he would be needing as much of it as possible in the future.

Similar doubts about his aptitude to become a Commando were also flooding through William Bennett's mind as he pondered on the vagaries of life which had brought him to Euston Station. Not so long ago he had been a guest of His Majesty in Pentonville Prison, not a stone's throw away, with the prospect of spending seven more years in an over-crowded, insanitary cell in the grim, fortress-like building that had been built by Napoleonic prisoners of war. As the British penal system was based on retribution, not rehabilitation, nothing had been done to improve conditions inside since the day the first inmates had arrived. Even with full remission, hundreds of days lay ahead when he would have to slop out in the morning, walk round the stamp-sized exercise yard before settling down to sew countless mailbags, and be banged up at night at an hour when children were still playing in the streets outside.

Not that he reproached the Home Office for not being more enlightened; he accepted it as the price one paid for being mug enough to get caught. In any case, prison was nothing new to him. He had spent much of his youth in Borstal institutions, and a fair amount of his adult life behind bars. But, he had to admit, he had been rather surprised when the Old Bill had turned up at his pad and caught him red-handed appraising the value of jewellery he had stolen from a safe in a side avenue off Hampstead Heath that was known to the criminal fraternity as Millionaire's Row. Someone had obviously put the squeak in, because he was too good a 'peterman' to have left any trademarks behind.

He had been weighed off at the Bailey by a boring old fart of a judge, aptly named Payne, who hadn't even had the decency to listen to his defence – flimsy thought it was – or the plea of mitigation his brief had spouted. No! He had been too fucking busy making notes for his summing-up to the jury, which would leave no doubt in their minds that the accused should be locked up at once and the key thrown out of the window. He had also done the carrot bit: ten years might seem a long time, but if Bennett behaved, saw the error of his ways and resolved to become an honest and upright citizen, he could be out in time to get his old-age pension.

He had only served three years, when, to his astonishment, one of the top screws unlocked his cell and escorted him to the Governor's office, saying: 'God is in His Heaven and He's tossed you a lifeline, you horrible little bastard.'

The Governor, plump, bland and untainted by constant contact with habitual criminals, had gestured him to take a seat. 'Well, Bennett? How're you enjoying life here?'

Bennett who was proud to have been born within the sound of Bow Bells, replied. 'It ain't exactly the Ritz but I've known lousier nicks.'

The Governor rubbed his hands together. 'Believe it or not, Bennett, you have been given the opportunity to change your uniform for another one which you can wear with pride.' He smiled, as if pleased with his own sharp sense of humour.

'I ain't quite cottoned on to wot you're suggestin',' said Bennett suspiciously.

'It seems the army are in need of men with your specialist skill.'

'*Safe blowin*'?' he asked, incredulous.

'Demolition, to be more precise. If you enlist, the slate is wiped clean and when the war's over you'll be a free man.'

Bennett needed little time to decide this was an acceptable proposition. He was sick to death of lying on his bunk night after night, unable to sleep for the drone of aircraft engines, the crash of bombs and the thunder of ack-ack guns. The aeroplane had not been invented when the prison was built so naturally there were no air raid shelters, and it had not occurred to anyone that its modern inmates might be entitled to protection.

Bennett had completed his basic training and then, even more astonishingly, had been invited to volunteer for the

Commandos, where he could use his knowledge in the service of his country without the slightest danger of ending up inside again. There had been more than a vague hint that if he declined Pentonville was waiting with open arms to welcome him back. But he had jumped at the opportunity, because he figured out it would enable him to keep his hand in until the war ended.

He turned to the dark-haired young soldier sitting immersed in thought on a kit bag beside him. 'Wot carrot they dangle in front of you, son?'

'I don't quite understand.'

'Wot they promise you if you volunteered? Couldn't 'ave been a pardon or remission, 'cos I see from your 'ands you never done bird.'

'Bird?'

'*Porridge*! Stir! Chokey!' said Bennett, amazed at the ignorance of the soldier.

'Sorry, but I've never fallen foul of the law.'

'Why you here, then?'

'I've got a friend in the Commandos.'

'I've got mates, tons of 'em, in Pentonville, but I couldn't get away from them sharp enuff. What's your monicker – sorry, name?'

'Ted Luck.'

'Bill Bennett.'

They shook hands.

'You strike me, Ted, as bein' a bit wet behin' the lug 'oles: kinda innocent of the facts o' life. I'd better take you under my wing. Apart from that, a bit of your name might rub off on me,' said Bennett. He winked in an exaggerated fashion. 'Fancy wettin' your whistle?'

'Very much, but look at the queues.'

'Lesson number one, Ted: never follow the common 'erd,' he said contemptuously. 'Loada pricks! No need to line up. You just keep an eye on my kit an' I'll nip outside to a boozer and get a quart o' Newcastle – much quicker than quein'. Got half a dollar on you? Be back before those poor sods 'ave 'ad a sniff of the barmaid's apron.'

Private Luck handed over the coin, wondering what on earth could have induced a man like Bennett to volunteer. He did not seem the type who would deliberately seek hazardous action.

Private Bunny Warren was a thin, almost cadaverous, regular soldier who was known as a 'hard case'. In peacetime he had spent more time in the glasshouse than on the parade ground, and had been discharged as being totally unsuitable to army life. But he knew no other and, like the recidivist who has become so accustomed to prison life he will commit a crime simply in order to get back behind bars, he had enlisted again under a fictitious name. In France he had emerged as an outstanding fighting soldier. He had fought in the rearguard at Dunkirk and been awarded the Military Medal for outstanding gallantry, which had surprised him: being rewarded for doing something that gave you immense pleasure did not make a lot of sense.

But when he returned to England he lapsed into his old habits through sheer boredom. Marking out soccer pitches with a service issue penknife, painting stones white, and saluting everything that moved, was not his idea of soldiering. So when volunteers for the Commandos were called for, he had not hesitated and his courage in the face of the enemy had been enough to guarantee his selection. Apart from actually deriving immense pleasure from fighting, he misguidedly thought that the glamorous-sounding Commandos would help him in his constant, but unsuccessful, pursuit of women. What sex he had enjoyed had always been with prostitutes long past their prime and forced to ply their trade in the red light districts that were an eyesore in every garrison town. That, however, did not prevent him from talking incessantly about his amatory conquests; boasts that his comrades took with a massive pinch of salt, for he was a most unlikely Cassanova. He had rat-like features and a habit of punctuating his speech with loud sniffs and foul-mouthed expletives.

A sergeant came through the barrier and said, in a surprisingly hushed voice as if anxious not to be overheard: 'You the special party for you-know-where? Don't want to say it aloud. Walls have ears. You take the first three carriages. Change at Glasgow . . .'

'Where to from there?' asked an inquisitive soldier.

'You'll be told when you arrive,' said the sergeant conspiratorially. 'Careless talk costs lives.' He gave the side of his nose a tap with his forefinger.

The soldiers shouldered their kit and trudged through the barrier, and staggered up the platform to the carriages allotted to them. They had not been cleaned since their last journey and the corridors were carpeted with dog ends, empty crisp packets, and bottles. As the train had often spent hours at a time stationary in sidings, the notices asking passengers to refrain from using the toilets when the train was immobile had been studiously ignored. Consequently the whole train stank of excreta, beer-laced urine and sweaty unwashed bodies.

'Not enough room in the coaches, so some of you'll have to kip down in the corridors. You'll have to pack your kit in too, because the luggage van is chocker-block,' said the sergeant, in a voice that mirrored his indifference.

Lance-Corporal Reginald Temple, with a nonchalant ease that belied his sense of purpose, was first into the carriages to grab one of the few available seats. He tossed his kit bag onto the netting luggage rack, and yawned contentedly. Despite the long journey he had already endured, he looked remarkably fresh and clean. His battle dress was sharply pressed and managed to look different to those worn by the other soldiers, as if it had been tailored to his own requirements. His hair was carefully groomed and, although short enough to comply with regulations, had obviously never seen an army barber's clippers. On his left wrist he wore a watch with a solid gold strap and on the little finger of his right hand was a signet ring on which was engraved a cat-like creature wearing a coronet. It signified nothing: he had had it made specially as part of his stock-in-trade, like the uneducated conman who wears an old school tie.

Private Luck sat beside Temple while Bennett also managed to grab a seat. Warren too managed to settle into one before an unholy scramble developed for those remaining. Kit bags were hauled off luggage racks and tossed into the space between the seats, and men clambered up and turned them into precarious hammocks. Temple eyed the heaped-up luggage between the seats and thought it could be turned into a makeshift table. He produced a new pack of cards from his breast pocket and casually enquired: 'Anyone fancy a few hands? We've a long and tedious journey ahead of us, so it'll help us pass the time.' He opened the stiff outer case and removed the wrapping from the cards. 'Bought them in the station kiosk.' He winked broadly. 'When I play I like the cards the way I prefer my women – virgins.'

He spoke in a refined voice: not the accent of the ranks, the habitual tones of the officer classes. He was aware of that, but made no attempt to conceal it because he had found nobody in the least minded. A phoney they could spot a mile off and nothing would make them take to one – but Temple was all right. Why he was only a lance-jack was his business.

'Name the game and stakes,' he said, tenderly fingering the cards like a man caressing a woman after a period of enforced celibacy. He split the pack in two and dexterously rifled them in a manner Private Luck had only previously seen in Wild West films.

'That's pretty expert,' he said.

Temple, realized his error. 'Been practising,' he said hastily. 'Not much else to do in barracks. First time I've managed to do it – normally they fly all over the place.' He reminded himself not to be so careless again; he was playing with mugs, not money-to-burn experts who saw the red light blinking when someone pretended they could not even shuffle a deck of cards.

Warren and two other soldiers expressed a willingness to make up a school, but only on the condition that the stakes were modest. They played pontoon for an hour before switching to the more serious business of poker.

Temple won steadily, but not so steadily as to arouse suspicion. He was too skilled for that. In peacetime he had made a lucrative living, fleecing wealthy punters on trains taking them to race meetings, and in the card rooms of the more fashionable hotels and gaming rooms. The two important lessons he had learned were: one, to appear lucky; two, not to be too greedy.

They played late into the night and the train had still not left the station. Private Warren yawned to indicate he had had enough. 'Either you married Lady Luck, or those cards talk to you. I don't care a fuck either way, because I'm going to get my fucking head down.'

Temple did not mind, he had not played to win money. The stakes were so low he would not have contemplated playing for them in normal circumstances. He just liked to keep his hand in. In his profession, you needed extremely supple and dexterous fingers, and you could soon lose your touch if you were doing nothing but work the bolt of a rifle, or dig trenches, or peel spuds.

He leaned back and closed his eyes, thinking: You must have been out of your mind. When you were called up you said: 'Don't volunteer for anything. Lie low and get yourself a soft number, and come out at the end of it in one piece.' He had done just that; got himself an easy number in the battalion office, and with it a few lucrative sidelines: access to weekend passes – no one seemed to count them or miss a man who was absent when he should not be – a backdoor source of NAAFI cigarettes and sweets which he sold off cheaply, and a business arrangement with a local garage owner to whom he sold siphoned-off petrol from the vehicles in the transport section.

He had not done it for the money. Just the excitement; he had always needed that. Then he had suffered a totally unexpected and uncharacteristic fit of remorse. He was cheating his comrades. If he craved excitement, there was a far more honourable way of getting it, but he would have to get himself posted – a task that proved much harder than anticipated. It was only when the notice appeared asking for volunteers for the Commandos that Temple managed to find a way out. When asked at the selection board why he had volunteered he had been embarrassed to tell the truth and replied: 'For the extra money, sir.' That had been a good enough reason.

He opened his eyes and saw that he and the dark-eyed young soldier sitting beside him, his face intense and intelligent, were the only ones awake. 'Might as well get acquainted. We're going to be seeing a lot of each other.' He held out his hand. 'Reg Temple.'

'Ted Luck.'

They shook hands. 'I always think hands tell you more about a person than their face,' Temple said. 'You've got very good hands. I'd guess you're not accustomed to manual work.'

'I'm in the army,' said Luck with a grin.

'Maybe, but you obviously look after them. Play cards?'

Luck shook his head. 'Not a gambling man at all: don't mind the odd game of chess if you ever feel like it.'

'Not for me. Needs brains! No money in it either.'

'People don't always do things for money, Reg.'

Temple sounded genuinely surprised. 'They *don't*? What other reasons are there?'

Private Luck to his annoyance found himself on the defensive. 'Well, satisfaction for one thing. Even a sense of vocation.' He shrugged. 'A compelling urge that can't be suppressed.'

To his surprise Temple said: 'I know what you mean. Like compulsive gambling. So tell me, what did you do before the balloon went up?'

'I was studying to be a concert pianist. I've still got a long way to go though,' he said earnestly.

'You play highbrow stuff then?' Temple nodded approvingly. 'Not averse to it myself in small doses. The easy-to-listen-to bits, not a whole concerto. Acts like a sleeping pill on me.'

'And you?'

'Have a guess.'

'Without wishing to sound offensive, I'd say you were a salesman of some kind. You're so self-assured.'

'Not a bad long shot. I agree I could pass for a second-hand car dealer, but the only thing I've ever sold is myself,' he said, adding enigmatically, 'Plus a lot of dreams.'

Luck frowned. 'Are such things saleable?'

'There's a limitless market, Ted. The promises of easily made money . . .'

For some unaccountable reason, Temple felt the urge to confide in the earnest young soldier. He wanted to befriend him, and to do that he needed to be totally honest.

'I was, for lack of a better phrase, a con-man. Not a very acceptable profession, but very rewarding.'

Ted found the immaculately dressed man intriguing. 'What kind of things did you do, Reg?'

68

'Anything that offered easy pickings – you name it, I did it.'

'Were you ever caught out?'

'Never. All you need is confidence. It's got to ooze out of every pore if the suckers are to fall.' He leaned forward and lowered his voice. 'You may not know it, Ted, but you're a very fortunate young man. Not many people in this world are content with what they're doing. The majority are motivated by greed: some because the need to acquire wealth is compulsive, others because they see it as a means of breaking loose.'

'And just how did you – fleece them, if that's the right word.'

'By offering favours. "Hand me a thousand and in a month I'll guarantee to turn it into ten thousand." Go to race meetings and drop the names of a few trainers, mention jockeys you're really pally with, tell punters you've laid a fortune on a horse that can't lose. And, being big-hearted, offer to place their bets with your own bookmaker who's offering over the odds.'

'And people fell for it?'

'Not all of them, but most of them did.'

Luck laughed, fascinated by the man who spoke so openly about his dishonesty. 'How on earth did you become a con-man, Reg?'

'Easy as falling off a log. You may find this hard to believe, but my old man is a rather distinguished KC, and well-heeled into the bargain. He sent me to a very good public school with high hopes that I'd follow in his footsteps. Well, I suppose I did, because barristers are con-men too, in another shape or form. The only things I inherited from my father were a certain suavity and a liking for the gee-gees. At school I used to listen to the racing results on my portable radio, and I discovered that if you sent a telegram from the local post office it was always stamped to the nearest quarter of an hour. It didn't take long for me to discover that I could often hear a result and still have time to get a telegram off to a bookmaker which showed it had been sent before the off. It was too good to last and I was caught out and expelled – the old man disowned me. You could say that from then on I never looked back. I became a stooge for a man who ran a find-the-lady game – you know, the chap in the crowd who proves it isn't a con – and it wasn't long before I was running my own game outside the bigger football stadiums. I made enough to be able to hob-nob with the well-breeched punters at race meetings, and frequent the better class of casinos and gaming houses. But it wasn't just the money, Ted – I enjoyed the challenge and the excitement. If there are two flies crawling up the wall I've got to open a book.'

'Why are you telling me this, Reg?'

'Because I want your friendship, and I'd hate it if you found out the truth by accident. It could happen, because the leopard really can't change its spots. Also to let you know that if you stick with me you'll be all right. Fall into a barrel of shit and you'll come out smelling of roses!'

They solemnly shook hands, like two gentlemen binding an agreement.

Private Luck considered himself extremely fortunate. He now had two guardian angels who were determined to guarantee his survival. All he needed was a third: Sergeant Keith.

At last there was a mournful hoot from the engine and a guard went along the platform slamming doors with a deafening crash. Men who had nipped out of carriages to stretch their cramped legs, or seek a break from the foul stench, made an unseemly dash to clamber aboard to avoid being left behind.

A whistle trilled and the train jerked. Buffers and couplings clanked and rattled before it moved sluggishly out of the blacked-out canopy into the starlit night, further illuminated by the searchlights probing for audible but unseen bombers.

Wartime demands had played havoc with the timetables, and the would-be Commandos found they were spending as much time motionless in sidings as they did travelling. They also spent long periods in anonymous stations, where detached voices announced over the loudspeaker systems that no passengers were permitted to leave the trains as it might depart without warning.

There were so many bodies stretched out in the corridors that access to the toilets was impossible, so the soldiers and sailors were forced to urinate out of the windows. A solitary voice broke into song, singing incongruous but appropriate words to Dvorak's *Humoresque*:

'Gentlemen will please refrain from passing water while the train
Is standing in the station in full view.
Workmen on the line beneath may catch it in the eyes and teeth
And they won't like it, nor I think would you.
We encourage constipation while the train is in the station
. . .'

It was soon taken up in unison: an antidote against the squalid conditions they were forced to endure without complaining because there was no one to whom they could complain. The verses seemed endless, and just when it seemed that the song would at last peter out someone would come up with another scatological rhyme that outstripped all the previous ones in its vulgarity.

Eight hours had passed since the train left London, and although no one had the faintest idea where they were, they knew for certain they were still a long, long way from Scotland.

Lord William Mappin woke from a disturbed sleep with a pounding headache and a mouth that felt as if it were filled with sand. He had imbibed too freely at the farewell party he had given before departing to become a Commando. He glanced around at the other passengers who were occupying one of the train's few First Class carriages. Directly opposite him was an elderly man, fast asleep with his mouth wide open, his upper denture perilously close to dropping out. Propping him up was a lieutenant-commander, heavily sedated with booze to blot out for as long as possible the awareness that he was returning for another thankless and terrifying spell on the Northern Patrol, and a boyish sub-lieutenant, too young to need anything to induce sleep; he would have slept on a clothes line.

On Lord William's left and also dead to the world, were two subalterns. To his right was a pretty Wren officer immersed in a book that was covered with brown paper. He wondered when she had boarded; she had not been there when the train left London. He studied her with a long sideways

71

glance. She had a small oval face with wide-set hazel eyes, an attractive mouth devoid of any lipstick and a nose that he imagined fitted the description *retroussé*, so often used in the magazines to which his mother was addicted. Her copper-coloured hair was drawn back in a severe bun and held in place by a tortoiseshell comb. He wondered whether it had been a deliberate attempt to add a touch of severity and maturity to her appearance; she could not have been more than twenty-one, twenty-two at the most. There was a single blue band on each sleeve and a three-cornered hat in the style favoured by highwaymen rested on her lap. He was not unused to being with beautiful women, but he could not recall one who had made such an immediate impact on him.

He feigned sleep so that he could let his head slump against her shoulder. He felt her stiffen and move away, but she could not distance herself too much because the window was in the way. When she realized her silent disapproval was having no effect she tried to shrug him off, but that did not work either.

She lowered her book and turned her head. She thought he was rather foppish-looking, although undeniably handsome. A strand of lank fair hair draped across his forehead and he sported what she called a Clark Gable moustache; neither one thing nor the other. She thought: I know who you remind me of. One of those handsome young actors in blazer and flannels who leap through stage windows saying, 'Who's for tennis?' Then she told herself not to be so critical; she had never set eyes on him before, and as the saying went, you could never tell a book by its cover. That brought a wry smile to her face, because that adage certainly applied to the one she was reading.

She heaved more energetically, and he sat upright. 'Sorry, making a nuisance of myself?'

'It's hot enough in here without you using me as a pillow,' she said haughtily.

'I'd move if there was anywhere to move to,' he said amiably.

'You could always lean the other way.'

'True, but the young man might get the wrong idea. I'd rather risk offending you than him.'

The remark brought a smile to her face. 'I'm not offended – just irritated. I know damn well you weren't asleep. What are you after, a cheap thrill?'

'Cheap is the last word I'd apply to you.'

'Well, you certainly can't expect any more in a crowded carriage.'

'We could talk.'

'I'd rather read my book.'

He produced a gold cigarette case from the breast pocket of a smartly tailored uniform that had clearly not seen much wear and tear. She noticed the case had a coat of arms embossed on it.

'Join me.'

'Don't you think it's stuffy enough without us adding to the smog?'

'Might be an improvement: take away the smell of booze and the old boy's halitosis.'

She accepted a cigarette which he lit with a gold lighter, and drew on it in a hesitant manner, like someone unused to smoking. She wrinkled her nose in mild distaste. 'Bit too pongy for my liking!'

'Black Russian: an acquired taste.'

She thought that sounded rather snobbish. 'I don't think it's one I'd want to acquire.'

'They are rather ghastly, aren't they? An unwanted, and unasked for present. Five hundred, but you can't look a gift horse in the mouth when there's a shortage. Frankly I'd swap them for fifty Players.'

She warmed to him and began to think she had been hasty in her judgement. 'Where're you going?' she asked.

'You should know better than to ask me that,' he replied with mock seriousness. 'Careless talk and all that.'

'I'm not likely to meet any German spies where I'm going,' she retorted tartly. She did not need anyone to remind her about security.

'Where's that?'

'Scapa Flow: a terrible place by all accounts. The sailors have a rather crude name for it. They call it the backside of the British Isles.'

'That's hardly crude. Wouldn't even shock my maiden aunt.'

73

She flushed slightly. 'Matelots are very down to earth. They use a more vulgar term.'

He found her primness rather refreshing. He was used to girls who used 'fuck', 'arsehole', and 'shit' without blinking an eyelid considering it fashionably *risqué*, and admirably suited to the pursuits of hunting and shooting. He wondered what she would be like in bed. Would she talk in euphemisms to describe the act of love making?

She said, as if reading his mind: 'You think I'm a prude, don't you? Well, I'm not. I didn't use the word the sailors employ because it might have offended you – no other reason. Some people have a natural antipathy to coarse language, and I see no point in deliberately offending them.'

'I'm afraid that in the army one can't afford to be that sensitive. Where the men are concerned everything is prefixed with a four-letter word. Their rifles, their boots – even their officers.'

She laughed joyously. 'The same applies in the Andrew – or should I say Navy, seeing as you're a landlubber?' She added, quite unexpectedly: 'I've told you, now you can tell me.'

'Tell you what?' he asked, slightly confused because his mind was still mulling over the significance the word servicemen used to describe everything they found to their dislike. It was such an odd choice of word; he could not imagine anything more pleasurable than making love.

'Where're you going?'

'I can't tell you, for the simple reason that I don't know. All I do know is that it's a Commando training school.'

'You're a Commando?' There was a note of incredulity in her voice.

'What's so odd about that?' he asked, slightly aggrieved.

'Well, to be perfectly honest, you don't look the type. I thought you had to be some kind of superman: a real tough. Fearless, and all that.'

'You don't think I fit the bill?'

She sounded slightly flustered. 'Since you ask, the answer is no. I can visualize you in some posh regiment playing polo and drinking endless toasts to long forgotten battles.' She saw the dismay in his eyes, and added hastily: 'Not that I'd question your courage. I can see you leading a cavalry charge, but not indulging in dangerous clandestine operations.'

'Perhaps you're right. I'll have to find out for myself.'

He decided to drop the subject; her criticism was too close to the truth for comfort. Whilst he had never served in what she called a 'posh regiment', his life until the outbreak of war had been one of indolent luxury. He had certainly played polo, and been brought up to believe that life centred around 'huntin', fishin' and fuckin''. But it was not his fault that he had been born with the proverbial silver spoon in his mouth, even though he would no doubt have continued in the same hedonistic way but for the war. He had joined the army because it was the done thing, and unavoidable if the things that really mattered were to be preserved, but it was only when he had met other soldiers, men from all walks of life, that he realized how shallow his life had been. He had never had to worry about work or security, or where the next meal was coming from, and he was surprised to discover there were so many who did. Yet they were astonishingly patriotic, although they would never openly admit it, and were quite happy to fight and die for a country that permitted such social inequalities and privileges. He wondered whether he had volunteered for the Commandos out of a sense of guilt.

He leaned over and prised the book from her fingers, raising his eyebrows when he read the title. '*Lady Chatterley's Lover*! Not the kind of literature a well-brought up young lady should be reading,' he chided. 'And here we've been skirting around the use of that word Lawrence used so recklessly.'

'I'm only reading it because my old tutor told me I ought to! I'd never been able to get hold of a copy before. But this one has gone the rounds of my old mess and I've promised to post it back when I've finished it.'

'Enjoying it?'

'No, and frankly I don't think I'll bother to finish it. I'm finding it laughably implausible and rather badly written. I know it's fashionable to admire Lawrence for his integrity and applaud his effort to make sexual relations precious instead of shameful, and a monument to what he called "phallic tenderness". But I'm afraid I find the gamekeeper a fraud. When he uses four-letter words they sound so false and unnatural. And when he speaks in the vernacular I want to throw up. It's music hall stuff.'

'I must say I found it rather exciting, but then I read it by torch light under the sheets at school. But it wasn't wrapped in brown paper.'

'I'm not ashamed. Just being discreet: the better part of valour. After all, it *is* banned.'

'I must confess I read it for the thrills, whereas you seem to be approaching it from a purely literary point of view.'

'I was reading English Literature before I volunteered. I'll continue when the war's over, but meanwhile I don't want to let my brain atrophy. But that's enough of me, and Lawrence. What did you do?'

'Before the war? Very little, I'm afraid.' He was glad she had jettisoned the idea of a literary discussion. She would have left him floundering.

'What was that on your cigarette case?' she asked unexpectedly.

'Family crest.'

'You're having me on!'

'Not at all. Been with us since the Dissolution – the reward for giving unquestioning allegiance to a despot.'

'You have a title, then?'

'Only by courtesy of being the son of an earl. But I don't want to trade on it. I need to *earn* respect, not command it.'

'A wise decision,' she said earnestly. 'A different world is going to emerge when this is over. People are not going to be satisfied with a return to the old order, they'll want a fairer share of the cake this time.'

He was amazed at her vehemence; he had never before encountered it in a woman. He found himself saying: 'I suppose you're right.'

She detected a note of hesitancy in his voice. 'I'm not a Red or anything like that; I'm just stating the obvious. If they're being asked to fight in the hills, on the beaches and in the streets etcetera, they'll want to feel they have a stake in them. They won't be fobbed off.'

'Do I detect a note of bitterness, resentment?'

'Good grief, no! It's only because I've never wanted for anything – anything material, that is – that I can appreciate the unfairness of it all.'

'That doesn't make a lot of sense to me.'

'I'll explain as best I can. My father is a circuit judge with an over-large sense of his own importance. He believes that the essential impartiality and integrity which his position demands can only be achieved by total detachment from the contaminating influence of everyday life. He even chose my friends for me, in case I became too chummy with someone who might put him in a compromising position.'

'You make him sound like some kind of ogre.'

'He's not that – just a pompous fool. The kind of man who asks a witness: "And pray, who is Ronald Colman?" He sees unworldliness as some kind of virtue; he knows all there is to know about the law, but very little about justice. If he was only a little more human he'd be a better judge.'

'But he let you go to university! That seems contradictory.'

'My mother insisted, and she's the only person who can overrule any of his decisions. University for me was like breaking out of a crysalis, for the first time in my life I felt free. Most of the students came from well-to-do families, but they were bubbling with ideas; ideas that would have sent a chill of horror through my father.' She sounded wistful. 'Oh! we were so outrageously Bohemian, or so we thought, but we did little more than sit cross-legged on the floor drinking gin and cheap plonk and putting the world to rights. It was marvellous. When war seemed inevitable, my father decided I should go to Canada to stay with his brother, who is an Anglican bishop. But I had had a taste of freedom, and I wasn't going back. So I joined the navy where, to coin a phrase, I discovered how the other half lives.'

Before he joined up he would have found her earnestness rather boring. The women he knew would have been branded ill-mannered if they had raised such views; they were best left to the cloth-cap politicians who did nothing but stir up class hatred. Now he found it rather refreshing.

He wondered what his father would say if he took this beautiful girl home to meet him. He would be pretty shocked to hear some of her views; he was a traditional 'backwoods' peer, cocooned from the realities of life on his vast estate which he left only occasionally in order to attend the House of Lords to vote on some issue that threatened his privileged existence. He was not a selfish person; he simply loved the life he led and wanted no other. He sincerely believed the war was being fought to preserve the status quo.

Lord William thought: *And I was pretty much the same.* Aloud he said: 'You and I are birds of a feather.'

'What an odd remark! What prompted that?'

'Simply that we seem to have fathers who are cast in the same mould. I had to join the army to find out that life isn't all cake and ale.'

They were so engrossed in their conversation that they failed to notice the train was slowing to a halt. There was a sudden flurry of frenzied activity as the sleeping passengers got to their feet and began reaching for their luggage. The door slid back. 'Glasgow Queen Street!' bellowed a guard.

Lord William scrambled upright. 'We'll have to finish our chat some other time. This is where I change trains.' He reached up for his luggage, which included a sizeable food hamper. 'What's your name? We must keep in touch.'

'Third Officer Hazel Payne. Look me up if you're ever in Scapa.'

He tumbled out onto the platform, calling back over his shoulder: 'I certainly will.'

She went to the window, leaned out and called after him, 'What about *your* name?' but he was lost amidst a melée of khaki and navy blue.

She returned to the carriage, wondering if she would see him again. She rather wanted to. After her initial feeling of dislike she had thought he was the kind of man she would like to get to know much much better.

She shrugged and said to herself: Ships that pass in the night.

As he scrambled out of the carriage, Private Bennett gazed around him. 'All this time an' we've been travellin' roun' in circles,' he said.

'What's that supposed to mean?' said Ted Luck.

Bennett chuckled loudly. 'Every time we stopped an' I peeped out of the winder we was at a place called Bovril or

Horlicks.' He pointed at an advertisement. 'An' that's where we are now!' He nudged Luck in the ribs. 'Only larkin'. Every prick knows they've taken down all the place names and left the adverts. Gotta confuse old Jerry if he invades. An' if he does I 'ope 'e uses the railway, 'cos if 'e do it'll take 'im a month of Sundays to get nowhere. Jus' like the bird wot flies in ever decreasing circles till it disappears up its own arse.'

Chapter Five

The party of would-be Commandos were met by a brusque sergeant.

'This way, you load of dozy wankers.' There was no real belligerence in his remark; it was an automatic response, one he used to every batch of men in transit. He led them over a bridge that spanned the platform to a siding where a much shorter train with two engines attached – a 'pusher' and a 'puller' – was waiting for them to board.

A railway worker was walking along the track, tapping the wheels with a large hammer. Private Bennett peered down at him, and said jocularly: 'Trust the army to put us on a train wot needs to be checked for wheels an' don' know wevver it's comin' or goin'.'

'Where this wee train is taking you, laddie,' the wheel tapper said, 'you'll have reason to be grateful for both of them.' He made it sound as though hell was their destination.

The train was even more cramped than the one they had just left, and again there was an interminable delay before it pulled out. But at least it was daylight and they were able to lower windows and draw some fresh air into their lungs.

The train chugged slowly through the grimy slums of Glasgow and in a short time was skirting the placid water of Loch Lomond. Towering above it like a watchful sentinel was the impressive bulk of Ben Nevis. The visibility was crystal clear, and the undulating countryside looked crisp and beautiful, presenting a kaleidoscope of colour. Apart from some shaggy-haired cattle it appeared uninhabited, and after the claustrophobic journey from Euston it seemed idyllic.

There were no First Class carriages and Lieutenant Lord William Mappin found himself sitting with a group of other ranks. He regretted it, not for snobbish reasons but because he felt his presence would act as a dampener on their conversation. Soldiers liked to moan about the army: not with any genuine sense of grievance, but simply because it was a time-honoured custom. An officer in their midst prevented them from indulging in what they considered was their right and privilege.

Aware of the sullen silence, he attempted to break the ice. He turned to Lance-Corporal Temple. 'This is breathtaking,' he said amiably. 'Worth all the discomfort we suffered getting here.'

Temple nodded towards the open window. 'Frankly, sir, I'll swap all "yon bonny banks and braes" for a cup of tea and a bite to eat. It never occurred to anyone that we might get a little peckish on the way here. But that's the army, sir. Thinks we can live on fresh air!'

Temple waited for the expected reprimand. Not that he was in the least bit worried; it was his way of reminding the effete-looking officer that such cock-ups were inevitable as long as they continued to hand out commissions to the likes of him.

But there was no rebuke. Lord William smiled broadly and wagged a reproving finger. 'And *you* are aiming to become a Commando? No grub provided, so you go hungry! Where's your initiative? I anticipated the usual lack of foresight and planned accordingly.' He stood up and took down a wicker hamper from the luggage rack. 'Fortnum and Mason. What I think they call their Henley hamper.'

'I'm afraid the pay we get doesn't run to such luxuries, sir,' Temple said caustically.

'All the more reason why I should share the contents with you,' said Lord William. He opened the hamper with a flourish. 'Fill your boots, lads! Not exactly a beanfeast, but enough to stop our bellies flapping against our backbones.'

The hamper contained legs of chicken, a pot of caviar, a tin of ham, some paté in a ceramic bowl, a box of assorted sandwiches, several kinds of biscuits and two bottles of white wine. 'Sorry about the plonk. It should be chilled, but as they forgot to pack any glasses we'll have to swig from the bottle, I'm sure you'll overlook such a minor vulgarity.'

Temple immediately warmed to him. He might look a prick, but he had a sense of humour and his heart was in the right place.

Private Warren, however, looked at the food with suspicion. 'If you'll pardon me asking, sir – how comes it, sir, with rationing and what not, sir, a shop can still sell stuff *we* haven't seen for donkey's?' He had liberally larded his question with 'sirs' to avoid any suggestion of disrespect, and scrupulously watched his language. By no stretch of the imagination could his favourite word have been used to describe the contents of the hamper.

Lord William realized his harmless lie had boomeranged. It would have been better to have said nothing and simply shared his food. He had made up the story about the famous store on the spur of the moment; the truth would have been too embarrassing. When he had volunteered for the Commandos he was determined not to trade on his title. He wanted to be treated no differently to anyone else, which meant he could hardly tell the soldiers in the carriage the truth which was that he had telephoned his mother when he knew he was leaving for London, and told her that if she could make it they could meet for a brief chat at Euston Station. She had arrived from her London home accompanied by her butler carrying a hefty hamper. To have told his new comrades this would have put up an impregnable barrier between them, and that was what he was desperately anxious to avoid.

He smiled at Private Warren. 'You certainly caught me out then!' He shrugged. 'The truth is, my old batman bought it from a chap who said it had fallen off the back of a lorry that happened to be parked outside a rather posh looking house. He gave him a fiver and asked no questions.'

Warren said, 'Good for you, sir. No crime in robbing the rich to feed the poor, says I. If we weren't noshing it, some fucking titled geezer would be.'

Lord William felt quite relieved at unexpectedly finding himself in the role of Robin Hood.

There were nine men in the carriage, and Lord William made certain that everyone got an equal share. As the food was passed round, Private Bennett said: 'As we're goin' to be in the same mob, sir, we oughta get to know each other. Private Bennett, sir.'

'Lieutenant Mappin. Glad to make your acquaintance.'

One by one the soldiers introduced themselves, and when it came to their turn to take a swig of wine called out: 'Your good health, sir!'

Christ! thought Bennett. I never thought I'd live to see the day when I took a shine to a' officer.

As the train chugged deeper into the heart of the Highlands, the need for two engines became apparent. One minute it was wheezing up inclines that were so steep it seemed the train would never make it to the top, the next it was descending so swiftly the sparks flew from the brake shoes like shards of molten metal from a knife grinder's wheel. It passed through lonely glens, drab areas of peat moors, past turbulent streams and hills that were covered with pine forests or carpeted with heather, and the occasional much bigger mountains that had grey screes at their base and were snow-tipped.

When it left Fort William the train headed due west on a single line track that followed the Road to the Isles. As they passed the northern end of Loch Shiel the mist cleared just enough for them to catch a glimpse of the statue of a solitary kilted Highlander, commemorating the men who had died in the Jacobite Rising, and the spot where Bonnie Prince Charlie landed by boat to raise his standard. It was a beautiful yet desolate setting; one of the most unpopulated areas in Great Britain, full of memories, never-to-be-forgotten defeats, feuds and massacres.

They all saw it through different eyes.

Bennett, who liked the comforting presence of bricks and mortar, pavements underfoot and the smell of exhaust fumes and smoking chimneys, sat wrapped in a blanket of despondency as heavy as the mist that shrouded the surrounding peaks. He knew nothing of the strange people who chose to live in such a remote and inhospitable land. The Scots were a closed book to him; strange men, wearing old bonnets, who descended on Wembley Stadium every now and again and tossed coins out of the windows of their charabancs to the cadging children below.

It appealed enormously to the hunter in Lord William Mappin. He saw himself sliding, snake-like, in pursuit of a prize stag. Private Luck saw it in terms of music, mystical and haunting: a Hebridean overture. Whilst Private Bunny Warren saw it as the

84

ideal terrain in which to fight a guerilla war. If Jerry ever did invade and overrun the south he would never, in a month of Sundays, gain a foothold in this part of Britain. One man with a sniper's rifle could really fuck up an entire army.

For Lance-Corporal Temple, with a vague schoolboy recollection that it was this scenery that had inspired Johnson or Boswell – to write some unreadable journal – it was a place that in normal times he would never dream of visiting. Race courses and casinos would be as rare here as igloos in Arabia.

One thing they all had in common: a deep apprehension as to the kind of place that awaited them at the end of the journey. If it was anything like some of the terrain they had passed through, the men would soon be sorted from the boys. Only the toughest would survive.

Suddenly, without warning, it became very dark, as if a giant hand had blotted out what little daylight there was. Then it began to rain, so torrentially that the windows had to be pulled up and the soldiers felt as if they were travelling down an endless unlit tunnel. Eventually the train juddered to a halt at the small fishing town of Mallaig, where the railway ended. Beyond was the sea.

When they clambered out visibility was no more than forty or fifty yards. The only sound was the mournful cry of countless seagulls wheeling overhead. A figure in a rain-glistening gas cape emerged out of the gloom, and barked: 'Fall in. Follow me.'

He turned and strode briskly through the small booking hall into the street outside, where the rain was battering the cobbles. Private Luck recognized his walk immediately and hurried forward. '*Harry*! It's me. Different name; same face. It's good to see you.'

Sergeant Harry Keith stopped and turned. 'Hullo, lad! Good to see you've fully recovered; we must have a chat some time. But let's get one thing quite clear – from now on, it's Sergeant. No familiarity. No favours. No "for old time's sake". To me you're just a name and number. Got it?'

Private Luck felt dejected and betrayed. He had imagined this would be a joyous reunion, one in which he could explain the reason for his presence. 'Very good, Sergeant, if that's how you want it.'

'That's how I want it, and that's how it's going to be.'

He formed the new arrivals into a marching column, making no attempt to distinguish officers from NCOs and the privates. The soldiers fumbled for their waterproof capes with fingers that were now white with cold, but Sergeant Keith stopped them. 'You can do that after I've said a few words. I'm Sergeant Keith, and I'll be your senior instructor for most of the time. I'm going to start out as I intend to finish: a real case-hardened bastard. You're going to wish you'd never volunteered, because I'm going to make your lives sheer hell. You'll hate me, and you'll go to bed praying that something awful and painful happens to me. But at the end you'll thank me – because I'm going to teach you how to kill and, just as important, how to stay alive.'

He produced a list and called out their names. By the time he had finished the rain had soaked through to their underwear.

'Don't bother about getting wet. This is an April shower compared to what you can expect, so you might as well start getting used to it. Now all you've got to do is follow the tail lights of my truck, and in three hours' time, maybe less, you'll be enjoying a nice, hot meal.'

'Where's our transport, Sergeant?' Lord William said.

'You're standing on it, sir.'

'You mean we 'ave to march through this?' said an anguished Bennett.

'Correct.'

They stood watching glumly as the sergeant got into the truck, started the engine and set off at a speed that indicated they would almost have to run to keep up with it. Three hours later they arrived at the school, where they formed up on a primitive parade ground, uneven and dotted with deep rain-filled potholes. Their calves and thighs screamed in agony, and their shoulders ached from the weight of their backpacks. They had all done a fair amount of route marching but never at such a pace, nor over such punishing ground. Around the perimeter of the parade ground they could barely discern the dim shapes of Nissen huts, and in the distance the dark hulk of what appeared to be a large house or mansion, gaunt and foreboding.

'Jesus Chris' Almighty!' Bennett said. 'I reckon that bloke Dracula lives 'ere.'

Sergeant Keith pointed into the gloom. 'You can't see it, but over there is the mess hut. First you'll be allocated huts, where you can get your brass polished and your boots and webbing cleaned. Then, if you pass my scrutiny, you can eat. After that, what's left of the day is yours to do as you please with. And make the most of it – you'll not be having much time to yourselves from now on. First thing in the morning the Colonel will give you a little pep talk, then the real job of turning you into Commandos begins.'

He turned to Bennett. 'For your edification, lad, Dracula *doesn't* live in the castle. But the Colonel does, and by the time he's finished with you you'll be wishing someone as friendly as a vampire *was* in residence.'

The Nissen huts had been erected with a total disregard for comfort. On either side of the bare concrete floor were rows of metal beds with rock hard palliasses, even harder pillows, and a single blanket neatly folded at the foot. By each bed was a small steel locker for personal belongings. The windows were ill-fitting and blacked out, and the wind whistled through the gaps in the corrugated iron walls. In the centre of the hut was a cast iron stove, but there was no fuel for it.

As the new arrivals were allowed to decide among themselves with whom they wanted to share hut space, Privates Luck, Bennett, Warren and Lance-Corporal Temple ended up together.

Private Bennett collared two beds – one for himself, the other for Private Luck – at the far end of the hut away from the door, where the draft was not quite so Arctic. He sat on the foot of his bed, tugged off his boots and massaged his aching feet. 'Fuck me, Ted, Pentonville was luxury compared to this dump! I wouldn't be at all surprised if we don' 'ave to slop out in the mornin'.'

He wearily removed his pack and contemplated with some dismay the prospect of cleaning his filthy uniform and equipment with materials that were soaked.

Lance-Corporal Temple, who had bagged a bed on the other side of Luck's, said belligerently: 'I've put up with being half drowned, but I'm buggered if I'm going to freeze to death. I'm going to find some fuel and get that stove going. There must be some trees around.'

Privates Luck, Bennett and Warren agreed to help, and half an hour later they had collected a sizeable pile of fallen branches and several handfuls of fir cones. They started the fire with the cones, which burned quickly and gave off a pleasant smell, but the wood was wet and soon the hut was filled with choking smoke. They decided that they preferred being wet to being asphyxiated.

'I 'ate the thought of it, but I'm goin' to turn out as if I was goin' to meet a girl', Private Bennett said. 'I'm not lettin' that sadistic fuckin' sergeant grind me into the dirt – no way. I got my pride to fink of.' It was a view that was silently shared by the others.

When they trooped into the large mess hut for their first meal, they were surprised and somewhat aggrieved when Sergeant Keith gave no more than a cursory glance at their efforts to look smart. They mistook his seeming indifference for callousness, not realizing that his experienced eyes had noted the trouble they must have gone to, and that mentally he was recording the fact that they had passed his first test with flying colours. They showed they possessed an essential quality, one without which no soldier could hope to last the course: personal pride.

The meal was extremely good, and when after a few beers in the 'wet' canteen they returned to their hut, they were surprised to see the stove burning brightly, the scuttle filled with coal. There was an unsigned note saying:

'Initiative! Any potential Commando would have figured out that where there was a stove there had to be fuel. Try the bunker at the rear.'

Lance-Corporal Temple stood warming his backside. 'I don't know who's been playing Fairy Godmother, but I bet my bottom dollar it wasn't Sergeant Keith.'

Private Luck thought differently, but did not contradict him. Sergeant Keith, like God, clearly moved in mysterious ways his wonders to perform.

Chapter Six

Reveille was at six thirty. It was still raining when the new intake marched to the mess hut for breakfast followed by Colonel Rutherford's pep talk.

When the tables had been cleared away they were called to attention as the Colonel strode in and stood on an upturned crate that had been provided as a makeshift rostrum. He signalled them to sit down, then launched into a twenty-minute lecture, in which he listed all the requirements needed to become a fully-fledged Commando. They were daunting requirements, which few of the men listening felt they could possibly meet: the spirit might be willing, but they secretly doubted if the flesh would be able to live up to the demands. He seemed to be asking the impossible.

'On parade discipline will be rigid. Off parade there'll be a degree of familiarity which few of you will have experienced, but it has a real purpose. You'll be fighting in relatively small units, and complete faith and trust in each other is essential in order to build up that special spirit of comradeship. There'll be no punishment: self-discipline is what counts. Any man who commits an offence or fails to meet the standards I demand will be RTUd. As the course progresses I hope that each of you will look on that as the worst possible punishment, something that can never be lived down. By the same token, you can jack it in any time you wish and there'll be no recriminations. Just one final point: don't for one moment think you've finished with spit and polish. You haven't. Every day will be harsh and unrelenting, but next morning you'll be expected to turn out again looking spick and span. Know why? It's to instil a sense of pride: the pride that made the Guards march ashore after Dunkirk looking as if they were about to attend Church parade.'

When the Colonel had gone, the new arrivals were split into small units, each with an instructor in charge. Bennett, Luck, Warren, Temple and Lord William Mappin were among the twenty or more men under Sergeant Keith.

'The first thing I'm going to do is sort out those of you who aren't George Washingtons. We're going to look at the loch,' he said, to their utter bewilderment.

They were marched along a rough track through a dense pine forest that led to a narrow, boulder-strewn path that finally came out at the edge of the loch, which was narrow at the inland end, but became wider as it stretched out to the unseen sea. The surface of the loch was sullen-looking, slate grey; on both sides the mountains rose cliff-like from the water's edge.

Sergeant Keith halted them at a precarious-looking pier with a ramshackle boathouse attached. Under the boathouse were several clinker-built rowing boats, and flat-bottomed paddle-propelled assault craft.

'When you volunteered you all stated that you could swim,' he said amiably. 'Well, this is where we find out if you told the truth. When I give the order I want you, one by one, to jump into the water.'

'That's a bit harsh on men who may have been economical with the truth in their enthusiasm, Sergeant,' Lord William Mappin said.

'Correct, sir. But necessary. You see, a man with full equipment who can't swim is committing suicide if he falls into the water during a real raid.'

Private Bennett groaned. 'I volunteered, Sarge, but in what yer might call unusual circumstances. It was volunteer or stay in the nick.' He shrugged. 'No point in beatin' about the bush. I can't swim.'

Sergeant Keith sighed audibly. 'There's only one way to find out if you're telling the truth *this* time, or just trying to avoid a ducking.'

Private Bennett said, with genuine anguish: 'Sarge, I swear it on me mother's grave! If you make me jump off of there I'll 'it the bottom before you can say "poor sod".'

'Sorry, Private Bennett, but if I don't put you to the test I'll never find out if there're others in the group who can't swim.' He did not sound at all contrite.

Bennett pleaded. 'At least try askin' 'em, Sarge! Surely they wouldn't want me to drown. It'd look bad for you on the very first day.'

'My way is much more reliable,' said the sergeant drily.

Three men slowly raised hands above their head, and said almost with one voice: 'I can't, Sarge.'

'Does that mean we'll all be RTUd?' one man asked.

'Not if you learn to swim before the course is over.'

Keith marched them back to the parade ground. On the way Lance-Corporal temple turned to Private Luck. 'Do you really think he'd have made everyone, non-swimmers included, jump in?'

'Yes.'

'You share my view that he's an inhuman bastard.'

'No – I think it was his way of telling us that from now on there must be total honesty, as a life may depend on it.'

'Jesus, that's attributing human emotions to the bastard!'

'Oh, Keith's human, all right. I'll tell you why some time.'

When they arrived back they were issued with specialized equipment, including a Wilkinson fighting knife, a toggle rope, a set of blue dungarees, a pair of plimsolls, shorts and a singlet, and rubber coshes which the sergeant explained came by courtesy of London Underground; they had originally been intended for the use of straphanging passengers during the rush hours until someone realized they could be put to a more lethal use.

From that moment on their lives were dedicated to the task of becoming Commandos. From early morning until late at night and sometimes through it, they were taken to the brink of human endurance. Some asked to be returned to their units. Others failed to measure up to the required standards of training and behaviour, and to their chagrin were sent back to their regiments.

They were taught boat handling in the loch, in which all types of craft were used. They did long, lung-bursting speed marches with full pack, and were taught to fire all types of weapons including German ones. They climbed the mountains, scaled the cliffs around the loch, learned how to hang

91

on to primed grenades before throwing them so that there was no risk of them being tossed back. On the parade ground they did punishing exercises and discovered muscles they never knew existed. They became proficient at demolition, laying booby traps, linking toggle ropes together to make a primitive bridge, and killing silently with their bare hands, the knife or a length of wire. There were survival exercises, when they spent long days and nights on the mountains learning to exist on what they could snare or dig up. Nothing was considered too revolting – worms, beetles and all kinds of edible fungi that would make normal people throw up in revulsion were devoured with gusto. They waded across icy streams, and slept rough in gale-force winds and freezing sleet, and became nonchalantly adept at negotiating the 'Death Slide', a length of wire stretched taut across a deep ravine from a tree thirty feet high on one side to a low stump on the other. There were lessons in unarmed combat where they were taught how to kill with the edge of the hand, the rim of a steel helmet, and from finger pressure applied to vulnerable nerve points.

Lieutenant Mappin thought he must have incurred the sergeant's displeasure, he was continually reprimanded, expected to be twice as good as everybody else. He did not know, and was not told, that this was a deliberate ploy. If officers were to lead they had to be able to inspire their men by example.

One morning, when the rain had called a temporary truce, Sergeant Keith formed his class up on the parade ground. 'Today is something special,' he announced with evident relish. 'You'll be taking part in an opposed landing, which will be as near as possible to the real thing. Good luck – because, believe me, you're going to need it.' He grinned broadly. 'Thank God I'll be a spectator!'

With full pack and bulging ammunition pouches they were marched down to the boathouse where they clambered into flat-bottom boats equipped with hand paddles. Rifles were piled into the bottom, and they were ordered to paddle half a mile out into the loch, then turn and make their way shorewards. Their hearts were beating like trip hammers; when Sergeant Keith forecast a rough time they knew something very unpleasant indeed was in store.

92

As Private Bennett plunged his paddle deep into the water, he forced a smile on his face. 'Don't let 'im scare shit outa you, Ted,' he said to Luck. 'This is gonna be a piece o' cake. Like bein' on the Serpentine.'

'Stop talking like his ruddy nannie,' Temple said. 'Ted doesn't need cotton-woolling. He knows bloody well that when Sergeant Keith grins like a Cheshire cat he's got something really shitty up his sleeve.'

'Thanks, Reg! It's time someone told him he's not my wet nurse,' Luck called over his shoulder.

He had hardly finished speaking when the water around the boats erupted into small gouts caused by tracer bullets from Bren guns firing on fixed lines. Everyone dug deeper and paddled more furiously: the bullets were dangerously close. But their efforts to avoid the fusillade were in vain. As they got closer to the shore the gunfire intensified and tracers passed inches over their heads as more automatic weapons opened up.

As they neared the shore they were confronted by an even more nerve-jangling ordeal. Grenades were lobbed into the shallow water, followed by smoke cannisters which enveloped them in an impenetrable fog. They heard the voice of Sergeant Keith bellow from the shore: 'Remember your boat drill. Don't panic. That's the surest way of getting yourself killed.'

The leading men in each boat leaped out, just as they had been taught, and hauled on the bow lines until the boats grounded and the rest of the men were able to leap ashore.

Keith roared, 'Knock out the Brens!' He pointed to a high mound topped with steel plates painted white. 'That's them.' Each was no bigger than a shoe box. The men rushed forward and flung themselves on the ground with such force that what breath they had remaining was knocked out of them. As they began firing they heard Keith bellow: 'A shilling deducted from your pay for every target missed!'

As Temple fired round after round in rapid succession and heard no rewarding sound of metal striking metal, he figured out that it would not be worth his while attending the next pay parade. Bunny Warren, on the other hand, hit every one of his targets. Although the adrenalin was flowing through his veins, giving him the strength of ten men, he fired slowly and methodically like the old sweat he was. He had not enjoyed himself so much since the retreat to Dunkirk. In his mind's eye the plates were real, flesh-and-blood Jerries.

Lieutenant Mappin, remembering his days on the grouse moors, held his breath before every shot and squeezed the trigger, resisting the urge to pull it. Bennett also did well; in his case the plates were not Germans but Sergeant Keith. Private Luck was praying silently to himself: Please God, don't let me make a complete mess of things.

They heard Sergeant Keith's voice above the rifle fire: 'That'll do. Now charge them.'

They rose and pounded up the steep incline, only to see more steel plates ahead, and even more live rounds whizzing over their heads.

'Get flat! Fire!' Keith roared.

Some of the men, firing erratically or inaccurately, felt the firm pressure of his boot in the small of the back. 'Steady now. Imagine they're real Jerries who'll get you if you don't get them first!'

When they had hit sufficient targets to satisfy him, he yelled: 'Up on your feet. Fix bayonets – charge!'

They bent low and ran forward, painfully aware of the bullets humming like hornets around them. Suspended from timber uprights were straw-filled sacks. To Keith's encouraging cries of 'In-out. In-out. Disembowel the bastards,' they thrust and withdrew their bayonets with unbridled savagery, venting their pent-up anger on the sacks, which far from resembling Germans had an uncanny likeness to Colonel Rutherford, the perpetrator of their misery. Then, when they thought it was all over, Keith shouted: 'Back to the boats. Attack repulsed. Prepare for a fresh assault.'

They scrambled back to the beached boats. As they began to paddle out into the loch, grenades exploded around them and the Brens again opened fire. At times the firing was so accurate paddles were splintered into matchwood.

They repeated the landing, which apparently met with the sergeant's approval, for he ordered them to march back to the parade ground. There he said: 'Now, once around the assault course and we'll call it a day.'

94

The totally exhausted men scaled walls, clambered over obstacles, crawled under pegged-down tarpaulins, and endured the ear-splitting bangs of thunder flashes that were thrown in after them, tiptoed over greasy logs eight feet above muddy pits, and finished off with a swift descent down the 'Death Slide'.

Keith studied his stopwatch. 'Not bad – not bad at all. But next time I want you to do it a damn sight quicker. If you don't manage it, we'll keep on doing it until you do. Because if today had been the real thing not many of you would still be here.'

Tired as they were, they completed another circuit of the assault course to his satisfaction. When they eventually tumbled into their beds, far from feeling bitter and resentful, they experienced an enormous glow of pride.

That night Sergeant Keith learned from Colonel Rutherford that the Prime Minister and his party of VIPs would be arriving by Sunderland flying boat in a few days time.

'Pick a good section, and put on a show. Remember, there's a lot at stake.'

Keith decided that Lieutenant Mappin's section would provide an ideal showpiece. They had all displayed well above average ability and enthusiasm, and were well on the way to becoming fully-fledged Commandos.

Five days later they were formed up on the parade ground where Keith told them about the visit later in the day. 'There're still a lot of people who don't approve of us, and we're going to show the Prime Minister they're talking out of their fundamental orifice. When he arrives I'll be giving you a lesson on the Tommy-gun, making out it's your first. There's logic behind the little bit of cheating: I want Winnie to be impressed at the way you pick things up so quickly, and prod him into speeding up the production of the weapon. It's a criminal shame they're in such short supply.'

They stood on the parade ground kicking their heels for two hours before they heard the throaty roar of aircraft engines and the massive bulk of a Sunderland flew low overhead to begin its descent to the loch. Ten minutes later Colonel Rutherford's jeep appeared. The Prime Minister sat beside him in the front, and there were three senior officers in the back with several more following in a truck behind. The Prime Minister was instantly recognisable. He wore a hard-topped hat, a cross between a bowler and a top hat, and his portly figure was clothed in a woollen siren-suit. He followed Rutherford to where Keith stood in front of his class holding a Thompson sub-machine gun. His entourage followed a dutiful three yards behind.

Keith called his class to attention and whipped off a parade ground salute. 'Just about to start a lesson, sir.'

'Ignore me,' Churchill growled. 'Carry on as if I weren't here.'

Sergeant Keith gave the weapon a pat and launched into a description he had given so many times he had lost count. 'This is not, as you may think, a modern weapon. It was invented by General John Thompson during the First War as a 'trench broom' but it never saw active service because the first prototypes were due to leave New York for France on November 11th, 1918, the day the war ended. But it's seen a lot of action since. The IRA use it, and it was popular with Al Capone and other gangsters who christened it the 'Chicago piano'. *Time Magazine* called it the deadliest weapon, pound for pound, ever devised.'

He then went on to describe how it worked, its rate of fire and its lethal capabilities. 'Ironically, this perfect weapon for close-quarter fighting never found favour with our own War Office, who dismissed it as a gangster's weapon: an unsporting weapon to use even against an enemy intent on destruction.'

He cast a discreet glance at the Prime Minister to see what reaction his words were having, for he knew that Churchill had been one of the gun's most outspoken critics. But the Prime Minister's face gave nothing away. He seemed preoccupied with the unlit cigar clamped firmly between his teeth.

'To add to the chronicle of shortsightedness, in 1938 the Birmingham Small Arms Company, which had a seven year option from America to manufacture them, pressed the War Office to place an order, but it was turned down. Thank God, the Mayor of New York had greater vision, for on the outbreak of war he presented us with several that his police

96

force had confiscated from gangsters. Now we'll see just how much we owe to him.'

Sergeant Keith marched his class to a long low-roofed building, the interior of which had been turned into a narrow cobbled street lined with shops and houses. From the corner of his eye, he saw Churchill and his entourage following.

He waited until they had taken their places in the area set aside for observers before balancing himself on the balls of his feet and slowly advancing up the street. String-operated plywood figures of uniformed Germans suddenly began to pop out from windows and doorways. He fired in short bursts as the figures emerged. The force of the .45 bullets tore great jagged holes in the models.

The observers who had anticipated his action were nevertheless still taken by surprise at the violence and noise of the demonstration, and their hands flew to their ears to shut out the brutal thud-thud-thud of the bullets. The acrid tang of gunpowder hung in the air, tickling their nostrils, and thin wisps of blue smoke spiralled upwards.

He attached a fresh magazine to the gun and handed it to Private Warren, the undisputed crackshot in the class. 'Now let's see what you can do with it.' Private Warren hit every target with the accuracy and nonchalance of someone who had been born with the weapon in his hands.

The rest of the class then took their turn at firing, and when they had finished Churchill turned to Rutherford. 'I'd like to have a go with this weapon I was apparently so contemptuous of acquiring for our fighting soldiers.'

He fired it and missed every target. 'Your men are much quicker to learn than I am,' he said to Sergeant Keith. 'It's hard to believe they have never fired it before.' Keith saw the suggestion of a smile flicker across the puckish face. 'I think, Sergeant, that I must withdraw my original reservations about the sub-machine gun. When you're waging a war to the death against gangsters and thugs – which is what the Nazis are – it's only right and proper to fight them with their own weapons.'

The class then demonstrated their skills at unarmed combat, aimed grenades to explode on impact, negotiated the 'Death Slide', went round the assault course, and attacked and demolished an enemy strong point.

Later, over glasses of malt whisky in Rutherford's office, the senior officers indicated that what they had witnessed had been an eye-opening experience. It had made them consciously aware of the vital contribution Commandos could make to the war effort. Churchill, drinking brandy, growled belligerently: 'The backbiting and bellyaching must cease forthwith. The Commandos must become a recognized force. Serious consideration should be given to the question of them having their own insignia and distinctive headgear, something they can wear with pride.'

On the way back to the flying boat he said to Rutherford: 'I was most impressed by the Sergeant and his class. When will they complete the course?'

'They have another week, I think, sir.'

Churchill stabbed him with his still unlit cigar. 'Thought as much. That wasn't the first time they've handled a sub-machine gun, was it? Now, I want the truth.'

Rutherford grinned sheepishly. 'No, sir. I needed to impress you and your party as to the contribution Commandos can make to the war effort.'

'You've done that, Colonel. But aren't you being a trifle unfair? I needed no persuading, even if some of my military advisers did. I was instrumental in the formation of the Commandos.'

As he waited for the launch to ferry him and his party out to the Sunderland, he turned again to Rutherford. 'There's a very special mission to be carried out in Norway. It'll call for the greatest courage and initiative, for the risks are great, but if successfully accomplished the rewards will be beyond calculation. It'll require a small party, no more than eight men, and I cannot think of any group of men better suited to the task than the ones I've watched today. A senior officer will visit you in the not too distant future to give a full briefing.'

When the Sunderland had departed, Rutherford returned to his office and sent a messenger to find Sergeant Keith immediately. When he arrived, Rutherford said: 'I think we've silenced our critics once and for all. You did a splendid job, Sergeant.'

'With the help of a little cheating, sir.'

'Forget it. That wily old bird saw through it, but he was still impressed.'

'Thank you, sir. Can I remind you of your promise!'

'No need to: you can join Lieutenant Mappin's section. He'll be pleased to have you, especially when he learns that the PM has something very hush-hush in mind for him and his lads. Specifically mentioned you too, so I've no option about granting your request.'

'Any idea what it is, sir?'

'Not the foggiest. All I know is that it's in Norway and is extremely hazardous. If you want to change your mind and stay here teaching, I can wangle it, otherwise you're welcome to go and get your balls shot off.'

'No change of heart, sir. Can I remind you I've also been teaching them how to stay alive?'

'I'll let you *and* the lieutenant do the actual picking and choosing. Select twelve of the best. Only eight will be needed, but it's safe to err on the side of caution. People do fall out for various reasons, through no fault of their own: a broken leg or arm, or a bullet in the head because they didn't keep it down during the harsh training that lies ahead.'

Chapter Seven

The twelve men Keith had recommended to Colonel Rutherford sat around a stove in an informal group in one of the
Nissen huts. They included himself, Lance-Corporal Temple
and Privates Luck, Warren and Bennett. An armed sentry
stood outside to prevent anyone else entering.

A young looking brigadier from Combined Operations
Staff was standing, legs astride, in front of them. He had the
hard, lean frame of a fighting soldier, typical of the new brand
of leader gradually being introduced into the army.

'Smoke if you want to, lads, because this is going to take
some time. I want to tell you as much as I possibly can about
the operation, that's the only way you'll appreciate how
important its success is. The background is this: very early in
the war America was supplying us with much needed equipment and war materials under the Cash and Carry scheme,
which meant we had to pay in dollars for what we wanted. A
straightforward business transaction which didn't affect
America's precious neutrality.'

He paused to add cynically: 'It also lifted America out of
the Depression, because it did a lot to put her industry back
on its feet. We invested in their plants and paid for new
factories. To accomplish this, all the gold we possessed was
secretly shipped to Canada in warships and fast liners. We
also shipped out what gold was rescued in Belgium and
Holland. Later, when we were running out of gold, we had to
ship all our negotiable securities to Canada to meet the
mounting bills. In order to fight on we've near bankrupted
ourselves.' He lit a cigarette. 'When Norway fell the Royal

101

Navy rescued their Royal family, together with a great quantity of gold which has enabled Norway to continue the struggle from here. There is a very strong Resistance Movement there and agents and equipment are regularly ferried over from the Shetlands.

'Well, quite recently some Norwegians arrived in a fishing boat with a remarkable story: hidden in a disused railway tunnel is a large quantity of gold bullion. It was being transported to one of the northern ports to be put aboard a British cruiser before the country collapsed, but the ship was forced to sail before the gold arrived, so it was taken inland and hidden. Your job will be to bring it back. Ideally we want you to do it without the Germans ever knowing. That means avoiding a fight if at all possible; if it isn't, then you'll be called upon to use all the skills and cunning you've acquired here. Just don't come back without it. We need it badly, but Adolph needs it more. And for God's sake don't get caught; Hitler has issued a personal directive that Commandos are not to be treated according to the rules of war, they're to be summarily executed. In his eyes you're not soldiers but cold-blooded murderers. A view, I might add, that's still held by some of our own military hierarchy, despite your efforts to convince them otherwise.'

This provoked a burst of humourless laughter.

'How do we get there, sir?' Lieutenant Mappin asked.

'By submarine from Scapa Flow. Transport will be laid on to take you to Scrabster near Thurso where a ferry will take you to Stromness in the Orkneys. You'll be based near Kirkwall until the off.'

'When will that be, sir?'

'Not sure yet. It depends to a large extent on the weather, and the latest information from Norway. There'll be a final briefing before you leave.'

Sergeant Keith raised a hand. 'What's this Op called, sir?'

The brigadier smiled. 'Sorry – one of the first things I should have told you. It's named Midas. You shouldn't need to ask me why. Now, any more questions?'

There were none.

'Right. I'll see you all in Kirkwall then.'

Early next morning, long before anyone else was up and about, they were formed up on the parade ground and marched to where a large army truck with a canvas hood was waiting with its engine ticking over. They tossed their equipment over the tailboard and clambered in after it.

Colonel Rutherford who had risen early to see them off, called out: 'Don't let me down, lads! Remember, you're Commandos.'

It was a long and circuitous drive to Thurso and dawn was just breaking over the Pentland Firth when they arrived at the small harbour where they boarded the ferry.

The Firth was considered by sailors to be one of the most inhospitable stretches of water in the world. That morning it certainly lived up to its awesome reputation. No sooner had the steamer left the comparative tranquillity of the harbour than it began to roll and pitch with such violence that half the Commandos were prostrate with sea sickness. They lay on the exposed decks and in the lounge, their battle dress fouled with their own vomit, feeling like death.

After what seemed an endless voyage to the stricken soldiers, one of the crew went round the ship calling out: 'On your feet lads!. We're nearly there.'

Somehow the Commandos found the strength to move legs that seconds before they had been sure would never respond again. They struggled to their feet and peered over the heaving bow to get their first glimpse of the vast land-locked anchorage that was capable of holding all the navies of the world. The barren, blizzard-swept hills encircling it had an Arctic bleakness about them, and the shrieking of the sea birds wheeling above the ship sounded like cries of utter despair.

A sailor tapped Sergeant Keith on the shoulder. 'Now you can see why matelots call it the arsehole of the Admiralty.'

The sky was dotted with barrage balloons; so many they gave the impression they were supporting the island with invisible strings and preventing it from sinking into the water. The hill tops bristled with shore batteries, and the Flow itself was littered with anchored flak ships. There were sleek destroyers straining at the anchor cables like greyhounds on the leash, their paint work daubed with red lead, an indication of how long they had spent at sea and how little time there was to give them their customary dashing appearance.

There were cruisers too, solid and reliable, but also looking jaded and neglected. Dwarfed by them were tubby corvettes, the navy's mongrels on whom the convoys were so dependent. Drifters and supply boats scuttled across the surface like water boatmen on a village pond; the unsung heroes of the war, daily fulfilling the inglorious chores without which the fighting ships could not survive.

As the ferry approached Kirkwall, the main town, Keith pointed to the top section of a main mast rising like a cathedral spire from the water. 'What's that?' he asked a sailor.

The sailor replied with a voice that was laced with a mixture of awe and fury. 'All that's left of the battle wagon *Royal Oak*. War hadn't ben on a dog watch when a U-boat slipped in and tinfished her. Went down with the loss of eight hundred hands, most of them still in their hammocks. Fucking disgrace – someone should have been keel-hauled for negligence. Three days later the Luftwaffe sank the *Iron Duke,* Jellico' old flagship. She's beached in Longhope Sound, as useless as a nun in a knocking shop. But they still fuck about with Divisions, and marines blow bugles every other minute. Blocked the gap where the U-boat slipped through: call i' Churchill's Barrier. Talk about bolting stable doors! After the total balls-up of letting two capital ships be sunk without a shot being fired, it was decided the Flow wasn't safe enough for battleships, so they've moved them to Rosyth and Loch Ewe.'

'You sound bitter.'

'So I ought to be. I was in *Royal Oak*. Lucky for me I was on the upper deck when the tin fish hit.' He suddenly changed the subject. 'Where're you going to be based, Sarge!'

'No idea.'

'Well, I hope for your sake it isn't in one of those corrugated iron huts that survived the First War. They have steel hawsers stretched over their roofs staked to the ground to stop them blowing away. And the mud is just as bad as it was in Flanders. I'm telling you, it's cold enough to freeze the balls off a brass monkey.'

'You've made my day.'

'Forewarned is forearmed, cock.'

As soon as the Commandos stepped ashore they made a remarkable recovery from their sea sickness, and were acutely aware of their filthy condition. Bennett said in a voice entirely devoid of humour: 'Anyone seen my arse'ole? I fink I left it on the boat when I frew up.'

Lieutenant Mappin had formed them up on the quay when the Brigadier who had briefed them came striding towards them. He returned Mappin's salute. 'Glad you made it in one piece. Can be a sod of a crossing on a bad day. You were lucky.'

Mappin raised his eyebrows. 'If today wasn't bad, sir, I'd hate to think what it's like when it is.'

The wind was causing the Brigadier's trousers to flap against his legs, and he was having trouble keeping his cap on. 'This, I'm led to believe, is the tail-end of a very fine spell of weather.' He saw Mappin's expression and added, 'Cheer up. I've laid on transport to take you to your billets. I know it's customary for Commandos to find their own digs, but as you're all so whacked I think the rules can be bent a little. You'll find the Orcadians are very hospitable and extremely generous: lots of fresh fish and lobster and grub you don't see on the mainland. I've got you a room in a small guest house: nothing fancy, but clean and comfortable. When your men are dropped off at their billets, tell them they've got to hand in their ration books and remember to settle their bills before they leave. I don't want to hear that anyone has buggered off without paying – the whole billeting system could be ruined if word gets round that Commandos don't honour their debts.'

Lieutenant Mappin assured him that would not happen. The scheme was too prized to risk ruining. It was something the ordinary soldier looked upon with envy and ill-concealed disapproval; it smacked of privilege. It was a justified resentment, for the set rate for a billet was ten shillings and eightpence a week, which meant billeted soldiers were far better off financially than the ordinary ranker. With beer at sixpence a pint and cigarettes sixpence for twenty, they could consider themselves very fortunate.

Sergeant Keith was dropped off at a small cottage on the outskirts of the town, and Lance-Corporal Temple and Privates Luck and Bennett at a large house in the centre of

Kirkwall. Bunny Warren, to his dismay, was billeted at the home of a Church of Scotland Minister. The rest of the section were dispersed in various other homes.

Lieutenant Mappin stood in the hall of the guest house wondering how he could attract someone's attention. The place seemed deserted. There were one or two framed pictures on the wall, enough brasswork to wear out the strongest elbows. There was a tiny reception desk in one corner with the silver-framed photograph of a petty officer in Number One uniform resting on it. Next to it was a bell. He banged it and the peal echoed round the confined space.

A woman emerged from the door behind the desk, wiping her hands on her apron. She was a short dumpy woman, with greying hair and sharp, work-tired features. She smiled, and her face was transformed into one of homeliness and friendliness.

'Now you'll be Lieutenant Mappin, I should think.' She wiped her hand again and held it out. 'And I'm Mrs Moray who'll be looking after you like your own mother.'

She spoke with a broad Scottish brogue. 'I'll show you to your room first. Then I expect you'd like a wee bite to eat. She eyed the heavy revolver in a holster on his belt. 'I wouldn't be asking too much of you not to wear that in the house, would it? I don't have too many residents just now, but the few I have might be a trifle put out.'

'I'll put it somewhere safe,' he promised.

The room she led him to was small and sparsely furnished with a sloping ceiling. A chest of drawers stood against one wall, and there was a china wash-basin with matching jug on marble-topped table. There was a single cast-iron bed with handmade patchwork bedspread. He felt it and decided he would sleep like a log on it. He parted the black-out curtain in the one window, which overlooked a small flagstone patio dotted with rather sorry-looking potted plants.

'Not much to look at,' said Mrs Moray, 'but we don't have the weather here for nice gardens.'

'It'll do splendidly, Mrs Moray. Home from home!'

'See you in half an hour, sir.'

Mappin put his .45 Webley revolver under the mattress along with the six grenades he carried in pouches, and the seven-inch long fighting knife specially designed for the Commandos by Captain Fairbairn and Major Sykes of the Army Intelligence Corps. They had both served in the Shanghai Police, where they had daily faced death from the knives of thugs and organized gangs who frequented the narrow alleys and back streets. The knife had been made to their specification by Wilkinson, the famous swordmakers. He shuddered involuntarily every time he touched the blade, experiencing the same chill of fear as when the barber used a cut-throat razor to shave his neck.

When Mappin went down she had laid a table in the dining room. 'Will a wee smoked haddock be to your liking? The man who cures them is the best in the Orkneys.'

'It certainly will,' said Mappin, his mouth watering at the prospect.

Mrs Moray poured strong tea from an enormous pot. When he had finished the fish she emerged from the kitchen with two plates piled high with piping hot bannocks and mealie puddings. 'I don't want to see any of that left on the plate,' she said. 'You'll not be well accustomed to our weather, so you'll need plenty inside you to keep the cold out.'

Mappin tried his best but was unable to clear the plates, and she tut-tutted rebukingly.

While she was clearing the table he asked her, as casually as he could: 'I have a friend stationed here, a Wren. Any idea where she might be based?'

'There's only one Wrennery that I know of, and that's *HMS Friendship*. Some of them drop in here from time to time for a meal. They call it *HMS Hardship,* and I can well understand why.' She gave an exaggerated shudder. 'My, it's a barren spot they've chosen to put the poor wee lassies!' She sighed. 'But, sailors and soldiers being what they are, it makes sense to tuck them away out of sight and harm.'

'I think I'll stroll up there. I could do with the exercise after that meal.'

'Feel free to come and go as you like, sir. And don't worry about what time you get back. The front door is never locked.'

Sergeant Keith's billet was little more than a crofter's cottage, primitive but spotlessly clean and comfortable. It was the home of a fisherman and his wife, Tom and Sheila McIntosh.

The living room, also used for meals, was low, with thick beams that had been blackened by the smoke from the peat fire. A large oil lamp was suspended from one of the rafters, and a big well-scrubbed table stood in the middle. Two straw-back chairs, unique to the Orkneys, stood on either side of the open hearth.

The man of the house, said Mrs McIntosh, was down in the harbour baiting his crab and lobster pots. 'You'll not be meeting him this day.'

She was a comely-looking woman in her mid-forties, with a mass of ginger hair held in place by an abundance of pins and combs which she was constantly touching, as if she doubted their ability to remain in place.

She led him up a flight of rickety stairs that were not much more than a ladder; the rungs were rough-hewn and there was no bannister. The room was windowless and the bed was a hard mattress on a row of planks. 'It's more comfortable than it looks at first sight,' she said anxiously.

'It's better than I'm used to.'

'I'll bring up some hot water, and when you're washed I'll have some food ready and waiting.'

He stowed his equipment in a corner, covered it with his greatcoat and went down the crude staircase.

He could not remember the last time he had eaten with such pleasure, eating not for sustenance but pure self-indulgence. There was home cured bacon and ham, fresh eggs, newly baked bread, and tea that was liberally laced with whisky. Mrs McIntosh hovered over him, rubbing her hands together, enjoying each mouthful as much as he was. 'I thought you'd like something to warm the cockle of your heart after that boat trip.'

'That was really marvellous,' he said, wiping his mouth with a paper napkin. 'Now, if you'll excuse me, I'd better nip out and see my lads are comfortably settled.' He felt the need to create a warmer image of himself. 'You know what great big softies they are; they like to be tucked into bed and kissed goodnight by their sergeant.'

She smiled coyly. 'Lucky boys.'

'I've covered my personal stuff, Mrs McIntosh, and I'd be grateful if you didn't disturb it if you clean the room. Some of it is rather lethal. I shouldn't let it out of my sight, but I don't want to parade through the streets looking like someone who's had a tip-off that Jerry's about to land.'

'It's safer here than in the Bank of Scotland, Sergeant. Now you just trot off and administer to your bairns.'

Keith consulted his list of addresses and decided to call on Private Warren first. He found him sitting alone in a book-lined room looking morose and bad tempered. The Minister and his old lady, he said, were over at what they called the Kirk. 'Glad to see the fucking back of him, although she's not too bad. Bit long in the tooth, but I wouldn't kick her out of my bed.'

Keith ignored the sexual jibe, knowing that Warren was incapable of mentioning a woman without hinting at the possibility of a conquest. 'Place to you liking, Bunny?'

'The room I'm in couldn't be better. But I've got a picture of Jesus above the bed keeping an eye on me, and a bible black as the ace of spades on the table. I flicked through it, Sarge, and came to the conclusion there's a fucking lot to be said for illiteracy. The grub is great, but I reckon the old boy waded through half the Old Testament before we got round to actually noshing. When we finished he asked me if I'd like to attend Evening Service, and when I explained that I had to meet my mates to sink a few pints in thanks for our merciful deliverance from that fucking crossing, he sounded real narked. Told me that liquor and the devil were bedmates.'

'And so they are, Bunny.'

'Now don't you go giving me that old Sally-Ann crap, Sarge. If the beer in the town is anything like the piss we get in the wet canteen, I'll drown before I can get half legless.'

'Don't tell him that, Bunny, let him think you're an abstemious lad who values money too much to waste it on beer. Come to think of it, that's not too far off the truth when it comes to you buying a round.'

'That's not fair, Sarge. If I wait till it's my turn to buy the last round, it's only because I like to get my money's worth. Been in the army too fucking long to buy the first, second or third, because I know from bitter experience there's always the tight-fisted fucker who waits till Last Orders is called and it's too late for him to stand his corner.'

'You make my heart bleed, Bunny. Now stop weeping on my shoulder and we'll rouse the other lads and find a decent pub where we can all have a real sup.'

Together they set off to round up the other men in the section before beginning the serious business of finding a pub that distinguished the men from the boys. Their final call was at the big granite house near the centre of Kirkwall where Temple, Bennett and Luck were billeted.

Sergeant Keith banged the big brass knocker that was shaped like a lion's head. The door was opened by a short plump man wearing a shapeless cardigan and a pair of well worn slippers.

'Just called to see my lads aren't making a nuisance of themselves, sir.'

'Don't you sir me, Sergeant, I'm not in the army. Only too glad to have them. Get sick and tired of the sight of women round the place. Love them as I do, a man can still get bored with having three women under his feet most of the time – two daughters and a wife – all telling him what he can and can't do. All for his own benefit, of course.' He winked conspiratorially. 'First thing I did when they arrived was get a bottle of pure malt out. My wife and the girls daren't complain: Scottish hospitality, I said. Bundled them off to the flicks, thank the Lord.' He held out a hand. 'Stewart Ferguson. I've told your lads to call me Stewart, you can do the same.'

He led Keith and Warren into the sitting room. It was a high-ceilinged room with an ornately carved centre-piece from which was suspended a massive chandelier ablaze with candle-shaped electric light bulbs. There were also wall brackets, supporting more imitation candles, and the big bay windows were blacked out with heavy velvet tasselled curtains. The three soldiers were comfortably settled in deep armchairs and on a sofa, and a big coal fire glowed in the hearth. Each of them was nursing a well-filled tumbler, the colour of which suggested that water was strictly rationed.

Mr Ferguson poured stiff drinks for the visitors and an even stiffer one for himself. He raised his glass. 'Here's to a speedy end to the war and your safe survival!'

110

Warren took a long deep swig, coughed and muttered: 'Jesus, Mr. Stewart, that's better than a bunk-up without a Frenchie on!' There was a stunned silence at the inappropriate attempt at a compliment, but Mr. Ferguson smiled. 'I discern the true connoisseur.'

When they had finished their drinks Ferguson said: 'Don't think you've got to stay here and keep me company. I expect you want to see a bit of the town. The watering hole I'd recommend is down the first turning on the left when you leave here: best ale in Kirkwall, and no shortage either. I only wish I could come with you, but Mrs Ferguson can only be pushed so far. She hates the cinema, and if she thinks I'm overstepping the mark the gentle kitten turns into a tigress. That, Sergeant, tends to make life a wee bit intolerable.'

'You certainly seem to have struck oil,' Keith said as they walked down the road.

'You can say that again,' Temple said. 'I only hope we're here for some time – time to get to know his daughters. Wait till you see them! A couple of real corkers. Legs like Betty Grable and tits like that sweater girl everyone is raving about.'

'Reg 'as staked 'is claim with Moira; I rather fancy Aileen myself,' Bennet said. 'Private Luck, you could say, ain't goin' to 'ave neither. But the old boy 'as a joanna, an' Ted says 'e'll settle for that.'

'Don't count your chickens,' Keith said. 'They could be the type of well-brought-up girls who'll want to see a ring on their finger before they fall to your undisputed charms.'

'One of them matelots on the ferry said the only virgins 'ere are the sheep wot can run faster than a sailor in sea boots. I reckon if Reg an' me play our cards right we'll leave 'ere 'avin' filled our boots.'

The pub was a picturesque single-storey building at the bottom of a steep, cobbled street. As they pushed through the heavy black-out curtains that screened the door to the saloon bar, their ears picked up the hum of animated conversation.

There were fishermen in thick blue jerseys propping up the bar, and seated around the tables playing cards and dominoes were other regulars. In an alcove sailors were playing table skittles. On the walls were framed photographs of famous warships and an assortment of cap tallies, bearing the names of battleships and cruisers which had visited the Flow.

Two of the fishermen moved apart to make room for Sergeant Keith who placed a five pound note, liberally covered with signatures, on the bar. 'Give them all a pint of your best bitter, please.'

The landlord held it up against a light and studied it carefully. 'Don't get many of these,' he said, 'especially from soldiers. Sorry to be so suspicious, lad, but I served in the last lot and we didn't get that kind of pay.'

Keith grinned, not at all annoyed. 'Where I've been there was nothing to spend money on!'

'And where would that be, Sergeant?'

'Place you'll not have heard of, and one I'm not allowed to mention.'

'Should have known better than to have asked,' said the landlord. He glanced at the sheathed fighting knife Warren had deliberately forgotten to leave behind and which was dangling from his belt. 'You wouldn't be one of those Commando types, would you?'

'We could be, but I wouldn't want it spread around. Just forget you saw his knife. He shouldn't be parading it like that. We don't want to advertise our presence.' He turned to Warren and said harshly: 'Put it out of sight.'

'Sorry, Sarge – slipped my mind,' Warren said. He removed the knife from his waist and tucked it inside his blouse.

'Do something as stupid as that again and I'll have you RTUd.'

The landlord handed Keith his note back. 'From what I've read yours could be a short and far from happy life, so the first round is on the house. And don't worry about anyone letting on about your presence here; our mouths are as tight as our purses.'

Keith eyed the note that had been handed back. 'You could say that's cause for alarm.'

The landlord smiled. 'Much tighter than our purses, then.' He tapped the side of his nose. 'I'm being serious. We take a stupid kind of pride in being accused of meanness, but we can hold our tongues. A lot of people here rely on the services for a living, and no one's going to jeopardize that by talking out of turn.'

112

A fisherman interrupted. 'And if tongues did wag, who would they wag to, the bloody seals? There's no Jerries here, 'cos no one can arrive or leave this place without someone noticing. Only the seals can come and go as they please, and they're not likely to swim across the North Sea with a message stuffed up their bottoms.'

His crude humour brought guffaws of laughter which the soldiers tactfully echoed. They stayed until long after Last Orders had been called and the doors bolted against further customers. When they eventually left they were all slightly unsteady on their feet.

Private Luck was stupidly elated. Sergeant Keith had taken him aside and said: 'The training's over. Off parade you can call me Harry. I don't need to be a bastard any more.' Luck felt as if Sir Henry Wood had personally asked him to perform at one of his concerts.

Temple and Bennett were hoping that the two daughters would still be up and about and that Mr and Mrs Ferguson had gone to bed. The beer had made them feel randy and in the mood to chance their luck.

Private Warren was wondering what he would do if he woke up in the middle of the night bursting for a leak. He had not bothered to find out where the toilet was. He need not have worried, because when he arrived back to his billet and tiptoed up the stairs to his room, he found a cryptic note on his pillow: 'There is a chamber pot in the bedside cupboard.'

It occurred to him that the Minister might not be such a miserable bastard after all.

Lieutenant Mappin stood looking at the board which carried a painting of a fouled anchor and the words *HMS Friendship* on it. A sailor with a white belt and gaiters and the badge of a leading seaman on his sleeve emerged from a sentry box. 'Anything I can do for you, sir?'

'I'm looking for a friend: Third Officer Payne. I promised to look her up if I was ever in Scapa.'

'Name rings a bell, sir, but no callers are allowed at the Wrennery except on official business.'

'It's rather important.'

'Not supposed to bend the rules for anyone; orders from the old dragon who rules them with a rod of iron. Poor cows might just as well be in a nunnery.' He winked. 'I'll take you to the guard room, sir, and maybe the PO will let me give the Wrennery a buzz.'

He led Mappin to a nearby building and nodded to an upright wooden chair. 'Take a pew, sir.' He went into a glass-sided cubicle and drew the sliding door behind him. A petty officer was sitting behind a desk reading a well-thumbed copy of *Lilliput*. He did not bother to look up as the killick spoke to him. He was used to horny young officers turning up out of the blue asking to see one of the Wrens; he knew the rules, but had long since given up taking any notice of them. The girls were not prisoners of war, and it was no skin off his nose to give them the opportunity of saying yes or no when someone called.

Mappin saw the sentry lift the earpiece of an old upright telephone, dial and speak into the trumpet-shaped mouthpiece. He saw his lips moving but could not hear what he was saying. He replaced the earpiece, then opened the sliding door. 'They've located your party, sir, and she wants to know who's calling. What name shall I give?'

'Lieutenant William Mappin.'

The sailor returned to the cubicle, picked up the phone again, spoke and replaced it. He came out. 'She's on her way, sir, but she says she don't know you from Adam.'

Mappin dredged up an unconvincing smile. 'Her memory is notoriously bad. She'll remember me as soon as she sees me.'

'Hope so for my sake, sir, because I don't want a rocket from her·ladyship. If she gets to hear that one of her ladies has been chatted up against their wishes she screams blue murder. Not to the Wren and not to the caller, but to the poor sod on sentry go, and you can take it from me she knows how to hand out a bollocking.'

Mappin sat in the guard room for twenty minutes before Hazel Payne walked in. She took one look at him and said: 'Good grief, you didn't waste much time looking me up!' She looked across at the rating. 'It's all right, Leading Seaman, we're old friends.'

'Any chance of nipping out for a while?' Mappin said. 'This isn't the most cheerful place to have a chat.'

'No problem – I'm off duty. I'll have to sign the In and Out book though. Won't take a jiffy.'

While he waited for her, Mappin felt relieved to find that she was every bit as attractive as she had appeared in the railway carriage. He had feared he might have made too much of their brief encounter. But he was even more delighted at her evident pleasure at seeing him again.

When she returned she said: 'I hope you and the sentry don't get into hot water over this. I gather the 'old dragon' is a bit of a martinet. Treats you like pieces of Dresden china.'

'All huff and puff. She knows what goes on and knows she can't stop it, so she puts on a bold face and cracks the whip to silence anyone who thinks she's running an escort agency.'

'I'm glad you wanted to see me.'

'I've thought quite a lot about you and wondered if we'd ever meet again. The chances seemed so slim. Did you ever think about me?'

'To be honest, I haven't had much time to think about anything except the course – but, yes, I did whenever I had a few minutes to myself. I wondered how I could wangle a trip up here.'

'And you did?'

'Not really. Line of duty.'

'Something special?'

'Mustn't be talked about.'

'Dangerous?'

He shrugged. 'What isn't in wartime? If you want to avoid trouble you don't join the Commandos. Simple as that.' He smiled with genuine warmth. 'You look lovely, Hazel. The Orkney air obviously agrees with you.'

'It really is a strange place. Sometimes you look over the Flow and think it's the most beautiful place on earth: so serene and out-of-this-world. The next morning it can be the most awful place. The wind cuts through you like a scalpel and your lungs feel as if they're about to burst. The rain and mud can send you round the bend, and there are times when you lie on your bunk wondering if you haven't caught the dreaded Orkneyitis which can turn grown men into gibbering idiots.' She glanced at the sky. 'But today it looks as if the sun has got his hat on, so let's make the most of it.'

'I'm a stranger here, so I'm in your hands.'

'To be frank there isn't an awful lot to do here. There're some lovely walks, and if you like bird watching it's an ornithologist's dream. St Magnus' Cathedral is splendid and worth a visit, and Kirkwall has some quaint streets and houses.' She spread her hands apart. 'You pays your penny and takes your pick.'

'I'm in no mood for bird watching, and I've done enough walking in the past few weeks to last a lifetime. As for the cathedral . . .' he pointed a thumb towards the ground. 'If I hadn't just eaten I'd suggest a meal. So what about a drink in a secluded picture-postcard pub?'

'A quiet pub in Kirkwall is as hard to find as a four leaf clover. All packed to the gunwales with soldiers, sailors and airmen.'

'Why don't we just take a slow saunter around the streets until we find some place to sit down and have a chat? That's all I really want to do.'

They strolled slowly through the pavementless streets, admiring the Scandinavian-style houses, a reminder of the Norsemen who once occupied it, and poking their heads through the doors of the numerous pubs they passed. Eventually they found a hotel near the harbour that boasted a lounge bar in which non-residents were welcome. There were several people, civilians and servicemen, sitting on stools at the bar, and more customers around the carefully spaced-out tables. But at the far end was a log fire with an inglenook which afforded some privacy.

Mappin led her to the hard stone seat. 'What'll it be?'

'I rather fancy a Harry Pinkers with lots of water.'

'What in God's name is that?'

'A pink gin, the navy's favourite wardroom tipple.' She giggled girlishly. 'Sorry, but everything in the navy is prefixed with Harry. You don't sleep, you have Harry crashers, and spirits without water or soda is Harry neaters. All rather childish, but one quickly slips into the habit. Makes you feel you've been around a long time and aren't still wet behind the ears.'

He ordered a pint of bitter for himself and when he came back with the drinks she patted the space beside her. 'Now let's take up from where you made a rather undignified departure from the train. You didn't even tell me your name.'

'You know it now.'

116

'Lieutenant William Mappin! Somehow that doesn't quite fit in with the son of an earl bit.'

Reluctantly he told her more about himself and his reason for not wishing to use his title. 'It might go down well if you're a ruddy general or a field marshal, but it's bloody silly when you're a humble two-pipper.'

'Isn't that a form of inverted snobbery, William?' she said mildly. 'Everyone must know who you are.'

'It's on my record, of course, but not many people have access to that. Colonel Rutherford obviously knew, but he respected my wishes and he's not the kind of man who goes around nudging and winking and dropping hints. The men I'm with certainly don't know, and as far as I'm concerned that's all that matters. If they respect me it's because I make a bloody great effort to be as good if not better at everything than they are, and that's a ruddy tall order. If you ever have the good fortune to meet Sergeant Keith you'll know what I mean.'

'So you're just one of the lads. Isn't that rather naive? You can never be that, and you know it. When the war's over you'll go back to being – what do they call it – a member of the ruling class.'

'I'm determined to do something useful. I want to *contribute*. That may sound corny, but I'm quite serious.'

'There aren't many options open to you, William, unless you stay in the army. Titles go down quite well there.'

'Out of the question. I'm strictly an hostilities only soldier. But I think you're wrong about options. For a start there's an estate that's been mismanaged for years, and a very large workforce that deserves more than it's getting. There's also business – by that I don't mean just lending my name to a letter heading, being a prestigious name on a board of directors and nothing else.'

'What about politics?'

'I don't think so. I honestly think I lack the ability to say one thing and mean another.'

'Politics needn't be like that. A lot of people will be expecting real changes.'

'I'll think of something. After all, there's no rush.'

She gently patted his arm. 'I wish you all the luck in the world, William. It's a terrible cross to bear.'

His voice hardened. 'Hazel, please don't be so bloody patronising!'

'Sorry – I shouldn't tease. But I do understand what you mean. Remember, being a judge's daughter isn't a piece of cake. That can be a millstone too.'

'So how're you going to break the shackles?'

'Like you I'm not really sure. If it doesn't go on too long I'd like to go back to college, then try my hand at journalism: a job with a paper that reflects my own views. The *News Chronicle*, for example. The kind of paper my father wouldn't allow in the house: too "woolly-minded and molly-coddling". Pampering to the masses, and spouting impractical pie-in-the-sky nonsense.'

She glanced at her watch. 'I really ought to be heading back. Kirkwall is no place to be stranded if there's an air raid and the Orkney barrage opens up. I won't be able to hear for a week.'

On the way back to the shore base he drew her to a halt below a large tree and kissed her. He was delighted at the warmth of her response. As she pulled away she said sweetly: 'That *was* nice.' Then like a child who has enjoyed an unexpected treat, 'More, please.'

He kissed her again, more ardently, and he felt her tongue, warm and moist, probe into his mouth. As she pressed herself close to him he felt the yielding softness of her breasts beneath the serge jacket.

'How about meeting tomorrow?'

'I think I can wangle that,' she said. 'There's a lot of duty-swapping goes on. Some of the girls have boyfriends at sea and they like to save up their shore leave for when they return to Scapa.'

'Same time, same place?'

She nodded. 'When,' she asked, 'does your little jaunt take off?'

'No idea, as yet. Depends on so many things. You'll only know when I don't turn up.'

'I might know before that. There's a buzz going round that something is going to happen soon – an amphibious landing.'

He sounded alarmed. 'I don't like the sound of that. This is supposed to be hush-hush.'

118

'Don't worry, there's been no breach of security. But it's impossible to keep things secret for too long here. Contrary to the general opinion, Wrens are not just pretty faces. We do a lot of jobs that were once only open to men. We work as armourers, in supplies, operations and signals. It's therefore par for the course if we occasionally hear things that are highly classified. I do a regular spell of duty on the submarines depot ship, that's where I heard the buzz.' She saw the look of concern on his face. 'Don't look so anxious, William! We're all clued up on the need for security.'

'How much do you know?'

'This may sound silly, William, but we've had orders not to discuss it with outsiders.'

'I'm hardly that.'

'You're not in the navy, and that's what they mean by outsiders. Would *you* discuss it with *me?*'

'Of course not, but it's got nothing to do with trust. It's orders.'

'Point made,' she said, and grinned.

He saw her to the main gate and watched as she turned and waved before disappearing in the distance.

He walked back to his billet with a new found spring in his step, convinced that he had met the woman he intended to marry. When next he wrote to his mother he would tell her so. He smiled to himself: he could almost anticipate her reply. There would be no reproach, no appeal for caution, just an acceptance that he knew what he was doing. He remembered the day when his father had presented him with a set of Purdey guns, when he had put the stock against his cheek and followed the flight of an imaginary flock of partridge and known instinctively there were no other guns for him. He felt the same certainty about Hazel Payne.

His father, he knew, would adopt an altogether different line: he would ask about her suitability, being long accustomed to believe that marriages were arranged affairs, more concerned with things like lineage and breeding. In his eyes women were very much like horses – you couldn't go far wrong if the blood was good. If you were lucky, love would follow; if it didn't that was no great calamity. You had preserved the line, and there was nothing to prevent you

119

finding happiness elsewhere, as long as you did not forget your obligations. And if he did not wholly approve of his choice he would have the consolation of having her father, the judge, as an in-law. That he would not jib at because they had so much in common.

He passed a pub and saw a group of unsteady soldiers pour out of the bar into the street. He saw one stiffen and salute, and immediately recognized Sergeant Keith. He did not return the salute, pretending not to have noticed; he did not want any of them to think they had let him down by getting drunk. In a week – perhaps more, maybe less – who was to know which of them would still be alive?

Chapter Eight

Five days had passed since the group arrived in Scapa, and Lieutenant Mappin had summoned Sergeant Keith to the privacy of his small room to explain as best he could the reason for the delay in Operation Midas.

'The brigadier called earlier,' he said as he poured coffee. 'Seems there's been a slight hiccup. The weather's been foul in Norway, the winds have been blowing Force Nine, and the sea's so bad a night landing has been out of the question. On top of that, the people over there seem to be having trouble getting in touch. It could be the weather, or their wireless is up the spout. Anyway, a new transmitter-receiver has been sent over. The brigadier didn't seem at all put out, though; said the gold had been there so long now that a few extra days was neither here nor there. He's a pretty cool customer.'

Keith shrugged. 'No point in getting hot under the collar, sir, but I'm worried about the men. I don't want them getting bored and losing their edge, like a fighter who's reached his peak and finds the contest is postponed. He knocks off training and gets stale.'

'That's one of the reasons I asked you to come over. I want you to organize a strict training routine. Lots of boat work, and plenty of really tough marches and exercises to keep them on their toes. There're several places they can work without being seen – don't want to arouse unnecessary curiosity.'

'I'll draw something up as soon as I get back to my billet, sir. We'll start first thing in the morning. I'll keep you informed of what I plan to do.'

'No need for that, Sergeant, I'll be with you. We'll work them hard, but we won't flog them to death. They'll have their evenings free.'

For the next eight days the small group imagined they were back at the training school. They marched and ran across the windswept hills, climbed the daunting tower-like sides of the Old Man of Hoy, recognized as one of the most challenging rock climbs in the world, fired their weapons, demolished imaginary strongpoints, sharpened up their unarmed combat, and made landings in conditions similar to those they might expect to find in Norway.

At night they returned to their billets, where their hosts got accustomed to the sight of filthy, weary men cleaning and oiling their weapons in the kitchen, putting grenades in the oddest places so as to be out of harm's reach, then cleaning their uniforms and polishing their equipment to be ready for inspection next morning. The nights were free to be spent as and how they wished.

Bennett and Temple regularly dated the two sisters, while Private Luck seemed content to spend hours playing the Ferguson's piano. The Minister and his wife gave up Private Warren as a hopelessly lost cause, and let him go his own way, placated by the thought that sooner or later he would depart from their sight and memory. Meanwhile they accepted his presence as a patriotic duty and placed an extra chamber pot in his room.

Sergeant Keith spent much of his time reading, although he occasionally dropped in to see Private Luck and listen to him play. But he soon tired of the prolonged spells of classical music and persuaded him to turn to something more pleasing to his ear. Luck cheerfully indulged him, playing Jerome Kern, Irving Berlin and other popular songsters. Sometimes Mr and Mrs Ferguson joined in the impromptu sing-songs, at which there was always a plentiful supply of drinks.

Most evenings Lieutenant Mappin managed to meet Third Officer Payne, whose duties ended in the afternoon. They went to the cinema, held hands on long walks along the deserted shoreline, and ate together in the guest house where Mrs Moray went out of her way to provide meals she assured them would 'help to build their strength up'. She never asked

122

about their relationship, although she thought to herself that they made a 'bonnie couple' and secretly hoped the time would come when the lieutenant would confide that they were more than friends. Youngsters, she told herself, should grab what happiness they could – because in wartime the most awful things could happen. As she knew to her cost. She had married her own petty-officer husband before the war, and when he retired they had opened the guest house, contemplating a blissful future. But, as a reservist, he had been among the first to be called back – and among the first to die when the *Royal Oak* was torpedoed. She consoled herself with the thought that they had at least shared some happiness, something that had been denied to so many of his younger shipmates.

One night, as he was walking Hazel back to the base, Mappin stopped.

'Does marrying into the aristocracy appeal to you, Hazel?' He tried to sound flippant.

'William, you are a scream. Is this some kind of proposal?'

'Not really, just putting out feelers. But I am expected to marry, for obvious reasons, and I wouldn't want to share my life with anyone other than you.'

'Isn't that a bit rash? We hardly know each other.'

He took her face in his cupped hands and kissed her. 'I'm being serious. I'm prone to making quick decisions. I know what I want, and when I set my mind on something I usually get it.'

'War,' she said seriously, 'makes people a little foolhardy. There's always that awful feeling that time's running out and one should make hay while the sun shines. There's something to be said for that attitude, but not a lot. "Marry in haste, repent at leisure", is not just a stale cliche.'

'I'm not suggesting we dash off and get married tomorrow by special licence. I'm just thinking it would be rather nice to have some kind of agreement – something to look forward to. It'll keep us both on the straight and narrow.'

'A formal engagement.'

'Not even that. Something either of us will be free to revoke if we think we've made a mistake. Although I'm certain I haven't.'

123

'It's far too serious a step to take just like that! Give me time to think about it.'

'Of course, darling, but don't take too long over making up your mind.' He fumbled in his breast pocket and produced the cigarette case she had admired on the train. 'I'd like you to have it.'

'Don't be silly. It's far too valuable. Anyway, I hardly smoke.'

'Never mind, I want you to have it. It'll remind you of what you'll be letting yourself in for if you decide to marry me.' He saw a tear glistening in the corner of her eye, and added with a smile; 'Apart from that, if I don't come back it'll remind you of the narrow escape you've had'

'I don't appreciate that kind of joke, William. It's emotional blackmail.' Even so she put the case in her handbag 'I'll – look after it till you get back.'

She turned and waved to him as she passed through the gates. It's ridiculous, she told herself, for people who have known each other such a short time to get emotionally involved to such an extent. Sod the war, she muttered angrily It makes the heart rule the head.

As she undressed she felt slightly heady and wondered whether it was the three gins she had drunk or the excitement of his unexpected confession of love. *He's handsome, charming, and a feather any girl would be proud to wear in her hat* But was that love? Or was it the devil-may-care mood that the war brought about; a mood encouraged by a surfeit of weepie movies in which people fell in love without any logical explanation. An inner voice told her that such things did happen; a voice she tried without success to stifle. She tumbled into her bunk but found she could not sleep. *Don't torture yourself What is so terrible about saying yes?* As he had said, it would not be binding. You're young, free and twenty-one, and i you make a mistake it won't be the end of the world, for God': sake. She felt immensely relieved at her decision and fell into a deep untroubled sleep.

Two mornings later, as Mappin was preparing to go out on an exercise, he was surprised by the unexpected appearance o the brigadier. 'Your chaps can have the day off. It may be the last they'll have for some time,' said the brigadier. 'Give them time to say goodbye to their ladies – and any other friends they may have made here.' He eyed Mappin with a twinkle. 'That goes for you, too. That pretty Third Officer you've taken in tow will expect it.'

Mappin wondered how he knew about Hazel. The Brigadier provided the answer.

'I've seen you both around town. I've also had the odd word with her on the depot ship. She'll be expecting you to line up something special tonight; she's one of the few who knows we're under starter's orders. As soon as it's dark tomorrow, you and your lads will muster on the jetty by the oil storage tanks where a navy boat will take you to the depot ship. Don't want to attract attention, that's why we're doing it at night. I know this place is more security-minded than most, for the simple reason that nearly every family has navy connections, but there's no point in taking unnecessary risks.'

'No point at all, sir.'

'Good. I'll leave it to you and Sergeant Keith to make sure your chaps aren't nursing too many sore heads in the morning.'

When Mappin met Hazel later in the afternoon, he said: 'We ought to do something special tonight – it'll be our last meeting for some time.'

'I know. You must be pleased the waiting's over.'

'We all are. If it hadn't been for you I'd have no fingernails left.'

'Why don't we have a quiet meal at your place? We'll stop on the way and get a bottle of wine and something stronger from under the counter.'

He grimaced, not really angry, but irritated by what he misconstrued as her morbid fatalism. 'Don't go overboard! It's not the last supper.'

'What put *that* thought into your head? I'm thinking more of a celebration.'

'I'm relieved, but it's hardly an occasion for pushing the boat out.'

'I've been thinking of what we were talking about. The answer is yes.'

'That's different! Oh, Hazel, that's wonderful. Let's see if we can dig out some long-buried hoard of champagne.'

They called in at the hotel where they had enjoyed their first night out together and bought a bottle of claret. To their amazement the manager also unearthed two bottles of Moet & Chandon left over from a long forgotten wedding reception.

When they eventually arrived at Mrs Moray's guest house, Mappin asked: 'I know it's rather short notice, but do you think you could rustle up something a bit extra for tonight? I'm leaving tomorrow.' He handed her the champagne. 'And if you could chill this, I'd be extremely grateful.'

'No problem at all, sir.' She nudged him gently in the ribs with an elbow. 'If you don't mind waiting, and promise not to breathe a word to anyone, I'll see what I can do. First, you'll have to help me carry a table up to your room, because I daren't risk offending my other guests. They've got fish again: can't have them reporting me to the food office.'

Lieutenant Mappin and Third Officer Payne carried the table up and Mrs Moray followed with a snow-white table cloth and some of her best cutlery tucked into the pocket of her apron. She went down again and came back with some glasses which had not been used since her husband's death. She laid the table with meticulous care and reappeared an hour later with the champagne, sunk neck-deep in ice in a massive casserole. 'It's not the proper utensil, you'll mind, but it'll not affect the flavour.'

'You'll stay and have a glass, won't you?' Hazel said.

'The weeniest dram, dear.' She laughed awkwardly. 'My husband said one sniff of a cork and I was half-seas over, and I'm afraid he was right.'

It was the first time she had mentioned a Mr Moray. Although Mappin had often been tempted to ask about her husband in the past he had never done so; now he took his opportunity.

She said quietly, in reply to his question as to his where abouts: 'He's close, sir – very close,' and left it at that.

Mappin opened the first bottle with a great flourish. As the cork shot across the room Mrs Moray applauded. When she had finished her drink she went out, calling over her shoulder 'Now don't expect me to rush things. Good fare, like prayer shouldn't be hastened!' She glanced at the table to satisfy

126

herself she had not overlooked anything. 'Anyway, I'm sure you two sweethearts have lots to talk about.'

It was the nearest she could bring herself to telling them that life was short, happiness something to be grasped before it was too late. She was not, as she would be the first to admit, very good with words.

Mappin and Hazel sat at the table chatting nervously about things of no consequence, anxious to avoid mentioning what was uppermost in their minds. They drank the first bottle of champagne, enough to make them feel pleasantly light-headed, and when Mrs Moray knocked and asked if it was all right to come in they were surprised to discover an hour and a half had passed.

When Mappin opened the door she was standing with a triumphant expression on her face, holding in front of her, like a sacrificial offering, roast chicken on a carving dish. It was surrounded by the crispiest of roast potatoes, parsnips and green peas.

'You're a miracle, Mrs Moray,' said Hazel delightedly. 'Where did you conjure that from? I haven't tasted chicken for God knows how long.'

'They don't grow on trees these days, that's for sure. But my neighbour keeps a few birds for laying and he's not opposed to a wee bit of bartering. A friend brings me a salmon and the fellow next door is partial to that.'

Mappin held up the claret and nodded to her.

'I won't, thank you, sir, I've lots to do. Now I'll leave you to enjoy your meal.'

They toasted each other and the future, eating slowly, relishing each unaccustomed mouthful. When they had finished Mappin glanced at his watch. 'I suppose you'd better be thinking of getting back,' he said mournfully.

He had hardly finished asking when the silence of the night was shattered by the stomach-churning wail of the sirens, followed almost immediately by the shattering boom of the shore batteries and the anti-aircraft guns of the warships and flak-ships opening up. The gathering gloom was brightened by muzzle flashes and the looping tracers that carved a multi-coloured filigree in the sky; the bare hills were outlined by the probing fingers of searchlights scouring the damson-coloured horizon.

'It could be a heavy one,' said Mappin calmly.

'That settles it,' she said. 'I'll have to stay till the All Clear. We're expected to take shelter if we're ashore when there's a raid, not try and get back.'

The windows rattled as the gunfire intensified. 'It would look bad for both of us if the guest house got a direct hit,' Mappin said.

'Jerry doesn't often drop bombs. He knows the chances of hitting anything are so remote. But I'm grateful he's turned up.'

'*Grateful*?'

'Yes. I've been wracking my brains for an excuse to stay: too nervous to suggest it in case you disapproved and thought I was throwing myself at you.'

'Are you sure?'

'Positive. You said we should do something special; well, I can't think of anything more special than making love.'

'Do you think it's a good idea?' he said apprehensively.

'I've thought about little else since you said you'd like to marry me. There're too many people around these days who've had the chance and regretted not taking it while they could. All they have to cling to is a letter saying, "I'm writing this just in case anything should happen. . ." Of course, they're young enough to get over it, but the regret will always be there.'

He eyed the narrow single bed. 'Not very big.'

'We'll be taking up no more room than one person,' she said placing a hand over her mouth to stifle the laughter that erupted.

Without any warning she began to remove her uniform, gracefully and with slow deliberation: first her jacket, which she neatly draped over the back of a chair, then wriggled out of her skirt which was placed on top of the jacket. She then undid her tie and unbuttoned the masculine white shirt. The white underslip followed, leaving her standing there in just a pair of panties, black stockings, suspender belt and bra. She sat on the chair, unclipped the stockings and carefully rolled them down. 'Not service issue, and as rare as gold dust. Can't risk laddering them,' she said casually.

Mappin's heart was thumping so violently he felt sure she could hear it. It seemed as loud as the guns outside and he wondered how she managed to seem so relaxed. Was it something she was accustomed to doing? The thought cut into him like a dagger thrust.

She let the panties fall around her ankles and kicked them away. Her legs were long, slender, as creamy white as alabaster, and her buttocks were firm and rounded. She moved her hands behind her back and deftly removed her bra to reveal breasts that were pertly erect, with small rosy nipples.

Mappin, who had made love to many women – love was perhaps the wrong word for those purely physical couplings – felt nervously awkward, acutely aware of the hard bulge that threatened to burst through his trousers. he knew without doubt that he was deeply in love with her and wanted her to know it, but he was afraid of openly declaring his emotions. He had done so too many times in the past and not meant a word of it, feeling it was expected of him; it spared the woman from thinking she was promiscuous. Instead he said: 'I'm quite serious about wanting to marry you.' It did not sound so deceitful.

She slid into the bed and propped herself up on one elbow. 'You've seen all there is to see of me. Now it's my turn.' He thought her voice did not sound as confident as she would have liked. He found that comforting.

He undressed quickly, letting his clothes lie in a heap on the floor. She looked at his erect penis and whispered: 'Quickly.'

He sidled almost shyly into the bed beside her, then reached up with one hand and unpinned her hair, letting it cascade down her shoulders. His other hand ran down her spine, then onto her flat stomach, as smooth as satin. She parted her legs and he felt the moistness of her.

He rolled her gently onto her back and penetrated her easily and deeply. She said, as if by way of explanation: 'There's only been one other.'

He thrust hard and fiercely, feeling her respond in unison as her buttocks rose and fell. He gave a deep groan of pleasure as he came explosively, and experienced a stab of guilt at having disappointed her. It had never happened to him before; he had always prided himself on his self-control.

He rested his head against hers. Her hair felt moist but smelt sweet. 'I'm sorry, darling.'

129

She ran her fingers through his tangled hair and murmured: 'It's all right. It really is – I finished when you did. The very first time it's ever happened to me. It'll be even better next time.'

They parted, and only then became aware of the guns still battering away in the night sky.

Her lips closed on his, and her tongue darted in and out of his mouth like a hot flame. His hands moved up to cup her breasts, and he gently teased the nipples until they were again as hard as acorns.

She propped herself on her elbows. 'Do you want to know about the first time?'

'Not really. It doesn't matter,' he said, although he knew it did.

'It does to me, because there was nothing to it, and I want you to know that.'

'Who was it, then?'

'I can't even remember his name. It happened after a college party. Most of the girls liked to boast of their affairs and tended to ridicule anyone who was still a virgin. It was interpreted as a sign of intellectual weakness and conformity. So I said to myself, "Hang it, why not get it over and done with?" So I did, and I couldn't for the life of me understand why they made such a fuss about it.'

'I didn't really need to know,' he said gently, 'but the truth is preferable to some cock-and-bull story about too much strenuous horse riding. If you listened to some women you'd believe that more hymens have been lost in the saddle than in bed.'

'Have there been many women in your life, darling?'

'A few in the past. But no more in the future.'

'Promise?'

He made a childish sign across his chest. 'Promise.'

He got out of bed and retrieved the unopened bottle of champagne, carrying it and two glasses back to the bed where they sat upright with their backs against the headboard.

'This is very decadent,' she said. 'Quite abandoned'

They finished the bottle. He felt her hand move down between his legs and he became aroused once more. She pushed him onto his back and sat astride him, impaling herself on his manhood. It was better than the first time; the time after that was better still. Hazel, who had been almost impassive during her first ever orgasm, now gave full rein to her feelings; she writhed, softly moaning and gently sank her teeth into his shoulder.

They fell asleep locked in each other's arms, blissful and satiated. When they awoke they were amazed at the strength of their need for each other and even more delighted at their ability to gratify it before they fell asleep again.

They did not hear the guns cease firing or the sirens sound the all Clear. They did not stir until Mrs Moray rapped lightly on the door and called through: 'I've left your tea outside, Lieutenant.'

When he got up to get it, he was surprised to see two cups on the tray.

Hazel giggled. 'And there was I thinking I'd have to shin down the drain pipe'

They sat up in bed sipping the tea. Hazel leaned over and nibbled the lobe of his ear. 'You *do*, don't you?'

'Do what?'

'Love me.'

'I wouldn't have thought you needed reassuring – it's pretty obvious.'

'I know, but I just want to hear you say it.'

'I do. Very much.'

'Me too. . .'

When they eventually went down, Mrs Moray greeted them as they tried to slip past the reception desk. 'Now don't think you'll be going off without a bite of something to eat, young lady. I think it was very sensible of you not to attempt to get back in that awful raid. But it couldn't have been very comfortable in that wee room: hardly space to swing a cat round.'

They were grateful for her tact.

'The armchair was a trifle hard on the back, I must admit,' Mappin said. And he rubbed his back to give veracity to the patent lie.

Mrs Moray's face was expressionless, although there was just a hint of banter in her voice. 'I'm sure it was, sir, I'm sure it was. Others might not have been so considerate of a young lady, but you being an officer and a gentleman. . .'

Mappin saw Hazel as far as the front door. 'Mind if I don't come any further? I ought to stay here in case of any messages.'

'Of course not. I know the way back with my eyes closed.'

'You'll be all right?' he asked anxiously. 'No awkward questions?'

'Don't worry, I'll give a graphic description of life in an underground shelter. But I don't for one minute anticipate anyone being sufficiently interested to ask.'

He said earnestly, a look of deep concern on his face: 'And if anything happens as a result of last night – you're not to worry.'

She laughed gaily. 'You mean if I get pregnant? Not a chance. Wrens who get a bun in the oven are dismissed the service, so we've all learned how to avoid it, even those like me who never felt the need for it. But, like boy scouts, it's better to be prepared.'

She kissed the tips of her fingers and pressed them against his lips. 'Promise me you'll come back in one piece?'

'Hand on heart. Sergeant Keith has taught us how to survive, and I paid particular attention to what he had to say. I've too much to lose not to.' He added; 'I just wish I knew when I can expect to see you again.'

'Much sooner than you imagine, my sweet.'

'I never imagined that I'd have cause to be grateful to the Luftwaffe,' he said.

'I don't think it would have altered things if they hadn't turned up.'

'I thought you said you were glad of the excuse.'

'I was, but I think I'd already made up my mind I was going to stay. As a precaution I asked one of my oppos to sign me back aboard if I didn't turn up.'

'You were prepared to take the risk?'

'No risk, really. No one ever really studies the In and Out book: just a lot of scribbled signatures. We stand in for each other all the time, like workmen clocking each other on and off.'

Mrs Moray watched Hazel's receding figure through a chink in the curtains, a faint smile on her lips. When the girl had disappeared from view she walked across to the desk

132

where the photograph of her husband stood. She picked it up, dusting it with the corner of her apron. 'I hope they'll be as happy as we were,' she said. She wondered why she was so concerned with the happiness of others. It had not always been that way.

As Hazel walked down the steep hill a chill wind funnelled through the narrow street, lifting the hem of her skirt and cutting through her like a knife. She experienced a sudden tremor of fear and shivered involuntarily. From the distant past she heard her mother, who was accustomed to such spasms, saying cheerfully; 'Someone's just walked over my grave.'

She dismissed the doom-laden thought from her mind. Her mother had uttered it so many times, but it had never been an evil omen. she was now a hale and hearty fifty-five year old, which to a young girl in love was as old as Methuselah.

Chapter Nine

The Commandos stood on the wooden jetty, grateful for the looming presence of the massive oil tanks which provided some protection from the biting wind that blew across the flow, whipping the tops of the waves into angry white crests. They stamped their feet, slapping their arms around themselves to ward off the cold that seeped deep into their bones. They carried all they possessed in their backpacks, pouches and kit bags, and looked forward to the time when they could get shot of some of it aboard the depot ship.

'Enjoy your last night on the tiles, lads?' Lieutenant Mapin said amiably.

Private Warren, who had spent the evening at a local hop, said morosely; 'I'd have been better off going to the Minister's prayer meeting, sir. Piss-awful night I had, and that's no bullshitting.' It was not strictly true; he had set his cap at several attractive ATS girls and been studiously ignored, finally settling for one who was overweight but, fortunately for him, also over-sexed. He had enjoyed what he called a 'knee-trembler' against the outside wall of the dance hall to an orchestration of ack-ack fire. But, true to the inbred habits of an old regular, he was loathe to admit that life in the army offered any pleasure whatever.

'Sorry about that, Warren.'

'I didn't join with the idea of enjoyment uppermost in my mind, sir. Blood, sweat and tears was all I was promised, and that was years before Churchill pinched the idea.'

'Bennett and I have no complaints, sir,' Lance-Corporal Temple said. We said a long farewell to the Ferguson sisters in the air raid shelter at the back of the wet canteen! Only time I've had reason to be grateful to Jerry. But I'll tell you something, sir; that matelot was right about virgins being rare here. Some rotten so-and-so had got there before we did.'

'And you, Private Luck?'

'I was with the Fergusons in the closet under the stairs listening to a Henry Wood concert on their portable radio, sir. Myra Hess was the soloist. Wouldn't have missed it for anything.'

'She ain't the sister of that mad sod wot flew to Scotland in a Messerschmitt, Ted?' Bennett said.

It was the signal for everyone to laugh out loud, laughter in which Private Luck heartily joined. 'How about you, sir?' Sergeant Keith said. 'Enjoyable evening?'

Mappin felt himself blush in the darkness. 'Feet up with a good book – nothing to write home about.'

'Wish I'd been as sensible, sir. I spent too much time and too much cash in the pub.' He did not like to say he had spent much of the evening having a quiet meal with his landlady and her husband, and the rest checking and rechecking his arms and equipment: that would have sounded pious and over zealous.

The crisp tones of the Brigadier floating out of the darkness ended their casual chatter. 'Are we all present and correct, Mr Mappin?'

Mappin saluted the as yet invisible figure. 'Yes, sir. All upright and as bright as new buttons.'

They heard boots stomping on the planking before the figure of the Brigadier emerged. He was wearing a short trench coat, more fashionable than practical, and the mist had formed thin transluscent drops that dripped off the peak of his cap. He stamped his feet and blew on his gloved hands. 'Brass monkey weather, and no mistake.'

'Jus' 'ad a quick slash, sir, an' I 'ad to break the dribble off of the end. Frozen solid,' Bennett said.

The Brigadier was unruffled by the familiarity. 'Never mind. Boat should be alongside any time now, then in half an hour's time you'll be enjoying a nice hot drink which, if I know the navy, will be laced with something that'll put a bit of lead in your pencils.'

Their ears caught the watery chug-chug-chug of the drifter as it approached the jetty, followed almost immediately by a voice calling; 'Ahoy there! Party of brownjobs for the depot ship ready to embark?'

As the fendered bow bumped into the jetty, a sailor in oilskins leapt ashore with a mooring line which he secured to a bollard. An engine telegraph clanged like a fractured bell, and the single propeller churned the water white as the coxswain manoeuvred the stern in. Another rating jumped ashore and secured a line aft, and the drifter bumped alongside, old car tyres suspended over the gunwales cushioning the impact.

A petty officer peered out of the wheelhouse window. 'All aboard the Skylark! Dump your clobber in the welldeck, lads, and we'll be off. One of the hands will give you a tot of Nelson's blood to keep your own from congealing.' He began intoning tunelessly:

'Cold as a frog in a frozen pool,
Cold as the tip of a polar bear's tool,
Cold as charity,
And that's fucking chilly,
But it ain't as cold as our poor Willie,
He's dead, poor bastard.'

Look lively, lads,' the Brigadier said.

The soldiers heaved their belongings over the gunwale and climbed aboard, carefully nursing their rifles and the grenades they carried in pouches on their chest. As they slumped down on the deck a rating came round with enamel mugs, followed by another carrying a wicker-covered rum jar. As he splashed a liberal tot into each mug, he said; 'Captain's compliments, lads. He's arranged for the Master at Arms to write it off as spillage.'

The Brigadier grinned. 'I was right, lads. Didn't I tell you the navy looks after the pongoes?'

'We've had plenty of practice, sir,' the rating with the jar said saucily. 'Dunkirk, then Norway. They've had to increase rum production because of you thirsty buggers.'

'Aren't you forgetting something?' the Brigadier said tartly.

The rating with the rum looked bemused. 'Don't think so sir.'

'The Lieutenant and I haven't had a tot.'

'Sorry sir, but rum is only for the ranks and lower deck, no officers. King's Rules and Regulations.'

'They don't apply to this outfit. No rules and no regulations.'

The rating grinned and bellowed to his oppo; 'Two more mugs, for the Brigadier and the Lieutenant. Only trying it on sir,' he said to the Brigadier. 'But take it easy, it's pretty strong stuff. Separates the men from the boys. That's why they don't allow the officers to have it'.

The Brigadier took the mug and downed the contents in one gulp. 'Less of your cheek, lad. When I was with the Gurkhas we had a bottle of this before breakfast. Kept our serious drinking till the evening.'

The rating was impressed by the Brigadier's casual downing of an eighth of a pint of neat rum. 'Christ Almighty, sir you sure you ain't in the wrong outfit? You knocked that back like a real old rum rat.'

Lieutenant Mappin tried to emulate him, almost choking as the fiery spirit flowed down his gullet like molten metal. He wheezed, blinking back the tears that welled in his eyes.

'Not bad. Not bad at all.'

The coxswain gave the order for the moorings to be slipped and turned the bow towards the open Flow. As it buttered through the choppy water, the soldiers were drenched with the spray that was thrown over the bow and stung their faces and brought tears to their eyes. The depot ship loomed out of the darkness like an iceberg. Berthed in trots alongside, barely discernible in the darkness, were the cigar-like shapes of submarines. As the drifter passed close to them, their paint-peeling hulls indicated the long periods they had spent at sea, serving as a grim reminder of the all too short spells in harbour. The depot ship was anchored fore and aft, and the coxswain skilfully steered the drifter round the stern to the bottom of a steep gangway that zig-zagged up the side.

When the drifter had been secured, the coxswain emerged from the wheelhouse. 'Mind how you go, lads! Those stairs are as slimy as a Maltese pimp.'

138

The Brigadier was the first to disembark. When he reached the top of the ladder a bosun's pipe shrilled, welcoming him aboard. He returned the brisk salute of the Duty Officer, who said 'I'll show you to the Captain's cabin, sir.'

'I'll find my own way, I've been here enough times. First I want to see the troops comfortably settled. They're as wet as a Manchester weekend.'

'A petty officer has been detailed to show them to the mess deck where some hammocks have been slung.'

'I think they'll opt for the floor. Never stay in a hammock.'

'No danger of them falling out, sir. This old lady never moves,' the Duty Officer said with a wide grin. 'She's aground on her own gash, she's been here so long.'

The petty officer led the soldiers along the cluttered deck, down hatches and steep ladders, and along passageways that were lined with insulated pipes, ventilation shafts, coiled hoses and crimson fire buckets. The mess they had been allocated had no port holes and was stiflingly hot. The bulkheads were lined with battered lockers, and there were rows of well-scrubbed tables. several hammocks were suspended from hooks in the deckhead and the whole place smelt of diesel oil and overcooked cabbage.

'Make yourselves comfortable,' the petty officer said, 'and if you can do that you're better men than I am. The *Altmark* was a luxury liner compared to this old tub.'

'It'll do,' the Brigadier said. 'They won't be here for long.' He made his way to the captain's quarters which were surprisingly spacious and comfortable. There was a large rug covering much of the deck, and two deep armchairs of rich brown leather. Photographs of several submarines adorned the bulkheads, together with a larger one of the King and Queen in their coronation robes. It was silent but for the whirr of the ventilation fans.

A large sandy-haired man, sporting four gold rings on the sleeves of his reefer jacket, rose from behind a desk and moved across the cabin to a bulkhead bell. 'Fancy a drink, sir?'

The Brigadier, although senior in rank, was aware that the captain was the monarch of his floating kingdom. He said respectfully; 'Thank you, sir, after that rum I could do with something civilised. Nearly took the lining off my stomach: daren't show it though. Your lads were watching me like hawks.'

'They're hard bastards – but they need to be, marooned out here for weeks on end with no chance of real action, having to listen to the tales of derring-do the submariners regale them with when they return from patrol.'

'Know where I'd rather be,' said the brigadier. 'I'm claustrophobic. Couldn't bear the thought of being entombed hundreds of feet under water.'

'Sailors are no different to soldiers. Boredom is their greatest enemy. You wouldn't believe it, but I get men volunteering for hazardous service just to get away from the brain-numbing monotony of life aboard a depot ship. I know exactly how they feel; I'd like a more active appointment myself, but someone has to do the chores. But you wouldn't appreciate that.'

The Brigadier became as angry as he ever allowed himself to be. 'I'd give my right arm to be going with the men who've just come aboard, sir. I find little satisfaction in sending men to what could be certain death when I know there's a comfy billet waiting for me in Whitehall. But someone decided I'd be more gainfully employed as a planner and I wasn't given the chance to disagree.'

'Sorry. Spoke out of turn. What about that drink?'

'Whisky, please, and I'll leave the size to you.'

The captain pressed the bell. 'My steward doesn't know the meaning of moderation when it comes to pouring drinks. Only knows one size: that's half-pints, and it doesn't matter to him whether it's gin, whisky or sherry. Wouldn't part with him for anything.'

A white-coated steward appeared before the bell had stopped ringing.

'The Brigadier would like a Scotch. I'll have a pink gin, and I *don't* mean half and half.' The steward withdrew to his pantry. 'Silly bugger,' the captain said. 'Doesn't believe a bottle of Angostura should last more than a week.'

He sat in one of the armchairs, motioning to the Brigadier to take the other. When the drinks arrived the Brigadier took a long sip before asking: 'Any last minute changes to our plans.?'

'Nothing this end. What about yours?'

'Nothing since I was last aboard. The weather's moderated over there, although it's still on the roughish side. The new W/T set we delivered is functioning, we've received all their transmissions and they've picked up ours. They're standing by to be told the submarine's ETA.'

The captain shrugged. 'That's it then: no turning back. The whole thing's in the lap of the gods now. *Otter* will finish provisioning in the morning and will be ready to sail soon afterwards.'

'In that case,' the Brigadier said, 'as soon as the men have finished eating we'll assemble everyone for a final briefing.'

In the small cabin that had been allotted to him, Lieutenant Mappin was making last minute arrangements with Sergeant Keith.

Keith handed him a sheet of paper on which he had written six names. 'It was a hard decision, sir, but I've done what you asked and selected the ones I think best.'

Mappin studied the list which contained the names of Lance-Corporal Temple and Privates Bennett, Luck, Warren, Foster and Buchanan.

'I've no quarrel with that, Sergeant: just sorry we've got to leave some behind. I asked the Brigadier if we could all go, but he was adamant.'

'I did call for volunteers, and they all put their hands up. Can't say I was surprised after all that training. Four of them almost chose themselves, sir. They're so close I can't imagine any one of them letting the others down. Foster and Buchanan are not quite so chummy, but they're solid and reliable.'

A voice came over the Tannoy. 'D'you hear there? The military personnel who have recently embarked will muster in their mess to await escort for a briefing.'

'Better put our skates on,' said Mappin.

A rating who had been standing outside the cabin led them through a labyrinth of passageways deep down into the bowels of the ship to the mess deck where the Commandos were already seated on rows of bench seats. On separate benches alongside sat two of the submarine's officers, the coxswain, some petty officers, and several ratings.

The soldiers stood when Mappin entered, but with a brusque gesture he indicated they should sit down. He strode across to a trestle table that had been set up in front of the seated men, while Keith found himself a space at the end of one of the benches. Then, as if by some unseen signal, the Brigadier and the captain entered, followed by a young lieutenant-commander who was wearing a white polo-neck sweater under a well-worn reefer jacket.

The captain nodded to the two-and-a-half striper. 'Over to you.'

The captain of the submarine stood up, placed his hands behind his back, and introduced himself. 'Lieutenant-Commander Cotton, captain of *Otter*, the boat that'll be taking you to Norway.' He saw the puzzled expression on the faces of the soldiers and smiled. 'Sorry – I ought to explain. We always refer to submarines as boats.' He was a slim man with a pronounced stoop, brought about by the need to adapt his considerable height to the limited headroom in a submarine. 'Our job is the easiest: we've simply got to deliver you safely to Norway. It's a trip we've made many times, so you'll be in safe hands. If you look at the flag on the side of the conning tower when you come aboard in the morning, you'll see our previous visits have not been without success. This time we won't be hunting, just running a bus service, but we appreciate to the full how important it is to get you ashore undetected and in one piece.'

Keith studied the careworn face of the young naval officer. He seemed almost too young to have the responsibility for the success of such an important mission resting on his shoulders.

'It won't be a comfortable trip, because space aboard the boat is very limited, but we'll do our best to make you feel at home. There'll be nothing for you to do and you'll find it extremely boring. When we've submerged you won't even be able to relax over a smoke.'

He spoke briefly about the voyage, the course they would steam, the estimated time of arrival, and the procedure for disembarking. Then he looked at the captain. 'That's about all I have to contribute, sir.'

The captain glanced at the Brigadier. 'Ball's in your court.'

The Brigadier rose, 'You'll be going ashore in inflatable dinghies which have already been put aboard the submarine –

142

you're all very well acquainted with them, so I needn't say any more about that. You'll be met by our Norwegian friends who'll take you to the gold. Once ashore you'll be pretty much on your own, because most of the time our friends will have to maintain radio silence. The reason for that is too obvious to need explaining: Jerry has very efficient detector equipment. However, they'll contact us when you and the gold are ready to leave. Then an MTB will be sent across to bring you home. Can't use another sub because there's no way of getting the gold aboard, whereas an MTB can go alongside and lift it inboard with her torpedo hoists. Even more important is the fact that it is *very* fast – show any enemy ship a clean pair of heels.'

He spoke for another twenty minutes, covering points he thought needed elaboration. Then, 'Any questions?' There were none. 'Right, then. Now we'll go to the armoury where you'll be issued with extra weapons and explosives.'

The armoury, which normally dealt with the needs of the submariners, was a large cavernous area amidships with heavy secure doors, and two armed sentries on guard. When the Commandos entered they saw that four tables had been laid out at one end. On top of one lay three Thompson sub-machine guns and several drums of ammunition. On another were two wooden boxes bound in brass bands; one was coloured green, the other black. Behind each table stood a chief petty officer. A PO sick berth attendant stood behind the third table with a cardboard container the size of a shoe box in front of him. Behind the last table was a young Wren officer.

Mappin caught his breath as he recognized Hazel Payne. If she recognized him she gave no sign.

The Brigadier turned to Mappin. 'Three Tommy-guns was all that could be spared – still in sort supply. Pick the three men you think will make best use of them.'

'Maybe only three, sir, but I'm glad to see them. I thought we were being sent off without any automatic weapons.' Then without hesitation Mappin called out: 'Sergeant Keith, Lance Corporal Temple, and Private Luck, take one each.'

'I'm more of a dab hand with one of them than anyone else, sir,' Private Warren said plaintively. 'I was the one picked to demonstrate it to the Prime Minister.'

143

'Maybe you are, but there's no one to match you at long range with a .303 sniper's rifle.'

'That's true, sir,' the private said, mollified.

The CPO standing behind the coloured boxes spoke almost parrot-fashion about their contents: 'This here green one holds high explosive: TNT, amatol and a few sticks of honest to goodness dynamite, some special limpet grenades, gun cotton, primers, a bag of emery dust, a quantity of ground glass, and a jar of potassium. You don't need me to explain what they're for – if you do, you've no right to be going on this caper.' He paused, then hurried on. 'There's also some odds and sods which you'll recognize.'

Private Bennett said audibly: 'Crikey, there's enuff stuff there to blow up the vaults of the bank of Englan', wiv enuff left over to do wot Guy Gawkes couldn'.'

'When you've finished nattering perhaps I can be permitted to finish,' the CPO said stiffly. He tapped the black box. 'This one here contains an assortment of detonators: some electrical, some percussion. Treat them gentle, because the fulminates are so unstable a fart could trigger them off.'

'They'll be your personal responsibility, Bennett,' Sergeant Keith whispered. 'You're the expert'

'Ave a 'eart, Sarge I can't carry that lot on my Jack Jones.'

'Not expected to. We'll take turns. I'm just telling you, they're your baby.'

'Jesus Christ, I can't hear myself talk for your ruddy nattering' the CPO bellowed. 'It might seem an awful lot of stuff to lug around, but no one knows for sure what you'll need and what you won't. No doubt the time will come when you'll be able to decide you can ditch some of it, or pass it on to the Resistance.'

The soldiers moved on to the sick bay attendant, who unsmilingly handed each of them two small brown envelopes containing navy issue Durex, known to the ratings as 'dreadnoughts'.

'If it's goin' to be that kinda jaunt ashore I'll 'ave a extra 'alf dozen,' Bennett said loudly.

'They're to put over the end of your weapons, and I mean the one you fire bullets out of. Makes it waterproof when you go ashore.'

144

Sergeant Keith's staccato 'Move along, Bennett,' ended the bantering exchange.

When the soldiers came to the table manned by Third Officer Payne, each was handed a large manilla envelope. 'All personal belongings are to be placed inside,' she said. 'They'll be kept in the safe in the ship's office and returned to you when you get back.' She also handed each man a small tube resembling a toothpaste container. 'It's dark make-up: makes you as black as Othello. There's such a shortage of proper camouflage cream we had to requisition this from a Wardour Street theatrical supplier.'

When Mappin stood in front of her he whispered: 'I didn't expect to see you here.'

She smiled. 'I'm in the silent service. I've been working for the captain for some time. I did drop the odd hint. . .'

He returned her smile. 'There'll be a letter from me to you in the envelope that's only to be read if I don't come back.'

'Don't be silly. Of course you will.'

'Will I see you before we go?'

'I'll have a word with the captain, but I don't hold out too much hope. Security. We'll all be going into virtual quarantine when we've finished here.'

The captain of the depot ship sat in his cabin enjoying a post-briefing drink with the Brigadier. 'Third Officer Payne, the one who was dealing with personal belonging –'

'Pretty little thing,' interrupted the Brigadier.

'She came to see me to ask if I would make a special request to you on her behalf,' continued the captain.

'What on earth can I possibly do for her?'

'Wants permission to spend a little time alone with Lieutenant Mappin. Seems they're rather more than friends.'

The Brigadier shook his head. 'I'd got an inkling of that, but the answer's no. Put yourself in my shoes, sir. What would you expect me to say if one of the Commandos requested permission to phone his wife or nip ashore and see his girlfriend?'

'Turn it down, of course, quite out of the question. Too risky. But the girl's in a different position – she's been in on this from the start. Anyway, she's confined to the ship like the rest of us.'

145

'That may be so, but in my eyes it wouldn't be fair. He shouldn't enjoy something denied to the others. Just tell her I'm sorry. Anyway, tearful partings are the last thing any of us want.' He smiled ruefully. 'At a time like this, a soldier's farewell is the best solution.'

The captain thought: You are a hard bugger. Only a desk wallah could take that view.

He might have altered his opinion if he had known that the Brigadier had not been allowed to see or speak to his wife and children from the time he was first appointed to plan Operation Midas.

Chapter Ten

The Commandos were roused from an uneasy sleep by the brassy blare of a bugle and a petty officer storming through the mess deck, upending hammocks and bellowing in a far too hearty voice: 'Rise and shine! Hands off cocks, on socks!'

The soldiers grabbed towels and shaving gear and shuffled off to the heads.

After breakfast they assembled in full battle kit on the upper deck opposite the midship's gangway. Below them lay *Otter*, the outboard boat in a trot of three. A black flag with a crude white skull and crossbones stitched on to it was draped over the side of the conning tower. Spaced around the Jolly Roger were strips of canvas denoting her kills: red for warships, white for merchant vessels. The soldiers felt a sense of relief when they saw the impressive tally.

Derricks were swinging out from the depot ship, delivering last minute perishable stores. The upper deck of the submarine was swarming with sailors wearing grimy white jumpers of oiled wool who were lowering the stores through the torpedo-loading hatches. The waist of the ship was lined with sailors who waved and shouted encouragement as the small group of soldiers descended the steep gangway and clumped across the two inboard boats to *Otter*.

Lieutenant Mappin looked up and saw the solitary female figure of Hazel. He waved and she blew a kiss in return. He hoped it would not be his last glimpse of the woman he loved.

They scaled the ladder on the outside of the conning tower and slowly descended the one that led down into the submarine, finding themselves in a world utterly different to any they had previously encountered. It was incredibly small and claustrophobic; every inch of space seemed to be taken up by some item of equipment. Pipes ran in all directions, and there were gauges and dials of varying sizes, stopcocks, and more levers than would be found in the signal box of a railway terminal.

A sub-lieutenant standing in the control room where the search and attack periscopes were housed, said: 'Follow the PO. He'll take you to your quarters.' To Mappin he said: 'I'll take you to the wardroom, sir.'

The petty officer led them through the various mess decks – ERAs, petty officers and leading hands – into the torpedo stowage compartment which also served as the mess for the junior ratings. 'It's going to be a trifle cramped, but you may prefer to doss down on the deck with a blanket over your head. Most of the off-duty ratings do.'

Bennett eyed the glistening 21-inch torpedoes with misgiving. 'They safe, mate?'

'You could belt them with a sledge hammer and nothing would happen. Not primed. But don't try it, because I could be wrong,' he replied cheerfully.

As the soldiers dumped their backpacks and weapons on the deck, they wondered how the sailors could live with the strange cocktail of aromas that permeated the boat. It was as if they were standing by the exhaust of an old bus which was burning too much oil and to which had been mixed the smell of grease, oiled wool, salt water and stale cabbage. There was also the sweet smell of rum and human sweat.

Lance-Corporal Temple pinched his nostrils between a thumb and forefinger. 'Crikey, what a pong! I bet the old slave traders smelt like eau de cologne in comparison.'

Sergeant Keith was already feeling slightly queasy. 'Find something else to talk about before I throw up, he said morosely.

'You'll find a bucket over there,' said the PO, nodding vaguely in the direction of the stern.

The first lieutenant escorted Mappin to the small wardroom which was separated from the rest of the ship by a curtain. Lieutenant-Commander Cotton was studying a chart spread out on a table. 'You can have my bunk because I don't

148

contemplate getting much sleep myself. This is what we call a "hot bunk" boat: officers and men coming off duty simply take over those vacated by their reliefs.'

'How long will it take us to get there, sir?'

'Depends on a number of things. In the darkness and on the surface we can make twelve knots on our main engines; submerged we have to go over to the motors and that reduces our speed to about six knots. A lot of course depends on Jerry. If we're forced to remain submerged for any length of time we can run the batteries down, and we'll have to wait till we surface to recharge them.'

'Are you anticipating any trouble, sir?'

'I won't be looking for it, that's for sure,' said Cotton with a smile. 'But Jerry has a constant air patrol on the lookout for British warships; fortunately they can't operate at night. But they have a very tenacious force of anti-submarine vessels on round-the-clock patrol.' He tugged his ear lobe. 'The important thing is not to be detected, because that means taking evasive action, perhaps lying doggo on the sea bed for a long time, and that can bugger up the whole schedule.' He straightened and rolled up the chart. 'Now, if you'll excuse me there're one or two things I must say to your men.'

He left the wardroom and minutes later his voice came over the intercom. 'I've a few words to say to our army guests before we sail. Life aboard a submarine is a bit arse-upwards, as you'll discover. Everything is reversed. Breakfast is served at night when the boat is surfaced, and dinner is around midnight. Cooking is dicey when we're submerged. Most important – there's no smoking when we're submerged. When we're about to surface you'll hear the order "Switch to night lighting" and the white bulbs will be replaced by red ones – that's to enable lookouts to adjust their night vision. This will be followed by "Carry on smoking". In the unlikely event of us having to remain below for any length of time, remember this: just relax and do as little as possible, because there'll be a need to conserve oxygen. Especially as we're carrying more bods than normal. The amount of carbon dioxide in the air will increase and this will make you tired and listless, but you'll recover very quickly once we've surfaced and some fresh air is pumped aboard.'

149

An hour later the voice of the first lieutenant came over the intercom: 'Stand by for leaving harbour.'

There was a flurry of activity as men hastened to their duty stations: lookouts to the conning tower, ERAs and stokers to the diesels and motors, the telegraphists to the wireless and Asdic room, the coxswain and second coxswain to the hydroplane controls.

Mappin was invited by Lieutenant-Commander Cotton to join him on the bridge, where half a dozen ratings stood on the main deck waiting for the order to cast off the mooring lines. Cotton called through a megaphone: 'Let go fore'ard, let go aft.' There was a loud splash as the wire hawsers hit the water.

Mappin glanced round the crowded conning tower. In addition to the captain and the lookouts, there was a signalman and the first lieutenant. He feared he might be in the way.

'Would you rather I went below, sir?'

'Not at all. You won't be here for long; as soon as we pass through the boom you'll have to leave. So enjoy the fresh air while you can.'

Two minesweepers appeared in the distance and an Aldis lamp blinked on the bridge wing of the leading ship. The signalman repeated aloud each word as he read the morse: 'Escorts – to – *Otter* – ready – and waiting'

'Send: am joining you now,' Cotton said. He turned to Mappin. 'The sweepers will take us through the boom and into the swept channel. They'll also clear any mines Jerry may have laid without our knowledge.'

Cotton used *Otter*'s motors for the complicated manoeuvre of leaving the depot ship, but as soon as she was clear he switched to the main diesels and fell in line astern of the sweepers. As the three vessels approached the anti-submarine nets marked by a line of buoys, the boom defence ships began to open the boom with the heavy lifting equipment on their bows. The Asdic could clearly be heard pinging away below; it was always an anxious moment. Enemy U-boats often lurked outside the boom waiting for the opportunity to slip through undetected below the hulls of the outgoing ships.

150

When they were clear of the minefields the sweepers signalled their intention to return to harbour. Their Aldis lamps flashed a 'bon voyage' message.

Free of the escorts, Lieutenant-Commander Cotton increased speed to twelve knots. A creamy white bow wave sent the sea rippling over the upper deck. Half an hour later he turned to Mappin. 'I'll have to ask you to go below now – this is always a dicey time. Jerry has a whole fleet of Focke-Wulf reconnaissance bombers patrolling the sea between here and Norway on the look out for subs; we've wreaked sheer havoc among their coastal convoys taking iron ore and other valuable war supplies to Germany. The bombers themselves are no great problem, unless they catch us on the surface and have time to dive-bomb. That's unlikely, though. We can crash-dive in less than twenty seconds. The real problem is that they'll report our position and request sea-borne support, and their anti-submarine ships are tenacious sods – very difficult to shake off.'

Mappin went below into the control room, where he stood watching the first lieutenant, who was standing behind the coxswain and second coxswain, operating the hydroplanes which controlled the trim of the boat, his eyes intently fixed on the bubble in the inclometer.

He was amazed at the calm efficiency of the sailors as they went about their duties. No one spoke, except to repeat the orders of the captain when they came down the conning tower voice pipe. There was little movement in the boat apart from the vibration caused by the massive diesels and the rotation of the twin propellers.

They had been at sea a little over two hours when the comparative silence was suddenly shattered by the voice of the captain filling the control room, now no longer quiet and matter of fact, but urgent and incisive. 'Emergency diving stations! Enemy aircraft approaching!'

There was a clatter of feet on the steep ladder as the first man descended. On the way down he pressed the alarm button to sound off the klaxon and its strident blast rang out through the boat.

Men were already at their action stations before his feet hit the deck. He was followed by the captain; the others followed

151

in quick succession. The last man called out: 'First clip on,' meaning the upper lid on the conning tower had been secured. Cotton was already shouting: 'Dive, dive, dive! Blow Q.'

As the quick diving tank was blown, a rating in the motor room swiftly broke the running charge that had been pumping amps into the batteries, and threw the grouper switches into the Up position to give maximum diving power.

It took a mere sixteen seconds to reach periscope depth.

Cotton took over control of the rapidly diving boat. 'Take her down to ninety feet, please. Steer 070 degrees,'

As the order was repeated by the coxswain and the second coxswain, the ship seemed to tilt at an alarming angle as the bow went down. Then a sound like a muffled drumbeat filled the boat, and seconds later it shuddered from the shock waves caused by the explosion of two 1,100 pound bombs. For a brief moment some of the lights flickered before resuming their normal brilliance.

'One hundred feet, please,' said Cotton. He turned to Mappin. 'Nothing to get hot under the collar over – just a shot in the dark. hasn't a hope in hell of hitting us. He'll hang around for a while hoping I'll go up to periscope depth and he'll get another chance, but he won't.'

Two hours passed and nothing happened. Cotton then gave the order for the boat to revert to watch-diving routine, which meant that one third of the crew could relax.

The first lieutenant turned to Mappin. 'I'll take you aft to where your lads are quartered – I expect they'll be wondering what the hell's going on. I'll explain that it's nothing to get tight-arsed about.'

Mappin followed him through the hull of the boat to the torpedo storage compartment.

Only the eyes of the Commandos revealed their apprehension. They had been trained to fight and kill a visible enemy, and they found it unnerving to be attacked by one they could not even see, let alone hit back at. The first lieutenant grinned cheerfully. 'The first time's always the worst, and we can't promise you it'll be the last!'

They relaxed perceptibly, assured by the calm composure of the officer and the indifference of the off duty sailors to the attack.

When Mappin and the first lieutenant returned to the control room, Sergeant Keith, who was lying fully stretched out on a torpedo, turned to a petty officer who was polishing some already gleaming equipment. 'Jesus, I hope the officer meant what he said and you do get us there in one piece! This Op means a lot in more ways than one – we can't afford to fail.'

The PO paused in his polishing. 'We can only do our best, mate. Every time we set off from Scapa we know it could be our last trip. No point in dwelling on it and losing your bottle.'

'I'm not talking about fear. I'm thinking that there're still some people who'll be quite happy to see this fail, because it'll prove their point that Commandos are a luxury we can't afford, carrying out hare-brained schemes that are doomed from the start. But I don't expect you to understand that. No reason why you should.'

'I do understand, mate – and I have every sympathy. Submariners are in the same class. The big ship men resent us, think we're an elite. They're envious of the extra pay we get, the casual way we dress, and the informal bonhomie there is in a sub. They want us to be inflicted with the same pointless bullshit they have to endure.'

'I wasn't thinking so much of other soldiers, more the big chiefs in Whitehall.'

'Then we're on the same wavelength, Sergeant. I'm not only talking about the lower deck. The Admiralty's run by big-gun men who think submarine warfare is a shitty business, unsporting. They've still got the Jutland mentality: battle wagons steaming in line ahead, blowing shit out of each other. That's how the war at sea should be fought. But they're a load of wankers: place their faith in sixteen-inch guns but won't allow the battle wagons to go to seas in case they get sunk.'

Keith was relieved to hear that there were men in the Senior Service who had as low an opinion of the Admiralty as he had of the War Office.

In the control room, Lieutenant-Commander Cotton decided to take the boat up to periscope depth. As the submarine was making less than five knots on her motors, the periscope would create little more than a feather-like wake, almost invisible to an aircraft.

'Periscope depth, please.'

There was an audible hiss as the search periscope shot up.

Cotton pressed his eyes against the view finder and focused the periscope, making a 360° sweep of the sea. There was a fair swell running which limited the extent of his vision, and he decided to take the boat up until the conning tower was exposed. It was a practice most submariners disliked; there was always the danger of the boat porpoising when it dipped, sending water cascading over the tower. But there was no other way of finding out whether or not the aircraft had gone.

He gave the order for the boat to be taken up to thirty feet, and the first lieutenant was just about to commence the process of trimming down when the Asdic operator called out: 'I've picked up something, sir. Very definite echo bleeps.'

'Belay that order,' snapped Cotton. He turned to his Number One. 'Check if anything has been picked up on the hydrophone.'

Asdic was still in its infancy, and its complicated dials and knobs were viewed with mistrust and regarded as something of a mystery by the old hands who preferred the tried and tested hydrophones.

When the first lieutenant went into the wireless room, the Asdic operator said, 'Getting it loud and clear, sir. Very positive, and getting closer.'

The leading telegraphist operating the set had a reputation for possessing the finest ears in the service, capable of picking up things that others were incapable of hearing, and the first lieutenant had unquestioning faith in his ability. Nevertheless he donned the earphones just long enough to confirm it for himself. 'Looks as if the F-W has summoned up a search party.'

He went to a rating operating one of the hydrophones and asked if he had detected anything.

'Yes, sir, no doubt about it. Whether it's someone looking for us, or just passing ships, is anyone's guess.'

'We'll soon know,' said the first lieutenant.

He reported back to the captain, who said: 'I'll take her up and have a quick look – better to know for sure what we're up against. Then at least I'll know what to do.'

He ordered the boat to go up to periscope depth, and as he swept the horizon his worst fears were confirmed. Spread out on the surface were at least four anti-submarine trawlers – known to submariners as UJ boats – carrying out a zig-zag sweep.

'One hundred feet, please,' he said. The men operating the hydroplanes responded as casually as two men taking a leisurely stroll through the countryside. They had been through it all so many times that they gave no thought to the possible dangers. They knew the boat could descend much deeper if the need arose and that her hull had been designed to withstand the most tremendous pressure: so great that a depth charge would have to be extremely close to inflict any lethal damage. Behind them the first lieutenant kept a watchful eye on the inclinometer and the trim of the boat.

Cotton gave continuous alterations to the course in a desperate attempt to confuse the pursuers. He knew they did not have sophisticated Asdic and relied on the more primitive hydrophones which meant they had to shut off their engines before they could be operated. Being aware of this, he simply switched off his own motors, along with every other moving part of equipment, when his listeners reported silence above. It meant considerable discomfort to the crew, for the fans and ventilating equipment had also to be shut down.

The deadly cat and mouse game continued for several hours, the Commandos sitting immobile in their quarters like spectators at a sporting conflict, aware of every tactical move but impotent to affect the outcome. As the trawlers above homed in on their quarry the tension mounted, and the interior of the submarine became hotter and more airless by the minute.

Throughout the desperate game of chess, the crew carried out their duties with unhurried movements and unruffled calm. Watertight doors were secured, separating one compartment from another: an unspoken reminder that if one part of the boat became flooded the remainder would continue to function despite the terrible fate that had been inflicted on their shipmates.

Then depth charges began to explode around the hull like great claps of reverberating thunder. The boat shivered and shuddered from the terrible impact. The lights dimmed and some went out as another pattern of depth charges exploded.

Sergeant Keith, who had sought refuge below one of the torpedoes, found himself gazing at a row of cups dangling from

155

bulkhead hooks when the first explosion came. Then, to his astonishment, he was looking at just their handles, as they shattered in the force of the blast.

Huddled on the deck the Commandos put their hands over their buzzing ears to cushion the shock, wishing they had the chance to go into action against the bastards up above who were making their lives such a misery. They cringed, grabbing at anything solid as the depth charges exploded with such venomous power it seemed as if the plates and rivets were groaning in agony.

Private Bennett called across the deck to Warren: 'Bunny, if we don' get outa this little caper, you can forget the dollar you owes me.'

'That's right fucking generous of you. And if we *do* get out?'

'You'll still owe me five bob!'

Keith was amazed, and not a little proud, that they could still joke under such circumstances.

In the control room Cotton remained unflappable. When the engines of the hunting trawlers stopped he shut down his own motors and went into 'silent routine'. When they restarted he did likewise. The depth charges, however, continued to explode around the boat.

'Take her down, Number One.'

'How far, sir?'

'Until we can't go any deeper. We'll rest on the bottom until they get tired of playing silly buggers and go home. We can't run for it, they've pin-pointed us.' There was an almost tangible silence as the submarine dropped lower and lower, and there was no more than a gentle bump when she settled on the seabed.

'Total silence will be maintained throughout the boat,' Cotton said. 'Just relax and take it easy.'

No one needed any encouragement to do that; there was already too much carbon dioxide in the thinning oxygen. It made the men so listless the slightest effort called for the utmost concentration, and the least exertion made them feel as if they had sprinted a hundred yards.

In the torpedo compartment the soldiers were feeling dizzy, incapable of clear thinking. All they wanted to do was fall asleep, but they resisted the temptation when a sailor warned 'Don't. Do that and you won't wake up.'

156

A further series of explosions hit the submarine, and it was shaken like a rat in the jaws of a terrier. There was an agonizing scream of pain as Private Buchanan was hurled across the compartment. His head struck a pipe with the sound of a dinner gong being sounded and he cannoned off and slumped in a heap on the deck, blood streaming from a deep gash on his forehead.

Keith, who had been knocked flat by the shock waves, crawled to his side and cradled Buchanan's head in his lap. The private's eyes were staring blindly at the deck head, blood seeped from the wound.

Keith called to a rating, 'Can you get the doctor?'

'Don't carry a sawbones. The coxswain's the nearest we have to one, and all he's got is a First Aid Manual and a medicine chest.'

'Get him anyway.'

'Why not? He won't be doing anything seeing as we're on the sea bed.'

Another series of explosions rocked the boat and more lights went out.

The rating said: 'You'll find some torches in that locker above the portside torpedoes. Better help yourself to some – all the lights may go any minute now.'

The sailor weaved an unsteady path through the boat to the control tower, and a few minutes later the coxswain arrived in the compartment. He knelt beside the injured man, loosened his blouse and pressed an ear to his chest, at the same time feeling for his wrist. When he was unable to detect any pulse, he placed his fingers against the side of his neck. He stood up. 'He's had it. I'll tell the captain. You'd better tell your officer.' He picked up a blanket from the deck and placed it over the dead soldier.

Together they made their way through to the control room, and broke the news to the two officers.

Cotton merely nodded, too engrossed to give much thought to something he could do nothing about.

'I'd better have a look,' Mappin said.

They returned to the compartment where Buchanan's blanket-covered body lay on the deck. His protruding boots reminded Keith of Dunkirk. The other soldiers were trying in vain to avert their eyes from their dead comrade.

'Get two of the lads to move him out of sight,' Mappin said.

'Bennett, come and give me a hand,' Keith called. 'I'll take his head, you take his feet.'

He put his hands under Buchanan's lolling arms while Bennett took hold of his feet, and together they dragged him across the deck and pushed him out of sight below one of the torpedoes.

Keith had never been close to Buchanan, who was very much a private person, but he had been a good soldier and would be missed. The group was small enough as it was and could ill afford to lose a member before they had even started.

Further explosions battered the hull, throwing everyone off their feet, and water began to seep through leaks in the ruptured plates and loosened rivets. A leading seaman entered the compartment and said to Mappin: 'Number One's compliments, but can you send half a dozen of your men to the midship's mess to give a hand with the bailing? It's flooding badly. Better strip off first.'

The soldiers removed their battle dresses and underclothes and followed the sailor to the mess deck, where they were appalled at the sight confronting them: shattered tables, benches and lockers, and items of clothing swilling around on the surface of two feet of thick, oily water. Under the watchful eye of a junior officer, several naked sailors had formed a bucket chain and water from the flooded mess was being passed back to be poured down the bilges. The soldiers joined the chain, filling buckets and passing back empty ones.

'Daren't use the pumps because of the noise,' the officer said.

The soldiers and sailors worked in total silence until they were utterly exhausted, and when they paused for a brief rest they realized they had made little change to the level of the water. But they returned to their labours with renewed effort, knowing their survival depended on it. Meanwhile, the depth charges continued to plummet down and explode with pulverizing force against the hull.

In the control room, Cotton listened anxiously as report from various parts of the boat were delivered. Not only was there flooding amidships, but one of the fore'ard compartment was also taking water. He turned to the first lieutenant. 'Prepare the confidential books for destruction, please, Number One.

158

When the men in the control room heard his words they knew the captain accepted there was little chance of escaping the relentless barrage. They also knew that the only way to destroy the confidential books while submerged was to use hydrochloric acid, which in itself presented a grave hazard because there was always the risk of a chemical reaction producing chlorine gas.

Cotton saw the look of resignation on their faces. 'Belay that order, Number One. We'll try the old dodge of firing some gash from one of the torpedo tubes and hope Jerry falls for it. Nothing to lose.'

The first lieutenant summoned three torpedo ratings and a senior ERA and hastened to the bow. Debris from the flooded mess was pushed into the starboard tube: bits of broken lockers and benches, a couple of life jackets, some odd bits of clothing and several caps.

The first lieutenant paused, then said calmly: 'Might as well make it look really authentic. Get some of the soldiers to strip the dead man and bring the body here.' He saw the expressions of horror on the faces of the torpedo party. 'Believe me, I'm not being callous, just sensible. If he were able to say anything, I'm sure he'd give his blessing.'

'Why strip the poor so-and-so, sir?' asked the ERA.

'Don't want Jerry wondering what a soldier is doing on a sub, do we?'

When the body was brought through it was lifted into the tube. The tube was flooded, and the internal pressure equalized to that outside the boat: then compressed air was released into the tube to act as a propellant and the bow cap opened. When the contents were forced out, the cap was closed and the water in the flooded tube was vented back into a special tank. At the same time, the engineer released a quantity of oil.

The first lieutenant crossed his fingers. When the contents of the tube reached the surface, followed by a slick of oil, the enemy might be misled into thinking they had made a 'kill'. It was a ruse often successfully employed by U-boat captains, who had found that the sight of the sea littered with bits of equipment and human clothing often had a psychological effect on hunters who, anxious to see positive proof of a kill, were only too ready to accept floating jetsam as evidence. A dead body would make it even more convincing.

Lieutenant Mappin stood in the control room studying the captain's expressionless face, hoping that no one would notice his own nervousness. He had a dread of slowly suffocating. He knew nothing about submarines, except for the little he had read, but he knew that the only method of escape for men entombed below the surface was by means of a special apparatus which propelled them to the surface like corks out of a champagne bottle. But that was of only academic interest; neither he nor his men had been taught how to use such equipment.

The boat's company settled down to play cards and Ludo while they waited for the captain to make a decision. The soldiers tried to follow their example, but found it difficult. Cotton allowed an hour to pass, then another, before he told the Asdic operator to switch on his set. When he reported that he could not detect anything above, Cotton told the operators on the hydrophones to switch on their equipment. When they too confirmed that they could hear nothing, Cotton waited another hour before giving the order: 'Ascend to periscope depth.'

The partially-flooded ship shuddered and heaved as the pumps started emptying the buoyancy tanks and the boat rose slowly.

Darkness was approaching and visibility was poor, but as Cotton swung the search periscope in a bow to stern sweep, a slight smile puckered his mouth. There was no sign of the sub hunters.

'Stand by to surface,' he said cheerfully. The seamen moved to their tasks like automatons, their brains fuddled by the lack of oxygen. They panted like tired dogs as they operated their levers and switches.

'Shift to night lighting,' said Cotton, and the boat was filled with a dim rosy hue.

'Ready to surface, sir,' the first lieutenant said.

Cotton was first up the steep ladder, climbing like an aged arthritic, and as he opened the hatch the welcome smell of fresh air flooded into the boat.

'Lookouts on the bridge. Start the generators.' He then opened the voice pipe stopcock and the helmsman below opened another and drained water from the pipe into a bucket.

As the generators pumped more fresh air into the submarine and began to recharge the batteries, pipes in the control room

160

froze and what looked like particles of snow dropped onto the deck. The boat was filled with the heavy thump-thump-thump of the pumps clearing water from the flooded sections.

The soldiers experienced sudden and severe headaches. Some vomited and feared their brains would explode. But their sudden panic dissolved when a CPO said: 'Nothing to worry about – a normal reaction after you've been starved of oxygen. Just relax and don't gulp it down like it's going out of fashion.'

The first lieutenant called out, 'Pipe, "Up spirits", and "Carry on Smoking".' The craving for nicotine was so great that men who minutes earlier had found difficulty in breathing reached for pipes, cigarettes and tins of 'tickler' to make roll-ups. When the soldiers struck matches to light their cigarettes, they were surprised when they spluttered and went out, not realizing there was still a shortage of oxygen.

As they smoked, inhaling deeply into protesting lungs, a petty officer and a killick appeared carrying plates piled high with corned beef sandwiches. 'Fill your boots, there's plenty more where this came from,' shouted the PO. The soldiers stretched out eager hands and ravenously devoured the food.

A rating asked the first lieutenant: 'Permission to ditch gash, sir?'

The first lieutenant nodded, and hands carrying buckets filled with accumulated refuse tipped the contents over the side of the conning tower, a ritual that was carried out only in darkness so as not to give away the presence of a submarine.

Otter had reverted to a normal routine as if nothing exceptional had happened. The signalman came down the conning tower ladder and spoke to Mappin. 'Captain's compliments, and would you like to join him on the bridge?'

When he appeared on the bridge, Cotton, a dark hulk against the parapet, called out jovially: 'Bit of a blow coming up! Couldn't wish for anything better. No aircraft to bother us, and not a trawler in sight.' He spoke as if the events of the past few hours had never happened.

Mappin felt his flagging spirits soar as the cold spray bounced off the bow and descended on the bridge in a fine spray that stung like nettles.

'That was a bit hairy, sir,' said Mappin.

'Known worse,' replied Cotton. 'But it's all in the past now. We're back on our original course, and not too far behind schedule. After a while the batteries will be recharged enough to get the electric ovens started, then everyone can have a hot meal. After that I suggest your chaps get their heads down.'

'I'd like to express my gratitude at the way you handled things, sir,' Mappin said hesitantly.

The captain patted him gently on the shoulder. 'I'll tell you something, Lieutenant, I'd rather go through that a dozen times than face what you've got coming.'

'I'm looking forward to it. Those bastards have really got me mad.'

'I'm sorry about the soldier we shot out of the tube,' Cotton said softly. 'But he probably made all the difference when it came to fooling Jerry.'

'I'd better get below and grab some shut eye,' Mappin said.

'You do that. I'll see that everyone gets a call in plenty of time.'

'How about you, sir? Don't you ever sleep? You've been on your feet since we left Scapa.'

Cotton chuckled. 'The navy has some funny customs. A captain is always responsible for his ship; even if something happens when he's got his head down, he still takes the can. So the simplest course is to do without sleep.'

As Mappin made his way below he felt sure that he would be unable to sleep: his fear of being entombed below was too great. But no sooner had he laid down on his bunk than he drifted off into a deep, untroubled sleep.

Chapter Eleven

Mappin was shaken awake by a seaman who handed him a cup of tea. 'Captain's compliments, sir, he'd like to see you in the control room.'

Mappin glanced at his watch: it was two in the morning. He swung his feet off the bunk and made his way fore'ard.

The control room was silent except for the occasional softly-spoken orders. Cotton motioned him to join him at the chart table, where he stabbed at a small cross with the point of a pencil. 'We're *here*.'

Mappin looked at the spread-out chart, marvelling at the skill required to navigate the submarine with such pin-point accuracy. The coast off Norway seemed to be dotted with thousands of offshore islands, some large, others no bigger than a football pitch, but each a lethal hazard.

'God,' he murmured, 'It's worse than a minefield.'

'They're better than an escort of destroyers,' said Cotton cheerfully. 'Jerry hates carrying out sweeps in the dark with all those islands around. They can rip a ship open like a tin of sardines.' He glanced at the chronometer on the bulkhead. 'We'll be surfacing in about an hour's time, so your lads should be ready to go ashore soon afterwards. It's a good time to land. The vigilance of the sentries will be at its lowest ebb, waiting for their reliefs and thinking of getting their heads down.'

'I'll go and warn them, sir.'

He made his way aft to the spare torpedo compartment, where he found his men just finishing a meal and joking among themselves in a light-hearted fashion. Mappin suspected they were doing their best to conceal their ragged nerve ends and the tight knot of fear that gripped their stomachs. He was experiencing the same symptoms. He assumed that a 'buzz' had reached them that action was imminent.

He called Keith aside and repeated the captain's message.

'Thought something was in the wind, sir,' said the sergeant. 'The matelots who served the grub warned us to stand by.'

'See the lads check their weapons and equipment carefully – don't leave it to the last minute. I don't want it to develop into an unseemly panic.' He tried to sound jovial. 'And see they don't forget their make-up! I want them looking their best for Jerry.'

'They've done that half a dozen times every hour, sir, just for something to do. Sitting around doing nothing gives them too much time to think.'

Mappin returned to his cabin to check his own equipment and smother his face with the dark grease paint. He found himself offering up a silent prayer that everything would go without a hitch. They had been silent spectators so far; now the moment was rapidly approaching when they would have to prove their worth.

He walked through to the control room, aware of the sound his boots made on the steel deck, and grateful for the assurance Cotton had given him that the enemy did not mount surface searches at night. Cotton had moved from the chart table and was now standing by the periscope. 'Take her up to periscope depth.'

The first lieutenant repeated the order, and Mappin saw the needles on the depth gauges move like the second hands on a clock as the submarine began to rise.

'Thirty feet, sir,' said the first lieutenant.

Cotton said quietly; 'Up periscope.'

Cotton rotated it in a full circle, then ordered it to be lowered. He muttered, as if to himself, 'Not much to learn from that – black as Newgate's knocker.' He replaced the periscope handles. 'Take her up, Number One.'

Cotton seemed to sense when the conning tower had broken through the surface of the water, for he grabbed his night glasses and snapped; 'Take over, Number One. Bunts, you follow me up. Duty lookouts, to your posts. You'd better follow them, Lieutenant.'

164

Cotton shinned up the vertical ladder. There was a metallic clang as he released the huge clips on the watertight hatch and cold invigorating fresh air flooded into the submarine.

Mappin saw the feet of the second lookout disappear through the hatch and he began to climb up himself. The figures on the bridge were dark blurred shapes; the only thing he could see as he peered fore'ard was the fluorescent glow of the bow wave.

A heavy sea mist, cold and clammy, enveloped the surface of the water like cotton wood. 'We could do without that,' Cotton growled angrily. The people ashore will have the devil's own job spotting our signal. I was hoping to have got your lads topsides by now, Lieutenant, but I'll have to leave it till the very last minute now. Can't have them standing on the upper deck, in case I have to dive suddenly.'

There was a nerve-tingling silence on the bridge, broken only by the gentle purr of the electric motors. When Cotton spoke again it came as such a surprise that Mappin felt his knees jerk as if he had been suddenly startled.

'See if you can raise anybody, Bunts.'

The signalman lifted the shaded night signal torch and flashed in morse. The reflection of the signal bounced back greenly off the thick mist. 'They'll be lucky to see that, sir,' he said glumly.

Every man on the bridge peered intently into the distance, watching anxiously for the recognition signal. Five minutes passed and there was no response.

'Start on the port bow, Bunts, and repeat it every half a minute until you've got round to starboard.'

The signalman's fingers worked the trigger on the torch, cursing to himself as the cold stiffened them. He had almost reached the end of his sweep when one of the lookouts whispered; 'Light, fine on the starboard bow, sir.'

The signalman raised the binoculars that were suspended from his neck and trained them on the faint flickering light. 'That's them, sir,' he said excitedly. 'They're flashing the code word; Midas.'

'Thank God for that,' said Cotton. 'Get the dinghies up and inflated before your lads come up.'

Mappin called down the conning tower to Keith, who was standing at the bottom of the ladder. 'Get the inflatables passed up, Sergeant.'

Sergeant Keith and Privates Luck and Warren clattered up the ladder and grabbed the dinghies as they passed through the hatch. Then they shinned down the ladder on the side of the conning tower and stood on the deck as the dinghies were lowered down to them. They attached the footpumps and began to fill the three dinghies with powerful thrusts of their legs. When they were fully inflated they attached the bow lines to cleats on the upper deck and slid the boats gently into the water.

Mappin lowered his head over the hatch. 'Right lads – up you come.'

There was a clatter of steel-shod boots on the rungs of the ladder as the Commandos made their way into the fresh air. The sudden change of temperature, from the clammy warmth of the submarine to the chilling sea mist, made their lungs ache.

'Luck and Temple, you'll be with me in the first dinghies,' Sergeant Keith said quietly. 'Lieutenant Mappin, Warren and Foster you'll man the second boat. Bennett, you'll be on your own in the last one with the boxes of explosives.'

'Trust me to get the shitty end of the stick,' said Bennett.

'Count yourself lucky. You'll be so busy stopping those boxes going over the side you won't have to paddle – we'll be towing you.'

As soon as the dinghies were secured to each other by lengths of rope the soldiers clambered into them gingerly. Water lapped over the sides, and when they knelt they felt it seeping through their trouser legs.

Cotton called down from the conning tower; 'Just keep heading towards the light. They'll flash it every two minutes.'

Lieutenant Mappin cupped his hands over his mouth and called back. 'Thanks a million, sir! Couldn't have worked out better.'

'Good luck. See you back in Scapa.'

Sergeant Keith released the rope securing his dinghy to the submarine. 'Right lads, Put your backs into it.'

The soldiers plunged their paddles into the water, and with firm powerful strokes propelled the dinghies away from the submarine. Keith chanted: 'In – out. In – out,' as the soldiers bent to their task, but there was really no need for him to call out encouragement. The men worked in complete unison; the reward of the endless hours spent in practice.

Through the darkness they heard the muffled clang of the submarine's hatch being closed and the slight turbulence that rocked the dinghies told them that *Otter* had submerged. Sergeant Keith kept his eyes firmly fastened on the light in the distance, which flashed with the regularity of a marker buoy. They paddled hard and furiously until they could feel the perspiration pouring off their bodies and dripping off their foreheads into their eyes. But despite their strenuous efforts their fingers remained half frozen from the sub-zero sea water.

Keith could hear their breath becoming more and more laboured, and he called out encouragement, 'Nearly there, lads.'

Bennett's voice floated through the mist in what he thought was a posh accent. 'Stick with it, chaps. You've just passed under 'ammersmith Bridge. Mortlake brewery next stop. Ten to one on the light blues!'

Warren, without pausing in his labours, called back; 'Put a fucking sock in it. If you think this is some kind of sodding boat race, you can change places. You'll know then what a fucking galley slave went through.'

'Save your breath for paddling, Warren,' Mappin said softly.

'Sorry, sir – but he pisses me off, sitting back there like Cleopatra in her bleeding barge.'

Sergeant Keith feared that his eyes were playing tricks. It seemed that it had suddenly grown much darker. He wondered if it was exhaustion, for the muscles in his back were screaming in protest and he imagined the others were suffering similar agonies. He turned his head and called back to Lieutenant Mappin, 'Permission for a short break, sir. No point in us arriving completely knackered.'

'Good idea, but everyone keep their eyes on that damned lamp,' Mappin said, 'We haven't come this far to get lost.'

The kneeling men hunched forward in the dinghies, their chests rising and falling from the continuous effort of paddling. Despite the perspiration that dripped off them, their breath seemed in danger of freezing solid.

Keith glanced anxiously around him, increasingly concerned with the deepening darkness. Then his anxiety vanished; he knew the answer. Now that he was no longer preoccupied with the strength-sapping task of propelling the unwieldy dinghy through the water, he could see that they had entered a fjord, the sides of which rose like cliffs on either side.

'We're home and dry, sir,' he called out excitedly. As he spoke, the sea mist suddenly began to clear as if some gargantuan fan had been switched on to disperse it. For the first time the flashing light ashore was clearly visible.

'Bend your backs, lads!' Mappin called out.

The soldiers returned to their task with new found energy, digging the paddles deeper and making much longer strokes. The surface of the water was now as placid as a boating lake, and the towering cliffs were clearly visible, dark and daunting, but at the same time giving the feeling of comfort and protection from the open sea.

Then Keith heard a strange sound. 'Cease paddling!'

He felt chill fingers of fear tighten round his intestines and he cocked his head to one side, desperately worried about the noise, which sounded very much like someone approaching them with considerable stealth and caution. He rested his paddle on the bottom of the boat, picked up his Tommy-gun and moved the safety catch to fire. He peered at the spot where he knew the torch had been flashing, but a full minute passed and there was no sign of it. *Shit*, he said to himself. *We've got this far only to be rumbled at the last minute.* He tried to disguise the fear and disappointment which flooded through him. 'Get you weapons ready, lads. We might have a fight on our hands.'

'You heard something too, then, Sarge,' Warren said. 'If you ask me, it's a boat.' He groped for a grenade, muttering 'They'll wonder what fucking hit them when this lands in their laps.'

The creaking and splashing continued and Keith raised his sub-machine gun to his shoulder. A dark shape loomed ahead

168

and his finger tightened on the trigger. 'Don't fire until I do,' he whispered.

Then a voice wafted out of the darkness and his fear dissipated like the sea mist. 'Follow closely behind me,' called a foreign voice, in perfect but heavily accented English. 'There are many rocks that will rip holes in your rubber boats.'

A row boat manned by two muffled figures loomed out of the darkness and Keith realized that the sound he had heard was that of oars in rowlocks. A heavy clinker-built boat drew up alongside the dinghies and a big powerfully-built man leaned over the gunwale and extended his hand. 'Welcome to Norway! You are, how do you say it, spot on the time?'

Keith grasped his outstretched hand. 'Are we glad to see you! For one moment we thought it was the Germans.'

The man laughed without humour. 'They do not venture into the fjords at this time of the day. They are likely to collect a bullet from a hunter's rifle – there is no closed season here where Germans are concerned. I am Olav Svenson, and my companion is Lars Ulricson, but we will more formally introduce ourselves later.'

'Lieutenant Mappin is in the boat astern' Keith said. 'He's the officer in command.'

'Our meeting must wait. Any minute now the Jerry will turn on his searchlights and sweep the fjord. But do not worry – he will not find us. We have timed to the exact second how long each sweep lasts. They are stupid creatures of habit.' He spat contemptuously. 'They always think that people will arrive when daylight is approaching, never in darkness which is the best time. Come. We have friends waiting.'

The row boat turned and began to head for the shore, and the line of dinghies fell in astern of it. They had been travelling for less than ten minutes when a cone of light cut through the darkness and began a systematic search of the placid water. The row boat sought shelter behind a cluster of razor-edged rocks, and Svenson began counting slowly in a monotonous voice. 'When I have reached one hundred it will be with us, and then it will take as long as two thousand before it returns. By then we will be safe.'

The small convoy of vessels stayed behind the misshapen rocks until the beam had swept past. The Norwegian whispered: 'They do not have their hearts in the job because they never find anything. Now we shall go.'

Five minutes later the dinghies struck pebbles. The soldiers leapt out and began to haul them up a steep narrow strip of pebbled beach.

'Do not bother with the boats,' said the big Norwegian. 'Fill them with stones and then cut the sides. We will sink them in deep water. They are of no further use.'

Sinking the inflatables presented no problem, for the strip of beach ended abruptly and the water at the end was fathomless. There was a sudden eruption of air bubbles, then the inflatables were no longer visible. Svenson tied the row boat onto one of the piles of a nearby jetty which led to a rickety fisherman's hut. 'We will stay in the fishing house until it is dark once more. That is not long.' He shrugged. 'Now, at this time of the year, we have seventeen hours, perhaps more, of darkness. We will have time to discuss our future actions.'

He led the small group of soldiers along the pier to the wooden hut, half of which projected out into the water on green, slime-covered stilts. The planks were covered with deep crisp snow and Ulricson, who was at the tail end, carefully smoothed away the imprints their boots had left. The interior was cluttered with nets, marker buoys and large drums which reeked of fish oil. On wooden pegs on the walls were suits of oilskin, and the whole place stank of seaweed, rotting wood and mould. A hurricane lamp gleamed dimly from a beam in the centre of the room. Seated around a bare scrubbed table were two more Norwegians.

Svenson left the room and returned with two bottles which had been buried up to their necks in the snow. The liquid was the colour of strong milkless tea. He boomed jovially: 'First we will drink Aquavit to warm ourselves, then we will drink to the success of our mission.'

For the first time since leaving the submarine, the soldiers felt safe enough to relax. They placed their weapons carefully on the floor and shrugged out of their webbing.

Svenson lit another oil lamp. It was the first occasion anyone had had to get a good look at him. He was well over

170

six feet tall, with shoulders to match: dressed in ski clothing, his face was covered by a pointed yellow beard and side-boards. He reminded Keith of the school book drawings he had seen of the ancient Vikings who had sailed their long boats across the waters to England and Scotland on their bloody conquests so many centuries before. All he lacked, he thought, were a pair of curved horns on either side of his woollen bonnet.

The big Norwegian poured deep measures from the bottle into cracked and stained glasses which he passed round, demonstrating that it should be drunk in one swallow.

The glasses felt ice-cold in the soldiers' hands, but when they swallowed the liquid it burned a molten course to their stomach. Though it was a taste they have never before encountered, they were grateful; the warming glow restored their vigour and enthusiasm.

Svenson brushed his mouth with the back of his hand. 'You know me and my compatriot Ulricson, both of the University of Oslo.' He gestured to the two people sitting at the table. 'The rest of my party are Ollie Nordhoff and Christina Ross.'

The couple rose and formally lifted their glasses, and Keith let his eyes rest on the woman. Corn-coloured hair cascaded from her woollen bonnet, and even the shapeless jumper could not conceal the fullness of her breasts. He estimated she was about thirty years old, perhaps younger. The man was in his late twenties and looked lean and muscular; his face had a weather-beaten look, suggesting long hours spent at sea.

'Ollie is our local hero,' Svenson said. 'He was captured very early on and tortured by the Gestapo in an unsuccessful attempt to make him betray those who objected to the Occupation. Even though they burned him with cigarettes and pulled out his toe nails with pliers, he would not talk.' Svenson's massive shoulders heaved. 'Not that it mattered. There were only too many prepared to provide the information, and Oslo echoed to the sound of the firing squads. One day Ollie has promised to show me his scars.'

Nordhoff nodded in acknowledgement of the tribute. 'You will have to wait, Olav. They are not a pretty sight.'

Mappin saluted, feeling rather awkward. 'Lieutenant William Mappin.' He nodded towards Keith, 'Sergeant Keith. The rest of the soldiers will introduce themselves.'

There was a disorderly flurry as people shook hands, forgetting almost immediately the names that had been exchanged.

Svenson sat at the table and said to the woman: 'Christina, pour out more Aquavit.' He patted the seat beside him. 'Lieutenant Mappin, be pleased to sit beside me. I have much to explain before we move off.'

Sergeant Keith's eyes moved towards the girl who had removed her woollen cap and was shaking her head like a retriever emerging from water. She had a pale oval face and the bluest eyes he had ever seen. Her mouth was wide, and her cheeks were speckled with freckles – he wondered how she had got them in a land which the sun seemed to have forsaken. Her brow was furrowed as if the effort of pouring more drinks demanded her full concentration. Then it seemed as if she were aware of his scrutiny because she turned and smiled. The smile transformed her, so much so that Keith could not remember seeing a more attractive woman. Christ, he thought, how did you get mixed up in this caper?

He moved across the cluttered room and took the bottle from her hand. 'Here, let me do that. A pretty girl like you shouldn't be waiting attendance on a scruffy bunch of soldiers.'

She smiled again, revealing perfect white teeth. 'I don't mind, Sergeant. I am so overjoyed at meeting British soldiers again. The last time I saw a Tommy they were being chased out of Norway by the Germans.'

Keith said, with a smile, 'You speak very good English, Miss Ross.'

'Very good Scots, you mean. My father is Scottish. How else would I have the name of Ross? He was attached to the Embassy here, but he and my mother managed to get out before the Germans captured Oslo. He went to England with the King on *HMS Devonshire*.

'You couldn't leave with them?'

'No. I was working in the Central Bank and was one of the people selected to escort Norway's gold reserves to one of the ports, where it would be put aboard a British warship. I won't bore you with the details, but the lorry I was in, together with another, got separated from the main convoy. By the time we

172

got to Molde all the warships had gone and we were forced to hide the gold in a disused tunnel.'

'I've heard that a lot of Norwegians have since made their way to Scotland. Didn't you want to?'

'Of course, but I was one of only three people who knew were the gold was. The other two were captured and tortured in an effort to make them reveal the hiding place. They died under interrogation.' She shrugged. 'That meant I had to remain. I was not being heroic – I simply knew that sooner or later an attempt would be made to rescue the gold, and I had to be here to show the way.'

Their conversation was interrupted by Mappin, 'I think you'd better listen to this, Sergeant.'

'Excuse me, we'll have a long chat later,' Keith said. He added flippantly, 'Duty calls.'

He walked across to the table were Mappin sat hunched over his drink, having a heads-together conversation with the three Norwegians. Svenson was saying: 'Here it is best to move at night. Everyone is now issued with an identity card and the Germans scrutinize them very carefully. You must have a valid reason for travelling any distance.'

'What are the defences like?' Mappin said.

'Very thorough, especially along the coastline: plenty of pill boxes with artillery and machine gun emplacements, anti-aircraft batteries, minefields. But they will not bother us.' He dismissed the dangers with a brusque gesture. 'They are not aimed at us, but a possible invader. What we have to fear most is the enemy within.' He saw the look of stark astonishment on Mappin's face. 'Did you not know we have acquired a new word in our vocabulary – quizling?' He spoke contemptuously. 'Derived from Major Vidkun Quizling, the collaborator who has proclaimed himself Prime Minister. There is no shortage of traitors anxious to serve him.'

Nordhoff spoke for the first time, his voice tinged with bitterness. 'That is why we have to work in such small groups – the Germans would give their eye teeth to infiltrate a traitor in our midst. They will do anything to get their hands on the gold.'

Keith felt a stab of fear pierce him like a dagger thrust and he found his gaze settling on the girl. 'That makes Christina a much sought-after prize.'

'Not really,' said Ulricson. 'What would they do if they captured her? Torture her? But they could not be sure she would talk. No, they will let us go about our task until we recover the gold. Then they will strike – and that is when we will need your skills.'

Christina laughed merrily. 'But they will not catch us. It will be like looking for a single snowflake in a blizzard.'

Svenson turned to Mappin and said gravely: 'We are glad you are here, but I am disappointed that those who sent you did not take greater precautions.'

'I don't quite follow you,' Mappin said.

'You are so ill-equipped for work in Norway. You have no snowshoes, and I doubt you can ski. You will find the going very hard.'

Mappin smiled apologetically. 'We've done just about everything but learn to ski. But we've worked in conditions every bit as hard as we're likely to meet here, so we'll cope.'

'Crying, as you English say, over spilt milk will not solve anything. We'll just have to manage. I will go to the hotel and borrow all the sheets.' 'Sheets?' said Keith.

'Yes. We will turn them into smocks which will make you invisible in the snow. Now your men should rest before we set off, they must be tired. We will keep watch.'

The soldiers stretched out on the hard floor, their weapons by their sides within easy reach. Ulricson and Nordhoff picked up heavy carbines which had been smuggled in from England and went outside to keep watch, while Svenson fell asleep at the table with his head resting on his forearms. Sleep also overcame Lieutenant Mappin.

Keith, unable to sleep, sat beside the girl on the floor, their backs resting against the wall.

'How far is the gold from here, Christina?' he asked.

'Not far as a bird flies, but it'll take us three to four days, perhaps more.' She gave a slight shrug of her shoulders. 'It'll depend on the weather. The country is very harsh: glaciers, mountains, rivers and deep snow. When we get further north we can travel in daylight because the areas are very sparsely populated and the Germans don't bother to mount patrols; but if they send a spotter aircraft we'll have to hide and that'll delay us.'

'Surely that's unlikely? They don't even know of our existence.'

She nodded. 'They *will* know. Nothing happens without them hearing about it sooner or later – there're too many people anxious to please them. Someone sees a group of people moving across open country and they cannot wait to get on the telephone. The Germans reward traitors very generously.'

'It's a dangerous life you're leading,' he said quietly.

'Not as dangerous as that of an informer. We shoot them.' she made an almost imperceptible frown. 'That's murder, for we're not soldiers at war – but one day the war will end and there'll be no room in Norway for those who betrayed their country.'

Keith felt a weariness seep through his body. 'It seems wrong somehow that war can be so cruel.'

'War is always wicked.'

'I didn't mean that. I was thinking it was all wrong that a girl like you should be forced to kill, and talk so calmly about it. It alters us all.'

She sat upright. 'That's not fair, Sergeant. You look to me like a man who could kill and still sleep, so why shouldn't I do the same?'

'I'm a professional soldier. I've spent my life preparing for war.'

'I could have guessed that,' she said quietly.

'Why?' he asked, feeling surprisingly wounded.

'There's something about you that sets you apart from the others; a quiet confidence in the way you do things, and there's something in your eyes that's disturbing.' She hesitated, seeking the correct word to express her feelings. 'A cold – ruthlessness . . .' She stopped and shook her head. 'I'm being most unfair. I don't even know you.'

'It's a pretty fair assessment,' he said.

He felt her head slump against his chest, and from the rhythmical rise and fall of her breast knew she had fallen asleep. Sleep, however, eluded him. He found himself thinking of her words and experienced a mounting anger that she had judged him so unfavourably, even though he had to agree with her assessment.

Chapter Twelve

Sergeant Keith was suddenly aware of boots stamping on the wooden floor and he realized he had dozed off. He looked up and saw the two Norwegians who had kept vigil standing at the door kicking the snow from their boots. The girl was still asleep; the arm against which her body had rested had lost all feeling. He shifted her weight and began to massage life back into it. The sudden movement roused her and she sat upright.

'I'll prepare some food,' she said drowsily. She stood up, yawned noisily and stretched like a cat, then produced a comb and ran it through her hair. 'I hope you managed to sleep too, Sergeant Harry?'

He felt an unexpected glow of pleasure at her use of his Christian name. 'Let me give you a hand,' he said.

'Not unless you know how to cook *torr fisk*.'

'Never even heard of it.'

'Dried cod. Smells awful, tastes wonderful, although you may not think so. But it's ideal for people who're continually on the move. One person can carry enough to feed several for many days. It's like the biltong of the Afrikaaner.'

'I'll let you get on with it, Christina.'

The sentries clomped across the floor to the stove where they warmed their hands. Svenson was at the table in quiet conversation with Lieutenant Mappin, and the Commandos were silently checking their equipment in an engrossed thorough manner which suggested they feared someone might have tampered with it without their knowledge. Keith was pleased to see that even among friends they had not forgotten the warning to be ever vigilant, which had been drummed into them at the training school.

Mappin beckoned to Keith to join him, and he saw that the Norwegian had spread a large scale map out on the table top. You can't fight a war, he thought, without charts and maps. Oh, for the days when they were fought in a single field and lasted a matter of days, not years.

He took a seat beside Mappin, and Svenson jabbed at the map with a grimy forefinger. 'We are at the mouth of this fjord.'

Keith craned forward and saw that the nearest port was Namsos, but the black and white map gave no indication of the terrain.

He watched intently as the Norwegian traced a course on the map. 'From here we go inland for some twenty kilometres, then we head almost due north in the direction of Narvik. I do not know exactly where our final destination is because I have insisted that Christina alone knows it. The reasons are obvious. If one does not know, one cannot betray its whereabouts. Only in the event of her life being endangered is she to pass on the information. We will move off as soon as we have eaten.'

'How far is it?' asked Keith.

'If we could follow a straight line, about one hundred and fifty of your miles, but we will zig-zag sideways and upwards. Some of the lakes and rivers are frozen and can be crossed, others aren't, which means a detour. There are places where the snow is soft and almost impassable. Then we look for hard snow, or even a glacier. But our real friends are the forests, for there we cannot be spotted. Occasionally we shall stop at farms and fishing places where we know the occupants will not betray us.'

'And food?' Mappin said.

'No problem. There are people willing to provide. We can also take a quantity of dried fish. Apart from that, Norway abounds with game, deer, elk, fox, hare, and plentiful bird life. Your men will not starve, Lieutenant. We are all good hunters.'

'So are we,' Mappin bridled. 'We've been trained to live off the land.'

'Good. Perhaps you can teach us something,' he said blandly. He gestured to a pile of sheets and pillow cases on the floor. 'When we have eaten I will get Christina to show your men how to make smocks. Not as good as those we have, but better than nothing.'

Mappin asked anxiously: 'Did the hotelier mind you clearing him out of his linen? More important, did he ask any questions?'

Svenson patted his carbine. 'No questions at all. He even drove me here in his van. He said he was just like the three monkeys. I replied that he was also a very wise monkey, because they were virtues that guaranteed his continued survival.'

When they had eaten the unappetising meal, Christina gathered the soldiers around her, took a sheet, cut it in half with a pair of scissors, then snipped a circular hole in it. 'That you slip over your head,' she said, 'the rest you tuck into your belt. Crude but practical. You should now feel like kings.' She saw the look of blank astonishment on Lance-Corporal Temple's face. 'Just a joke. When King Haakon was being pursued by the Germans, who had orders to capture him dead or alive, he and his party eluded them by dressing up in bedsheets.'

The Commandos used their sharp-edged fighting knives to fashion their smocks, and half an hour later they resembled children playing at ghosts.

'Bloody difficult to get at a grenade in a hurry,' Warren mumbled.

'Clip a couple onto your belt, you bonehead,' Keith said sharply. 'They're only meant to conceal you from a distance. If someone gets close enough for you to toss a grenade, he's not going to mistake you for a ruddy snowman.'

The Norwegians then donned army issue white smocks and slung big backpacks over their shoulders. They were also white.

Bennett said: 'One problem, Sarge. The explosives an' wot-'ave-you're too 'eavy for me to lug aroun'.'

'We'll have to unpack it and distribute it among ourselves. Wrap it in anything that will cushion it from sudden shocks; socks, spare underwear. Anything you consider too fragile we'll have to leave behind.'

'Leave it to me, Sarge. I'll sort through it and chuck the dodgy stuff in the oggin.'

When Bennett had sorted through the boxes and jettisoned what he considered too sensitive to be carried, Svenson said brusquely: 'We should go now.'

The party slipped out of the fishing hut and made their way up a narrow gully that cut through a dense thicket of fir trees. Occasionally they caught a glimpse of the searchlight's beam as it continued its relentless sweep.

They trudged in silence through the trees which were so close together the sky above was completely shut out. The branches acted as an umbrella so that the snow underfoot barely covered the soles of the soldiers' boots. A stiff wind whistled through the topmost branches dislodging great lumps of snow which showered down on their hunched shoulders. It was eerily silent except for the crunching sound of the pine needles underfoot. In the pitch darkness the soldiers kept colliding with each other, and Keith called a halt. 'Use your toggle ropes. Pass one end to the man ahead, otherwise you'll be knocking each other senseless.'

Despite the inky blackness, Svenson was as sure footed as a mountain goat as he weaved a path through the trees. He reminded Keith of a blind man following a familiar route. The sergeant was suddenly aware of Christina walking beside him. 'He's like a cat in the dark,' he whispered. 'Not bad for a university tutor. What was his subject?'

He heard her laugh quietly. 'English. But he also happens to be Norway's finest elk hunter, and his other hobby is the study of bats. As you know, they're virtually blind and fly in the dark with the aid of an inbuilt sonar system. He must have acquired the habit too.'

They travelled slowly but steadily through the forest, stopping every two hours to eat or enjoy a hot drink. When dawn approached, crayoning the sky with a pinkish hue, the Commandos burned patches of moss to warm the ground and lit fires under stones to make improvised hot water bottles before they settled down to sleep, just as they had been taught to do in Scotland. The Norwegians did not bother; they slid into sleeping bags which provided ample protection from the bitter cold. In the silence of the dense woods they felt extremely safe.

When the time came to move on they kept well clear of towns and villages which still bore the ravages of German

180

bombs and artillery, but after three days were forced to leave the cover of the forests and venture out into the open where the snow was deep and treacherous. The Norwegians found the going relatively easy in their snow shoes, but the soldiers sunk into it up to their knees; despite their fitness, they were exhausted with the effort of dragging one foot after the other.

Christina could not help noticing what a tower of strength the sergeant was and how inexhaustible he seemed to be. When a man was in danger of falling well behind, he urged him on with words that bore more than a hint of mockery. She thought him brutal until she realized he was not being deliberately callous, but was aware that ridicule acted as a greater spur to a man's pride than calls of encouragement: something that had not occurred to Lieutenant Mappin, whose shouts were full of sympathy and understanding, indicating he too was suffering.

The howling wind, as mournful as a wolf's cry, was bitterly cold, and there were frequent snow squalls which reduced visibility to a few yards. Svenson was anxious that the ill-equipped soldiers would become too exhausted to continue. He called Mappin over. 'Nordhoff and I will go into the next town to obtain snowshoes for your men. It is a risk, but one we must take. He says he has friends there.'

They trudged on for several hours before Svenson called a halt. 'We will go and get the snow shoes.' As they set off, Ulricson showed the soldiers how to construct snow houses. They were invisible from a short distance, and when the soldiers huddled inside them the warmth of their bodies generated so much heat that their clothing began to steam. Svenson and Nordhoff were away for several hours, and by the time they came back the soldiers were so rested they felt like new men.

Svenson said to Mappin: 'The town was almost deserted and we had a great deal of trouble finding what we set out for. The damage is so great that many people have moved off. The streets were littered with burnt out vehicles and most of the houses are uninhabitable.' He shook his head sadly. 'There is no water and no electricity. Perhaps the Germans think it is better to leave them in such a terrible state – they do not have to keep an eye on anybody. Nordhoff went off on his own for a short time which angered me until he showed me the reason for his absence.' He grinned widely. 'Show them, Ollie.'

The weather-beaten Norwegian groped in his backpack and produced two large bottles. 'This will warm us better than any fires,' he said with genuine relish.

'Ollie, we are proud of you! One day a medal will be struck in your honour.'

The soldiers were shown how to attach the snow shoes and given the basic instructions on how to use them. At first they felt as if they had tennis racquets on their feet, but after a short time they became more adept. The snowshoes made the going much easier, because their weight was more evenly distributed and they no longer sank up to their knees.

Svenson encouraged them with the news: 'Tomorrow night we will reach a farmhouse where we will be among friends. Nordhoff knows them well. There we can rest and eat good food.'

The small group set off with renewed vigour and made excellent progress. Everyone was confident that they would succeed in their mission, for they had not set eyes on a solitary German soldier; nor, for that matter, any Norwegians. But when they rested, Keith insisted that all weapons had to be checked and cleaned and a foot examination held. Even with the snow shoes there was still a grave risk of frost bite.

The brief period of daylight was rapidly approaching, and Mappin fearful that they might be spotted, said anxiously to Svenson: 'Don't you think it's time we halted and took cover?'

The Norwegian gestured vaguely with his mittened hand in the direction of a steep line of rugged peaks about four or five miles away. 'On the other side is the farm where we will shelter. It is better to press on.'

The news seemed to give the Commandos new-found energy and they strode forward with dogged determination. When they reached the crest of the hills they found themselves gazing down into a wide snow-covered valley. Nestling in the centre of the valley, safe from avalanches, stood the farmhouse, a solid building constructed from the whole trunks of pine cut in half length-ways. It was built on a pile of big stones so that the occupants were never snow bound. The roof was made of turfs which in summer sprouted flowers. A ramp ran from the house to the *fjos* where the cattle were housed, and the *laver* where fodder and equipment was stored. A wisp of grey smoke rose like a signal from the chimney.

A man appeared at the doorway, he waved, and everyone automatically quickened their pace.

Svenson and the farmer shook hands, then embraced each other like old friends. The farmer was a powerful, raw-boned man whose bare forearms indicated a total disdain for the sub-zero temperature. With a sweeping gesture he invited everyone inside.

The main living room was sparsely furnished with solid looking pine furniture and the ceiling beams were smoke-blackened. A fire smouldered in the large hearth, above which hung some blackened hams and strips of eel that were being cured.

Svenson said: 'Meet Edvard Bjørnson, a true patriot. We are safe here.'

The soldiers saluted in a gesture of greeting while the Norwegians exchanged handshakes and embraces.

The farmer called out something in Norwegian, and a plump woman in a shapeless dress emerged from the kitchen drying her hands on her apron and smiling with genuine warmth. She spoke to Svenson, who turned to Mappin. 'She will prepare some food. Meanwhile, we will drink.'

The farmer left the room and returned with two large bottles; he poured liberal measures into chunky glasses which he took from a large dresser.

Svenson licked his lips. '*Hjemmebrennt* – a drink for real men. Edvard distils it himself. Strictly illegal – but wonderful, like all forbidden things.'

Like the Aquavit it was ice-cold and had to be downed in one swallow, but there the similarity ended, for in comparison the Aquavit was a mild, pleasant-tasting aperitif. The home-brewed spirit burned a passage down their throats; when it reached their stomachs it felt as if they had swallowed a red-hot rivet.

When the glasses were replenished, they raised them in a 'To Norway' toast.

Suddenly Svenson stiffened and cocked his head, like a dog sensing the approach of something unfamiliar. An almost palpable tension filled the room as he made a signal calling for silence. Then they all heard the unmistakable growl of an aircraft and Svenson moved swiftly to a window and cautiously drew back a shutter.

Circling above like a gull was a German spotter plane, the black cross insignia clearly visible on the underside of its single wing. The wing was mounted above the cockpit to give the pilot an uninterrupted view of the ground below, and Svenson could see quite clearly the goggled and helmeted head of the pilot gazing down.

'I can't believe it,' he muttered. 'He has not been following us. It is most disturbing that he should arrive just when we did; almost as if he were expecting us.'

'I am sure it is just a routine patrol,' Nordhoff said.

'We will soon know,' said Svenson grimly. 'We cannot move for at least six hours. Time for a German ski patrol to get here. We will have to be ready for them.'

'It is pure luck,' persisted Nordhoff. 'He could not have seen us. We have been too careful.'

The sound of the aircraft gradually receded and Svenson said: 'I hope you are right, Ollie.' He motioned to Ulricson and Nordhoff. 'You will each keep watch for two hours, then I will take over.'

The woman called them to the big well-scrubbed table, where she served out massive portions of *fiske-molje*, which the soldiers had difficulty in getting down; it seemed to be dominated by the taste and smell of cod liver oil and it was only a continuous flow of the fiery ice-cold spirit that enabled them to get through the meal.

As the time passed, with no sign of the spotter plane returning, and no harsh warning cries from the sentries announcing the arrival of German troops, they visibly relaxed. The soldiers loosened their webbing and stretched out on the hard floor, but kept their weapons close at hand.

Keith sat with his back against a wall, a position from which he could raise himself slightly, and peeped out of the shuttered window. Christina came and sat beside him. 'I don't think we need fear the arrival of any Germans,' she whispered.

184

'That's comforting,' said Keith wryly. 'Unfortunately, I don't share your optimism.'

'I'm not being optimistic,' she said in a low voice. 'I'm being quite practical. Someone – don't ask me who or how – warned them of our movements. They don't want to capture us; just follow us because they want us to lead them to the gold.'

'Who could have warned the Germans?'

'Quite a lot of people had to be taken into our confidence when Olav planned the route with me. There had to be safe houses where we could rest, and people with transmitters we could use in an emergency because our own was too heavy to carry. There's another group of patriots who'll provide us with sledges once we've retrieved the gold. We had to trust them. It only needs one traitor, though.'

'That still doesn't explain the aircraft.'

She shrugged. 'It could have been someone from the town where they got the snowshoes.'

'Has it occurred to you that it could be someone in your party?'

'Out of the question. Olav only chose those who've been tried and can be trusted.'

'Maybe Ollie was right and the plane's appearance was sheer luck, but it can't do any harm if you let Svenson know of your misgivings.'

'Not just yet. I'll see if it turns up again.'

The hours dragged and the aircraft did not reappear. There was no sign of any suspicious activity around the farmhouse.

'Soon it'll be dark again and we can move off,' Christina said. Keith did not reply.

'Are you angry with me, Harry?' she said.

'For expressing your fears? Of course not.'

'No, not that – for saying unkind things about you.'

'Water off a duck's back as far as I'm concerned.'

'I wasn't being critical,' she said earnestly. 'Just saying how different you are to the others. Lieutenant Mappin gives the orders, but I notice he looks anxiously towards you to make sure he's said the right thing. The soldiers also look to you – they don't have your assurance and confidence.'

'They're all damned good soldiers,' he replied, 'otherwise they wouldn't be here.'

185

She gently patted his hand. 'Of course they are. I'm not expressing myself very well. They're *depending* on you, you give them strength. You should be flattered.'

'I'm just a soldier, and so are they.'

'Oh dear. The more I try to explain the worse I make it sound.'

'Why not stop trying and just accept we're a group of men all doing the same job?'

'But you *are* different, Harry,' she said, 'and I'm sure they're grateful for that. Take the dark-haired boy with beautiful hands. He's someone who obviously dislikes what he's doing but knows he *must*. He's always looking towards you, seeking approval. You, on the other hand, have utter confidence in your own judgement.'

'That's not very flattering.'

'I'm not being offensive,' she said. 'I'm not saying you're an arrogant man: just one who has faith in his own ability.'

'That's what being a regular is all about.'

'Do you have a wife and children? A home to return to when the war's over? Is it the thought of them that makes you so determined?'

'No family at all, I'm afraid. Not through choice, though – I've never been in one place long enough to put down roots. One day I will.'

'I don't think so, Harry. You're making excuses. One does not need time to fall in love. It can be as sudden as switching on a light, no longer than it takes to glance across a room.'

'Can't we just drop the subject? It bores me.'

'I was right; are *are* a hard man.'

'I'm a soldier! I know soldiers don't make wars, but they do fight them, and if they're worth their salt they want to win. Victory won't put anything in their kit bags, but they'll have the satisfaction of knowing they're the best.'

'That's a very narrow view,' she said desperately. 'Don't freedom, democracy, the victory of right over might, mean anything to you?'

'They don't to the Jerry, and he's top dog right now.'

'You must believe in *something*.'

'Revenge will do for the time being.' He heard the bitterness in his voice and felt the need to explain. 'When you've

186

trained for something all your life it's humiliating to end up the loser, and that's what happened to me in France. We were out-classed and out-fought, our generals made to look like muddling amateurs. The army I'd devoted my life to was reduced to nothing more than a rabble.'

'You're a bitter man.'

'The only sensible thing you've said so far.'

She squeezed his arm. 'I should feel the same, but I don't. I share your sense of shame because I witnessed the same things.'

She paused and continued in a low voice. 'When the Germans invaded we capitulated without a struggle. We even queued up in orderly lines to hand in our own wireless sets. We stood idly by as our universities were closed and the students sent off to labour camps. We didn't know what hunger was, and we watched in surprise as the Germans spread butter on bars of chocolate they had been given, they were so ravenous. Yet they were the conquerors!'

'Norway wasn't in much of a position to put up any real resistance.'

'Harry,' she said miserably, 'you don't understand how wretched I felt. When war in Europe was imminent I was all for Norway being neutral. I even objected when Britain wanted to mine the Leads to prevent the Germans shipping iron ore to their ports, for fear it would be interpreted as a belligerent act. Then, when the Germans did invade, I looked to the Allies to come to our aid. They did, and were defeated. The Tommies were prepared to die for us, but we were not prepared to die for Norway. It was only with that realization that I found the will to fight.' She closed her eyes and said, with sudden unexpected venom: 'Now I'm prepared to die for Norway – just as you're ready to die for your country.'

Sergeant Keith remained silent. How could he explain to his beautiful, ardent young woman that patriotism had never entered his mind? He had joined the army to escape the dole queue. It was only later that the Regiment became the hub around which his life revolved. It was to him what heaven was to a devout church-goer; a comfortable womb from which the outside world was excluded. It was a world where the air was fresh, where a man was prepared to lay down his life for a comrade, or the pride of the Regiment, but certainly not for something as abstract as King and Country. To the average soldier, the ideals expressed by romantics like Rupert Brooke were hogwash.

Perhaps, he thought, I ought to make the effort to explain. But when he glanced down at Christina she had fallen asleep. Why the hell, he thought, do I need to explain myself to anyone? We'll win this ruddy war, and when we do no one is going to ask Sergeant Harry Keith why he had fought with such determination.

He sat there musing until darkness descended on the valley like a velvet cloak and Svenson announced it was time to move on.

Keith shook Christina. 'You going to have a word with Olav?'

She shook her head. 'There's no need. I was letting my imagination play tricks. There's nothing to fear.'

Keith was not so sure. It was strange how the plane had arrived dead on time. If it turned up again, he would have a word with Lieutenant Mappin.

Chapter Thirteen

As they assembled in the inky darkness outside the farm-house, Svenson announced a slight change of plan. 'We will move inland further than originally intended. There is a large lake which at this time is frozen over and we can cross it at much greater speed. I did not like the appearance of that spotter aircraft. If it comes again I think we will need extra vigilance.'

Keith, standing alongside Lieutenant Mappin, heard the words with growing unease. They meant that Svenson too now suspected the plane's appearance might not have been sheer coincidence.

They trudged through deep snow for what seemed an eternity before they reached the lake, fringed by ranges of black snow-capped mountains. The going was surprisingly easy; the ice was as smooth as a sheet of slate, and once they had adjusted themselves to the slippery surface they found they could best cope by moving their legs in a skating motion. However, the wind was bitterly cold. Their breath froze in the air and their feet lost all sense of feeling. Apart from an occasional glimpse at the luminous dial of his pocket compass, Svenson seemed as sure of his direction as a homing pigeon.

Then, just as everything was going smoothly as a Swiss watch, Nordhoff let out an agonizing cry of pain as he slipped and hit the solid ice with such a cracking impact everyone feared he would fall through into the icy water below.

Svenson knelt beside him, asking anxiously: 'Are you all right, Ollie?'

Nordhoff replied through gritted teeth, the pain evident in his voice: 'My ankle. God, I hope I haven't broken it!'

He tried to struggle to his feet but slid back onto the ice with a suppressed groan of agony. 'You'd better continue without me, Olav. I will catch up when I have rested.'

'There is no question of us abandoning you, Ollie. We will carry you, if necessary.'

'Please Olav, I will only hold you back.' His teeth gleamed white in the darkness as he attempted to make light of his injury. 'I am dispensable.'

'None of us is that,' said Svenson grimly. 'We cannot desert you. You had better let me have a look.' As he bent low over the prostrate figure, Nordhoff brushed aside the hands that were trying to loosen his boot laces.

'I am not worth risking the gold for, Olav. *Please*, let me follow you.' The group clustered anxiously around him as he gingerly felt his ankle. 'I am certain it is only a sprain. There are no broken bones. I promise, I will catch up. We have not come so far to fail because I have been stupid enough to fall over. How many times have we had a tumble skiing and quickly recovered? You must press on,' he said urgently.

'Are you sure, Ollie?' asked Svenson. 'Soon it will be daylight, and it would be folly for us to be trapped like sitting ducks on the open lake.'

'The ice will soon numb the pain. I promise you, I will join you.' His voice became angry. 'Christ, Olav, I demand it! Think of the gold. Only that.'

Svenson shrugged in the darkness. 'As you wish. We will wait for you at the rendezvous. If you do not arrive, we will come back.'

They set off with heavy hearts, fortified only by the sound of Nordhoff's voice calling out after them: 'All for Norway.'

Bennett turned to Sergeant Keith. ''E's a right spunky bastard, Sarge, an' no one can deny that. I wouldn' fancy bein' left on my Jack Jones in the middle of fuckin' nowhere with a busted leg.'

'Svenson is right though,' Keith said brusquely. 'He'll only hold us up.'

'Tell you wot, Sarge; if I was doin' a big job and my mucker couldn' get away because 'ed 'urt 'isself, I'd say fuck the loot an' make sure I got 'im to safety.'

Keith slapped him on the back, and said with a grim smile: 'But you're a criminal, Bennett, and they always look after their own. What do you call it – the code of the underworld?'

'Common decency, more like.'

'I hope you're not going soft in your old age, Bennett.'

The girl appeared at Keith's side. 'I'm worried for Ollie. This is a very wild part of the country – there are packs of wolves. He could be attacked.'

'He's got a gun,' said Keith laconically. 'And he had the chance of being helped but declined, so he must feel pretty confident he'll make it.'

'You're very harsh, Harry. If it had been one of your men, would you be so ruthless?'

'Better ask Private Luck,' he said.

"I'm asking *you*,' she snapped angrily, 'and you're being evasive. Are you afraid of facing up to the truth?'

'Let's get moving,' was his reply.

The party moved on in total silence, their thoughts on the man they had abandoned in the solitary waste of the frozen lake. They all knew Nordhoff would soon be as stiff as a board if he was unable to summon up the strength to get up and keep moving.

They lost all sense of time as they struggled across the glass-smooth surface, with limbs that grew stiffer and stiffer as the cold crept deep into their bones, and the effort of sliding one foot before the other was sheer torture. When they eventually reached the shore of the lake they simply slumped down, hoping sleep would engulf them.

'We cannot stay here,' Svenson said. 'We must find shelter.'

Lieutenant Mappin called out: 'Get them on their feet, Sergeant, otherwise they'll freeze solid.' Keith did so with solid kicks from his heavy boot. The stick, he figured, was far more effective than any dangled carrot.

Svenson found a deep ravine that was almost a cave. No light penetrated the overhanging rocks, and it was sheltered from the biting cold. He considered it safe enough to light a fire and cook a meal; Ulricson was told to keep the first look-out.

When they had finished eating, Svenson said: 'I am going out to flash my signal torch so that Ollie, if he is still with us,

191

will know in which direction to head.' He rummaged in his backpack, then solemnly announced that his torch was missing.

'In the morning we must all agree to being searched,' Christina said.

'No,' said Svenson firmly. 'I am not going to allow mistrust to creep into our venture.'

'You might have to,' said Keith grimly, 'whether you like the idea or not. We've all had misgivings about the sudden appearance of the spotter plane, and the torch may be the explanation.'

'Let us sleep on it,' Svenson said. 'Ulric, you will keep watch. One of the soldiers will relieve you in two hours' time.'

The night passed uneventfully, and when the first rays of morning sunshine tinted the snow-capped peaks, Svenson reluctantly conceded that everyone must be searched. 'That is just to prove I have no suspicions – none at all.'

The Norwegians and the soldiers readily agreed to emptying their packs. Keith thought it a pure waste of time; if anyone had stolen the torch he, or she, had had ample time to hide it in order to recover it later. This theory was confirmed when the missing torch remained missing.

Then, suddenly, any suspicions they may have harboured dissipated like snow on a fire. The sentry called out that he had sighted something in the distance. It was no more than a minute dot that seemed to be moving in an erratic manner, like a winged insect that has been immersed in water trying to fly.

Svenson took his binoculars out of their case and focused them on the distant object. There was an agonizing period of suspense before he said, with evident pleasure: 'It is Ollie!'

Two of the soldiers struggled to their feet. Despite the cries for caution from Svenson they hurried across the ice to support the staggering Nordhoff. His face was ashen, ice-caked; somehow he had managed to get some sticks which he had made into an improvised splint to put on his injured leg. Svenson half carried him to the meagre warmth of the fire and poured him a massive tot from the bottle the farmer had given him on departure. 'You will feel better after that, Ollie.'

The injured man gulped it down and wiped his crusted lips 'I feared at times I might not make it, Olav, he muttered. 'I

192

have never known such cold. Now I must sleep for half an hour.' He went to the back of the ravine and lay down beside the heap of backpacks.

When he awoke, Svenson said: 'I must insist on looking through your backpack, Ollie. Everyone else has agreed to being searched and I cannot make any exceptions.'

'What are you hoping to find?' asked a bewildered Nordhoff.

'I will tell you only if I find it.'

But there was no torch in the injured man's pack.

Half an hour later the ominous sound of an aircraft engine filled the silence. The white spotter plane appeared once more, swooping over the ravine where they lay concealed. It flew low in repeated circles before gaining height and disappearing into the distance.

'What on earth is he up to, Sergeant?' Mappin said to Keith.

'Just keeping tabs, if you ask me, sir.'

'We could have a crack at shooting him down,' said Mappin hopefully.

'Waste of time, sir. He'll be in radio contact with his headquarters, so even if we did knock him off his perch they'd send another to replace him. Apart from that, he may not have actually spotted us – he just knows we're somewhere in this area.'

'What do you suggest?'

'Play him at his own game, sir. He wants us to lead him to the gold and when that happens, Jerry will pounce. All we have to do is make sure we're ready and waiting. In this kind of terrain we can hold off a ruddy battalion of troops.'

They kept to the lower slopes of the mountains, where there were numerous deep crevices to provide complete protection from the howling wind, also furnishing hiding places from any German patrols. As long as they continued to travel by night they had no need to worry about aircraft. Not that that continued to worry them, for the plane failed to appear on two successive periods of light since they had left the lake. Nordhoff seemed to have recovered completely from his bad ankle, no longer requiring the splint to give it added support.

193

On the third night after leaving the lake, they found shelter in a deep cave where they were able to light a fire without fear of being spotted. Great icicles descended from the roof; the steady drip-drip-drip as they began to thaw from the heat of the fire sounded like the beat of a metronome.

Svenson spread his map out on the hard floor and summoned Mappin and the girl to his side. As he studied the map by the flickering flames, he exclaimed angrily: 'God, what wouldn't I give for my torch! I can hardly read it.'

Ulricson suddenly appeared at his side saying apologetically: 'Is this it, Olav?' He extended a hand holding the missing torch. 'I was just checking my pack when I found it among the explosives.'

'I did not unpack the explosives when I made my search,' Svenson said coldly. 'That was very foolish of me. It just did not occur to me.'

'On the sacred life of my mother, Olav, I did not put it there,' Ulricson protested.

'Have you ever let your pack out of your sight, Lars?'

Ulricson began to bluster. 'I have taken it off to sleep and left it when I kept watch. I had no reason to mistrust anyone. You must believe me, Olav!'

'No one distrusts you, Lars,' Nordhoff said in a placatory tone. 'Perhaps Olav put it there by mistake. It is easily done in the dark, when all the backpacks are in one heap. For God's sake, do not let us mistrust each other when so much is at stake. What difference does a missing torch make, I ask you?'

'It can be used to flash a signal to send an aircraft.'

Nordhoff laughed loudly. 'And who could do that, when each of us knows every movement the others make?'

'We keep watch on our own, Ollie. We obey the call of nature without wishing to be observed. Christina's need for special privacy is observed.'

'You think there is a Quisling among us?' asked Nordhoff hotly. 'You know us too well to believe that. We have pledged our lives to Norway.'

Svenson shrugged as if it were a matter of no great importance. 'The bear is very cunning, Ollie, but he will always put his paw in the trap if the bait is tempting enough. Now, let's get down to business.'

Nordhoff shook his head in dismay. 'You are still not convinced, Olav. That is bad for morale.'

Svenson did not reply, bowing his head over the map and tracing his finger along a line parallel to the main railway line heading north. 'We will go this way for about nine hours, and will then rest in the place where the sledges will be provided. Then we will be close to our destination. After that, Christina will take us to the gold.'

'Then?' said Mappin.

'We head for the coast where we pick up two fishing smacks. We will hug the coastline and sail north until we reach the spot where we are to rendezvous with the British MTB.' He slapped his hands together, and the sharp crack echoed around the small cave. 'The rest is up to God, the Commandos and the British navy.'

Chapter Fourteen

They set off again as the sky was beginning to darken. They marched in silence for two hour stretches until Svenson announced: 'We are approaching the town. You wait here while I go and announce our arrival.'

'I will come with you, Olav,' Nordhoff said quietly.

'There is no need, I will be perfectly safe.'

'I am still worried about the story of the torch, Olav.'

'You suspect me?'

'If you have nothing to worry about you will not mind my coming,' said the young Norwegian. He smiled teasingly. 'You insisted on us all being searched, so it's only fair.'

'I have nothing to hide. So come.'

Keith watched them go. Only when their shapes had blended into the darkness was he aware of Christina standing beside him. 'It's a great pity that mistrust has entered into this,' he said solemnly. 'We have enough on our hands without having to look over our shoulders every five minutes.'

'Too much is at stake for anyone to relax their vigilance, Harry.'

'You don't honestly believe we've got a traitor among us, do you?'

'I don't know. He may not even consider himself to be one. There're many Quislings who have sided with the Germans for patriotic reasons – they sincerely believe it's for the good of Norway to collaborate. In their eyes it's the only way to establish stability. They see little hope of Norway being liberated. England is in no position to do it, and America seems determined to keep out of the war. Norway is the home of the suicidal lemming, and there're many people who see members of the Resistance as lemmings.'

'Are you voicing your own opinion?'

'Of course not. When we recover the gold I shall travel back to England with it.'

'Some people would say that's deserting a sinking ship.'

'I'm prepared to return if I'm asked to,' she said simply.

The cluster of wooden huts was more a village than a town, and as Svenson and Nordhoff approached it there was no sign of life; the windows were blacked out and the narrow streets shrouded in darkness. There was not a single footprint to mar the purity of the snow which carpeted them. Only the wisps of smoke spiralling upwards from the chimneys was evidence that it was inhabited.

Svenson said: 'We must make our way to the house of the mayor who will tell us where the sledges are concealed. On the surface he is helpful with the Germans and they trust him. He has even been allowed to retain his telephone for official business, so I will be able to inform the fishermen that we shall be arriving soon. All we have to do is dodge the sentries. But there is not a big garrison here – there is no need for one.'

No sooner had he spoken than he felt Nordhoff firmly grasp his arm, and heard him hiss: 'Careful, Olav. Two German soldiers.'

Svenson could just make out the dim shapes of two figures, unmistakably soldiers. Their helmets gave their heads a dome-like appearance and the barrels of their slung rifles were clearly discernable above their shoulders.

'Quick, down there,' said Nordhoff, jerking his head towards a side street. 'I will distract them.'

He suddenly began to stagger like a drunkard, singing loudly at the top of his voice a particularly ribald song that was a favourite among the fishermen. Svenson glided away down a side street as silently as a shadow, and as he did so he heard a loud command in German calling on Nordhoff to halt and identify himself or be shot.

Twenty minutes later Svenson was safely inside the mayor's house, where he was given a drink, told where to collect the sledges, and shown the telephone should he wish to use it.

An hour later Nordhoff arrived grinning broadly and looking none the worse for his brush with the sentries. 'I showed them my papers describing me as a fisherman, which is true, and said I was on my way to join a whaler when I fell among thieves and got drunk. I showed them my ankle to prove I had fallen over, they propped me up and I promptly fell down. They laughed their silly heads off. I was so convincing, Olav, even though I say so myself! When they found they could get no sense out of me they made me dance, and I did so, shuffling around like a bear at a carnival. Eventually they tired of their silly game, and the sergeant said it wasn't surprising they had been able to walk into Norway as easily as into a house where the front door has been left open, as Norwegians think only of getting drunk. Then they threw me out into the street. However, I did learn that they only patrol the streets every three hours because it's so cold, and as there's a curfew it's a waste of time in any case, so we have plenty of time to make our way back to the others.'

'I am proud of you,' Svenson said.

Nordhoff smiled boyishly. 'You are joking, Olav. I only did my duty. If you had been captured all would have been lost. Now I really do need a drink.'

'You have earned it. Now I must telephone and arrange the boats.' Nordhoff crossed the room to listen, but Svenson angrily gestured to him to move away and closed the door.

The two Norwegians returned to the waiting party and Svenson announced that it was time to set off and collect the sledges. They skirted the town where Nordhoff had been detained, and hugged a ridge of craggy little black hills, resembling the teeth of a saw, which ran a few hundred feet above the railway line some five miles to their left. The only sound apart from their heavy breathing was that of rushing water.

'That is the river they use to float the logs down from the timber mills,' Svenson said.

'We're not far from the gold now,' Christina whispered to Keith.

In the gloom they could barely make out the dark hulk of a large shed-like structure. As they got closer they were able to see it was a timber store with a massive roof that was supported by the enormous trunks of felled trees. It had no walls and was filled from floor to ceiling with logs waiting to be shipped down river. Two men emerged from the shadows, both wearing thick lumberjack coats, blue denim trousers and heavy logging boots.

One said: 'Come. We will show you the sledges.'

They moved to the rear of the timber store and the two men began shifting logs from a snow-covered pile. Underneath lay three sledges, solidly built, with whalebone runners and hauling ropes made from reindeer hide.

The second man, who had not yet spoken said: 'They have been well waxed and greased and will move as smoothly as eels in a bowl of herring oil.' He laughed at his own feeble joke.

Svenson thanked them, and turned to Mappin. We'll have to man-handle them down to where there is snow, then I will need some of your men to help pull them.'

'I knew there'd be a fucking catch somewhere,' Bunny Warren said. 'They don't want fighting soldiers, they want effing pack mules.'

Keith slapped him on the back. 'Never mind, Bunny You'll get a nice bundle of hay at the end of this.'

The roar of the water deadened the sound the sledges made as they were hoisted over boulders to more level ground where the snow was hard and crisp. Mappin detailed three men to assist Svenson, Ulricson and Nordhoff, who were in charge of one of the primitive modes of transport. To the soldiers' surprise and delight they moved as easily as curling stones, and little physical effort was needed to maintain steady speed. There was a tangible easing of the tension that had gripped them since they first set off, brought about by the conviction that they had now accomplished the most difficult part of their task.

Svenson called a brief halt and summoned Christina to his side at the leading sledge. 'You must guide me from here Christina. Only you know the way.'

'We carry on until we see a big water tower that was once used to fill the tanks of the railway engines,' she said. 'That' where the disused sidings are. The tunnel is at the far end

Twenty minutes later the top of the water tower loomed into view like the head of an enormous toadstool. The snow lay thick on the ground, and abandoned snow-covered wagons and coaches lay like stranded whales on the tracks. Many had jagged holes in their sides and roofs, reminders of the terrible strafing to which the Luftwaffe had subjected the rolling stock.

The disused and unfinished tunnel, cut deep into solid rock, stood at the furthest end of the siding. It resembled an enormous cavern in which prehistoric monsters had once dwelt. They went in cautiously, their weapons at the ready. It was clammy and foul-smelling, and condensation dripped in a steady stream from the curved roof, but it was surprisingly warm after the bitter cold outside.

'It's about half a mile long,' Christina whispered to Svenson. 'The war prevented its completion. The wagons with the gold are at the far end.'

Svenson's teeth gleamed in the darkness. 'I don't think there is any need to keep your voice down, Christina.' He barked his shin against a rock and cursed. he switched on his torch, but the beam scarcely penetrated the blackness. 'We're going to have the devil's own job to see anything in here.'

'There're ventilation shafts which give some light during the day,' she assured him.

'In that case we will wait until morning. The rest will do us good. I will keep first watch for two hours, then Ollie will take over, then Lars.'

Ulricson was keeping watch at the entrance to the tunnel when the sky began to brighten and narrow beams of dust-choked light filtered down through the ventilation shafts giving the occupants their first glimpse of the interior. Two railway wagons with thick steel sides stood on the track looking as impregnable as tanks and the sliding doors were secured by padlocks the size of a heavyweight's fist.

Sergeant Keith called Bennett to his side. 'Think you can shift them without making too much of a din or destroying the contents?'

'Jesus, Sarge, wot you take me for? I could do it wiv a tin opener, only I ain't got one. But leave it to me. Just tell everyone to stan' back in case somefink goes wrong – which it won't.'

He rummaged in his pack and sorted out the explosives, fuses and detonators which had been carefully wrapped in his spare socks and underwear. He spoke softly to himself. 'Bit o' plastic stuff, not much. Don't want no toxic fumes.'

There was a muffled bang not much louder than a large firework, and the tunnel was filled with choking dust which fell in flakes from the walls and roof. Bennett moved forward, slid back the doors and whistled in astonishment. 'They certainly made certain no one was goin' to leg it wiv the loot. Take a dekko at that.'

In the centre of each wagon stood a large steel safe about six feet tall and five feet in width. In the centre of each door was the dial of a combination lock.

'Unless someone knows wot the combination is, we ain' goin' to open them inside a munf of Sundays.'

Keith turned to the girl. 'Is there a combination?'

She shook her head. 'I don't know it.'

He turned to Bennett. 'Well?'

'I'd be collectin' me old age pension before I worked it out, Sarge. Wear me bleedin' fingers to the bone. If you ask me, it's gotta be a blowin' job.'

'Will that be difficult, Bennett?' Mappin asked anxiously.

'Not difficult, sir, just bleedin' dodgy. I don' wanna bring the 'ole bloody tunnel down on our 'eads, so it's gotta be given a bit of fought. Likewise, we don' wanna send the gold up in the sky like ruddy rockets, do we? Everyone'll 'ave to move up to the entrance. If you can find anyfing what we can fill with packed-down snow it'll be a 'elp: cushion the explosion. Make it go inwards 'stead of out.'

They all began a frenzied search which was rewarded by the discovery of a pile of heavy tarred sacks which had once been used for coal. They filled them with snow.

Bennett spent an hour preparing the explosives, whistling tunelessly as he carefully placed it around the combination locks, attached the cordtex to the charge, taped on the detonator and attached a long length of safety fuse.

'All done.' he called out cheerfully. 'All you gotta do now is bring up the sacks o' snow, then it's just' like Guy Fawkes Night. Light the blue paper an' vanish up your own arse. Then cross your bleedin' fingers and wait for the bang.'

202

When the sacks of packed-down snow had been placed in position around the two safes, everyone but Bennett retired to the entrance of the tunnel. He activated the fuse, then flung himself to the ground as it sputtered, covering the back of his head with his hands. An enormous explosion reverberated through the tunnel and a dense cloud of black smoke poured out of the entrance.

Bennett stood upright, his face blackened and his ears ringing. He surveyed the two safes with pride. The doors were hanging on their hinges, and the interior of the shattered wagons was filled with the tattered remnants of the sacks. 'Not bad,' he said to himself. 'Not 'alf bleedin' bad, Bennett, considerin' as how you ain' done a proper job for so long now.'

As the dust settled the group at the entrance began to run back, their boots clanging against the lines. Svenson hauled himself into the first carriage, knelt beside the safe and peered inside. In front of him, in neat layers, were gold ingots, looking for all the world like bars of yellow scrubbing soap.

'Let's get them onto the sledges without a moment's delay,' Mappin bellowed.

The sledges were hauled into the tunnel and the ingots lowered from the wagons. They were so heavy it required two men to handle a single bar, and it took two hours before the last ingot was placed into position and a tarpaulin secured over them.

Then their ears caught the sound they had all been dreading; the deadly drone of the spotter plane. It circled slowly above the sidings like a vulture patiently waiting to descend on its prey below.

'This is too much of a coincidence,' Svenson said. 'Only three people could have betrayed our whereabouts: myself, Lars, or Ollie. I know it was not me, and I know it could not have been Ollie for the simple reason that he did not betray me when the German patrol seized him.' He swung his head and fastened his eyes on Ulricson. 'That leaves only you, Lars. Why did you do it?'

'On my life, Olav, it was not me! I would die rather than be a traitor.'

'You will die, Lars. That is certain,' Svenson said coldly. He turned to face Mappin and held out his right hand. 'Your pistol, please, Lieutenant.'

Mappin removed the heavy black Webley from its webbing holster, saying hesitantly: 'Don't rush to conclusions, Olav. Give him a chance to explain.'

'There is no time, Lieutenant. Soon the Germans will arrive in force.' He motioned to Ulricson with the barrel of the pistol. 'Kneel, Lars, let's get this over and done with.'

Ulricson remained amazingly calm, his voice steady and his eyes holding not the slightest hint of fear as he knelt. 'You are making a terrible mistake, Olav.'

Svenson placed the muzzle of the heavy calibre pistol against the back of the man's head and slowly cocked the trigger. 'I am sorry it had to end like this, Lars. We were such good comrades, but you were foolish about the torch. You should have thrown it away.'

His finger tightened on the trigger and the chamber began to revolve with agonizing slowness. The tension was unbearable. Then it was shattered by an anguished cry from Nordhoff. 'No, Olav, no! It was me.'

Svenson lowered the revolver. 'I thought as much, Ollie. But I could not prove it. No man could have walked as you did with a bad leg – it is physically impossible. Courage and determination are not enough. You stole the torch and replaced it. And when the Germans find a man out in the streets after curfew, drunk or sober, they do not make him dance then set him free – they either shoot him or send him to the concentration camp. I think you told them we were close to the gold.'

Nordhoff nodded dumbly, then said, in a voice little more than a hoarse croak: 'I am not a traitor. I admire what you are doing, but it is a waste of time. The Germans are here to stay little pinpricks such as you are inflicting will not alter that The gold may reach England, but at what price? Two, three four hundred hostages? And even more sent to the concentra tion camps?'

'*That* from a man who was tortured by the Gestapo in Oslo for working for the Resistance?' Svenson said contemptuously. He gestured with the pistol. 'Remove you jacket and shirt, Ollie, I want to see the scars.'

204

'I was not tortured, Olav. The Germans persuaded me it was better for Norway if I collaborated with them. They even encouraged the stories that I had been tortured and had refused to betray my colleagues. They knew only vaguely about the gold and a plan to retrieve it, and they told me to infiltrate myself into the group that was planning it. It took some time to find you, but I did, and you readily accepted my offer of service.' He smiled wanly. 'With my record you could hardly refuse.'

'That is what I think they call in a court of law a plea of mitigation. It falls on deaf ears.'

'It was all for Norway.'

Svenson fired swiftly and without warning. The heavy calibre slug hit Nordhoff in the chest, blowing open a hole as big as a cricket ball. As he slumped to the ground, Svenson leaned over him and fired another shot into his skull, which burst like an over ripe melon.

'We must move,' said Svenson, without a second glance at the huddled corpse which had been flung backwards against the wall of the tunnel by the impact of the slugs. They manned the sledges and hauled them towards the circle of light. As they emerged from the tunnel into the daylight, there was neither sight nor sound of the spotter plane. Then, as they began hauling the sledges, a louder, more ominous sound filled the air. Just above the rim of the distant mountains the dark bulk of two cumbersome and ungainly looking Ju 52s, the work horses of the Luftwaffe, appeared. Each was capable of carrying fifteen fully armed men in its angular fuselage, but they were extremely vulnerable to accurate fire for their cruising speed was a mere one hundred and thirty miles an hour.

'Everybody down!' Keith bellowed. 'And hold your fire. Find what cover you can.' The Commandos slid below abandoned trucks and cranes, cocking their weapons in readiness.

The aircraft, with one engine on each wing and a third in the centre, dropped down until they were only four hundred feet above the ground. Then white-clad figures began to tumble out of the fuselage. Seconds later, parachutes ballooned above them and reduced their plummeting descent with a sharp jerk.

Below, the waiting soldiers and Norwegians watched in fascination as the paras feverishly worked on their guide lines to control their parachutes. As they steadied, their round crash helmets were clearly visible, as were the rubber-soled boots that laced halfway up their calves. They were heavily padded at the knees, chest and shoulders to cushion the impact of landing.

When they were two hundred feet from the ground, Keith shouted: 'Fire!' His order was immediately followed by a deafening fusillade from the Tommy-guns, rifles and carbines. It was almost impossible to miss at such close range, and the bodies of the paras twitched and jerked as bullets thudded into them. Canisters containing weapons thudded into the earth, and the men who had managed to land uninjured and free themselves from their parachutes ran for them and retrieved Schmeisser sub-machine guns and heavier weapons. Some of the Germans wore special glasses to protect their eyes during the fall, and they carried long-barrelled Mauser sniping rifles with telescopic lenses. As they collected their weapons, they fell flat, wriggled into the snow and opened fire.

'Take your time,' Keith called out. 'Select your targets.' Lying under a gantry and firing his Tommy-gun in short accurate bursts, he saw Private Warren in a kneeling position firing his rifle with the calmness of a man shooting tin ducks at a fairground gallery, seeming invulnerable to the hail of bullets that whistled past him and ploughed up the snow. 'Good shooting, Bunny,' he called encouragingly, 'but for God's sake keep down.'

Warren paused only long enough to grin and give a thumbs-up sign. He felt no fear – only elation and pride in his marksmanship. Not many men, in the heat of battle, could hit someone clean between the eyes.

Ulricson, standing upright at the entrance to the tunnel firing his carbine from the shoulder, suddenly screamed aloud as a burst of Schmeisser fire stitched a crimson pattern across his chest, turning his white smock into a vivid scarlet.

Private Luck had taken cover behind a hydraulic capstan used for shunting wagons and was firing his sub-machine gun in long sweeping bursts. His lips were drawn back, exposing his teeth in a white snarl. When one drum of ammunition was empty he quickly replaced it with a fresh one. He fired so many rounds he had to pause to cool the red-hot barrel in the snow. No other thought filled his mind but the need to kill as many of the enemy as possible; it was not blood lust, but the fear of letting down Sergeant Keith.

Bennett suddenly appeared, standing upright and precariously exposed. 'Down, you bloody fool!' Keith roared. Bennett was either deafened by the roar of the gunfire or he chose to ignore the warning, for he began to hurl short-fuse grenades, which exploded on impact, at the dug-in Germans. A helmeted head soared through the air like a punted football, and there were anguished screams as shrapnel tore great holes in the bodies of the prostrate paratroopers.

Mappin saw a sniper taking careful aim at Warren, and bellowed to him to hit the deck. But Warren simply carried on shooting, methodically working the bolt of his rifle as fast as he could. Temple also saw the danger he was in and fired a long burst at the sniper, relieved to see him topple slowly into the snow, a scarlet blanket slowly spreading around his inert figure. Then Warren gave a slow dull moan as the heavy calibre bullet took the top of his head away. His body fell forward to rest in a position that suggested prayer.

Although the Germans had superior firepower they were nonetheless at a disadvantage, being pinned down in open ground where there was no cover. Every time they raised their heads they were greeted with a hail of rifle and Tommy-gun fire, while Bennett's grenades continued to explode among them with devastating effect.

A whistle trilled shrilly, and Keith saw the paras struggle to their feet and begin a shambling dog-trot towards them, firing from the hip as they advanced, their ungainly boots slithering on the snow. The Tommy-guns and rifles created an ungodly cacophony as they fired into the almost solid line of Germans. The sub-machine guns, fired in sweeping arcs, scythed them down like ripe corn, while the Lee-Enfields picked off selected targets. Keith studied the advancing line of bunched men, his eyes searching for their officer. He spotted him, still blowing his whistle and urging his men forward with his Schmeisser. The sergeant took his time and fired a short burst that almost cut the German in half, but his death did not halt the suicidal charge.

One German literally disintegrated as he was struck on the chest by one of Bennett's short-fuse grenades. Flesh and limbs flew through the air to land among the Commandos with a sickening thud, staining their white smocks so that they resembled butcher's aprons. Mappin saw Foster, firing from beneath a wagon, suddenly stiffen and drop his rifle, then slump to the ground.

It seemed an eternity, but was in fact only minutes, before Mappin called: 'Cease fire.' The Germans lay in huddled heaps on the snow. Two or three groaned loudly, the rest were silent. Among the wounded was a young soldier, his head resting against a portable wireless transmitter. He looked up at Keith and croaked: 'Kamerad'.

Keith turned to Svenson. 'You speak his lingo. Tell him if he wants to live he's got to send off a message saying the gold has been recaptured. That'll give us time to press on before they rumble they've been conned and set off after us.'

Svenson spoke rapidly in German and the soldier nodded eagerly, then sent off the dictated message, not giving a thought to his treachery, only grateful that his life had been spared. 'The message has been received and acknowledged,' he said after a couple of minutes.

Svenson then calmly shot him, along with the other wounded. 'It's kinder. They could not survive the cold.'

Keith looked around for the girl and was relieved to see her at the mouth of the tunnel, her clenched fists pressed tightly against her mouth. 'Everybody all right?' he called out. 'Anyone been hit?'

'Got a nick in the arm, but nothing to write home about,' Temple called back.

Svenson checked on his own group and announced solemnly: 'Lars will not be coming with us.'

Keith walked over to Warren's body and removed the identity tag which hung round his neck, and picked up his rifle. Warren's wicked, curiously ageless face wore a triumphant leer, like someone who has died at the peak of the sexual act. He said to Temple: 'Collect his ammo and grenades.' Then to Bennett and Luck: 'You two help yourselves to a couple of Schmeissers – we may need them. Our own ammo is getting short.' He walked over to Foster's body, removed his tag and picked up his rifle, ammunition and grenades.

Svenson appeared at his side. 'We must move quickly, make the most of the time the signal has given us.'

Sergeant Keith looked at the red carpet surrounding the dead paras and was surprised to find a deep sense of grief flooding through him; he had expected a glow of triumph. Some of the Germans were little more than boys, but they had fought like veterans.

Bennett joined him. 'Poor little sods, 'ardly outa their nappies.' He rolled one over with his boot, exposing hair that was the colour of freshly churned butter. 'Don't suppose 'e ever 'eard of Norway till 'e arrived 'ere. Wonder wot he was finkin' when he copped it?'

'How many of us he could kill, and what he'd feel like when the Führer was pinning an Iron Cross on his tunic.'

'You ain't got a 'eart, Sarge, you got a bleedin' brick.'

'It was them or us,' said Keith bluntly.

'You all right, Harry? Still in one piece?' called out Private Luck, looking pale and tense.

'Couldn't be better, Ted. How about yourself?'

'Now it's over I feel like throwing up.' He lowered his head and did so.

Lieutenant Mappin lit a cigarette with visibly shaking fingers. 'The lads did well, Sergeant. Even you must feel proud.'

'What's that meant to be, sir, some kind of compliment?' Keith said viciously.

Mappin was bewildered at the unexpected antagonism. 'Sorry, Harry. Have I said something wrong?'

'No, sir.' He choked back the words he was about to utter. 'I know what you mean – they were more scared of me than the enemy.'

Lieutenant Mappin felt a deep stab of remorse pierce his heart like a bayonet. He could have expressed himself better. 'I didn't mean to imply that at all,' he mumbled apologetically. 'I'm as proud as you are, but I happen to know your approval means more to them than mine.'

'Private Warren certainly wouldn't have got my approval, sir: senseless waste of life. Silly bugger couldn't distinguish business from pleasure. Now, if you don't mind, sir, I suggest we call a halt to this pointless conversation and move off.'

'When we get back I'm going to recommend you for a gong,' said Mappin, humbled.

'If you do that, sir, I'll tell them where to stuff it,' he replied, with a laugh. The tension immediately eased.

The soldiers took up their positions at the sledge, and Keith took over the place of the dead Norwegian. Christina stood beside him, shaking uncontrollably, and he saw that she was carrying Ulricson's carbine on her shoulder. He patted her back. 'It was awful, but necessary.'

She gave a hurried glance over her shoulder at the heaped-up bodies. 'That's what I keep telling myself. They belong to the same race which has shot many hundreds of hostages, and turned our towns to rubble. I should have no feelings of guilt – it's stupid.'

Svenson lifted his hand and brought it down in a swift cutting gesture, signalling it was time to leave. The men heaved at the lather harness and the sledges with their priceless cargo slid smoothly over the crisp white snow.

'We must reach the safety of the forest before the spotter plane returns to see what has gone wrong,' Svenson said grimly.

The going became much harder as they made for the higher ground and the dense sweeps of pine that stretched in an unbroken line halfway up the mountains. The shoulders and back muscles of the men protested in agony, their hands red-raw from hauling at the leather harness. The cold seeped through to the marrow in their bones, and their feet had lost all feeling. But they pressed forward doggedly, spurred on by fear of the sound their ears were straining to catch, and it was only when the sky began to darken that they relaxed. It was a question of minutes before the light had faded and they were safe from the prying eyes of the spotter aircraft.

They penetrated deep into the forest and only halted when it was safe to light a fire and cook a meal. Private Bennett stretched out beside Lance-Corporal Temple. 'You know, it's a funny fing, but when I was a toddler I was shit-scared of the dark. Always went to bed wiv a light – one of those round, stubby candle fings you stand in a saucer. Min' you, it was a great 'elp when I did time. A light on in the cell all the time never bothered me.'

'I always liked the dark,' Temple said. 'An unlit room was the best place to learn how to palm cards.'

'Conjurin' tricks in the bleedin' dark! Come off of it, Reg.'

'Great practical use, my lad. When I was playing cards for a living it meant I could look at the other players, and when you do that you find they stare back, trying to read something in your eyes instead of looking at what you're doing with your hands.'

Keith listened to them, a faint smile of satisfaction on his face. He remembered Mappin's words. Yes, he was proud of his men. It was hard to believe that such a short time ago they had been fighting for their lives.

Christina lay down beside him. 'I'm so cold Harry,' she whispered. 'Warm me.'

He put his arms around her and felt her body nestle close. He would have liked to have done more, but that was impossible with an audience. Even so, he felt happy and content. Soon it would be over and there would be more suitable occasions on which to demonstrate his growing affection.

Chapter Fifteen

They had been travelling through the forest for several hours when Svenson called a halt and walked over to Lieutenant Mappin. 'Soon we will have to leave the protection of the trees and make our way to where we pick up the fishing boats.'

'How far away are they, Olav?'

The big Norwegian shrugged and held up three fingers. 'No more than that.'

'Three what?' Mappin said.

'Hours, of course. Certainly not minutes or days,' said Svenson, with a great bellow of laughter, but the levity concealed his obvious concern.

The Commandos felt a great surge of relief flood through them. Their boots, which had never had a chance to dry out, were literally falling to pieces, and the prospect of having to walk barefoot was a terrifying thought that had nagged at their brains for some time. Now they knew it was a fear that would not materialize.

Svenson continued. 'We will have no trouble with Germans because the town was completely destroyed by artillery and aircraft, so there was no need to maintain a garrison. Most of the population have moved away, but a few fishermen remain. The Germans permit them to work as normal – otherwise they would starve.'

The three hours proved to be four; a gale force wind blew up, creating snowstorms that reduced visibility to a few feet. They slithered across the high frozen ground that overlooked the fishing harbour, and Svenson called another halt. 'While you rest here I will walk down and see if the coast is clear for us to continue. One man in daylight will not arouse any suspicions.'

Svenson went down towards the harbour along a narrow road that was normally used by the fishermen to transport their catches. Both sides had high banks, providing welcome shelter from the howling wind. He sang at the top of his voice, anxious to establish the fact that he had nothing to hide and even less to fear. Then, to his dismay, he saw that a German pillbox had been erected on a flat piece of ground, giving it a commanding view of the town below. It was a dome-shaped structure with walls and roof at least four feet thick. Two heavy machine guns were strategically positioned to give a clear field of fire, and the turret of a Mark IV tank with a 75mm cannon was embedded into the ground. Around it were barricades of barbed wire and signposts with a white skull and crossbones on them and the words: 'Achtung Minen'.

Svenson stopped singing, the pillbox looked impregnable. He gradually retraced his footsteps, wondering how he could break the bad news to the Commandos.

When he got back he described what he had seen to Lieutenant Mappin. 'I cannot understand why our friends failed to inform us of the fortifications. We will have to revise our plans and make our own way to the rendezvous with the MTB.'

'Don't let's rush anything, Olav,' Mappin said. 'If we go by Shanks's pony it'll take days – days we can't afford. Furthermore, my men are almost barefoot.'

'I think I'd better have a look at the pillbox, sir,' Keith said. 'Better show me the way, Olav, and bring your binoculars.'

The two men moved stealthily across the ground above the road, slipping from rock to rock like lizards, sometimes squirming snake-like on their stomachs. When they reached a rugged crag overlooking the fortifications, Keith stretched out a hand for the glasses. He focused them on the pillbox, carefully noting every aperture and mentally working out the field of fire of each gun. 'Not as bad as it could be, Olav,' he whispered. 'Everything's geared up to an attack from the sea.'

They stayed there for ten minutes before Keith tapped Svenson on the shoulder, signalling it was time to leave.

'Only one sentry on duty. It takes him exactly seven minutes to do a complete circuit, and he never looked inland. If you ask me, Jerry erected that little lot more to put the fear of God into your people than anything else. The big gun isn't manned and neither are the machine gun emplacements. It shouldn't be too difficult to creep up from behind and catch them with their pants down.'

'It is very risky,' said Svenson apprehensively.

'Anything we do from now on is going to involve an element of risk. When he finds out what happened at the sidings, Jerry is going to come after us in force. He won't give a damn for the gold; he'll be wanting revenge.'

When they returned to the rest of the party Sergeant Keith described what they had seen to Mappin.

'What do you suggest, Sergeant? An all-out attack? We'd never get away with it. In the dark we would be completely at sea.'

'I suggest a dawn attack, sir. We make our way there in total darkness, hole up, then hit them at first light, when they're least expecting it.'

Keith unsheathed his fighting knife and drew a map of the fortifications in the snow. When he had finished he told each member of the unit the role he would be playing. 'Stealth and surprise are the important things,' he added.

There was only a short period to wait before darkness began to enfold them, but each minute seemed hours. Keith, anxious to destroy the impression that he and not Mappin was in command, said: 'Let's know when you're ready to go, sir.'

'We seem to have forgotten one thing, Sergeant. What'll we do with the gold while we're giving Jerry a bloody nose?'

Keith smiled ruefully. 'Good point, sir. We leave it here. If we pull it off we come back for it, if we don't, it'll have to be hidden again. Olav will have to see to that end of things.'

'Let's go, then. Might as well get it over and done with.'

They lay in a snow-covered depression overlooking the fortifications and settled down until the sky began to brighten. Keith raised himself on his elbows and focused the binoculars on the pillbox. There was a tin-roofed wooden hut at the end of a roughly-made road which he assumed served as the mess room for the off-duty soldiers. The road would therefore be free of mines. A solitary sentry stood outside his shelter smoking a cigarette, occasionally glancing at his wristwatch. He tossed his cigarette end into the snow where it left a dark smudge, then began to patrol. Keith waited until he returned and went into his shelter.

'*Now*,' he whispered urgently. 'I'll take the sentry. You all know what you have to do.'

The soldiers moved swiftly and silently towards the emplacement, just as they had done dozens of times in Scotland.

The German garrison, conditioned into believing their presence was a mere show of strength, had lapsed into a casual, careless routine and were caught totally unawares by the attack. Bennett and Temple kicked open the doors of the mess hut and hurled in short-fuse grenades in quick succession, then hit the ground like rugby players diving for touch. The wooden building disintegrated in a sheet of flame, and glass and timber soared into the air.

The startled sentry emerged from his shelter groping for his rifle but Sergeant Keith was beside him before he managed to reach it. He held his knife in his left hand, his right raised to create the opening for an upwards thrust under the rib cage. He moved so quickly the scream of the sentry remained frozen in his throat as the knife pierced his heart. Blood gushed from his mouth, and he toppled to the ground.

One soldier, his uniform smouldering, ran out of what was left of the hut, his hands above his head. Bennett hit him hard behind the ear with his rubber cosh, felling him like a pole-axed steer. 'Courtesy of London Transport, Fritz,' he shouted, before crushing the butt of his gun into his victim's face. Then he sprinted, bent low, towards the tank turret. The big gun began to traverse, Bennett hoped and prayed that the sergeant was right and it could not fire inland. He planted a bell-shaped magnetic grenade on the side and dived head first against the concrete wall of the pillbox. Private Luck and Lieutenant Mappin scrambled up the steel ladder leading to the top of the pillbox and dropped grenades down the ventilation shafts.

Sergeant Keith flung himself beside Bennett below the apertures and together they tossed grenades inside. There

216

was a muffled explosion, a steel door soared through the air as if it were weightless and thick black smoke billowed from the chimneys. Miraculously, soldiers began to emerge from the pillbox, firing their sub-machine guns. Private Luck emptied a magazine of Tommy-gun bullets and saw three of them keel over; almost in slow motion. A siren wailed from somewhere in the distance, and Luck gesticulated wildly in the direction of the clearly marked minefield. Two trucks were careering through it at breakneck speed. The trucks were filled with grey-clad soldiers who were firing all kinds of weapons as the trucks bucketed over the uneven ground.

'Hit them with everything we have. Grenades – the lot,' roared Keith.

Grenades began to cascade down around the approaching vehicles, while the Tommy-guns, captured Schmeissers and rifles kept up a merciless fire. Some of the grenades detonated mines which erupted in black mushrooms of smoke. The leading truck caught fire and swerved violently, bouncing off the safe path into the mined area, setting off more land mines before exploding in a deafening boom. White-hot flames from ignited petrol soared high into the air and took hold of the second truck. The driver jumped out of the driving cab, his uniform a mass of fire, and began rolling in the snow, his screams rending the air. Dazed soldiers, all thought of action forgotten, were moving tentatively through the minefields and barbed wire, their hands above their heads, all croaking out the one word of German every Commando knows: '*Kammerad*'.

'Take your time, lads, and knock them off,' said Keith pitilessly. There was a concentrated volley of fire which ceased only when there was no further sign of life among the Germans.

Sergeant Keith listened for Mappin's voice announcing their withdrawal, but he did not hear it. Instead he heard Luck call out: 'Sarge! I think Lieutenant Mappin has been hit.'

He looked towards the voice and saw Luck kneeling over the Lieutenant. He ran to the pillbox. Mappin was sitting in an upright position, his back resting against the concrete. His face was a greyish colour and his eyes had a dead, glazed look.

'Better take over, Sergeant. Can't move my legs. Absolutely dead. No feeling at all.'

'Where're you hit?' asked Keith anxiously.

'Somewhere in the back. Didn't really feel much.'

'Help me get him to his feet, Luck.'

Together they hauled Mappin upright, and placed an arm around each of their shoulders. 'Try walking, sir. Take your time, there's no rush,' said Keith.

Mappin remained where he was. Then through gritted teeth said: 'No good. Nothing responds.'

'Keep trying, sir,' said Keith harshly, hoping that the ferocity of his voice would act like a surge of electricity to the stricken man.

'Sergeant,' said Mappin with surprising calm, 'I am trying, believe it or not. I'm sorry to say I seem to be paralysed.'

'Don't worry, sir. We'll stick you on one of the sledges.'

'Don't bother, Sergeant, I can't make it. Better leave me and press on. Jerry will treat me as a POW. He has to: Geneva Convention and all that.'

'Balls to all that! When he sees what we've done here he won't be taking any prisoners. Anyway, Hitler has decreed that Commandos, as they're not strictly soldiers, aren't covered by any convention.'

'That's an order,' said Mappin with cold deliberation. 'Do you hear me?'

'No, sir. The grenades must have punctured my ear drums.' Keith turned to Luck. 'Keep an eye on the Lieutenant while we go and collect the gold. See he doesn't do anything stupid.'

When they returned with the sledges, Mappin was still lying against the wall of the pillbox, with Luck pressing handfuls of snow against his forehead. They lifted him with the utmost care and lay him stomach-down on the top of one of the sledges.

'Better let me have a look at the wound, sir.'

'Don't bother, Harry, it'll be a waste of time. Something tells me my number's up.'

'Knock it off, sir!' Keith angrily retorted. 'There's no time for tea and sympathy.'

Lieutenant Mappin's head slumped forward; his eyes closed, but his chest continued to rise and fall. Keith rummaged in his backpack until he found the small package, issued to every man, which contained a cyanide capsule, morphine and a hypodermic syringe. He filled the syringe with morphine and emptied it into Mappin's arm.

'We must go now, Sergeant,' Svenson said insistently. 'We have come so far, it is senseless to throw it all way for one man. No one would appreciate that more than Lieutenant Mappin.'

Keith shouted out an order and the soldiers took up their positions on the sledges; but the one carrying Mappin refused to budge.

'It is overloaded, Sergeant. Better to put him out of his misery – I know that sounds harsh, but there is no other way.'

'Listen, Olav, and listen bloody carefully. He's coming with us. If anything is going to be dumped, it'll be your ruddy gold.'

Svenson could see that nothing would deter the sergeant, and he gave a shrug of resignation. 'All right. What do you suggest!'

'If we can't find anything to carry him on I'll do it myself,' said Keith grimly.

'We'll have a scout round and see if we can find anything suitable,' Private Luck interrupted.

A few minutes later he and Temple returned carrying a door. 'The only part of their mess hut which escaped undamaged, Sarge.'

'That'll do fine,' said Keith, 'and if we can't manage both sledges at the same time we leave one and come back for it.'

'I'll take his place at the sledge,' Christina said. 'I'm as strong as any man.'

'No objections to that, but it might be wiser if you went ahead and got a couple of your friends to come up and give us a hand.'

Svenson nodded in agreement. 'Do as the sergeant says, Christina. I know the numbers on the boats – the skipper in charge is Viggo Storstein.'

She hurried down the steep rutted road towards the harbour, her eyes glancing anxiously from side to side in a desperate attempt to catch a glimpse of a friendly face, her ears listening apprehensively for the ominous sound of a spotter aircraft. But she arrived at the outskirts of the once prosperous fishing port without seeing another human, and she deduced that the unexpected eruption of gunfire and explosions had sent everyone scurrying for shelter.

The small harbour was empty except for a solitary traditional Norwegian fishing boat at anchor. It was a stout weather-beaten vessel, about fifty feet in length with an upright wheelhouse aft. The sails were furled, and there was no sign of life aboard, but the diesel engine was turning over and small puffs of exhaust were coming out of the pipe which protruded like a periscope from above the wheelhouse.

She studied the stencilled numbers on the side; they were the same as those Svenson had given her. She thought of calling out, then decided against it, and instead looked around for something to throw against the hull to attract attention. She found a large stone which she tossed at the boat, only to see it splash into the water. The stone had been too heavy. She picked up a smaller one and managed to hit the roof of the wheelhouse; it landed with a thump she was sure could be heard a mile off.

A head emerged from a hatch just aft of the wheelhouse.'I am with Olav Svenson,' Christina called out.

'I'll bring the boat alongside,' the sailor replied. 'I've been expecting you. I am Storstein.'

He called through the hatch to someone below deck Another man emerged, went up to the bow and began to haul in the anchor on a small winch, while the owner went into the wheelhouse. Another man appeared and went into the cramped engine room. The engine chugged into life and he manoeuvred the boat alongside the stone jetty, then jumped ashore.'Where's the second boat?' Christina asked anxiously

'There isn't one. When the firing started the crew had second thoughts about the wisdom of their actions and put to sea with the other fishing boats. I suppose they thought the Germans had ambushed your party and there was no point in remaining.'

'But you stayed.'

'If you'd been caught there was nothing for me to worry about – I'd simply deny all knowledge of your existence.'

'All the Germans are dead, but we need help to get the gold aboard. There's one badly wounded British soldier who' being carried by two of his comrades – we need someone to replace them on the sledges.'

The skipper nodded and called out to the man who had hauled in the anchor. 'Wake Nordahl. You and he will follow the girl.'

The man bellowed down the hatch and a young man emerged rubbing the sleep from his eyes, complaining bitterly at having been disturbed.

'Hurry, the pair of you! We need to be away to sea before the Germans arrive.'

An hour later the gold was safely stowed in the hold.

Mappin was lowered down the fo'c'sle hatch into a dingy mess which housed six bunks in double tiers, and was carefully placed on one of the lower bunks. The skipper turned to Svenson. 'Some of the soldiers must hide here until we are well out to sea. The remainder can share my cabin aft.'

Storstein stepped into the wheelhouse and sounded a horn which emitted a goose-like honk. The young man released the mooring lines and the boat headed out towards the open sea.

Svenson standing beside the skipper in the wheelhouse, said angrily: 'Was it necessary to announce our departure?'

'Very much so,' said Storstein calmly. 'The Germans insist that we must always signal our intention that we are off to fish. They're very strict, so we should act as normally as possible.'

Svenson glanced shorewards, his eyes searching for grey uniforms, his ears waiting for the sound of gunfire; but he saw nothing, and heard only the chug-chug-chug of the diesel. 'Why weren't we warned about the pillbox?' he asked.

'For the simple reason that when the arrangements were made it didn't exist. The whole damn thing was erected in hours. The Germans recruited every able-bodied man they could find and forced them to work. Those who refused were shot. We had no way of getting a message to you because you were always on the move. Soon it'll be dark and then we will have nothing to worry about.' He gestured vaguely ahead. 'The sea is covered with scores of fishing boats similar to this one, so if Jerry comes looking for us it'll be like seeking a needle in a haystack.'

'You know where we are to meet the British navy boat?'

'Of course, but I can't understand these unnecessary complications. We should sail all the way to the Shetland Islands.'

He tapped the steering wheel. 'This boat can sail round the world without any trouble. We should do that.'

'I didn't plan this. Perhaps what you say makes sense, but I can't disobey orders. Perhaps the British thought that once the Germans knew it was a Norwegian boat that had spirited the gold away there would be terrible reprisals – perhaps a ban on all fishing.'

'It doesn't matter,' Storstein said indifferently. 'When we reach our destination I'll make radio contact with the British and say you have arrived.'

In the forward mess deck, Keith had stripped off Mappin's uniform in order to examine his wound. A cursory look told him that there was nothing he could do: the lieutenant needed the attention of a qualified doctor. There was a small wound, no bigger than a sixpence, in the middle of his back just above the crease of his buttocks. It was not bleeding, and was quite clean. He applied a field dressing and gave Mappin another morphine injection.

When daylight came, the fishing boat was just one more vessel in a large fleet of similar boats. The skipper turned to Svenson. 'What we have to look out for now are German patrol boats. They appear from time to time to search us and see that our papers are in order. What we need to pray for is a spot of really foul weather so they don't turn out.'

However, their prayers were unanswered. The sea remained relatively calm and visibility was good for the time of year. Lookouts were posted fore and aft for what remained of the daylight hours, but nothing was sighted.

The next morning the vigil was resumed, but after a time the strain began to tell. The lookouts thought they saw things that did not exist: rocks bore an uncanny resemblance to U-boats; the steel poles marking offshore wrecks were identified as periscopes. On one occasion a sperm whale surfaced unexpectedly, causing the skipper to give an order to the soldiers to grab their weapons and stand by to repel an imminent attack.

On the third morning the skipper found that he no longer had company. The other boats had gone. He was not surprised; the Germans imposed strict limits. He glanced sky-wards, the tension visible in his furrowed face; a solitary boat, if spotted where it had no right to be, was certain to arouse suspicion. Less than two hours of light remained when the fo'c'sle lookout called: 'Enemy aircraft approaching.' His finger pointed out over the port bow.

'Everyone below decks!' the skipper bellowed. The soldiers, who had been seeking a brief respite from the foul-smelling mess-deck, bolted down the hatch like rabbits.

The distant speck became larger and the roar of its engines louder and louder as it flew low over the fishing boat. 'A Dornier reconnaissance bomber,' Storstein growled.

It was a long slim aircraft with a bulbous nose and unmistakable twin fins and rudders on the tips of the high-set tail plane. It completed an investigatory circle, then came in aft of the boat, a signal lamp flashing from the perspex nose.

'He's telling me to heave to,' said Storstein.

'What should we do?' asked Svenson.

The skipper gave a humourless grin. 'Pretend I can't read his signal and hope for the best. The Germans know that very few fishermen can read morse.' He leaned out of the wheel-house door and began to wave in an energetic fashion, to show how delighted he was to see the aircraft. At the same time he called out to the two crewmen who were on deck, pretending to attend to some nets. 'Wave back! Look as if they're welcome.'

The two men waved both arms above their heads, jumping up and down like fans at a soccer match.

The Dornier completed another circle and came in lower, the lamp still flashing. As it passed overhead, the pilot's face was clearly visible. The bomber banked lazily and flew in even lower. This time there was no flashing lamp, but fiery spurts of machine gun fire as its two 7.9mm machine guns began firing. One of the waving seamen crashed down onto the deck, his legs severed above the knees. As the plane passed, the guns on the underbelly took over. Bullets ploughed into the decks and chewed great furrows in the hull. The glass in the wheelhouse shattered; the roof was churned into matchwood. The remaining seaman dived for the protection of the capstan, but was riddled with bullets before he reached it.

'Get the soldiers topsides!' the skipper screeched. 'They can give the bastards a taste of their own medicine.' Svenson ran to the mess deck hatch and yelled his orders. The soldiers scrambled out, their weapons cocked and ready for action.

The Dornier banked once more, coming in yet again with its machine guns spitting fire. The Tommy-guns and rifles opened up simultaneously but were as ineffective as a feather duster against a swarm of hornets. The mizzen mast toppled down like a felled tree and the deck hatches were ripped to pieces, but miraculously no one was hit. As the soldiers continued their ferocious firing the twin engines screamed like a banshee as the pilot sought to gain height.

Svenson gripped his carbine so hard that his knuckles showed white. 'I think we've driven them off,' he said to Keith.

'No such luck, Olav. He's gaining height so that he can bomb us. No point in risking being shot down when he can polish us off out of range.'

When it was no longer threatened by small arms fire, the Dornier levelled out to commence a bombing run from astern. Two black objects tumbled from the open bay and exploded with a deafening crump less than fifty yards abeam of the boat, causing great columns of icy water to erupt high in the air and cascade with enormous weight onto the upper deck, sweeping the soldiers off their feet. The water was so cold it immediately froze on their tunics.

Two more attacks were made, and although there were no direct hits the damage was extensive. The boat began to make water through sprung planking in the hull. Then providence intervened. Without warning the sky became as black as a shroud, heralding one of those freak storms that had been the bane of Norwegian fishermen for centuries and the maker of countless widows. A force nine wind began to blow, whipping the sea into angry white-topped waves which crashed over the boat with a deafening roar. Hundreds of tons of water pounded the deck, flooding the fish hold to such an extent that the gold was completely covered. The bomber, imperilled more by the weather than the boat, dropped two more bombs which exploded harmlessly in the sea, too far off to inflict any further damage. It then headed towards the distant shore.

The skipper called to Svenson to join him in the shattered wheelhouse. 'Take the wheel, I must examine the damage. Just try and keep her on this course. Have you handled a boat before?'

Svenson nodded. 'But only during holidays, and never in a storm like this.'

'Do your best. My boat can take a lot more before she gives up. I'll get the pumps working and the soldiers bailing.'

As the big pumps battled to reduce the water level in the fish hold, the soldiers formed a human chain as they used any object capable of holding water as bailers. They emptied the galley of buckets and saucepans, and even empty food tins. As soon as they were filled they were passed to the men on deck who emptied them into the bilges and over the side. Christina went to the aid of Bennett who, single-handed, was trying to operate the ancient vertical hand pump. Together they thrust the piston up and down with metronomic regularity. When darkness came the men continued to bail, and although they were unable to empty the hold they kept the flooding to manageable proportions.

The skipper relieved Svenson at the wheel. 'I'll head inshore and seek shelter in one of the smaller fjords. With a bit of luck we can carry out some make-shift repairs; enough to enable us to make the rendezvous.'

He swung the helm over and let the boat run before the storm, which showed no signs of abating. In the windowless wheelhouse the spray stung his face, drawing blood that froze immediately. In the hold the soldiers were so cold they had difficulty holding their bailing implements and the wind howled so loudly they could not hear each other. Only Mappin, heavily sedated with morphia, was unaware of the perils that beset them.

One minute the bow was rearing up almost vertically; the next the boat was in danger of being pooped. Then it would rise to the crest of an enormous wave and plunge with a bone-shattering crash into the trough. Lashed to the wheel by a stout length of rope the skipper, despite his incredible strength, was showing signs of the strain. He had great difficulty fighting against the sleep his brain and body demanded. From time to time he studied the chart by the beam of a hand torch muttering to himself: 'Please God, don't let my engine fail me now!' If it did, he knew his boat would be pounded to driftwood.

In the fish hold, Keith was urging the soldiers to put a bit more back into their bailing. he could not help thinking at the same time what a great pity it was that the whole mission should have to end in total failure. As the great waves pounded against the hull, hurling more freezing water into the hold, he knew it could only be a question of time before they all went down. He glanced at Christina, her arms and shoulders working in unison on the pump handle, her sodden hair lank, and her eyes closed. Her teeth were gritted and blood was seeping through her clenched fingers. Bennett was intoning, in a dead, monotonous voice: 'Up, down. Up, down.' It was a pity, Keith thought, that he and the girl would never have the chance to get to know each other better. He would have liked the opportunity; no woman had ever aroused so much interest in him.

Storstein, who had fished some of the most hostile seas in the Arctic region, could not recall encountering weather quite like it. The wheel felt like an angry wild animal in his hands – it seemed to have acquired an unruly will of its own, for when he spun it to starboard it spun back wildly of its own accord to port. But he knew the sea was like a temperamental and wilful mistress who could blow hot and cold according to her whims. One minute she could be a scolding virago; the next a loving, embracing charmer. Her tantrums were short-lived, so it was merely a question of time before her mood changed. All he and his beloved boat had to do was ride the storm. He whistled through his gritted teeth, praying that the groaning timbers understood the sea as well as he did, and did not decide to give up the ghost.

Then, just when he had decided that he might as well abandon all hope, the wind began to abate and the waves lessened their ferocious pounding. The helm responded; the elderly diesel engine began to take on a more regular thump and the screw no longer rose out of the water to churn thin air.

He called to Svenson lying in a heap on the deck in his own vomit. 'She has relented, Svenson! She has decided to spare me for a few more trips. Take the wheel while I take a depth sounding.'

Svenson, as green as the sea that now rose fitfully over the bow like the punches of an exhausted boxer, took over the helm while Storstein removed an ancient lead line from a locker and went aft to sound the depth.

He returned to the wheelhouse. 'We're in four fathoms,' he announced. 'I'm going to anchor here until I can move safely inshore.'

Just before dawn, Storstein weighed anchor and steamed towards the shelter of a narrow fjord where the cliffs rose perpendicular from the water. He anchored as close to the shore as he could, and the battered and weather-beaten boat was virtually invisible from seawards. 'When we have eaten,' he said to Svenson, 'I'll examine the damage and see what repairs we can do.'

The damage was extensive, but he was certain that the bigger leaks in the hull could be made more watertight if they hammered flat empty food tins and buckets, and nailed them into position. They worked tirelessly and ceaselessly to repair leaks. When they ran out of tins and other utensils they caulked seams with rope which they ripped apart with bloody fingers.

Five hours later, Storstein anchored in the narrow inlet where they were to meet the MTB.

Chapter Sixteen

Private Luck sat with his back resting against a bulkhead as he unlaced his sodden boots and removed his socks in order to examine his feet. As he peeled off his socks he gritted his teeth to prevent himself screaming at the excruciating pain. Pieces of flesh were adhering to the wool and the stench was nauseating. Two toes on his right foot were black and oozing a foul smelling pus and the big toe on his left foot was in a similar condition. He needed no doctor to tell him he was suffering from a bad attack of frostbite. Harry, he thought, is going to blow a gasket when I tell him. The sergeant had been so insistent about the importance of looking after your feet – and he had tried to do just that. But he had not bargained on standing for several hours in freezing water, passing up hundreds of buckets through the hatch. But Keith was not likely to take that into consideration; he would put it down to personal neglect.

He thought about putting his boots back on and keeping quiet, but when he saw Sergeant Keith approaching he decided against concealment. He was practically unable to walk and that made him a passenger.

'You all right, Ted?' asked Keith, glancing at the boots on the bunk and the exposed feet.

'Think I've got a touch of frostbite, Sergeant.' He extended his feet so that the sergeant could see them.

Keith pursed his lips. 'I don't like the look of that at all, ' Ted. Why didn't you mention it earlier?'

Luck waited for the explosion of wrath, but it did not come. 'It's the first chance I've had to see why they should have started to play me up,' he said apologetically.

Keith knelt and tenderly examined the grotesquely black-ened toes. 'Not your fault, Ted, so don't blame yourself.' He shook his head in bewilderment. 'I'd better get Olav to take a look at you – something new in my book. He's bound to have encountered it before, though. Christ, I hope so!'

'It could have been worse, Sarge,' Luck said, feeling sur-prisingly relieved. Somehow Keith's tolerance made his inju-ries seem less disastrous, the agony more bearable.

'I'm glad you can be so ruddy cheerful about it, Ted.'

'It could have been my fingers. That really would have had me worried.'

'The piano, you mean?'

Luck nodded. 'I can still work the pedals without toes!'

'I'll get Svenson,' said Keith, and as he moved off he called over his shoulder: 'Everyone on deck in half an hour. Foot inspection.' He knew his voice sounded firm and authorita-tive, but he wondered what he would do if he found half his men had blackened, putrefying toes that smelt like over-ripe Camembert cheese.

He found Svenson in the wheelhouse with the skipper, drinking a tea coloured liquid from a huge stone jar. He wasted no words. 'Do you have a cure for frostbite, Olav?'

The Norwegian spread his arms apart like a bird fanning wet wings. 'Of course, but it depends so much on the degree. In a trifling form it can be cured by an instant application of snow or water which will restore circulation. Direct heat only causes painful inflammation. If mortification has set in, then amputation is the only answer.'

'Who has it?' Storstein asked bluntly.

'One of my chaps. It looks bad.'

'I'll look at him. I've seen it many times, fishermen get it hauling in the nets or standing too long in cold water. Some-times it's the ears or nose – always the extremities. That's why fishermen always make bloody damn sure their cocks are well protected.' He bellowed like a buffalo in pain, laughing at his puerile attempt at humour. 'A man has ten toes, ten fingers, two ears – but only one cock.' He held up an index finger as if he feared that Keith was hard of hearing. 'Only one! God should have given him ten cocks and only one finger and toe,' he said coarsely, then noticed the pent-up fury in Keith's eyes. 'I joke, Sergeant. Bring him to the wheelhouse.'

230

'Why the hell can't you make the effort to go and see him?'

'Because it's better your men are not witness to what may be done to save him. Do you carry any medicines or drugs?'

'Field dressings and some sulphanilamide powder, which, if I remember correctly, is a new-fangled drug that acts as an anti-bacterial agent. It was never properly explained when or how we should use it.'

'Get it,' said Storstein brusquely. 'We can try it. If it kills him it won't matter too much, he'll probably die anyway.'

'You don't have to be such a callous bastard.'

'Callous! I have fought to save my boat and the gold and I have done that. Now you expect me to save one of your men. I'm a sailor, Sergeant, not a physician – I can only tell you what I know.' He paused. 'Have you ever had frostbite, Sergeant? It's like hungry rats nibbling at you, but you lack the strength to shake them off.' He stomped out of the wheelhouse, the stone flagon swinging in his hands.

'He's not a brutal man, Sergeant,' Svenson said. 'A lifetime of fishing has taught him to hide his feelings – it's a hard life. He took his young wife fishing once; her leg got caught in a trawl warp and he had to hack it off with an axe to stop her from being pulled overboard. She did not survive and he has never forgiven himself. I know that is true because he reported to the police in Oslo and asked to be charged with her murder. Of course, no action was taken. He was even more grief-stricken and remorseful when the newspapers told the story and described him as a hero.'

Keith went back to Luck and asked him if, with a little support, he could make it to the wheelhouse.

'I'd walk from Land's End to John O'Groats if I thought that at the end of the journey someone was going to do something about the pain, Sergeant.'

Keith put one of Luck's arms around his shoulder and helped him up the steep ladder. 'Ted, when this is over, if you ever decide to give up the piano, I'll personally recommend you for the Hop Pickers. We'd be proud to have you.'

'I've got a nasty feeling that my soldiering days are over.' He paused for breath, 'I'm sorry, Sergeant,' he added. 'I really am. I've been nothing but a burden to you since we met in France. You should have left me there – it would have saved a lot of trouble.'

'*Sorry!* You silly bugger, you've got nothing to apologize for.'

Even in the shelter of the overhanging cliffs the boat continued to roll and pitch. 'Lay him on the deck and hold him down,' Storstein said when Keith and Luck reached the wheelhouse. 'I don't want to slip and cut his legs off.'

Keith was about to say something to the Norwegian about his insensitivity but choked back his words. He had often, in the past, met men who hid their true emotions under a hard, almost cold exterior, it was possible the Norwegian was the same.

Keith spreadeagled Luck on the deck like a man about to be crucified. He knelt beside him and put the whole weight of his own body onto his biceps. Storstein unsheathed the gutting knife he wore round his waist and tested it by shaving some hairs off his forearm. Then he bent down and picked up the flagon of spirit. 'give him a good drink of this.' He forced the neck of the flagon between Luck's lips. 'Take a really good swig, Ted.'

Luck tried to swallow the fiery liquid but it made him cough and he turned his head away.

Storstein poured some of the spirit over the blade of his knife, muttering to himself: 'Damn waste of good liquor.' Then he knelt on the deck and with a swift movement of the knife severed the blackened big toe.

Then he did the same to the two frostbitten toes on the other foot. He picked up the foul-smelling pieces of flesh and bones and tossed them overboard. 'Might as well feed the fish!'

'Good lad,' Keith murmured. 'It's over now. Just relax.'

Luck's head slumped to one side and he lapsed into unconsciousness. Keith sprinkled the sulphanilamide powder over the wounds, then carefully applied field dressings. He turned to Storstein. 'The kid's got bags of guts. Not a whimper.'

'If you've ever had frostbite, Sergeant,' the Norwegian said, 'you'll know that any pain, no matter how bad, comes as a relief. Now take him below, keep him warm, and let him sleep.' He looked at the sergeant and held out the flagon. 'You look as if you need this, but leave some for me.'

He held out his hands and Keith saw they were trembling. 'I don't enjoy being called upon to play God,' said Storstein.

'The lad will be glad you did, and so am I,' Keith said. 'Thanks.'

Svenson helped him carry Luck down into the forward mess deck where they placed him on a bunk and Keith gave him an injection of morphia. He found two dry blankets in a locker and carefully wrapped them round Luck's legs, then made his way to the upper deck where the rest of the soldiers were standing by for a foot examination. He was immensely relieved to discover there were no other cases of frostbite.

He decided to look for Christina; a few minutes alone with her would take his mind off his own tormented thoughts. But when he found her she was sitting with Svenson and Storstein in the skipper's personal cabin just aft of the wheelhouse, ruling out the chance of a few comforting words in private.

Lying on the table, concealed in an ordinary suitcase, was an R/T set of the type smuggled to agents in occupied countries.

'We've been talking things over, Sergeant,' Storstein said. 'We should contact headquarters in England without delay, and say we're ready to be picked up.'

'That's fine by me,' Keith said.

Storstein lifted the mattress on his bunk and produced a code book. 'Olav will help me prepare a message. He is much more expert than I am.'

'Tell them to make sure there's a doctor on board,' said Keith.'

'I'm sorry, Sergeant, but that can't be done. We must keep our message as short as possible or the Germans will locate us.'

When the message had been completed, Storstein tapped out his call sign and an eternity seemed to pass before it was acknowledged. He signalled that he was ready to transmit and on receipt of the 'go-ahead' sent the message, which included their exact position.

They sat in huddled silence for what seemed hours. Then the reply came back that the MTB would soon be on its way.

'There's nothing now to be done except wait patiently for its arrival,' Svenson said. 'It is a very fast boat, so it shouldn't be too long.'

Twenty-four hours passed and there was no winking light from seawards to announce the arrival of the MTB. Nerves in the confined cabin became taut and edgy.

'Soon we will have to break radio silence and contact base,' Svenson said. 'An MTB should have been able to do the trip in a few hours. It's long overdue.'

Keith was also feeling the strain but trying hard not to show it. 'Give it a little longer. There could be many reasons why it hasn't arrived: an engine defect, a delayed departure.'

Svenson nodded. 'Four hours – no more.'

The four hours passed with agonizing slowness. Then the wireless set came to life and Svenson commanded silence with an urgent gesture. 'Our call sign!' He feverishly worked his key in acknowledgement, then scribbled as fast as he could on the pad in front of him.

When the message had been decoded he looked up with a wry smile. 'No MTB. It was attacked and sunk by E-boats, but it did manage to get a message away: a replacement vessel, this time a fishing boat, is on the way. I'd have preferred something a bit more menacing.'

Keith left the cabin to break the disappointing news to his men in the mess deck. Bennett and Temple were sitting on one of the topmost bunks, where Temple was trying in vain to explain the art of 'Find the Lady'. 'Of course *I* can find the Queen,' he said patiently. 'If I couldn't the mugs wouldn't be interested in shelling out good money in the hope that they can find her and pick up a fiver. They've got to be convinced it isn't a con.'

'If they *never* win, Reg, they'll soon rumble it's a swizz – stands to reason.'

'My dear boy, I do let someone win occasionally. When interest flags Her Majesty turns up quite frequently and the betting gets a new lease of life.'

Bennett shook his head ruefully. 'Fanks for tryin' to learn me, Reg, but it ain' my game. If I'm gonna be a crook at leas' I'll be a' 'onest one.'

Temple said, with the utmost patience: 'I'm not trying to impart my skill and know-how simply to impress you, I'm trying to open up a bright new future. I don't want you to go back to your old ways where you'll either end up behind bars again or blow yourself to bits.'

234

'An' where'll you end up if *you're* nicked? Tell me that. In chokey, jus' like me.'

'Wrong. I've been caught many times, but all I get is a hefty fine. I appear before the beak, plead guilty, and tell him it's an innocent game of chance which I sometimes win but often lose. I then offer to give a demonstration to the bench.'

'I know, Reg, an' 'e never fin's the lady – like me.'

'On the contrary, the beak has an astonishing run of good luck.'

'Knock it off for a minute, lads,' Keith called out. 'I've got some bad news.'

When he had told them he walked across to Mappin and saw that he was still sleeping soundly. He turned his attention to Luck. 'You all right, Ted? Need another shot?'

Luck propped himself up on an elbow. 'No thanks, Sergeant, I want to be compos mentis when that MTB arrives.'

'It isn't going to,' Keith said. 'It's been sunk. But another boat is on its way – we'll just have to be patient a little longer.'

'It never rains but wot it fuckin' pours,' Bennett said. 'Never min', it'll give me time to figure out 'ow this slippery-fingered bastard can work it so I never pick out the Queen but a soddin' beak can.'

Luck said, 'Tell me, Sergeant, it wasn't a bad dream I had and I only imagined I'd lost some toes?'

'Sorry, Ted. It wasn't a dream.'

'That's odd, because I can still feel them.'

'Try and get some sleep, lad. I'll wake you in plenty of time.'

He clambered up the ladder, recalling that he had read somewhere that people who had had limbs amputated were often aware of a 'ghost' limb. It was just another of the Almighty's cruel jokes.

Another twenty-four hours passed and Keith was still standing on the fo'c'sle peering into the darkness of the fjord. Christina who was standing anxiously beside him said, 'Harry, what'll we do if it doesn't arrive?'

'That's something I've deliberately tried not to consider. I suppose we'll have to get the skipper to make it on his own.'

'I've spoken to him about that and he told me there was little chance of his boat surviving the journey. Do you think we could . . .'

235

The sentence remained unfinished, for Keith cut her short. 'Listen!' he said urgently.

From out of the darkness the slow thump-thump-thump of an engine was clearly audible. 'Get Svenson,' he said. 'Tell him to bring the signal torch.'

He heard the muffled sound of footsteps on the deck and seconds later Svenson and the girl were standing beside him. Svenson cocked his head and listened intently, then called to Storstein to join them.

He too listened carefully. 'It's a fishing boat,' he whispered. 'I'd stake my life on that. Flash the password, Olav.' He chuckled grimly. 'If I'm wrong I hope I'll live to regret my confidence.'

Svenson held the shaded torch at shoulder height, flashing the series of dots and dashes that would disclose their identity. There was an almost immediate response from a shaded green torch sending the recognition signal. The three men and the solitary girl threw their arms around each other and literally bounced up and down in jubilation.

The throbbing of the engine grew louder and a dark bulk emerged out of the blackness.

'I'm coming alongside,' a muffled voice called out. 'Stand by to take my lines.'

Keith scurried to the mess deck hatch. 'Get Lieutenant Mappin and Private Luck up here smartish!' he yelled down.

The looming bulk grew larger until a wheelhouse and a funnel were clearly discernible, and there was a wheezing squeak as the wooden rubbing strakes of the two vessels met. Mooring lines landed with a dull thud on the wooden deck of Storstein's boat, and there was a frenzied rush as people hurried to secure them to cleats and bollards.

'Where's Lieutenant Mappin?' a voice called out cheerfully in English.

Keith stepped forward. 'He's badly wounded, sir. I've taken over – Sergeant Keith.'

He felt his hand being grasped and pumped in greeting. 'Sorry we took so long. Believe me, we haven't dawdled.'

'Better follow me, sir,' said Keith.

He led him aft to the skipper's musty cabin where an oil lamp burned dimly on the table. To his surprise he saw himself looking at a naval officer wearing a blue reefer jacket, a white roll neck sweater and a pair of knee-high sea boots. The two interwoven gold rings on the sleeves of his jacket indicated he was an RNR officer; a peacetime officer on a cruiser liner or trawler skipper who had been called to the White Ensign at the outbreak of war?

The officer glanced at the occupants of the cabin. 'Lieutenant Entwistle,' he said crisply. 'Pleased to meet you all.' His voice had an intonation that summoned up visions of the Humber and the North Sea; not one that would have been heard in a peacetime wardroom of the Royal Navy.

'Olav Svenson at your service,' Svenson said formally.

The girl inclined her head, and Storstein merely grunted.

'I understand you've got a very valuable cargo aboard which Jerry is anxious to get his grimy mitts on – in which case I'll get some hands aboard to get it shifted to my boat.' He turned to Keith. 'Anybody ready, willing and able in your party to give a hand?'

'Just three of us, sir.'

'Many hands make light work, as the Chinaman said when all the bulbs went out,' he quipped cheerfully.

'Temple, Bennett, give a hand to bring that gold onto the upper deck!' Keith bellowed. 'And pull your fingers out – haven't got all day.'

Several figures swarmed over the gunwale like pirates boarding an enemy ship. All were similarly dressed in thick serge trousers, heavy woollen jumpers and clumping sea-boots; some spoke in English, others in Norwegian.

'Get the gold topsides quickish, lads, and over the side to our boat,' Entwistle snapped.

Svenson, Storstein, the engineer, and even Christina helped with the transfer of the gold from one ship to the other. When it had been completed, some two hours later, Entwistle said cheerfully: 'How about nipping aboard for a stiff snifter? You can name your own poison. We don't have much in the way of personal comforts, but I always make sure we've got a well stocked bar.'

'I've got two badly injured soldiers who need to be transferred,' Keith said sharply. 'Would it be asking too much, sir, if we got them aboard your ship before you push the bloody boat out?'

The RNR lieutenant was suitably chastened. 'Jesus, I'm sorry, Sergeant. You must think I'm a callous sod.'

'No, sir – just a different sense of priorities.'

Willing hands passed the two injured men over the gunwales.

Entwistle was full of contrition. 'Put them in the messdeck and make them comfortable. Tell them we'll have them back home in two shakes of a donkey's tail.'

The approaching dawn was tinting the cliffs encircling the fjord with a cyclamen pink. As daylight increased, Svenson said with mounting apprehension: 'We should move before it is fully light.'

Entwistle slapped him on the back. 'Not to worry, squire, nothing to get in a muck sweat over.' He led him to the side of the boat. 'Peep over and have a look.'

Svenson did so, and saw that the hull and bridge of the fishing boat were painted a gleaming white.

'We're not exactly strangers to these parts, Mr Svenson. We've learned how to hole up and remain invisible in daylight – like a white hare in the snow, you might say. And at sea, from a distance, we're often mistaken for an ice floe. Still, we're better off waiting till it's dark.'

When the two injured men had been safely transferred and made comfortable in the warm, dry and fresh-smelling mess deck, Entwistle said: 'Now let's retire to the wardroom and fill our boots. It's not, I hasten to add, a real wardroom, it's a poky cabin, but I call it that just to remind myself that I'm part of His Majesty's Royal Navy.' He sighed like a man who has adjusted himself to life's unfairness. 'When war started I had visions of myself pacing the quarter deck of a battleship with a telescope under my arm, thinking of the next pink gin; instead I got this tub which hasn't even got a quarter deck. Someone discovered that I fished these waters and knew them like the back of my hand, so I was given the job of running agents back and forth to Norway.' The cabin was indeed small and spartan, but it contained a comfortable looking bunk, two chairs, and a bulkhead picture of the King and Queen.

Entwistle looked at the strained and exhausted faces of the people he had rescued. 'Find a spot to park yourselves. The young lady can sit at the captain's table.' He chuckled at his own feeble joke.

238

'Jenkins!' he bellowed at the top of his voice, and a rating appeared as if from nowhere.

'You called, sir?'

'Fetch some glasses, and give everybody what they want.'

The rating glanced at Bennett and Temple. '*Everyone,* sir? As I keep reminding you, sir, this is a wardroom.'

'As some sage once remarked, Jenkins, we're all in the same boat – so if you can forget your inbred snobbishness for one minute, give them a drink. If you can't, we'll grant them instant commissions.'

When the steward had scuttled off to get extra glasses, Entwistle winked. 'He worked in the Trocadero before the war and likes to keep the classes in their proper places. Me, I was a Grimsby skipper, I didn't give a monkey's who I supped and dined with, just so long as I could be back first with the biggest haul and command the highest price. Jenkins tries his best to reform me: an officer must be a gentleman. He's been so bloody subservient all his working life he doesn't salute, he touches his forelock!'

Keith warmed to Entwistle immediately; he would have made a good sergeant.

Jenkins, with an obvious but unexpressed air of disapproval, served whatever drinks were requested, but Keith noticed that Bennett and Temple were the last to be served. He thought: Most men I know would be grateful to serve under an officer as unorthodox as Entwistle, but Jenkins feels let down. He felt sorry for the man. But his sympathy quickly disappeared when he stretched out his legs on the rather threadbare carpet only to find Jenkins lifted them immediately to place an ancient newspaper under his boots.

Later as darkness settled round the boat like a comforting blanket, Entwistle gave orders for the boat to proceed to sea. Keith stood in the wheelhouse beside him, thinking how much more efficient it was compared to Storstein's trawler. There was a helmsman at the wheel, a rating by the engine room telegraph, another crouched over the Asdic, and yet another in a small cabin aft of the wheelhouse listening intently to a wireless set.

'This,' said Entwistle, 'is not, as you might have suspected, an ordinary run-of-the-mill fishing boat. We're something special. My Lords Commissioners of the Admiralty could have built a destroyer for what it cost to fit out this tub.' His pride was evident.

An hour passed without either of them speaking and Keith went to the mess deck to see how Mappin and Luck were; finding them both sound asleep, he went in search of Christina. But she too was sleeping, so he returned to the wheelhouse, just in time to hear the Asdic operator announce: 'Clear echo to port, sir. Loud and clear, and approaching fast.'

'Goodie, goodie,' said Entwistle, much to Keith's surprise, and rubbed his hands together like a miser who has just counted his gold. 'Twenty minutes to dawn,' he said, glancing at the chronometer on the bulkhead. 'Poor bastard couldn't have timed it better.'

A white cone of light probed the sullen darkness, illuminating the boat in a circle of dazzling white. A signal lamp flashed. 'Tell me what he wants, Bunts,' Entwistle said calmly.

'He's asking us to identify ourselves, sir.'

'Send him our registered number,' said Entwistle casually, 'and tell him we're fishing in approved waters and my papers are in order.'

An Aldis flashed brightly. 'Seems he's not satisfied sir,' the signalman called out. 'Says we're well beyond the approved limits.'

'Tell him I must have strayed off course and will remedy it immediately at first light when I'm able to take a fix and establish my exact position. Express my sincere apologies, and give my undying allegiance to the Führer.'

The signal lamp on the trawler winked a seemingly endless series of dots and dashes and the signalman read the response with obvious relief. 'Message received and understood, sir. He will be standing by.'

'Stupid bastard,' said Entwistle, much to Keith's surprise.

'What'll you do, sir? Make a run for it?'

'At ten knots top whack? You must be joking. When daylight comes I think you'll find we've got an E-boat sitting on our tail. She's capable of forty knots, so there's not a lot of point in trying to shake her off, is there?'

240

Keith nodded dumbly. 'I'll get my two fit men to stand by with their weapons. Might as well put up some kind of show, sir.'

Entwistle seemed remarkably unconcerned. 'If it'll make you feel a bit happier, Sergeant, by all means go ahead, but I don't think it'll contribute much to the final outcome.'

Don't tell me he's one of those crazy Navy bastards who can't think of anything but going down with his ship! Keith thought.

Entwistle glanced at the brass chronometer on the bulkhead. 'Do me a favour, Sergeant, and tell your Norwegians to remain below and not to panic if they hear a bit of gunfire. No point in exposing them to needless injury.'

Keith returned to the wheelhouse after delivering the message and was surprised to see that Entwistle had replaced his reefer jacket and peaked cap with a grimy anorak and woollen bonnet. 'Might have to parley with the Kraut,' he said by way of explanation.

Dawn came with unexpected abruptness, and Keith, peering out of one of the portholes, saw a sleek grey shape cruising steadily about two miles astern of the fishing boat. It looked menacingly lethal. He picked up a pair of binoculars dangling from the compass binnacle and focused them on the distant vessel.

'Don't bother to check,' Entwistle said. 'It's an E-boat, all right.'

'I'd still like to see what we're up against.'

Keith scanned the E-boat from bow to stern. A German ensign fluttered boldly from a jackstaff aft, and he could clearly see the figures of seamen hunched around an assortment of 40 and 20mm cannons. Forward were four enormous torpedo tubes, each containing a 'tin fish' capable of sinking the biggest ship. On the open bridge was the captain, wearing a white-topped cap set at a rakish angle, accompanied by two other officers and some ratings. Aft of the bridge was a manned machine gun. He whistled silently to himself. *I hope Entwistle can parley convincingly*, he thought, *otherwise we'll be blown out of the water in less time than it takes to say Kamerad.*

Suddenly the E-boat increased speed and roared towards the fishing boat. Her bows rose high out of the water, sending up great plumes of foam. The roar of her powerful engines was deafening. As she passed abeam she slowed down, and Keith saw the commanding officer put a megaphone to his mouth. The amplified voice echoed across the space separating the two boats telling them in impeccable Norwegian to 'Heave to'.

Entwistle turned to the Norwegian seaman who had been summoned to the wheelhouse. 'Nip out and see what he wants.'

The Norwegian went out and listened, then repeated what he had heard. 'He's going to lower a boat and send a boarding party to inspect us. He warns that he will sink us if we do not co-operate fully.'

Entwistle opened the wheelhouse door and tossed down a trumpet-shaped megaphone. 'Tell him he's welcome to search me – I've nothing to hide. Ask him if he's partial to fresh cod because I've got a hold full of the stuff.'

The seaman repeated the message and passed back the reply to Entwistle. 'He says thank you for the offer which he readily accepts. He will do his utmost to inconvenience you as little as possible.'

A bloody silly game if you ask me, Keith thought. What's going to happen when they come aboard and find British soldiers and a cargo of bullion? We'll fight to the end, but it'll be a bit one-sided. As soon as the German captain hears the gunfire he'll sink us, and the whole venture will have been a waste of time and lives.

Through the binoculars he saw men on the E-boat preparing to lower a boat, whilst a party of seamen, all carrying sub-machine guns, stood on the upper deck waiting to board. He also noticed that, despite the friendly exchanges, the E-boat's guns were trained on the fishing boat. At such close range it would be impossible for them to miss. In order to lower the boat the E-boat had reduced speed until it was almost at a standstill, bobbing up and down like a cork.

Entwistle's right thumb pressed down hard on a button on the bulkhead. The clamour of the bell shrilled loudly throughout the boat, and at the same time Entwistle shouted: 'Bunts, hoist the White Ensign!'

The signalman bounded out of the wheelhouse and hauled down the Norwegian flag, replacing it with the White Ensign.

Keith took his eyes off the E-boat and peered down at the deck below where men were squirming snake-like on their bellies across the deck. Four of them lifted the tops off big oil drums lashed to the deck and scrambled inside. He saw they were lined with concrete and contained twin Lewis guns which were raised by a system of counterweights. Four Norwegians emerged on the fo'c'sle and removed the tarpaulin cover on the harpoon gun to reveal a twelve-pounder cannon. Two other men, lying flat on their stomachs, removed planks from the decking and lifted out heavy machine guns, thrusting the muzzles through concealed firing slits in the gunwales.

Entwistle poked his head out of the wheelhouse. 'Open fire! Blow the bastard out of the water!'

There was an ear-shattering crescendo as the guns opened fire simultaneously. At such close range the E-boat was as vulnerable as a sitting partridge. A shell from the fo'c'sle gun took away the E-boat's mainmast which toppled onto the deck in a tangle of wires, while machine gun bullets thudded into the hull and raked the upper deck. Figures toppled into the sea like broken marionettes. A siren blared from the E-boat's bridge, and the boarding party was left stranded as the engines roared into life and the boat sped off, bows high out of the water, as it sought to evade the curtain of steel that continued to thud into the hull.

Entwistle smiled grimly. 'Maybe not Queensbury Rules, Sergeant, but bloody effective. See why I wasn't too impressed by your offer of supporting fire?' As he spoke he removed his anorak and bonnet and put on his uniform jacket and cap. 'Better look like what we are: the Royal Navy.'

Keith watched and thought: Some purists with outmoded ideas about chivalry in battle would be appalled, but I'm not. If we try to fight Germany on equal terms we haven't got a dog's chance – this is the way to cripple the bastards. And the thought occurred to him that Entwistle's boat was really no more than the navy's equivalent of the Commandos.

The E-boat turned sharply and came in fast, bows on to the fishing boat to minimize the size of the target. Red flames flickered from the muzzles of her cannons as they opened fire, and the machine guns followed with a rat-a-tat-tat of long bursts of fire. Keith was amazed at the accuracy of their fire in view of the damage that had been inflicted. The heavier guns gouged great chunks out of the fishing boat's gunwales, and the roof of the wheelhouse disappeared with a deafening whoosh. Bullets ploughed deep furrows in the deck, and one of the men firing through the scuppers screamed in agony as machine gun bullets painted a crimson landscape across his chest.

'Don't get jittery, Sergeant,' Entwistle said reassuringly. 'We can absorb more punishment than those bastards can dish out – we've got more armour plating than a ruddy tank.'

The E-boat, Keith guessed, was no more than half a mile away when two large black objects spurted from her bow like swimmers taking a racing dive from the edge of a pool, quickly disappearing from view below the surface of the sea. Seconds later their white track was clearly visible as they sped towards their target.

'Trying to tin-fish us,' said Entwistle. 'Not much hope of that. Target's too small and draught's too shallow.' Even so he gave a crisp order to the helmsman: 'Hard a' starboard,' which brought the bows of the fishing boat head on to the tracks of the approaching torpedoes in order to minimize the size of the target. Keith watched with surprising detachment as they sped harmlessly down both sides of the boat.

The E-boat veered away, creating an enormous bow wave which swept over her upper deck, drenching her crews. Entwistle gave another helm order and the fishing boat swung round so that most of her guns could be brought into action. They hammered out a remorseless tattoo of tracer, armour-piercing and high explosive shells and bullets. Thin wisps of black smoke began to trickle out of the side of the E-boat and it suddenly stopped moving like a wounded man. Then the black smoke turned crimson as tongues of flame licked their way along the hull. Seconds later there was a muffled explosion, and men emerged onto the upper deck struggling into life jackets before releasing the lashings on the life floats. The guns ceased firing as the crew abandoned their posts and formed in orderly groups along the upper deck. Some jumped overboard and started swimming towards the lowered boat containing the boarding party. The E-boat began to settle by the stern until her bows were entirely clear of the water.

244

Entwistle manoeuvred his boat until it was abeam of the stricken vessel less than a hundred yards away, considering it inadvisable to go closer in case of a sudden and violent explosion. He stood at the wheelhouse door and called across to the captain who was still on his bridge. 'Do you speak English?'

The captain, a young man with white-blond hair, was mopping blood away from a deep head wound. 'A little.'

'Good. I will, if you wish, send an open signal giving your position. I'm sorry, but I have no room for survivors.'

'Thank you, but I have already signalled my position. If you did have room aboard your vessel for my crew I would have to decline. You have fought in a below the belt manner. You are a warship masquerading under false colours – that is against the Geneva Convention. One of my officers will inform headquarters of that, and no doubt it will be forwarded to the Führer. This is against the tradition of fighting sailors.' He spoke with typically Prussian arrogance.

'You could not be more right,' said an unruffled Entwistle. 'You might also get him to pass on the message that when your beloved Führer's U-boats stop sinking innocent passenger ships we might have second thoughts about our own illegal activities.'

He wondered why the captain could not personally register his protest instead of delegating it to a junior. But he quickly dismissed it from his mind; he had more important things to worry about.

As he turned to re-enter the wheelhouse, he paused, shouting down to the crew: 'Release as many Carley rafts and life belts as we can spare. Don't want to see the poor buggers drown, although they won't thank me at the Admiralty for leaving anyone alive to report back on our tactics.'

Keith wondered what he would have done had he been in Entwistle's shoes. Was his hatred of the Germans so deep he would willingly have consigned them to a cruel death? He did not know, and was glad he had not been put to the test.

'Full ahead, and don't spare the horses,' Entwistle called to the seaman on the engine room telegraph. 'There's still enough light left for Jerry to send some bombers looking for us – he knows exactly where we are.'

As the fishing boat piled on the speed, Keith looked astern and saw the sea was a mass of bobbing heads as the sailors swam for the safety rafts and life belts. Through his binoculars he could see that the E-boat's bow had risen high out of the water; only part of the bridge was still visible, and upright on it stood the youthful-looking captain, his right hand raised in a rigid salute.

'Daft it may be,' muttered Keith, 'but it takes guts.'

Entwistle heard him and glanced aft in time to see the E-boat disappear. 'Well, that's answered one question that puzzled me,' he said.

'What's that?'

'He was determined to go down with his boat,' Entwistle said. 'That's why he said one of his officers would report me to old Adolf. Stupid sod! I'd want to live long enough to get my own back.'

Keith felt an unexpected wave of sympathy surge through him like an electric shock. It was a terrible way to die – standing saluting on the bridge, waiting for the water to engulf you, then filling your lungs, waiting goodness knows how long before pain and fear ceased to exist. Then he remembered Mappin and Private Luck and hoped the E-boat captain had lived just long enough to experience pain as terrible as frostbite, just long enough to reflect on how precious life was. Even then he would be better off than Mappin, who faced a wheelchair-bound future with ample time to reflect on how different it might have been.

Chapter Seventeen

What little daylight remained passed uneventfully. There was no heart-churning drone of aircraft, nor the sound of the predatory approach of an E-boat or destroyer intent on exacting revenge. The sea was benevolent, the wind no more than a benign Force Four.

Sergeant Keith realized how little sleep he had managed to snatch. The weariness in his limbs made him feel as if lead weights had been attached to them. He turned to Entwistle, who seemed as bright and energetic as when they first met. 'Do you mind if I nip below and get some shut eye, sir?'

'Fill your boots, Sergeant. Know exactly how you feel.'

Keith smiled. 'You don't show it, sir.'

'Don't let looks fool you. When I hit port I'll get as pissed as a pudding, then I'll sleep for twenty-four hours. In order to survive in this lark you've got to adopt a hedgehog mentality. Wide awake half the time, fast asleep the rest. No half measures.'

'Before I turn in, sir, and if it's safe, could you send a signal off asking for an ambulance to await our arrival? Those two men mean a lot to me.'

'I've already sent a signal requesting an aircraft to be standing by. We're berthing in the Shetlands and there're no hospitals there.'

'Thank you, sir.'

'Forget it, Sergeant. I'm a much happier man saving lives than I am taking them. The navy hasn't realized that yet.'

Twilight was approaching as the dark outline of the Shetlands appeared on the distant horizon. The sky was pewter-coloured and the sea as grey and desolate as a funeral cortege. Two hours later a motor gun boat approached at full speed, flashing a message. She was to escort them through the boom.

Once through the boom the fishing boat made her own way to her normal berth; an inlet sheltered by two low-lying humps of bleak and inhospitable land, uninhabited but for a colony of screeching gannets. Entwistle tied up alongside a near-derelict jetty where four similar fishing boats were moored. A lieutenant-commander sporting the straight rings of a 'pusser' officer, stood on the jetty. Standing beside him was a surgeon-lieutenant RNVR carrying a black Gladstone bag, looking for all the world like a GP about to set off on a maternity case.

'Well done, Entwistle,' the two-and-a-half ringer said in clipped tones. 'Quite splendid. You've delivered the golden eggs without losing one. I'm Lieutenant-Commander Lavender-Finch. Been sent up specially from the Admiralty to tell you that.'

Lavender-Finch was in his mid to late forties, and Entwistle knew that anyone of that age who was still a two-and-a-halfer was a passed-over man, no more than a glorified errand boy. Such types were invariably officious and self-opinionated, expecting everyone of lower rank to kiss their arse.

'If you're the best they could rustle up in the way of a welcoming party, I'd rather do without one.'

'See you in the debriefing hut,' the officer said, barely controlling his chagrin. Then he turned on his heel and strode away.

'He'll have your balls for breakfast, talking to him like that, sir,' Keith said.

'Not a chance. He'll swallow his pride and go back and bask in our reflected glory,' Entwistle said sourly. 'Can't exactly report that he had to bollock me for insubordination. Wouldn't go down very well, would it, not with a Press Officer standing by to issue a release about the wonderful coup that has been pulled off right under Jerry's nose, and Downing Street and Whitehall ready to take the credit for the brilliant planning. Couldn't allow some jumped-up prick who's too useless to be given a seagoing appointment to spoil it all by complaining I was rude to him! Would only confirm what a lot

248

of people already know: there are still too many square pegs running this war.' He slapped Keith on the back. 'Let's hear what the sawbones has to say about your injured men, then we'll see about getting them to hospital. Then after the debriefing we'll hang one on.'

The surgeon-lieutenant emerged from below deck. 'The private soldier will be all right after a good long rest,' he said to Entwistle. 'He'll have a bit of trouble learning to balance properly when he walks, but that's all – no gangrene and no infection. The lieutenant is a different kettle of fish.' He paused. 'You realize, of course, that this isn't an expert opinion. I'm not qualified to give one, and I can't be held responsible for any error in my diagnosis. . .'

Keith interrupted him. 'I know that, sir,' he said impatiently. 'Just tell me how bad he is.'

'I think he has a bullet or a piece of shrapnel lodged against his spine. Only an X-ray can confirm that, but there's definitely a considerable degree of paralysis.'

Keith looked at him searchingly, guessing from his age that he had not long been qualified and was desperately aware of it. This was confirmed when the surgeon said: 'I've been flown here from Scapa, Sergeant. My job is simply to keep an eye on your men while they're being transferred to a mainland hospital.'

'What are his chances of getting over the paralysis, sir?'

'Again, I'm not qualified to say. It may be operable, it may not be. It might even dislodge itself. From what I've read of such cases, that's not uncommon.'

'Thank you, sir. I hope you told Lieutenant Mappin that.'

'Well, I didn't as a matter of fact. Didn't want to hold out too much hope – that would be cruel.'

'And my lads?' Entwistle said.

'They got off remarkably lightly, considering what they've been through. Nothing more than cuts and bruises. Can be treated in your sick bay.'

'I'd like you to tell Lavender-Finch they need hospitaliza-. tion. They'll appreciate a trip to the mainland and a few nights on the town.'

Three lorries appeared on the road adjoining the jetty and a party of naval ratings jumped out. The petty officer in charge of the working party saluted Entwistle smartly. 'Orders to unload a highly secret cargo, sir. All very hush-hush, except we know it's gold.'

'It's stowed in the fish hold. For Christ's sake make sure none of our men drop one ingot over the side, because if they do they'll have to live to be one hundred and fifty before they can pay off the debt.'

The PO touched his cap and led his party aboard.

The sound of an ambulance bell was heard clanging in the distance. 'Let's see about getting the wounded ashore,' Entwistle said.

Lieutenant Mappin was fully conscious when Keith went down into the mess deck. Private Luck was grimacing with pain as he tried to fit his bandaged feet into his boots.

'Don't bother with that, Ted. You're going to hospital, where a nice pretty nurse is going to tuck you into a comfy bed with clean sheets, take your temperature and make sure that the most important part of your anatomy didn't get frost bite,' said Keith coarsely. With the assistance of Private Bennett and Lance-Corporal Temple, he carried Luck onto the upper deck and onto the jetty to the canvas-topped ambulance that had just arrived. Then they returned to get Lieutenant Mappin.

Mappin gave a curt nod to Bennett. 'Would you mind awfully waiting on deck till you're called? I've got something private to say to Sergeant Keith.'

Bennett winked in a conspiratorial manner. 'If you was to ask me to go an' dangle me chopper over the side of this 'ere boat in order to feed the seagulls, sir, I'd do it. I ain't met many gents in my time, an' not many orfficers wot is entitled to be called that, but you fit bof bills, sir, an' I ain't overdoin' it.' Then, embarrassed by his own volubility, he clambered up the ladder.

'Harry, you'll be going back to Scapa to collect our personal belongings?' Mappin said.

Keith nodded. 'Correct, sir.'

'Remember that Wren officer in the depot ship?' Keith again nodded. 'She'll ask about me, Harry. I want you to tell her I didn't make it back.'

'Why's that, sir?'

'Well, we had a kind of agreement. One that was pretty binding; it would have tied her to me for the rest of our lives. But she's too young to be lumbered with an invalid. She'll soon forget and make a fresh start.'

'I remember her, sir,' Keith said. 'Very attractive girl.'

'She is beautiful. It was, as that ghastly woman who writes all those romances is fond of saying, love at first sight.'

'You sure you want me to lie to her, sir?'

'Positive, Harry. I've had no feeling in my legs since I was hit, and I've read enough to know it's a million to one chance that I'll ever walk again. What do they call such cases – paraplegics?'

'Wouldn't know, sir. But I do know modern surgery can work miracles.'

'Not in my case. I don't need a surgeon to confirm it – I just *know*. Anyway, I could tell from the navy doctor's face that he didn't hold out much hope.'

'He's still wet behind the ears, sir, probably never seen a war wound before.'

'I can't take the risk Harry. It wouldn't be fair to Hazel.'

'There's plenty of women who'd put up with almost anything in order to share what you can offer, sir.'

'Meaning?'

'Colonel Rutherford told me all about you, sir, and made me promise not to let on to anyone that I knew because that was the way you wanted it. I respected you all the more for that.'

'You're talking about material things. In time she would want children; supposing I can't give them to her? I'd be forced to watch her become bitter and disillusioned. No, thank you. Now let's drop the subject. When I have to make my report, Harry, I'm going to recommend you for an award. I'll get one as a matter of course, not because I deserve it but because that's the way they do things. But you know as well as I do that none of us would have come through this without you.'

'Sir, you'll be doing me a real personal favour if you don't recommend me for anything. I'd feel ashamed accepting it, 'cos I did it for all the wrong reasons.'

'Come off it, Harry! Don't play the modest hero with me.'

'Quite frankly, sir, I didn't give tuppence for the gold, and I cared even less about what it meant to freedom-loving Norway. I just wanted the chance to get a little of my own back – well, I did that, and that's medal enough for me.'

'All right, I'll do as you wish, but only on one condition. That you'll tell Third Officer Payne what I've asked you to.'

Keith grasped Mappin's hand and shook it warmly. 'That's a deal, sir.' With the assistance of Bennett and Temple he carried him to the waiting ambulance.

'I don't suppose the army will have much use for a soldier who can't march properly, Harry,' Private Luck said ruefully.

'Never you mind, lad, there's always room on Forces Entertainment for lads with your talent. Maybe not that highbrow stuff you like to play, so you'll have to lower your sights and become another Charlie Kunz till it's all over.'

'I'll happily do that, but I'll still see you at the Albert Hall one day.'

Keith held up a thumb. 'You can say that again!'

He watched as the ambulance disappeared into the distance and thought: That's two promises I have to keep.

A twin-engined Avro Anson bomber which had been converted into a flying ambulance was waiting on the tarmac of a make-shift airfield, bulldozed into relative flatness with strips of heavy metal mesh laid down to provide the base for a runway.

Mappin, Luck and the other wounded crew members of the fishing boat were taken aboard and carefully laid on stretchers secured to the deck. As soon as they were strapped into position the engines fired into life and the aircraft took off, skimming the tops of the few sparsely leafed trees that lined the perimeter of the airfield, and heading for the Scottish mainland. Keith and the two soldiers watched as it soared over their heads, and stood there waving until it disappeared from view.

'Some of the Norwegians and sailors from the boat 'ave asked us to their mess for big eats an' a booze-up in their wet canteen, Sarge,' Bennett said. 'All right wiv you if we go?'

'Of course. Have a good time.'

'What'll you do?' Temple asked.

252

'I'd much rather join you, but Lieutenant Entwistle has invited me back to his quarters. He's laid on a meal and drinks for me and the Norwegians: can't very well refuse.'

The debriefing lasted less than an hour, prompting Entwistle to remark aloud: 'Well, it was brief, if nothing else.'

Lavender-Finch had been taking copious notes. 'I'm just jotting down the bare bones, he replied, irritated. 'Later, Lieutenant, you'll have to submit a more detailed, written report, as will the sergeant. I need just enough for a Press release, I'm not expected to write a ruddy book. For obvious reasons, no names will be mentioned, but I expect the hacks from Grub Street will have a field day.'

Entwistle's quarters were in a Nissen hut a short distance from the small shore base which housed the officers and ratings who crewed and maintained the clandestine fleet of fishing boats. It was surprisingly well equipped with an assortment of comfortable armchairs. A single bed stood at one end and in the centre was a stove. A table with a spotless cloth on it was laid for dinner with sparkling glasses and a full set of cutlery at each place.

Svenson and the Norwegian skipper Storstein, who occupied two of the armchairs, were nursing large tumblers of whisky. Christina was sitting in another and she rose when Keith came in. 'You sit here, Harry. I'll perch on the arm.'

As she made way for him, he noticed that she had found time to wash and brush her hair, and was conscious of his own dishevelled appearance.

Entwistle had changed into a pair of clean grey flannel trousers, a white shirt and blue blazer and looked quite the dapper host. 'Name your poison, Sergeant. I've got everything.'

Keith was loath to leave the armchair, conscious of the girl's close proximity and the warmth of her body resting against his, but he was also aware that he reeked of sweat. 'I'd like a really stiff Scotch, sir, but first I wouldn't mind cleaning up a bit.'

Entwistle gestured to a second door at the far end of the hut. 'You'll find a bathroom through there.'

When he had washed the grime away and shaved, he returned to his chair and was glad to see Christina was still perched on the arm.'

'I could have taken you all down to the wardroom,' Entwistle said as he handed him his drink. 'It's all pretty slapdash here, Sergeant, and no one gives a toss about non-commissioned ranks being there, but that stroppy two-and-a-halfer will be there and he's enough to put a dampener on any evening.'

Keith had little opportunity to engage Christina in any personal conversation, but during one slight pause in the general chatter he managed to say: 'Tomorrow, if you haven't anything better to do, perhaps you and I could do a little exploring. From the little I've read about this place it can be very beautiful at this time of year.'

'I'd like that very much, Harry.'

'That's a date, then,' he said happily, thinking: I'll tell her I'd like to see a lot more of her. I'm bound to get a spot of leave and she won't have much else to do.

Entwistle's steward had certainly not forgotten his years at the Trocadero. He served up a meal that would have met with the approval of his former employers, and after a final nightcap Entwistle announced that it was time to break up the party.

'I've arranged accommodation at the base, so when you're ready I'll lead the way.' He took Keith aside. 'You can kip in my bed, Sergeant. I'll borrow a bunk for the night in the wardroom annexe. Thought you'd prefer that to the Petty Officers' mess.'

Keith thanked him. 'Mind if I walk down with you?'

'Of course not. When you get back here, treat it as your own – help yourself to anything you need. You'll find a pair of clean pyjamas in the top of the chest of drawers.'

Entwistle led the party down the narrow unlit road towards the base, lighting the path with the pencil beam of a blacked-out torch.

Keith linked arms with Christina who rested her head on his shoulder. 'That was one of the most enjoyable evenings I can remember,' she said. 'Now I'll sleep like a top.' She laughed gaily. 'I wonder why we say that? Do tops sleep particularly well, Harry?'

'I always thought it was a log.'

'No, I distinctly remember my father saying "top".'

254

He realized she had stopped and turned her face to his. 'Would you kiss me, Harry? That'd be the perfect ending to the party.'

Her lips were warm and slightly dry against his, and he felt her tongue gently probing into his mouth. As his own lips parted in response it moved inside like a darting flame of passion. He felt himself growing hard and moved away, but she drew him closer. 'Tomorrow, Harry, we'll make love properly.'

'Sure you want to?' he asked hesitantly.

'Of course. You may not be too pleased at the news, but I've fallen in love with you.'

'I'm pleased all right! That's exactly how I feel.'

They reached the entrance to the shore base where an armed sentry paced up and down like a caged animal. He stopped and called out: 'Halt, who goes there?'

'Lieutenant Entwistle and party reporting aboard,' Entwistle said. 'And don't ask me what the password is because I don't ruddy well know.'

The sentry laughed. 'Pass friend – all's well.'

Keith held Christina until the others had passed through the barrier, then kissed her passionately. 'See you in the morning. Say about eleven o'clock because you'll need a good night's sleep.'

'Till then, my darling.'

Entwistle came back and handed him the torch. 'Find your way back on your own all right, Sergeant? If not, I'll come with you.'

'No need to, sir. I've got rather used to moving around in the pitch dark.'

Keith whistled as he walked back down the narrow road. The knowledge that he had at last found something to love other than the regiment made him forget his tiredness and put a youthful spring into his step.

Entwistle's steward woke him next morning with a steaming cup of strong tea. 'Eggs, bacon, fried bread and tram smash do you for breakfast?'

'The first three sound good, but I'm not sure I like the sound of tram smash.'

'Tinned tomatoes. Coffee or tea?'

'Coffee. You know, that's something they've still to hear of in the army.'

He shaved as he luxuriated in a hot bath, then asked Jenkins if there was such a thing as an iron around. 'I'd rather like to clean and press my battle dress and make myself a little more presentable, although there's not a lot I can do about my boots.'

'What size do you take, Sergeant?'

'Nines.'

'You're in luck – same as me. I've got a gash pair you can have. And don't worry about your clobber, I'll clean it. I'm a dab hand when it comes to playing the housewife. Need to be with the lieutenant to look after. He can't do a thing for himself.'

Keith looked down at his creased and pressed blouse and trousers and thought: It might not pass muster at Aldershot, but it's a damn sight better than it was. He thanked the steward for his help and kindness, and walked down to the shore base. He halted at the barricade. 'Sergeant Keith for Miss Ross,' he said to the sentry. 'She's expecting me.'

'So am I, Sergeant. You're to report to the Master at Arms office. I'll get someone to take you.'

A gaitered rating with a thick cudgel dangling from his wrist by a leather strap, led him to the office where the Master at Arms, without bothering to look up from his desk, said: 'Take him to the wardroom.' Keith wondered why there was any need for so much security when all he intended doing was spend the day strolling over the island with, and hopefully making love to, a beautiful woman.

As soon as he entered the wardroom lounge he realized from the glum expression on Christina's face that something was amiss. She looked, as Bennett would have said, like someone who had lost a quid and found a tanner. She got up and walked across to Harry and grasped his hands. 'Harry! I was so looking forward to it.'

Entwistle, he noticed, was wearing his best uniform and looking every bit as grim as the girl. Only Svenson and Storstein were smiling.

Lavender-Finch, looking like a Gieves display advertisement, said brusquely: 'There's been a sudden alteration to

256

plans. I've spoken to the Admiralty on the telephone, and it seems Downing Street wants to make a lot more of the incident. The gold and its gallant Norwegian rescuers are sailing for Scotland as soon as the bullion is reloaded aboard Lieutenant Entwistle's boat. From Scotland the bullion will be transported by rail to London. The Bank of England insists there should be no delay: apparently a warship is preparing to leave Portsmouth for Canada with some of our own gold, and there seems no point in not killing two birds with one stone.'

'Typical Whitehall cock-up, Sergeant,' Entwistle murmured out of the side of his mouth. 'Take it off my boat, then put it straight back aboard.'

'If you've got something to say, Entwistle, speak up. Don't mumble,' the Lieutenant-Commander said snappily.

'Simply explaining to the Sergeant, sir, that the whole operation seems to be being conducted with typical Whitehall thoroughness.'

Lavender-Finch gave a thin smile. 'Thank you, Lieutenant. I'm glad you give me credit for some things.'

'Always believe in giving credit where it's due.' He knew Lavender-Finch had had no hand in the switch of plans and was just carrying out orders.

The two-and-a-halfer turned to Keith. 'Well, that's all Sergeant. You're dismissed.'

'What about me and my men, sir?'

'You report back to Scapa, of course.'

'How do we set about doing that, sir?'

The officer sounded bored. 'I suppose someone here will find space aboard the next supply boat that's going to Scapa Flow. If not, you'll have to make your own way there. I've been led to believe that initiative is one of the prime requirements of a Commando.'

'We'll cope, sir,' Keith said stiffly. 'Thanks for your interest in our welfare.'

'I'm not a wet nurse, Sergeant, and stop being so ruddy petulant. There's a war on, remember.'

'Sorry. I tend to forget that, sir.'

'I'll fix up something, Sergeant,' Entwistle said. 'You won't have to swim.'

'That's it then. See that everyone is down on the jetty in an hour – time and tide wait for no man.' And with those parting words Lavender-Finch walked out of the wardroom.

Entwistle watched his retreating figure. 'When I meet pricks like that I realize my number here isn't so bad. Imagine having to serve afloat with someone like that, Sergeant!'

The girl came up to him. 'He didn't tell you, Harry, that the real reason for the hurry is that King Haakon has expressed a wish to personally meet us in London. He wants to honour us for what we've done.'

'And that,' said Entwistle with obvious disgust, 'is why we're being mucked about. The waiting warship is a load of bilge. Photographs of King Haakon dishing out gongs is too good an opportunity to miss. The outside world will know that Hitler can't ride roughshod over little people and get away with it.'

'I asked Olav if he couldn't get it postponed for twenty four hours,' Christina said plaintively. 'I said that having a little time alone with you meant more to me than any medal. But he wouldn't hear of it. He can't wait for the world to know that Norway is still in the war.'

'You can't blame him for that,' Keith said. 'He's a patriot first and foremost, he's not doing it for personal glorification.'

'I know that,' she said mournfully, 'but would one day have made all that much difference? And why didn't they let you come with us? The King owes as much to you as he does to us.'

'The people who plan these things don't always think the same way as we do. Perhaps someone in Whitehall thought the world didn't need reminding that Britain was at war – can't have us stealing the limelight.'

'You're bitter, Harry, and I can't blame you for that.'

'When we report back we're bound to get a spot of leave,' Keith said. 'Is there somewhere I can get in touch with you?'

'The Foreign Office will be able to give you an address for my parents. I don't have one; I wasn't allowed to write or receive letters. But I can write to you.'

'That's not without its problems either. Although I'm a Commando now, I'm still on the payroll of my old regiment. I'll give you the address of regimental headquarters and perhaps they'll forward any letter on to me, but it may take a heck of a time and my leave could be over by then.'

258

Entwistle nudged his elbow. 'Sorry, Sergeant, we haven't much time. Better make your farewells.'

He embraced Christina, but refrained from being more demonstrative, aware of the eyes of the other people in the room.

He walked over to Svenson and Storstein and held out his hand. 'It's been a privilege knowing you.'

'Without you the gold would still be in Norway,' Svenson said.

'I've told slops to make sure your lads can draw anything they need till they get back to base,' said Entwistle. 'Boots, clean underwear and socks: you name it, they'll get it. I've told them to put it down to me.'

Keith shook his hand. 'Thanks a lot, sir, they'll appreciate that.'

'Just report to the Master at Arms. I've had a word with him and he'll let you know when a boat of any kind is leaving for Scapa. meanwhile, the three of you can use my hut. Jenkins will do his nut, but he won't risk falling foul of me.'

'Keep your feet dry, sir.'

Keith walked down to the mess where the two soldiers had spent the night, finding them bleary-eyed but cheerful after a night of revelry.

'Have a good time, lads?' He smiled. 'A pointless question – I can see you did.'

'A whale of a time, Sergeant,' Temple said. 'Plenty to eat and as much as we could drink. But even better, the Norwegians here moaned they had so much money and nothing to spend it on! I just couldn't resist suggesting a card school.'

Bennett extended a foot enclosed in a shiny new boot. 'That lieutenant bloke said we could get wot clobber we wanted from wot they call slops, an' 'e'd pick up the tab. But there wan't no need for that, Reg 'ere was able to pay. 'E was rollin' in bees an' 'oney!'

Chapter Eighteen

The three Commandos arrived in Kirkwall in total darkness. Keith announced it was too late to try and get out to the depot ship so they had better set about finding digs for the night.

'In that case,' said Temple, 'we'll pop along to old man Ferguson. He said we'd always find "welcome" written on the mat if we were around these parts.' He winked lewdly. 'And we got the same message from his daughters.'

'I'll try Mrs McIntosh,' said Keith. 'She told me pretty much the same thing. See you down on the jetty about nine in the morning.'

As the navy pinnace approached the depot ship, Keith stood on the bow scanning the submarines moored alongside hoping to get a glimpse of *Otter*. They all looked alike to him – sea-battered and anonymous.

He clambered slowly and awkwardly up the steep slanting gangway on the ship's side and reported to the duty officer. 'We've got some personal belongings to collect, sir: our own and those of the lads who didn't make it back. We've also got some Tommy-guns to return.'

'Brigadier Howarth said he was to be told immediately you reported aboard,' the officer said.

A rating was detailed to take them to the cabin where they found Howarth, immaculate as ever, reading a thriller. He jumped up when they entered. 'Congratulations, lads!' he cried. 'Far exceeded our wildest dreams. I was informed immediately the news came through that you'd pulled it off, and by rights I should have headed straight back to London –

seems I was considered to have done my bit and that was the end of it. But I was determined to hang on and thank you personally. No one bothered to give me the details, the gold was all that mattered, so you'd better fill me in, Sergeant.' He produced a bottle. 'Not too early?'

'Never is, sir.'

The Commandos sat around the small table drinking their whiskies, and Keith told him about the operations, the deaths of Warren and Foster, the serious injury of Lieutenant Mappin and the grisly contribution Private Buchanan had made to the success of the operation.

'What about *Otter*, sir?'

'Didn't make it back, I'm afraid. The last we heard from her was a signal saying she was heading for home – then nothing.'

Keith felt a sudden emptiness. Just how much were bars of gold worth in terms of human life? They could certainly purchase arms and equipment for the Norwegian freedom fighters, but they could not replace one soldier or sailor.

The Brigadier read his thoughts. 'The value couldn't be measured in a tangible form, Sergeant. The newspapers here were full of it, and that's bound to boost morale when it's at a low ebb. Added to that, Jerry knows we're still capable of hitting him without warning where it hurts. They'll be forced to maintain extra vigilance in every country they've occupied, because they'll never know where the next blow will land.'

'You may be right, sir,' Temple said, 'but I didn't notice anyone falling over backwards to say what a good job we'd done.'

'You got a mention, Lance-Corporal: not an enormous one, but you weren't entirely ignored.' He paused and added solemnly: 'My father was in the last lot. He told me about a disastrous attack at Ypres; half his company was wiped out, but all his commanding officer was interested in was the pack horses. He said they cost ten pounds each, whereas a soldier cost only one shilling. Times haven't changed. The gold was the important item, and the sole purpose of Operation Midas. Now let's see about getting you some food. You must be famished.'

'First I'd like to collect all the personal belongings, sir, and also have a few words with Third Officer Payne.'

'Just collect your own stuff, Sergeant – the rest you can leave to me. I'll sort through it and return what's suitable to the next of kin. As for the girl, you'll have to go to the shore base where she's stationed. she didn't remain aboard: no point, but you should be able to find her without any difficulty.'

'Does she know about Lieutenant Mappin, sir?'

Howarth shook his head. 'No reason to inform her. She's not listed as next of kin.'

'That's one piece of news I'm pleased to hear, sir.'

Howarth looked bemused. 'Was she expecting to be told?'

'They'd got rather friendly, sir.'

'Not too much, I hope,' he said sympathetically. 'He sounds in a pretty bad way. When that kind of thing happens, women tend to think they're honour-bound to stick with them.'

'That's what the Lieutenant is anxious to avoid, sir.'

'Sensible chap! Harsh as it may sound, it's cruel to saddle a young woman with someone who could turn out to be a total invalid. Sympathy isn't a good basis for marriage.'

Keith walked to the shore base immersed in thought. The meeting with the Brigadier had not been at all what he had expected. Instead of being told he and his two comrades would be sent on leave, he had said they would have to make their way to Aldershot where they would be rekitted. From there they would go to Salisbury Plain and report to a new Commando unit which was being formed and trained for a special operation.

'I've arranged for you to collect some money from the pay office here – enough to provide you with digs and a few extras. I'd have liked to have sent you down by Pullman, but rules are rules. That's the way Commandos have to operate: initiative and enterprise. I'd have thought you've displayed enough of that to warrant a rail pass, but I was told there'd be no exceptions.'

Keith had grinned. 'We'll be there dead on time, sir.'

'It may be some consolation, Sergeant, to know that all the Commandos involved in Midas are to be recommended for an award.'

'With all respects, sir, you can scrub my name.'

'You don't have any say in the matter, Sergeant. I've been told to submit the names, and the King will do the rest. If you feel like telling him what to do with his gong you can – but I wouldn't if I were you, not unless you want to see the war out in one of the army's glasshouses.'

He had saluted and replied cheekily: 'After Norway, sir, I'm not so sure that's such a daunting proposition!'

He arrived at the barrier outside the shore base and asked to see Third Officer Payne, and the sentry said he would send someone to fetch her.

She came striding down the main drive of the base, her arms swinging, her head held well back. He recognised her immediately and felt a deep stab of guilt when he thought how wickedly he was going to deceive her. He had no need to introduce himself for she recognized him immediately. 'Sergeant Keith! How wonderful to see you.' Then she looked bewildered, and the smile disappeared from her mouth and eyes. 'Where's Lieutenant Mappin?'

'That's what I called to talk to you about.'

He could see that she sensed that something was wrong; her voice became harsh and matter-of-fact. 'We can't speak here. Let's go to the little guest house William and I got to know so well.'

As they walked towards Mrs. Moray's house, she said unexpectedly: 'It's bad news, isn't it?'

'I'm afraid so, but let's wait till we're somewhere more comfortable. I don't want to break the news in the middle of the street.'

'I knew something was wrong as soon as I got over the surprise of seeing you,' she said, quite calmly. 'If William had been all right he would have come himself.'

They remained silent until they reached the familiar house where a cardboard sign in one of the front windows said: 'Vacancies'. Hazel rang the bell and after the briefest of delays the front door opened to reveal Mrs Moray. If she thought that the young woman on the doorstep had transferred her affections rather quickly, there was no suggestion of it in her face or voice. 'Come in, my dear! I've been so hoping you'd pay me another visit.'

Hazel stepped inside. 'This is Sergeant Keith, a very close friend of Lieutenant Mappin. We were looking for some-where we could have a private chat, and I suddenly thought of here.'

Mrs Moray nodded to Keith. 'Go into the lounge and make yourselves comfortable. You'll be alone there. I'll put the kettle on for a pot of tea, then you can talk to your heart's content.'

Hazel removed her Dick Turpin hat, smoothed her hair, and sat down in one of the armchairs. Keith took one opposite.

'Let's not wait for the tea, Sergeant. I'd like to get it over and done with. He's dead, isn't he?'

'I'm afraid so,' Keith said. He felt a stab of shame as the lie came so glibly to his lips. Then he repeated the words he had rehearsed a dozen or more times in his mind. 'It was instant. He didn't suffer.'

He saw her lower her head and search the cuff of her uniform jacket for a handkerchief. Then her body shook with uncontrollable sobs, and she let out a low keening cry that was heart-stopping in its intensity.

He was relieved when Mrs Moray came in with a tray holding the tea and a plateful of scones. When she saw the girl's obvious anguish she put them on a table and sat beside her, drawing her close to her ample bosom. 'Oh, you poor wee thing. It's the Lieutenant, isn't it?' Hazel nodded dumbly, and continued to sob, dabbing at her eyes with the crumpled handkerchief.

'Just you have a good weep and don't mind me. I know just how you feel. I felt the same way when they told me my man was gone.'

Hazel wiped her eyes and blew her nose loudly. 'I'm sorry, Mrs Moray, I didn't know.'

'*The Royal Oak*, right on our doorstep.' She cradled the young Wren in her arms and rocked her gently to and fro. 'Now just you carry on crying – I know I did, for weeks. And don't let anyone try to tell you that time heals all things. It doesn't, and you'll be grateful it doesn't because when you've been lucky enough to find the right man you don't want to forget him.' She patted Hazel's hands and poured the tea.

'I told her he didn't suffer,' Keith said awkwardly. 'That's some consolation. better than ending up a helpless cripple.'

Mrs Moray's voice was crisp with anger. 'Perhaps from a man's point of view: certainly not a woman's. I'd give the world just to have my husband sitting where you are. Just to be able to hear his voice and hold his hand would be enough. It wouldn't be a burden but a pleasure. Men can never see that, though.'

Hazel looked up. 'You know, William and I once talked about young women being saddled with a crippled husband. He was strongly opposed to it – one should never let pity override common sense, he said. I thought he was talking rubbish; you shouldn't confuse love with sympathy. Right now I'd give anything to prove it.'

Keith was shocked at the intensity of her feelings. 'Would you mind leaving us for a few minutes, Mrs Moray?' he asked. 'I've got to leave shortly and there's something personal I have to say to Miss Payne.'

When she had left the room he turned to Hazel. 'Mappin made me promise to tell you he was dead. Well, he isn't. He's badly injured, perhaps crippled for life. But after what you've said, I couldn't let you go on believing the worst. Apart from that, I don't like lying. Anyway, I'd always be asking myself if I'd done the right thing. He may not want to see you again, but after listening to you and Mrs Moray I think you're entitled to some say in your own future.'

'Thank you, Harry. Thank you for being honest. I'll think carefully about it once the shock has worn off. Maybe I'll see it his way, but I don't think so.'

'I hope you do. That's what he wants.'

'We don't always get what we want, Harry. I think I'll want to have a say in things.'

He shook hands formally and walked out of the house, feeling sad and bewildered, wondering if he had done the right thing by breaking his promise to Mappin. He bought a bottle of whisky at an off licence, and when he got back to his billet he drank himself to sleep.

Keith met Temple and Bennett early next morning, and they set off for Aldershot. As they walked to the ferry point,

266

Bennett said: 'Pity we gotta leave this place, Sarge. We're gonna miss those sisters, an' we'll be real lucky if we ever meet up wiv two birds as accommodatin'. Only aim in life is to provide comfort for the troops. Never min', san fairy Ann.'

Temple tut-tutted. 'Bennet, old sport, it's *Ca ne fait rien*,' he said disparagingly.

'That's wot I said, Reg,' said an unperturbed Bennett, ''cept you make it soun' right funny. Ain't that so, Sarge?'

Keith did not answer; he was still thinking about Hazel Payne, hoping that once she had thought things out she would walk out of Mappin's life as casually as Temple and Bennett had walked out of the Ferguson sisters'.

Chapter Nineteen

It took Sergeant Keith and his comrades four days to reach Aldershot and another two to reach the tented camp on Salisbury Plain. But they arrived with buttons shining, webbing freshly blancoed, and their new battle dress perfectly creased. They felt justifiably proud of themselves because they had achieved it without the slightest help from the army.

They were subjected to a rigorous medical before they were passed A1, fit enough to be enrolled in their new unit. For the next few weeks they engaged in a brutal and exhaustive course of training which, they were told, was their preparation for an operation that would have significant impact on the outcome of the war. But what it involved no one was prepared to divulge.

During the training, Keith was told he had been awarded the Military Medal, and Bennett and Temple were to receive the DCM, but there would be no investiture at Buckingham Palace. So many gongs were being dished out that the King only had time personally to present the more outstanding awards for gallantry; theirs, it was stressed, were certainly not in that category. Keith was disappointed about Buckingham Palace – not because he would not meet the monarch, he could not have cared less about that, but a trip to London would have enabled him to find out the whereabouts of Christina's parents.

He had written to the Foreign Office requesting their address and had had a formal acknowledgement of his letter, but nothing else. He had also thought of writing to Lieutenant Mappin, but had always shied away from it at the last minute.

He still wondered if he had done the right thing. Mappin might be furious at his betrayal. Luck, too, he knew would be pleased to hear from him, and he wrote to him care of the War Office but simply had a curt reply saying Luck had been honourably discharged and had left no forwarding address.

The operation, when it was mounted, turned out to be no more than a hit-and-run foray across the Channel into occupied France, the sole object of which was to return with a handful of captured Germans for interrogation, in the faint hope that they might divulge information about Hitler's invasion plans. It was only after the successful completion of the raid that the Commandos were given fourteen days leave.

Keith travelled to Paddington with Bennett and Temple. They arrived in the middle of a particularly heavy air raid and spent the first night of their furlough in a street shelter not far from the station. They did not sleep a wink because of the scream of falling bombs, the rumble of explosions, the continuous crack of the ack-ack guns, and the non-stop singing of some of their fellow occupants.

When they emerged into the morning daylight, they had their first glimpse of the terrible havoc Hitler's bombers were nightly inflicting on the capital and the incredible courage with which Londoners were facing the ordeal. There were great blackened gaps where houses had once stood; others had been neatly sliced in half so that they resembled children's dolls houses. Some fires were still burning, and rescue squads were crawling over piles of rubble seeking survivors. The air was filled with the clamour of bells from ambulances and fire engines. Canvas hoses writhed across roads like giant pythons, and homeless people with dead-looking eyes trudged the streets carrying the few personal belongings they had managed to salvage. But, despite everything, an air of resilience and defiance dominated. There were numerous reminders that nothing Hitler could do would quell Londoners' sense of humour; this was borne out by the variety of crudely painted yet cheerful signs outside blitzed pubs and shops: 'Down but Not Out'; 'Business as Usual'; 'Free Beer – but Mind the Glass'; 'No Looting, Unexploded Bomb'.

Bennett paused outside a pub off Praed Street where the windows were boarded up with planks, and the sign hung lopsided from its support. On the pavement stood a black-board and easel that had once carried chalked-on lunchtime menus, but now bore the message: 'Back in a tick – have a drink on us – but don't pinch the glasses'.

'Bit early, but we surely ain' goin' to look a gift 'orse in the mouf, are we?' said Bennett.

They went into the saloon bar, where the floor was littered with broken glass and ceiling plaster. A solitary male was sitting on a bar stool drinking a pint of Guinness, a white moustache of froth adhering to his upper lip. Perched on the back of his head was a dented bowler hat, giving him the appearance of an out-of-work foreman.

He saw Keith's amused glance and took the hat off. 'Found it in the gutter – bomb blast. Too good to throw away. Fancy a pint on the house?'

They nodded, and he nipped behind the bar and pulled three pints of bitter. He wiped the collar of foam off the top of the glasses with the back of a none too clean hand, and topped them up. 'Landmine landed in the street at the back. Boozer was closed, thank God, but the guvnor's old lady was having a crap at the time and got blown off the throne. Came down screaming blue murder because she got some porcelain stuck in a place which her old man hadn't seen for donkey's years. The guvnor's visiting her now, in St. Mary's across the street. He don't know whether to celebrate or curse the pilot for being such a rotten shot! So here we are then, lads – beer's on the house.'

'Glad to see *you're* making the most of it,' said Bennett.

'Holding the fort till he comes back. Anyway, I haven't missed visiting this dump every day for the past twenty years, and I'm not letting Adolf change the habit of a lifetime. Not much point, is there? Life wouldn't be worth living if you let something like a bomb get you down.'

They drank their beers and thanked him.

'Have another. He'll claim it on War Damage.'

They declined and went out into the street. 'Sure you won't change your mind, Harry, and come to my place?' Temple said. 'Show you the sights and burn the candle.'

'Sorry, Reg, and thanks for the offer, but I've one or two things to sort out.'

271

'The Norwegian bit, Sarge?' Bennett said, and winked.

Keith nodded. 'Said I'd look her up in London. Not sure how to go about it, though.'

'The best of luck.'

Keith watched them head for the nearest Underground station before hailing a cruising taxi and asking to be taken to the Foreign Office. The taxi was forced to make numerous diversions to avoid streets that were cordoned off, and there were various signs explaining the reasons: 'Unexploded Bomb'; 'Burst Gas Main'; 'Rescue Squads at Work' . . .

The taxi stopped outside the Foreign Office. When he entered Keith was handed a printed form which had a space for his personal details and another asking him to state the purpose of his visit. He wrote: 'Private and highly confidential', hoping the official whose desk it would land on would be misled into thinking he had some valuable information and take the trouble to see him.

A uniformed porter with a row of World War One medal ribbons on his breast showed him into a small waiting room where half a dozen people were sitting against the wall on hard chairs, all apparently resigned to an indefinite wait.

Keith sat there for the best part of two hours before a young man in a smartly tailored blue pin-stripe suit poked his head round the door. 'Sergeant Keith – this way please,' he said in an effete public school drawl.

The young man led him into a tiny interview room and gestured to him to take a chair on one side of a bare table, whilst he took the chair on the business side. 'What have you to tell us, then?'

'Nothing. I want *you* to tell *me* something.' He saw the young man's jaw sag. 'I'm trying to discover the whereabouts of Mr Andrew Ross who used to work in our Embassy in Oslo. He left when the Germans invaded.'

'I'm afraid that's not the kind of sensitive information we can divulge to a casual caller. You'll have to state your reasons in writing. Even then it's doubtful if we can tell you anything.'

Keith restrained his mounting anger and frustration. 'I've already done that, without success. Now I've called in person, giving up an entire day of my leave. And I'm *not* a casual

272

enquirer – I'm looking for his daughter. I was one of a group of Commandos who helped to smuggle her out of Norway along with a large consignment of gold.'

The young man's face expressed renewed interest. 'Remember reading about that in *The Times* – caused quite a stir. King of Norway dished out medals.'

Keith felt ashamed as he touched the ribbon on his battle-dress blouse. 'Got this for my part in it, but from our own King.' He thought: You bloody liar. But his story might have some effect.

The young man was suitably impressed. 'I'll see what I can do. Can't have it thought that we're indifferent to the needs of our heroes! Back in a jiffy.'

The jiffy turned out to be some considerable time, long enough for Keith to have smoked three cigarettes. When the young man returned he handed Keith a typewritten address. 'Took quite a bit of persuading on my part before they coughed up with it. Can't understand their reticence as Ross has retired – permanently.' He pointed an index finger towards the ornate ceiling.

Keith rose. 'You've got all the makings of a fine diplomat. Tactful and with a delicate way of putting things.'

The young man beamed.

Keith showed the address to one of the doormen and asked for directions.

'Head for Belgrave Square, then ask again when you get there. It's a street somewhere off there.'

Keith decided to walk, thinking the fresh air would clear his head of the foul stench of the shelter still lingering in his nostrils. He walked across Horse Guards Parade, through St James's Park, past the Victoria Memorial and Buckingham Palace, then along Constitution Hill through to Belgrave Square where a passerby directed him to his destination.

It was a short street of small but dignified houses with carefully tended window-boxes, black doors and polished brass knockers: the kind of houses occupied by people of limited means who wanted an impressive address. In the centre was a charred space, like a drawn tooth in an otherwise perfect set. The numbers on either side of the bombed house told him all he needed to know. He knocked on the front door of the house on the left and got no reply. He tried the one on the right, and after a short wait it was opened by an elderly woman in a tweed skirt and jacket who was cradling a small dog in her arms.

'I'm making enquiries about a Mr Ross. I wonder if you can help?'

She glanced at the blackened shell of what had once been a house. 'I think that speaks for itself. A direct hit – Mr and Mrs Ross died instantly.'

'Was there anybody else in the house at the time?' he asked anxiously.

'Just the maid and the housekeeper. Both survived, thank God.'

'Do you know where I might find them?'

'The maid went off to join the ATS. The housekeeper I can help you with – she's staying with a sister in Primrose Hill. She gave me the address in case her missing cat turned up. Hang on, I'll get it.'

Keith flagged down a taxi and ordered it to go to Primrose Hill where the cabbie dropped him outside a dilapidated house at the foot of the hill, on which was sited a battery of anti-aircraft guns and a barrage balloon unit. He went up a flight of stone stairs and pulled a chain to set off a chime of bells. A woman opened the door. 'I'm looking for Mrs Armitage.'

'That's me. Better step inside.'

She led him into a comfortably furnished sitting room which was crowded with aspidistras in big brass pots.

'Take a seat and tell me what brings you here. Cup of tea?'

'No thank you, Mrs Armitage, I'm a bit pressed for time. I'm looking for Miss Christina Ross. Did she escape the bombing?'

'She wasn't there,' Mrs Armitage crossed herself. 'A miracle she wasn't.'

'Where is she now?'

'I can't help. I wish I could. A few days before Mr and Mrs Ross, bless their souls, were killed they gave a little party for Christina and some Norwegian friends. I remember thinking what a pretty young thing she was, and how a uniform suited her.'

274

'Uniform?'

'Yes. She was wearing one with "Norway" on the shoulders. You know, just like our own lads have the name of their regiment on their shoulders.'

'Did you know where she was going?'

'Not really, but if you were to ask me to guess I'd say Norway. There was a toast wishing her and the other Norwegians a safe return, and from the amount of tears Mrs Ross was shedding I gathered she was expecting Christina to be away a long time.'

'Was Norway actually mentioned?'

'Only when the Norwegians lifted their glasses and said, "All for Norway". I didn't need a crystal ball to guess that's where they were off to, and I remember thinking that we British would never be that emotional.'

Keith thanked her, wondering what on earth he could do with the rest of his leave. There was no point in going to the Norwegian Embassy – they would not give any information about a person who had returned to work with the Resistance. He could write to Entwistle, but that too would be a waste of time.

He walked back to the West End and found a YMCA hostel off Tottenham Court Road where he took a single room. He slept for two hours, and when he woke up he went to the big cinema on the corner which was showing a government-funded film about a group of soldiers escaping from Dunkirk. It was blatant propaganda. It was a different Dunkirk to the one he had experienced. The men were ludicrously patriotic, their stiff upper lips laughably stiff. He left in disgust after half an hour. He went into a pub where a heavily made-up tart solicited him. On a sympathetic impulse he bought her a drink, but said he was waiting for his girlfriend; she apologized and moved down the bar to where another solitary soldier was drinking.

Then he had an idea. He rushed to Reception and borrowed a set of out-of-town telephone directories.

Lady Hazel Mappin pushed her husband's wheelchair across the flagstone terrace at the back of the house. Below, stretching as far as the eye could see, was what had once been the famous deer park; it had now been put under the plough. The herd of deer, which had grazed there unmolested for centuries, had been heavily culled and sold as venison, only a handful being kept for breeding purposes when the war ended.

'Well, no one can accuse us of not pulling our weight!' Lord William said. 'We're digging for victory on a grand scale.'

'We've only just started,' Hazel replied enthusiastically. 'There's still a lot more we can do. The manager tells me the southern end of the estate is ideal for sheep and cattle, and a fair number of the big trees in Dowton Wood can be felled for timber without any permanent damage. There's a terrible shortage of good wood.'

Mappin groaned. 'He mentioned it to me, and I've agreed, but heaven knows what the old man will say. That's one of the finest game preserves in the country.'

'He'll have to learn to do without his pheasants! Anyway, he can't really object, seeing as how he's agreed to you running the place on a more economical footing. Even he accepts that we can't live in glorified isolation while the rest of the country is fighting a war.'

They were interrupted in their discussion about the future of the estate by the appearance of an ancient servant. 'Telephone call for you, my lord.'

'Tell whoever it is that I'm tied up just now. They can either ring back or leave a message.'

After a few minutes the old man reappeared. 'It's a Sergeant Keith,' he said, 'ringing from London.'

'The bugger's surfaced at last!' said Mappin with a wide grin. 'I wondered when he'd get round to it.' He propelled himself across the terrace with hands that could not spin the wheels fast enough.

He returned five minutes later. 'Wants to know if he can come and see me. Gave him the time of the next convenient train and said I'd meet him at the station with the car. Typical of him – he told me to save my petrol, he'd get a taxi. I told him petrol was the least of my worries.'

'Did you mention me, darling?' she asked apprehensively.

'No. I'm keeping that as a surprise.' He rubbed his hands together. 'We'll roll out the red carpet for Harry! Open up the banqueting hall. Best silver, the Jacobean glass, the Georgian candlesticks. Raid the old man's cellar. The works.'

'No, William, he'd hate that. Let's make him feel at home. We'll eat in the small dining room, as we always do. Good food and plenty to drink, no "ancestral home" stuff. You're Lieutenant Mappin, not his Lordship – don't embarrass him.'

'That, hand on heart, is the last thing I'd want to do,' said Mappin, chastened. 'I just thought I'd demonstrate my degree of affection.'

'Let's keep it simple, but warm, darling.'

'I've still got a lot to learn,' he said quietly.

Sergeant Keith stepped out of the carriage, peering along the darkened platform. He hoped he had got out at the right destination; no porter had called out the name of the halt, and there was not a sign in sight to indicate where he was.

A figure emerged from the early morning mist. 'Sergeant Keith, sir?' he enquired. Keith nodded, and the man who was wearing a chauffeur's uniform of peaked cap, cross-buttoned coat and old fashioned breeches and knee boots, heaved an audible sigh of relief. 'Thank God for that! So many people go straight through without realizing they've missed their stop.'

Keith looked at him and thought: I've never seen anyone dressed like that except in some old movie about murder in a fog-shrouded castle.

'If you'll hand me your luggage, sir, I'll put it in the boot,' the chauffeur said.

Keith held up a small suitcase. 'Like to travel light – all I need's in here.'

The chauffeur took it. 'Never mind, sir, if you find you're short of anything I'm sure we'll be able to do something about it.'

In the forecourt outside, Keith looked at the ancient Bentley, long and sleek, obviously washed and polished with infinite care, but looking rather incongruous with a sort of trailer attached to the rear.

A rear window slid down, and he hear the familiar voice call out. 'Hop in the back, Harry!'

Keith felt as if a fist had thudded into his chest and stopped his heart. As he slid into the car he really did feel Mappin's fist thud into his side, but there was no pain in it; it was an Englishman's embrace.

'Jesus, I'm glad to see you fit and well, sir.'

Mappin's legs were concealed beneath a tartan rug. 'What kept you so long, Harry?'

'Guilt, I suppose. I was never sure if I'd said the right thing to Third Officer Payne. I broke my promise to you, sir.'

'Thank Christ you did!'

'Why's that, sir?'

'All in good time, Harry. First, I want to hear what you've been doing with yourself.'

'Not a lot,' Keith said. 'Plenty of training and one minor op that was a bit of a damp squib.' He did not really want to talk about the army and peered out of the rear window. 'What's the weird contraption you're towing? Looks like a mobile kitchen.'

'Economy, Harry – the answer to petrol rationing. Some new-fangled thing the boffins dreamed up. This car is driven by the gas produced from either chicken shit or pig shit; not sure which.'

Keith laughed. 'They ought to try bullshit, sir! There's no shortage of that.'

'Harry, I'm out of it now, so call me William or Bill,' said Mappin earnestly.

'How're things going, Bill? The legs, I mean.'

'I've had two ops now, and they've removed the shrapnel. When they showed it to me I couldn't believe something so small could do so much damage. I've got some movement back, and the specialist says there's no reason why, in time, I shouldn't regain full use of my legs. Meanwhile, I'm confined to a wheelchair most of the time. I attend Stoke Mandeville once a month for treatment. They say a lot depends on my own determination – I assured them there was no shortage of that on my part.'

Keith thought of Private Luck, and how he had imagined he could still feel his missing toes, and he hoped that Mappin wasn't imagining things when he said he had regained some movement and that the specialist wasn't giving empty comfort to a hopeless case.

The journey from the station to the beginning of the estate was a short one and they had not been travelling very long when Mappin pointed out of the window. 'Nearly there. That's our boundary wall.'

It was about ten feet high, a masterpiece of the bricklayers' art. Its elegance, however, was marred by broken bottles on the top embedded into concrete. As they travelled alongside it, it seemed endless.

'Some wall,' Keith said.

'I can't make up my mind as to its real purpose,' Mappin said, 'whether it was erected as a physical reminder that it enclosed a private and privileged world to which outsiders were not admitted, or whether it was built to cocoon its owners from the realities of the outside world.'

'Bit of both, maybe,' said Keith tactfully.

'I'm trying to change things, Harry,' Mappin said. 'Open it up, make it more businesslike, less of a bastion against progress. My mother's all for it; my father asks, why? Says we've managed all right for centuries.'

The entrance to the main drive was marked by a massive pair of wrought iron gates, in the centre of which were the coat of arms of the family. There was a small lodge house on one side, and as the chauffeur sounded his horn a man emerged to swing them open.

The gravel drive was lined on both sides by towering trees that shut out the light: oaks, beech and cedars, their height an indication of their age. Keith had taken it for granted that Mappin would live in what for lack of a better phrase he called a stately home, but he was unprepared for the grandness of the reality. It reminded him of Hampton Court.

The house lay well back from an enormous manicured lawn, in the centre of which stood a fountain with mermaids and dolphins spouting jets of water. It was shaped like the letter H, the central facade was in white stone, the adjoining wings of red brick. A clock tower stood in the middle of the main building, and the gold face of the clock was at least eight feet in diameter. The corners of the wings had turrets with gleaming cupolas on top. But what came as an even bigger shock was the sight of the young woman he had last seen in Scapa standing on the top step of the flight that led to the main door.

Mappin saw the expression on his face. 'Didn't let on because I wanted to surprise you. As I said, breaking your promise to me was the best thing you ever did.'

While the chauffeur got a wheelchair from the boot and helped Mappin into it, Hazel skipped down the steps and embraced Keith. 'As you can see, Harry, you didn't manage to put me off!'

The informality of her greeting eased the apprehension he had been experiencing. But he still could not help thinking: This isn't what the war is all about – the preservation of old piles like this. This represents a way of life that should have gone years ago.

Hazel saw his expression. 'William has offered to convert one of the wings into a hospital, and the other into a convalescent home.'

Keith felt better for hearing that.

She linked her arm with his and led him into the house. 'You don't know how much this means to him. He's always talking about you and the others, wishing he was still with you. Seeing you again is the best thing that could have happened.'

He smiled back. 'The second best thing,' he said, thinking how happy and relaxed she was. That too came as an immense relief.

His mind went back to the time they had talked in Mrs Moray's guest house when he had decided to tell her the truth about Mappin; that he wasn't dead but might just as well be. He had frequently worried that he had done the wrong thing by breaking his word. Now, when he looked at her radiant face, he knew he had not.

Later, after he had been shown his room and they were relaxing over a drink, she said: 'William was furious with you – and, I might add, with me – when I turned up out of the blue and told him that as far as I was concerned nothing had changed. Which was true, of course.'

'I'm really delighted for both of you,' said Keith.

'It'll be three soon,' she said.

The news made him even happier. It meant that it was a marriage in every sense of the word.

Keith brought Mappin up to date with the news about the surviving members of the unit. 'Can't help you with Private

Luck because I've lost touch with him. All I know is that he's been discharged.'

'He's in fine form, Harry,' Hazel said. 'William tracked him down to the hospital and invited him to convalesce here. He refused until we told him we had a Steinway piano in the music room.'

'Where is he now?'

'That's another surprise we've got in store for you, but it'll have to wait for a couple of days. Don't want to spoil things by letting you into the secret too early.'

No amount of pleading and prodding would make either of them change their mind, and Keith had to be content with waiting. But he did it with the impatience of a child waiting for Christmas.

Chapter Twenty

Keith had never seen Luck out of uniform, but he recognized him immediately as he appeared from the wings and walked unsteadily across to the podium to shake hands with the famous conductor, then turn and bow to the audience before lifting the tails of his black swallow coat, and sitting down at the piano. He looked as young and vulnerable as ever, and Keith knew his teetering gait was due to a lack of balance caused by the missing toes. He glanced down at the printed programme and read the second item: Tchaikovsky – *Piano Concerto No. One in B flat minor*. Soloist – Emmanuel Gluckstein.

As the opening chords resounded throughout the hall, he was transported back to France. The notes of the piano were replaced by the sound of Ted's voice defiantly humming the same notes as he trudged along on his makeshift crutch, willing himself to keep moving.

Keith had catnapped through the first item, a symphony by the same composer, and was only awoken by the rapturous applause that greeted its conclusion. Now he listened enthralled as Ted, all assurance and confidence, fought a musical battle with the orchestra: one man against a vast array of brass and strings. When the final notes faded into silence, the orchestra rose as one and tapped their instruments in appreciation. The conductor pointed at him with his baton, then clapped, heralding the arrival of a new virtuoso.

The audience rose too, and Keith with them, applauding as loudly as the most fervent enthusiast there. The music meant little to him; he was paying tribute to a young man who had helped to fill an empty gap in his life.

Ted rose and bowed elegantly, then tottered off, only to be called back by the conductor and the demanding applause of the audience.

Afterwards, in the small, almost spartan dressing room behind the stage, Ted's manner was disarming. 'I was lucky to be given this chance. I'm not quite ready for the Queen's Hall yet, but I'm everlastingly grateful for having been given the opportunity. I think someone must have pulled a few strings.' He glanced at Mappin. 'Your father is a patron of the LPO, I hear.'

'That's true, Ted, but he's never been to a concert in his life. Doesn't know an oboe from a hobo,' he said unconvincingly.

'I don't know why he's being so coy,' Hazel said. 'William heard you play at home and thought your talents should be recognized, so he spoke to his father. That's what friends are for.'

'All I helped you get was an audition, Ted. The rest was up to you.'

Mappin insisted that he should take them all to dinner and Ted, in his gratitude and overwhelming delight at seeing Keith, readily accepted, although it meant reneging on a promise to dine with a well known impresario who wanted to discuss his future.

'He's already arranged another appearance at the Queen's Hall in a few week's time. Very short notice, but music-starved Londoners aren't too demanding nowadays. I'm sure he'll understand when he calls to collect me and I explain the situation. I can tell him I wouldn't be here but for Harry.'

When the impresario called at the dressing room and Luck explained the position, he was magnaminous. 'Emmanuel, you and I will dine together hundreds of times in the years to come. Tonight you should spend with your friends.'

The meal passed all too quickly for their liking, and Keith and Ted solemnly pledged that they would keep in touch.

'I promised we'd meet at the Albert Hall, and we shall', Ted said.

Afterwards, on the way home, Hazel put her mouth close to Keith's ear. 'William and I have decided that if it's a boy we'll christen it Harry,' she whispered. 'If it's a girl, Harriet. It'll be our way of saying thank you.'

284

Keith felt too emotional to speak.

He spent the next five days in blissful and total idleness. In a pair of borrowed corduroy slacks and sweater, he wheeled Mappin on his daily tour of the estate and listened intently as he outlined his plans for the future and his growing desire to be a useful contributor to the wealth of the country. Not once did he think of his unit or the war: and for the first time since the debacle of Dunkirk he was no longer consumed by a burning desire for revenge. But for Dunkirk he would never have met Ted. He would not have volunteered for the Commandos, which also meant he would never have met Mappin and Hazel, nor Christina. Of course, the war still had to be won, but it was no longer a deep personal issue for Keith. He had come to view it as a job that had to be completed as quickly as possible so the world could be restored to some semblance of normality and sanity. He had discovered there was a life outside the army to be cherished and shared. Now he happily contemplated a peacetime life that extended far beyond the narrow confines of the Hop Pickers; when his time expired he would not sign on, for by then he would have done enough soldiering, but he would not fade away. He had a new set of ideals to love and cherish.

Two days later, towards the end of his second week, half-listening to the BBC early morning news as he shaved, he heard the cultured voice of the announcer say: 'Music lovers throughout the civilized world will be shocked and saddened by the news that the Queen's Hall has been totally destroyed by enemy bombs. mercifully the hall was empty when the bomb hit it. Only hours earlier a large audience had listened to an afternoon performance of Elgar's oratorio "The Dream of Gerontius".'

It was an unusual breach of the security which was normally strictly enforced when it came to the naming of specific targets, so stringent that people joked: 'I see Random has copped it again.' – a reference to the frequently heard announcement that 'bombs were dropped at random last night'. Keith assumed that the destruction of the world famous concert hall would cause such widespread indignation in neutral countries that the breach was a deliberate decision by Downing Street. It would certainly stiffen resolve at home.

Later, at the end of the bulletin, it was disclosed that members of the London Philharmonic Orchestra who had left their instruments in the band room in readiness for the next performance, were appealing to the public for replacements. It was going to be 'business as usual' as far as they were concerned.

When he joined Mappin and Hazel for breakfast, he announced, without any preamble: 'I'm reporting back. Cutting my leave short.'

'Why?' asked Mappin.

'Didn't you hear the news? The Queen's Hall has been destroyed.' Keith felt anger surge through him like an uncontrollable torrent. 'That bomb could have landed when Ted was playing, and you and Hazel were listening. All three of you – not to mention Harry, or Harriet – could have been killed.'

'We weren't, though,' said Mappin calmly.

'That's not the point. It was on the cards.'

'You're forgetting one thing, Harry. You've left yourself out of the list of possible casualties.'

'Well, I can't wait to give the bastards another crack at getting me. But I'll take a few of them with me.'

Mappin was witnessing a Keith he never knew existed. Even in the tightest corner he had always been calm, collected and professional; now he was unable to control his fury.

Keith could feel himself quivering. He had come perilously close to losing the three people who meant more to him than anything else, and his love for them had rekindled his hatred of the enemy and his burning desire for revenge.

The war had once again become a personal vendetta for Sergeant Harry Keith.

p